Ab

Chantelle Shaw e[...]
up stories in her hea[...]
discovered Mills & [...]
times when her ch[...]
pace the floor with [...]
other! Twenty yea[...]
her own. Writing takes up most of Chantelle's spare time, but she also enjoys gardening and walking. She doesn't find domestic chores so pleasurable!

Born and raised on the Wirral Peninsula in England, **Charlotte Hawkes** is mum to two intrepid boys who love her to play building block games with them, and who object loudly to the amount of time she spends on the computer. When she isn't writing – or building with blocks – she is company director for a small Anglo/French construction firm. Charlotte loves to hear from readers, and you can contact her at her website: charlotte-hawkes.com

Ann McIntosh was born in the tropics, lived in the frozen north for a number of years, and now resides in sunny central Florida with her husband. She's a proud mama to three grown children, loves tea, crafting, animals (except reptiles!), bacon and the ocean. She believes in the power of romance to heal, inspire and provide hope in our complex world.

Postcards from Paradise

January 2023
Caribbean

April 2023
Costa Rica

February 2023
Brazil

May 2023
Australia

March 2023
Hawaii

June 2023
Bali

Postcards from Paradise:
Brazil

CHANTELLE SHAW

CHARLOTTE HAWKES

ANN McINTOSH

MILLS & BOON

First Published in Great Britain 2023
By Mills & Boon, an imprint of HarperCollins*Publishers,* Ltd
1 London Bridge Street, London, SE1 9GF

www.harpercollins.co.uk

HarperCollins*Publishers*
Macken House, 39/40 Mayor Street Upper,
Dublin 1, D01 C9W8, Ireland

POSTCARDS FROM PARADISE: BRAZIL © 2023 Harlequin Enterprises ULC.

Master of Her Innocence © 2016 Chantelle Shaw
Falling for the Single Dad Surgeon © 2020 Charlotte Hawkes
Awakened by Her Brooding Brazilian © 2020 Ann McIntosh

ISBN: 978-0-263-31868-5

MIX
Paper | Supporting
responsible forestry
FSC™ C007454

This book is produced from independently certified FSC™ paper to ensure responsible forest management.

For more information visit: www.harpercollins.co.uk/green

Printed and Bound in Spain using 100% Renewable electricity at
CPI Black Print, Barcelona

MASTER OF HER INNOCENCE

CHANTELLE SHAW

For *New York Times* bestselling historical romance author Sarah MacLean, who gave brilliant workshops at RWA 2015 and inspired me to go with my crazy ideas and write bonkers! Thank you, Sarah.

CHAPTER ONE

'SISTER ANN, DO I really need to wear a habit?' Clare
Marchant looked doubtfully at the Mother Superior. 'It
seems wrong to pretend that I belong to the Holy Order
of the Sacred Heart. I feel like I am an imposter.'

'My child, I strongly advise that for your safety you
should dress as a nun. Torrente is one of the most dangerous places in Brazil. Its close proximity to the border
with Colombia has made it a route for drug smuggling
and people trafficking and I have heard of young women
in the town who have been forced into prostitution. It
is a lawless place where even the police are too scared
to visit. The men who run the drugs cartels have little
respect for life, but they do at least retain some respect
for the church.'

The Mother Superior smiled gently at Clare, noting
the signs of strain on the young Englishwoman's face
and the shadows beneath her eyes that told of too many
sleepless nights of worry.

'There is no need for you to feel like an imposter.
You have come to Brazil with the selfless intention to
search for your sister and pay the ransom her kidnappers have demanded. You are bravely prepared to put
yourself in danger to help someone you love, and at least

the church can offer you some small measure of protection.' Sister Ann's expression became grave. 'I'm sure I don't have to remind you that the men who took Becky are utterly ruthless.'

Clare followed the nun's gaze to what looked like a jewellery box on the desk, and a feeling of nausea swept over her as she pictured the gruesome contents of the casket. *Don't think of it*, she ordered herself. But her mind visualised the severed tip of an earlobe wrapped in layers of tissue paper like some ghastly mimicry of a gift from a lover. Surely it wasn't a piece of Becky's ear? She could not bear to think of her beautiful sister being mutilated by whoever had snatched her from the street outside the five-star hotel in Rio de Janeiro where Becky had been modelling for a photo shoot.

She tore her eyes from the box and stared at what she could see of her reflection in the small mirror hanging on the wall of the Mother Superior's office. The grey habit Sister Ann had lent her fell to just above her ankles to reveal a pair of flat black lace-up shoes. She watched the Sister place a veil on her head. With her auburn hair covered up she looked different—more elegant and sophisticated like Becky—although the sprinkling of freckles on her nose were a giveaway clue to her vibrant mane hidden beneath the veil, she thought ruefully.

'If it helps your conscience, I have given you a white veil; they are worn by novice nuns before they take their final vows when they change to a black veil,' Sister Ann explained. 'That way, it is not entirely untruthful for you to appear to be a young woman who is contemplating a religious life. And, after all, you were drawn to seek comfort at the chapel of Santa Maria when you arrived in Rio de Janeiro. Many of us are called to our vocation in mysterious ways.'

Clare could not bring herself to admit to the kindly nun that she did not believe her future was to follow a life of religious devotion. Although the fact that she was still a virgin at the age of twenty-four meant that she fitted the requirement of chastity, she thought wryly. Mark had called her a prude, but she didn't think she was. She had simply wanted to be sure he was the right man for her, and it turned out that he hadn't been.

England and her break-up with Mark seemed a million miles away, and she wondered if she would wake up to find that her sister being kidnapped was a bad dream rather than a living nightmare. But, unbelievable though it was, the situation was real. On Monday morning she had arrived for work as usual at her parents' company, A-Star PR, and received a frantic phone call from her father with the astonishing news that her younger sister Becky, an internationally famous model, had been kidnapped.

'The kidnappers have sent a letter saying they will kill Becky unless I follow their instructions.' Rory Marchant had sounded shaken. 'They want me to go to Brazil and pay a ransom, but I can't leave your mother, and I daren't tell her that Becky's life is in danger. The specialist said it is important that Tammi doesn't suffer any kind of stress. She was lucky to survive the first stroke, and a second one could kill her.' Rory had broken down. 'Clare, I don't know what to do. I want to rescue my precious girl, but I don't want to lose my wife.'

'I'll go to Brazil and take the ransom money to the kidnappers,' Clare had said instantly. 'You can't leave

Mum, especially now that she is finally showing signs of recovering.'

She had dismissed the little voice in her head, which whispered that her father had never thought of her as his precious girl. It had always been her sister who had come first in their parents' affections, but it was unsurprising after Becky had been seriously ill and nearly died when she was a child, Clare reminded herself. She loved Becky and could only imagine how terrified her sister must be feeling right now.

She blinked back a sudden rush of tears and turned to the Mother Superior. 'Thank you for helping me. All the Sisters have been so kind. I felt scared and alone when Sister Carmelita spoke to me in the chapel in Rio.'

Clare's thoughts flew back to two days ago when she had arrived in Rio de Janeiro and, following the kidnappers' instructions, had checked into a rundown motel to wait for the gang to contact her. But, instead of receiving a letter telling her what to do next, as had happened when the kidnappers had contacted her father in England, this time she had been sent a package, and when she had opened it and seen the grisly, severed piece of earlobe, she had rushed to the bathroom to be sick.

The note sent with the box had instructed her to go to the town of Torrente, which she had found on a map was in the far west of Brazil, over two thousand miles from Rio and deep in the Amazon rainforest. It had been at that point, exhausted and fearful that the kidnappers had hurt her sister, that she had been inexplicably drawn to step inside the church near her motel, and she had broken down and told the nun she had met about Becky being kidnapped. Within twenty-four hours Sister Carmelita had arranged for Clare to catch an internal flight to the city of Manaus in northern Brazil, and she had been staying with the nuns of the Holy Order of the Sacred Heart while Sister Ann arranged her onward journey to Torrente.

'I wish you would reconsider your decision to try to rescue your sister alone and go to the police.'

'I *can't*. The kidnappers said they would kill Becky if I told anyone they are holding her. I'm scared I may have put her life in danger by accepting help from the Sisters—' Clare's voice trembled '—but I didn't know what else to do.'

'I am afraid the kidnapping of wealthy tourists is becoming a growing problem in Brazil, and it is sadly true that often the police are unable to track down the kidnap gangs,' the Mother Superior said heavily. The sound of a vehicle driving into the courtyard drew her to the window. 'Mr Cazorra is here and, God willing, you will soon be reunited with your sister.'

Clare picked up the rucksack she had packed with a few of her own clothes and other essentials. 'The gold prospector you have asked to take me to Torrente doesn't know why I'm going, does he?'

'Don't worry, your secret will remain within the walls of the convent. I have explained to Diego that you are to take up a post teaching at the Sunday school and you must reach the town by the weekend.'

Fear cramped in Clare's stomach. Sunday was when the kidnappers had said they would contact her again to tell her where she should take the ransom money. She picked up the leather briefcase that held five hundred thousand pounds in used bank notes. It was a terrifying thought that Becky's very life was contained in the briefcase and Clare gripped the handle tightly.

'I should warn you about the gold prospector,' Sister Ann said.

'Warn me?' Clare's tension ratcheted up a notch. 'You said I could trust him.'

'I don't doubt he will get you to Torrente safely. He knows that area of the Amazon rainforest better than anyone I can think of. Mr Cazorra is a good man who has helped the Sisters in the past, but he has a reputation for...' The nun paused before saying delicately, 'Well, let's just say that he enjoys the company of women. Many women. He is very charming.'

'You mean he's a flirt?' Were all Brazilian men Lotharios? Clare wondered, remembering the taxi driver who had driven her from Manaus Airport to the convent. The man had greasy hair and was wearing a sweat-stained T-shirt, but he had suggested that he would give her a free tour of the city if she went to bed with him. Needless to say, she had declined his invitation.

All she could think about was saving her sister and the news that her escort to Torrente was a womaniser was the least of her concerns. 'I'm sure I'll be able to handle your Mr Cazorra,' she said grimly as she followed the Mother Superior outside to the courtyard.

Diego Cazorra glanced up at the stained-glass window of the convent and noticed how the sunlight shining through the coloured glass reflected a rainbow effect on to the floor of the courtyard. It was strange how beauty was often found in the simplest things, he mused. At the diamond mine he owned with his close friend and business partner Cruz Delgado, he had discovered some of the most fabulous diamonds ever found in Brazil. But the purity of sunlight touched his soul in a way that glittering gemstones never could.

The two years he had spent in one of Brazil's most notoriously violent jails had taught him to appreciate the simple things in life: the feel of warm sunshine on his face every time he came up from a mineshaft, or the sight of a cloudless blue sky, which he hadn't seen the whole time he had been locked up in an overcrowded prison cell that stank of the sweat and fear of incarcerated men.

The memories of what had happened to him as a teenager had never faded, but Diego had learned to block out thoughts of the past, although he could not prevent his nightmares. He turned his mind to a recent phone call which was the reason for his visit to the convent on the outskirts of Manaus, the largest city in the state of Amazonas.

'I was wondering if you would grant me a favour, Mr Cazorra,' Sister Ann had asked him. And, like a sucker, he'd agreed, thinking that the Mother Superior wanted him to paint some walls or fix the roof. But no, it was nothing so simple. It turned out the favour was to escort one of the nuns to a town on the border with Colombia.

Diego frowned. Torrente was a godforsaken hellhole, and he doubted that a multitude of nuns could make a difference to the lives of the population of the town, who lived in extreme poverty and had pretty much all turned to crime because there was no other way of making money to feed their children.

The *favela* where he had spent his childhood had been as crime-ridden, disease-ridden and despair-ridden as Torrente, and he had no desire to visit a place that was a grim reminder of his past. But he never forgot that the only person who had helped him when he had been a young man in desperate need of salvation had been a priest, Father Vincenzi. Diego was not religious himself, but he felt a strong sense of loyalty to the church that had quite literally taken him from prison and given him his life back.

He was due to return to Rio next week to check up on the casino and nightclub he owned, before flying to Europe for a business meeting with Cruz to discuss his stake in the jewellery company Delgado Diamonds and the Old Betsy diamond mine. But he could spare a couple of days to drive one of the Sisters of the Sacred Heart up to the border. He might even get a chance to take a look at a site where geological survey reports showed there could be gold reserves. Maybe his good turn would be repaid with good luck and he would find gold in Torrente, Diego mused as he adjusted his battered leather hat and climbed out of the Jeep when he saw the door of the convent swing open.

The Mother Superior swept towards him, her grey habit and black veil flapping in the breeze. 'Diego, it's good to see you,' she greeted him in English, which was curious because they normally conversed in their native Portuguese. 'I would like you to meet Sister Clare, who has recently joined our holy order from England.'

So that cleared up one mystery. What was less easy to explain was why his heart felt as if it had slammed into his ribcage with the force of a speeding train. Diego stared at the diminutive figure, dressed from her neck to her ankles in unremitting grey, who followed Sister Ann across the courtyard. Sister Clare's white veil framed a heart-shaped face dominated by the bluest eyes he had ever seen. They had the dark intensity of sapphires, their colour emphasised by the fact that her skin was pale like cream and as flawless as porcelain.

He silently mocked himself. *Santa Mãe*, he'd be writing a sonnet next! He was shocked by his reaction to the English nun and surprised that she was so young. He guessed she was in her early twenties: only a few years older than him when he had been sent to the state penitentiary in Belo Horizonte. Of course prison was not the same as a convent, but he couldn't comprehend why a beautiful young woman would choose to shut herself away from the world.

'I'm pleased to meet you, Mr Cazorra.' Her voice was sweetly melodious, reminding Diego of a crystal-clear mountain stream.

'Sister—' He took off his hat and held out his other hand. He was suddenly conscious of his calloused palm when she placed her fingers in his. Her small hand was swamped by his much bigger one and her skin was as soft as satin. An image flashed into his head of her stroking her soft hands over his naked body. He wondered what her body was like beneath the shapeless nun's habit, which did not entirely conceal the swell of her firm, round breasts.

Whoa! Diego stopped his imagination in its tracks. She was a nun, he reminded himself, and strictly off limits. He was certain he was already damned in the eyes of whatever deity he might meet when the time came for him to leave this world, but having inappropriate thoughts about a holy maid was a step too far even for someone as disreputable as him. But, while he had a conscience, the drug lords in Torrente definitely did not. He doubted they would respect Sister Clare's innocence; they'd just as likely wonder how much money they could make by selling her virginity.

'I can read your thoughts, Diego.' Sister Ann's voice jolted him from those thoughts, and he sincerely hoped she couldn't. 'I can tell you are keen to get on the road before the bad weather that is forecast arrives. When do you estimate you will arrive in Torrente?'

Diego did not want to be responsible for taking the young nun to a town where her safety was by no means guaranteed and he quickly made a decision. 'It's not going to be possible to make the journey, I'm afraid. As you know, the wet season has started early this year and heavy rain is due in the next few days, which will make the roads impassable.'

'But we have to go.' Sister Clare stepped forward and stood directly in front of him. Her petite stature meant that she was forced to tilt her head to look up at him, and Diego was startled by the fierce expression in her blue eyes. 'You agreed to take me.' Her voice was no longer soft and soothing but shrilly demanding. 'I *must* reach Torrente by Sunday.'

He frowned. 'With respect, Sister, you're going there to teach at a Sunday school. It's hardly a matter of life and death and I don't fancy being trapped in Torrente for weeks, possibly months. The road up by the border is a dirt track that turns into a quagmire when it rains.' He jammed his hat on to his head and walked back to his truck. 'I'm sorry. You'll have to start your teaching post next spring when the wet season ends.'

He put his boot on the footplate of the Jeep, but as he was about to swing himself up into the driving seat, he felt a surprisingly firm grip on his arm.

'You're not listening to me, Mr Cazorra. I need to get

to Torrente by Sunday and apparently you are the best person to take me. But if you are worried about some wet weather, can you lend me your vehicle so that I can drive myself?'

Diego was riled by Sister Clare's snippy tone. 'Have you seen rain in the Amazon? It's not a light shower like you get in England; it's a deluge that frequently causes flooding and mudslides. I don't allow anyone to drive my truck, Sister. And even if I did, how would you return it back to me as you'll be living in Torrente?'

Clare bit her lip as she realised her mistake. She could not admit that she intended to catch the first available flight out of Brazil as soon as she had paid the ransom money and rescued Becky. 'I'm sure I could find someone who would drive your Jeep back to Manaus.' Her heart sank as the gold prospector shook his head. She knew of no other way of reaching Becky and this man was her only hope of saving her sister. '*Please*, Mr Cazorra. I *must* get to Torrente.'

Diego cursed beneath his breath when he saw the shimmer of tears in the nun's eyes. He could never resist a pretty face, although his usual response when he was attracted to a woman was to take her to bed until he had sated his desire for her. 'Is teaching at a Sunday school so important to you?'

Sister Clare's sapphire-blue eyes seemed to grow even darker in intensity. 'I…have been called to Torrente,' she said in an emotionally charged voice.

Diego appealed to Sister Ann for support. 'Torrente is a dangerous place, especially for a young woman.'

'Sometimes we are asked to show courage, as the priest who once helped you did,' the Mother Superior reminded him.

'Damn it,' Diego growled. It was true that if Father Vincenzi had not been brave enough to accept the role of chaplain at the violent prison where Diego had been an inmate he might still be rotting in a cell, or dead. Who was he to argue with what the English nun clearly believed was her religious duty?

'*All right.* I'll take you. But don't say I didn't warn you that Torrente is no place for innocents. We'll leave straight away and if we're lucky we might beat the bad weather.'

'Thank you.' Her smile was angelic and Diego felt a strange sensation in his chest as if a hand was squeezing his heart. His gaze dropped once more to the outline of her pert breasts and he felt as though another part of his anatomy was being squeezed! He'd obviously gone too long without sex, he thought derisively. When he went back to Rio he would remedy the situation and visit one of his casual mistresses, many of whom were dancers who worked at his nightclub.

His life as a wealthy entrepreneur was very different from the poverty and deprivation he had endured as a child, Diego mused. His mother had been a drug addict, and most of the time she'd been incapable of taking care of her son. From a young age, Diego had been left to roam the dark alleyways of the *favela*. He had witnessed things that no child should see, and sometimes when he'd felt really scared he'd taken shelter at his friend Cruz Delgado's home. By the time he was a teenager he had become hardened to the grim realities of life in a slum, but one night he had found his mother being beaten by her drug dealer because she did not have enough money to pay him, and Diego had lost his temper—with catastrophic results.

Deus, don't go there! He jerked his mind away from the dark pit of his past and glanced towards the Mother Superior, who had gone back inside the convent and now returned carrying a crate filled with bottles of drinking water. 'You'll need to take plenty of fluids with you for the trip,' she said.

Diego preferred a stronger kind of liquid refreshment, but he shrugged. 'Pack the water in the back of the Jeep,' he told Sister Clare, 'while I check over the engine.'

Clare's hands were shaking as she gripped the crate of water bottles, and her legs felt so wobbly that when she climbed into the back of the Jeep she sank on to her knees, overcome with relief that she had persuaded the prospector to drive her to Torrente. She was a vital step closer to rescuing Becky. Her heart was beating painfully hard in her chest, but not only from fear of what lay ahead when she met the kidnappers.

When the Mother Superior had said the gold prospector was a womaniser, Clare had visualised the slimeball taxi driver who had flirted with her when he had driven her to the convent. She could not have been more wrong! Diego Cazorra was the most gorgeous man she had ever seen. Working for her parents' modelling agency meant that she had met hundreds of good-looking guys, but none, including Mark, came close to the smoulderingly sexy Brazilian.

She studied him through the window of the Jeep. The first thing that had struck her about him was his height. He was several inches over six feet tall, lean-hipped, his long legs encased in faded denim jeans, which he wore with calf-length leather boots. His broad shoulders and powerful pectoral muscles were clearly defined beneath his tight-fitting black T-shirt.

The biggest surprise was when he had removed his hat and revealed an unruly mass of streaked dark blond hair that reached to below his collar. His European appearance was further enhanced by his silvery-grey eyes and sculpted features: razor-edged cheekbones and a square jaw covered by several days' growth of blond stubble. Add to that a blatantly sensual mouth and a wicked glint in his eyes when his gaze had lingered on her breasts that had made Clare feel flustered.

He was a fallen angel and he oozed sex appeal from every pore, but she was horrified by her reaction to the prospector when her thoughts should be totally focused on Becky. Even if Sister Ann hadn't warned her that he was a womaniser, she would have guessed as much from the way he had eyed her up as if he was imagining her without any clothes on. She could still feel a tingling sensation in her breasts and was thankful that the stiff serge fabric of her nun's habit disguised the hard points of her nipples. Suddenly the Mother Superior's advice to travel to Torrente in the guise of a nun seemed a good idea. She could not afford any distractions.

The slam of the Jeep's bonnet made Clare jump and she looked around for somewhere to store the bottles of water. There were no seats in the back of the Jeep, just a bench running down one side, a camping stove and cooking equipment and a couple of rolled-up sleeping bags. The Jeep was basic, but as long as it got her to Torrente she didn't care that it promised to be an uncomfortable ride.

The storage area behind the front seats already contained a large crate of beers. She moved the crate over to make room for the water bottles and discovered a pile of books and, out of curiosity, she glanced at the titles and was surprised to see her favourite novel, *Great Expectations* by Charles Dickens. There were a number of other classic novels by Orwell, Steinbeck and Tolstoy. She would not have guessed that the tough gold prospector's choice of reading material included *Anna Karenina*, the iconic tale of doomed love—which just went to prove the adage that you shouldn't judge a book by its cover, she mused, as she flipped through a well-thumbed book of poetry by John Keats before replacing it where she had found it.

The prospector called her, sounding impatient. 'Are you holding a prayer meeting back there? Let's go, Sister.'

Clare hurried round to the front of the Jeep and her heart gave a painful lurch when she realised that the briefcase containing the ransom money was no longer where she had left it on the floor of the courtyard.

'Where is my case?' she demanded in a panic-stricken voice.

'I put it on the front seat.' The prospector gave her a curious look. 'Take it easy. What are you carrying in that case that is so valuable—the Crown Jewels?' he asked in a teasing voice.

Five hundred thousand pounds to save her sister's life. Clare swallowed. 'Books for the Sunday school.' Technically, it wasn't a lie. Sister Ann *had* given her a few prayer books to take to Father Roberto, the priest in Torrente.

She was relieved to see the briefcase in the front of the Jeep. There was no elegant way of climbing up into the cab. She hitched her nun's habit up to her knees so that she could put her foot on to the step, and gave a startled gasp when two hands gripped her waist and the prospector lifted her off the ground.

For a few breathless seconds she was aware of the strength of his arms around her and the imprint of his fingers burned through the stiff fabric of her clothes and set her skin on fire. The scent of sandalwood cologne mixed with his musky maleness stirred her senses, and she felt an inexplicable urge to turn her head and press her lips against the blond stubble on his jaw.

'Thank you, Mr Cazorra,' she mumbled as he plonked her on to the passenger seat. Her face felt hot with embarrassment that he might have guessed her thoughts.

'Any time,' he said laconically. 'My name's Diego. We're going to be spending the next forty-eight hours together so let's drop the formality.'

'Forty-eight hours! Do you mean we won't reach Torrente today?' Clare stared at him and her stomach swooped as her eyes were drawn to the lazy curl of his smile. 'Where will we spend tonight?'

'I usually sleep in the back of the Jeep. Admittedly, it's not very comfortable for someone of my height, but it does for a night or two.'

Clare pictured herself and the prospector squashed into the small space and her heart gave a painful jolt. 'I can't sleep in the Jeep with you.'

Diego silently acknowledged the truth of her statement. There was only one reason he would spend a night with a woman and it certainly wasn't to sleep. Various inappropriate thoughts had run through his mind when he had lifted Sister Clare into the Jeep. His hands had almost spanned her tiny waist and he had been aware of the gentle flare of her hips and the swell of her breasts. He guessed that beneath the voluminous folds of her nun's habit she had the curvaceous figure of a Pocket Venus, but he would have to curb his imagination or spend the five-hundred-mile journey to Torrente in his current uncomfortable state of arousal.

'There is a settlement on the way to Torrente where we'll stop tonight. The villagers offer basic accommodation for tourists who want to explore the rainforest.'

He started the engine and Sister Ann spoke to Clare. 'Good luck, my dear. I will pray for your safekeeping and for your soul.'

As the Jeep turned out of the convent grounds Clare was gripped with apprehension that soon she would meet the kidnappers. She felt sad to be leaving the Sisters of the Sacred Heart, knowing she was unlikely to meet them again.

'Good luck?' Diego questioned. 'Torrente must be an even worse place than it was the last time I visited the town if the Mother Superior needs to pray for you while you teach at the Sunday school.'

He glanced at his passenger and wondered why she blushed. The soft stain of colour on her face emphasised the delicate lines of her cheekbones and made her look even lovelier. But something about the situation didn't feel right. He had an antenna for trouble, honed during his years living in the *favela* and the time he had spent in prison. His experiences of life had turned him into a cynic, he acknowledged. What could be suspect about a young nun who was as pure and beautiful as an English rose?

'It was a figure of speech.' Sister Clare turned her

guileless blue eyes to him. 'I'm sure Sister Ann prays for all souls, even yours, Mr Cazorra.'

He dismissed his strange feeling that she was not what she seemed and grinned. 'Heck, that's going to take a lot of prayers.'

CHAPTER TWO

CLARE WAS DETERMINED not to respond to the gold prospector's undeniable charisma. She looked away from his toe-tingling smile to focus on the road ahead. The highway was signposted to Boa Vista, which she remembered from the map was in the far north of Brazil, but soon they turned off the main road on to a dirt track.

'There are no paved roads going west,' Diego explained. 'Most people who want to visit the towns along the border with Colombia and Peru travel by boat on the Rio Negro.'

'Why didn't we take a boat instead of driving?'

'The river narrows as it flows into Torrente, making it easy for the drug lords to control the area. There's an airstrip at the edge of the town which they also control. Travelling by Jeep means I can go where I like and, more importantly, I can leave whenever I want to.'

Clare's heart plummeted at the news that criminals controlled the air and river routes into and out of Torrente. Once she had paid the ransom money she hoped to get Becky to safety as quickly as possible. She wondered if she should tell the prospector the real reason she was going to the town and maybe he would agree to bring her and Becky back to Manaus. But, although

Sister Ann had said he was trustworthy, Clare was afraid to trust anyone apart from the nuns who had helped her.

She thought of her father back in London. Rory Marchant would be desperately waiting for news of Becky but trying to pretend to his wife that there was nothing wrong. Tammi Marchant was only in her early fifties, but a year ago she had suffered a stroke that had left her partially paralysed. It broke Clare's heart to see her once vibrant and still beautiful mother now so fragile. Her father had insisted on caring full-time for his wife and had handed the running of A-Star PR over to Clare.

It had been a daunting task to take charge of the agency, but Clare had risen to the challenge. She'd enjoyed developing her PR skills and had discovered a natural talent for devising advertising campaigns. At least being busy meant she'd had no time to brood over her break-up with Mark. Her mother's illness and her father's devoted care of his wife had shown her that she wanted a marriage as strong as her parents' relationship, and she was prepared to hold out until she met a man she could love and trust with all her heart.

The one positive thing was that recently she had felt a deepening bond with her father as they'd shared looking after Tammi and discussed business together. For the first time in her life she sensed that her father was as proud of her as he was of her sister. Of course she was not in the same league as Becky, who was one of the world's most sought-after models, but it made a nice change to realise that being the brainy daughter rather than the beautiful one wasn't such a bad thing.

It was likely that Becky's fame and high profile were the reasons she had been targeted by the kidnappers. Perhaps they had tied Becky up—or worse, Clare thought sickly, as she remembered the severed piece of earlobe the kidnappers had sent her.

She took a deep breath and tried to calm herself down. Allowing her imagination to run away with her would not help Becky. In an attempt to take her mind off the situation she searched for a topic of conversation.

'What exactly does a gold prospector do? I mean, I realise that you search for gold, but there must be more to it than that.'

'Actually, it's pretty much as you described. I take my metal detector to areas where I think there might be gold deposits.'

'But how do you know where to start looking?'

'I have a good knowledge of geology and I know how to recognise signs of mineralisation. I carry equipment that allows me to analyse rocks, but often it's down to intuition. I've been looking for, and mining, gold and diamonds for many years.'

Clare's eyes were drawn to the prospector's darkly tanned fingers on the steering wheel and she recalled that when she had shaken his hand the skin on his palm had felt rough, as if he was used to manual work. 'Have you actually worked in mines? What made you choose such a dangerous job?'

He shrugged. 'I needed to make a living, but I left school with few qualifications, which limited my career options,' he said drily. 'Mining is dangerous but it's well paid.'

A poorly educated miner who read Tolstoy and poetry? Clare studied his chiselled profile and wondered where he had learned to speak faultless English, albeit with a sexy accent. She flushed when he turned his head and caught her looking at him. 'You obviously lead an interesting life, Mr Cazorra,' she murmured.

'My name is Diego,' he reminded her. 'I've got a question for you, Sister. What made you decide to become a nun?'

Oh, help. She bit her lip as she searched her mind for an answer.

'If you don't mind me saying so, you are a beautiful young woman and committing yourself to a life of chastity is not normal, in my opinion.'

She shot him a startled glance at the same time as he turned his head towards her, and their eyes met. Once again she was aware of a sizzle of sexual chemistry between them. Did he really think she was beautiful? For years she had compared her very ordinary features to her sister's stunning looks and she had never had much self-confidence in her appearance.

The Mother Superior had warned her that the prospector was a womaniser, Clare reminded herself. He probably flirted with every woman he met, but even if he did find her attractive, she could not respond to the gleam in his eyes without blowing her cover that she was a nun. She realised he was waiting for her to answer his question, but lying did not come naturally to her.

'All of us are on a personal journey, and this is the road I have chosen to take,' she said vaguely. It was not entirely untruthful because the road to Torrente led to her sister. She was eager to change the subject and at that moment a flock of brightly coloured birds flew out of the trees.

'Oh, look! Are they parrots? I've only ever seen a parrot in a cage. There is such a huge diversity of wildlife in the rainforest. I recently watched a documentary about the Amazon. Did you know that over a thousand species of birds are found in the Amazon basin?' Clare was determined to keep the prospector's attention away from her personal life. 'Sister Ann said you know the rainforest well. I suppose you must get the chance to see many different species of wildlife?'

He gave another shrug. 'I've hunted wild boar occasionally if I needed a meal and run out of supplies. And it's always a good idea to check your sleeping bag before you get into it in case a tarantula has crawled inside.'

'Really?' Clare paled. 'I hate spiders.' She winced as the Jeep hit a pothole in the road and she was jolted in her seat, only saved from hitting her head on the window by her seat belt. The dirt road was becoming progressively bumpier as they drove further west, and the trees on either side grew so densely that in places they formed a tunnel that the sunlight could barely penetrate. She did not want to think about spiders or any other deadly creatures that might be lurking in the humid gloom of the forest. Nor did she want to think of the evil men who had snatched Becky. She forced her mind to more pleasant thoughts. 'I believe there are many different species of monkeys living in the rainforest. Do you like monkeys, Mr Cazorra?'

'To eat?' he drawled.

'Of course not. You don't really eat monkeys, do you?' She gave him a horrified look, only realising when he grinned that he was teasing her. His smile should come with a danger warning, she thought, feeling the hard points of her nipples chafe against her lacy bra. Her inconvenient awareness of the prospector was making a stressful situation even worse. She could not bring herself to use his first name, preferring to keep a sense of formality between them. With a deep sigh, she turned her head and stared out of the window to remark on interesting flora and fauna as the Jeep bounced along the uneven road.

They had been travelling for a couple of hours when the first drops of rain landed on the windscreen and quickly turned the dust-covered glass opaque, despite the efforts of the windscreen wipers.

Diego cursed beneath his breath as within seconds the shower became a torrential downpour. From experience he knew the potholes in the road would soon fill up and the road would turn into a river of mud. He needed all his concentration to drive in these conditions, but his passenger hadn't stopped talking for what seemed like eternity.

'Sister Clare—' he interrupted her mid flow as she listed some of the different types of flowers that apparently grew in the rainforest; the woman was a walking encyclopedia '—have you ever considered joining a silent order?'

She blushed and Diego was fascinated by the rosy stain that spread across her cheeks. He couldn't remember ever seeing a woman blush before, but the kind of women he associated with were not sweet virgins, he acknowledged. He pictured Sister Clare's pretty face flushed with a glow of sexual arousal and shifted uncomfortably in his seat as his body reacted predictably.

'I'm sorry.' She nibbled her lower lip with her teeth, making Diego long to soothe the tender flesh with his tongue. 'I tend to talk too much when I'm nervous,' she admitted.

'You're right to be nervous. Torrente is not a nice place.' He wished she had taken heed of what he'd told her about the town before they had left Manaus. 'If you want to turn back, say so now. Once the road floods, I won't be able to turn the Jeep round without the risk of the tyres becoming stuck in the mud.'

'We can't turn back!' Panic made Clare's voice sharp. The prospector gave her a curious glance and she forced herself to speak in a calmer tone. 'I want to carry on to Torrente. I have a job to do there.'

'Couldn't you have taught at a Sunday school in England?' he muttered, followed by something in Portuguese, and Clare guessed it was a good thing she did not understand.

He had been right about the rain in the Amazon being a deluge. Five minutes ago the sun had been shining, but now it was as if a dam had burst and gallons of water were falling on to the Jeep and the road, which, as she peered through the windscreen, she could see was quickly becoming a river of mud.

She was jolted violently as the wheels went down another pothole and the truck came to a standstill. Diego revved the engine but the Jeep did not move and, looking out of the side window, Clare saw the wheels spinning round in the mud. When he rammed the gear lever into reverse she held her breath as the Jeep moved backwards a little way before it stopped.

'What are we going to do?' Clare had to shout above the noise of the rain hitting the roof. 'I thought the bad weather wasn't due for a few days?'

'It rains every day in the rainforest,' Diego said ironically. 'This shower will probably last for an hour. When the wet season starts properly it sometimes rains for days without stopping.'

'I suppose we'll have to wait until the rain stops before we can try to dig the wheels out of the mud?'

'If we wait, the Jeep will sink up to the axles in no time. I've got some wooden planks in the back that I'll put under the rear tyres.'

Diego pulled the brim of his hat down low to shield his eyes from the rain and opened the door. Within seconds of stepping out of the Jeep he was soaked to the skin. 'Slide across to the driver's seat,' he ordered Clare. 'When you hear me thump twice on the Jeep I want you to start the engine, select reverse gear and then accelerate slowly.' He looked at her closely. 'Do you know how to drive a car?'

'Yes, of course I do.' She had never driven a four-by-four or attempted to free a vehicle that was stuck in mud, but Clare tried to sound more confident than she felt. After some fumbling, she found reverse gear and when she heard two thumps on the bodywork she pressed her foot down on the accelerator pedal. Nothing happened, so she pressed harder until finally the Jeep rolled backwards.

They were free! Feeling a sense of achievement, she smiled at the prospector when he yanked open the door, but her smile faded as she took in his mud-spattered appearance.

'*Santa Mãe!* I told you to accelerate *slowly*. Look at me.'

Clare couldn't stop looking at him! Even covered in mud he was the sexiest man she had ever laid eyes on. She shifted across to the passenger seat so that he could climb into the Jeep. There was even mud on his face, but he still looked gorgeous and he exuded an air of toughness and raw masculinity that made Clare imagine being swept up into his arms and carried off to be thoroughly ravished by him.

His T-shirt was sodden and her heart skipped a beat when he pulled it off to reveal his tanned chest, covered with a fuzz of golden hairs. Heaven help her. He had an amazing body. She could not tear her eyes from his well-defined six-pack and powerful shoulder muscles. Her parents would snap him up on to A-Star PR's books, but she would feel a lot more comfortable if his toned physique was hidden from her view. 'Do you have a spare shirt I could find for you?' Her voice sounded annoyingly breathless.

'There's no point. It's likely the Jeep will get stuck again and I'll have to get out in the rain to free up the wheels.' His eyes narrowed on her pink cheeks. 'Next time, could you not stamp on the accelerator like you're a racing car driver?'

She was already overwrought with worry about Becky and felt ultra-sensitive to his criticism. 'I'm sorry you got covered in mud, but I thought you wanted to get the Jeep out of the pothole,' she said stiffly.

'You have no idea what I want, Sister,' Diego muttered. If she did not stop looking at him like she was doing—as if she had never seen a half-naked male before—he would be unable to restrain himself from showing her *exactly* what he wanted.

He dragged his gaze from her cupid's-bow lips and tried not to imagine how soft and moist her mouth would feel beneath his if he kissed her. It was likely she had never seen a man's bare flesh, he conceded. His skin was burning up, but for the first time in his life he could not succumb to temptation. If she had been any other woman he would have suggested they climb into the back of the Jeep so that they could alleviate their mutual desire.

For it *was* mutual. Diego's extensive experience of women meant he was infallible at recognising the telltale signs of sexual awareness. Sister Clare was desperately trying to hide her reaction to the chemistry fizzing between them, but her big blue eyes reflected her sexual interest in him that her chosen way of life commanded her to deny.

Deus, women were always trouble, he thought, reaching behind the seat for a beer. He flipped off the bottle top with the opener that, for convenience, he had screwed to the Jeep's dashboard and lifted the bottle towards his lips but, before he could take a swig, a hand grabbed his arm.

'Surely you are not thinking of drinking alcohol while you're driving?' Clare said in an outraged voice.

'I'd prefer not to be thinking about it, Sister,' Diego murmured as he lifted the bottle closer to his mouth and felt her fingers dig into his bicep. Her hand looked pale against his darkly tanned skin. He visualised her naked white body beneath him, her soft thighs spread in readiness for him to possess her. Tension coiled low in his gut and he shrugged her hand from his arm and put the bottle to his lips, his taste buds anticipating his first sip of beer. It was warm rather than ice-cold the way he liked it, but it was better than nothing.

Diego stiffened when Clare leaned across him and he inhaled a fresh lemony fragrance, which he recognised was soap. He supposed nuns did not wear perfume or make-up. Sister Clare's smooth complexion was entirely natural. Her long eyelashes were dark auburn and he wondered if her hair, hidden beneath her veil, was the same colour.

The jangling sound of metal jerked Diego from his fantasies and he frowned when he saw that she had taken the keys out of the ignition.

'Drunk driving is a despicable crime and potentially life-threatening to other road users,' she stated.

He tried to control his impatience. 'In normal circumstances I agree that driving after drinking alcohol is unacceptable, certainly in a town. But, in case you hadn't noticed, we are the only people on the road. We haven't seen another vehicle since we left Manaus, and we won't see another one because no one else is crazy enough to want to go to Torrente.'

He held out his hand. 'Give me the keys, Sister Clare, and let's be on our way. We can't afford any more delays if you want to reach Torrente by Sunday.'

She *had* to be there on Sunday to pay Becky's ransom. Clare remembered the instructions from the kidnappers to wait in a cave close to a waterfall just outside the town. She felt torn, knowing the gold prospector was right and they could not afford to be delayed. But she fervently believed that driving while under the influence of alcohol was wrong.

'My aunt was killed by a drunk driver,' she burst out. 'Aunt Edith was knocked off her bicycle one Christmas Eve. The driver of the car who was responsible for her death was found to be three times over the legal alcohol limit.'

Diego squinted through the mud-smeared windscreen at the torrential rain. 'I'm sorry about your aunt, but we're unlikely to come across a cyclist in the middle of the rainforest.' He looked at Clare, noting the stubborn set of her chin but also the faint quiver of her lower lip. She had the most beautiful eyes, twin sapphires that at this moment shimmered with a sheen of tears. 'Damn it.' He exhaled heavily. *'All right,'* he muttered as he wound down the window and poured the beer on to the ground.

'Satisfied?' He glared at Clare as she silently handed him the keys.

The word hovered in the hot, humid atmosphere inside the Jeep as sexual tension exploded between them. Clare's gaze locked with the prospector's grey eyes. *Satisfied* made her think wanton thoughts and imagine how it would feel to be satisfied by him. With his rugged good looks and to-die-for body, he was every woman's fantasy and, without consciously being aware of moving, she swayed towards him, her eyes unknowingly issuing an invitation as she moistened her dry lips with the tip of her tongue.

Seemingly in slow motion, he lowered his head until his face was so near to hers that she felt the whisper of his breath on her cheek. Another few centimetres and his mouth would brush across her lips. She held her breath, willing him, wanting him to kiss her.

Suddenly Becky's face flashed into her mind. Dear heaven, *what was she doing?* Clare silently questioned. Self-disgust swept through her as she realised she had not given her sister a thought while she had been panting over the gold prospector.

She jerked away from him and inched across her seat until she could go no further and was pressed up against the door. 'Please, can we continue our journey, Mr Cazorra?' she said in a low voice.

For a moment she thought he was going to refuse. When she peeped at him she was shocked by the feral hunger that tautened his features and gave him a wolf-like appearance that was further enhanced by the hungry gleam in his eyes. She was relieved when he inserted the key into the ignition and started the engine.

Diego forced himself to concentrate on steering the Jeep around the rain-filled potholes. It was impossible to tell how deep the holes were and he wanted to avoid becoming stuck in the mud again at all costs. The quicker they got to Torrente and he could deliver his beautiful, infuriating passenger, the better it would suit him.

He glanced at her sitting primly beside him, her body hidden by her nun's habit and her hair covered by her veil so that only her lovely face was visible. Her serene expression irked him. She was apparently unaffected by the fact that they had been a heartbeat away from kissing, while he was aware of a dull ache in his groin that felt as if he'd been kicked by a mule.

'You seem to have trouble remembering my name, Sister Clare,' he drawled. 'I'll remind you again. It's Diego. If you call me Mr Cazorra once more, I might be tempted to assist your memory.'

'Assist, how?' Clare was curious, despite her determination to keep her distance from him, something that was difficult to do physically while they were cooped up in the Jeep. She was intensely aware of him every time he moved his arm to change gear, and when he took off his hat and ran his hand through his hair, her fingers itched to brush back the dark blond strands that had fallen across his brow.

He took his eyes briefly from the road and sent her a smouldering glance that melted her insides. 'I'll have to kiss you until you have learned my name.'

CHAPTER THREE

HEAT SWEPT THROUGH Clare and she felt herself blush from the tips of her ears down to her toes as she visualised Diego carrying out his threat. This had to stop, she told herself firmly. She had come to Brazil for one reason only—to rescue Becky. She had no idea what kind of conditions her sister was being held in, but the severed piece of earlobe sent to her by the kidnappers made the situation very real and very dangerous. She could not allow herself to be distracted by the outrageously sexy man sitting beside her.

Unable to think of a suitable retort to what she assumed was his teasing remark, she turned her head to stare out of the window at the unending jungle. He would not really dare kiss her, she assured herself. But she remembered the Mother Superior's warning about him being a womaniser and decided not to give him any opportunity to take liberties with her.

They had been driving for some while—Clare had been absorbed in her thoughts and had lost all track of time—when the rain stopped as suddenly as it had started. The heat of the sun close to the equator caused the wet leaves to evaporate steam into the air so that the forest looked like a giant smoking cauldron. Even the huge puddles were steaming on the road that stretched ahead as far as the eye could see, like a giant brown snake wending through the green forest.

'When was your aunt killed?' Diego asked suddenly, his voice breaking the tense silence that had filled the Jeep for miles.

'Almost two years ago.' Clare remembered the cold grey day before Christmas when her mother had phoned to break the news that Aunt Edith had died after being knocked off her bike by a car. The fact that the driver was drunk at the time of the accident had only been revealed later at the inquest, and Clare had felt anger as well as grief that her aunt's life had been ended by a thoughtless, selfish act.

It was hard to imagine that when she had left England three days ago the weather had, typically for November, been freezing cold with the promise of sleet, while in Brazil the temperature on the dashboard was showing thirty-seven degrees centigrade and the humidity was so high that Clare's clothes were sticking to her.

'The car driver said that he skidded on a patch of ice, but the police breathalysed him and found he was over the alcohol limit and shouldn't have been driving,' she said tautly. 'My aunt was older than my parents, but she was fit and healthy until her life was cut short.'

'You were obviously fond of her.'

It was strange how it was often the way that you didn't appreciate what you had until it was gone, Clare mused. She missed Aunt Edith's sensible advice and dry humour more than she would have believed.

'I lived with her for part of my childhood.' She gave a rueful smile. 'At the time I hated being packed off to her cottage in a remote Kent village while my parents remained at our home in London. It never occurred to me that my aunt might not have enjoyed having her life disrupted by a stroppy kid.'

'Why did your parents send you away from home?' Diego could not explain why he was curious about his passenger. Usually he avoided personal discussions. He was never even mildly interested in his mistresses' private lives, and he discouraged curiosity about himself. His past was not a place he wanted to revisit or reveal to anyone.

'My sister was very ill when she was a child. She was diagnosed with leukaemia when she was six years old and underwent chemotherapy for several years before she was finally given the all-clear. My parents couldn't cope with spending weeks, sometimes months, in the hospital with Becky at the same time as trying to run their PR company and look after me.'

She sighed. 'It sounds ridiculous, but I felt abandoned by my parents. I was only nine when Becky became ill, and I didn't understand how serious her illness was. When my parents spent so much time with her I believed she was their favourite child.'

'That's understandable.' Diego could appreciate Clare's feeling of abandonment when she was a child. He had been abandoned by his father before he had been born, and his mother's dependence on crack cocaine meant that he had learned to fend for himself from a young age. 'You said your sister made a full recovery. Once she was better, did you return to live with your parents?'

'No. I visited them at weekends, but I had started at a secondary school in Kent and my parents decided it would be better not to disrupt my education by moving me to a new school in London.'

'You must have resented your sister because she lived with your parents while you were left with your aunt.'

Clare was surprised by Diego's perception. There *had* been times when she had felt jealous of all the attention Becky received, she acknowledged, but she had hated herself for her jealousy because, of course, her sister had not chosen to have leukaemia.

'I love my sister. It wasn't Becky's fault that I grew up feeling pushed out of the family. I was lucky that I hadn't been struck down with a horrible illness or spent chunks of my childhood in the hospital. My parents dealt with a difficult situation in the best way they could.'

Thinking about Becky and wondering if the kidnappers had harmed her made Clare's stomach contract. Becky had suffered so much as a child and it seemed desperately unfair that once again her life was threatened. Clare hoped her sister was not making the situation even more difficult. Becky had been over-indulged by their parents during the long years of her illness, and her subsequent career as a successful model meant that she was used to people rushing around after her. But it was unlikely the kidnappers would treat Becky like a princess.

The Jeep lurched as the wheels went down another crater in the road and Clare winced and rubbed her bruised spine. The continual jolting made her feel as though she was inside the drum of a washing machine on the fast spin cycle.

'How much longer do you think it will take us to reach the village where we are going to stop for the night?'

Diego glanced at the instrument panel. 'We've driven one hundred and forty miles. Inua village is two hundred and fifty miles from Manaus and because of the damned potholes in the road we're travelling at an average speed of thirty-five miles an hour.'

'So we should reach the village in just over three hours,' Clare said instantly. She caught Diego's surprised look. 'I have a freakish brain when it comes to maths. At school, when my friends were trying to decide what careers to choose, I always knew that I wanted to be an accountant.'

'So, did you go to university?'

She nodded. 'I have a degree in Accountancy and Marketing and after I graduated I was headhunted by a top bank in the City of London. I worked for the bank for eighteen months, before I became chief accountant at my parents' public relations company. Recently, I've become much more involved in the actual PR side of the business.'

Diego frowned. 'I'm trying to understand what made you give up a good career and cut yourself off from your family and friends. How do your parents feel about your decision, especially as you have chosen to leave England and join a holy order in Brazil?'

Clare regretted telling him so much about herself. It was a sign of her insecurity that she felt she needed to boast of her academic achievements to make up for the fact that she wasn't beautiful, she acknowledged ruefully. For a few moments she had forgotten that the Mother Superior had persuaded her to pretend to be a nun for her protection. She felt uncomfortable about her deception but she did not dare risk telling Diego the real reason why she was going to Torrente.

'My parents support what I am doing,' she murmured, remembering how her father had hugged her tightly when she'd said goodbye to him before leaving for Brazil. 'What about you?' She steered the conversation away from herself. 'Do you have a family?'

'No.'

When it became clear that Diego wasn't going to add anything more, Clare tried again. 'So, you're not married?'

'No.'

'I imagine being a gold prospector means you spend a lot of time on your own. It must be a lonely way of life.'

'I like my own company,' he drawled.

Clare gave up. She wanted to ask him how he had developed an appreciation of classic literature if his education had been as poor as he had said. There was something about him that made her think he was more than a rough, tough prospector. It was not just because of the books she had found. She could not explain why she sensed an air of mystery about him, but the idea that he was hiding something reinforced her decision to keep the truth about her identity a secret.

The surface of the dirt road grew worse the further west they travelled. Twice more the Jeep became embedded in mud. The first time, Diego managed to free the wheels by placing wooden planks beneath them, but on the second occasion he had to use a specially designed jack to lift up the front of the Jeep. It was a lengthy procedure and Clare had to get out to help and found herself ankle-deep in mud which dried to the consistency of cement in the sun.

By the time they reached Inua she was wilting from

the humidity and exhaustion and visualised a clean hotel room, hopefully with air conditioning and perhaps even a bath.

'Where is the rest of the village?' she asked Diego when he parked in a clearing in the forest where a few huts with thatched roofs were grouped around a larger hut that seemed to be a communal place for the villagers. The men sitting on the floor outside the large hut were mainly dressed in shorts and shirts, but the women were topless and the children who rushed up to greet the white-skinned strangers simply wore loincloths.

'This is it,' Diego told her. 'Inua is home to a small community called the Yanomami.'

'But you said that tourists stay here.' Clare looked at the ramshackle huts. 'Where will I sleep tonight?' Her visions of a comfortable bedroom and en suite bathroom were disappearing.

'The guest hut is over there.' Diego pointed to a hut set slightly apart from the others. 'Don't worry,' he said when he saw her expression. 'The wooden cubicle next to the hut is a shower. The Yanomami children find the shower fascinating because they bathe in the river.'

He walked away to talk to an elderly tribesman and came back to Clare a few minutes later. 'I'll get your bag from the Jeep and show you your accommodation. The tribal elder, Jacinto, asked if we would like to eat dinner with the Yanomami people, but they do actually hunt monkey and that's what's on tonight's menu. I guessed you'd want me to decline the invitation.'

'Thank you.' Clare shuddered. She hadn't felt like eating much since she had heard about Becky being kidnapped, and the idea of eating monkey destroyed all vestiges of her appetite. She followed Diego into the guest hut and was relieved to see a wooden bed frame. The mattress was woefully thin, but at least she would not have to sleep on the floor.

'I realise it's not the New York Hilton,' Diego drawled when he saw her expression, 'but I assume you are used to living a simple life at the convent.'

She looked at him suspiciously. 'How does a gold prospector and self-confessed loner know what the New York Hilton is like?'

He gave her one of his heart-stopping grins and ignored her question. 'I'm going to cook dinner on the camping stove. I only have non-perishable tinned food, nothing fancy. But you're welcome to join me.'

'Actually, I think I'll have a shower and an early night. It's been a tiring day.' The heat and her constant worry about Becky had made her feel drained both physically and emotionally. Her fierce awareness of Diego was not helping matters, Clare conceded as she watched him walk over to the Jeep. A brief spectacular sunset had streaked the sky with hues of pink and orange, but now darkness was closing in and she felt very alone in an alien environment.

It was a relief to take off the stiff serge habit and her veil. The shower was surprisingly powerful, but Clare was convinced she had glimpsed a snake slither out of the cubicle as she had entered and she did not dare hang around in case it came back.

Even at night the humidity was so high that she felt as if she was being smothered in a damp blanket. She had packed a light cotton chemise to sleep in, but she was still too hot and the mosquitoes were eating her alive. She lay on the bed, huddled beneath the mosquito net, and wondered where Becky was sleeping tonight. The rainforest was even noisier at night than during the day, as hundreds of species of insects and nocturnal creatures vied to make the loudest sounds.

What was that? Clare tensed when she heard a scurrying noise on the floor of the hut. Could it be a rat? Her muscles tensed and her heart was pounding. The noise came again and she switched on her torch and shone it on the floor. The beam of light revealed a huge cockroach, its hard black shell gleaming and its long antennae twitching as it moved purposefully towards the bed.

'Ugh!' Clare's nerve crumbled. The rainforest was a terrifying place. She loved the English countryside, but here in the jungle she imagined what other creatures might be crawling or slithering inside the hut. Panic engulfed her and, without thinking of anything but her desperate need to find a place of safety, she leapt out of bed and remembered to grab the briefcase containing the ransom money before she tore out of the hut. She sprinted over to the Jeep faster than she had ever run in her life. The rough ground hurt her bare feet and the beam from her torch picked out glowing pinpricks of light that she realised were the eyes of animals hiding in the dark forest. Frantic with fear, she pulled open the back door of the Jeep.

'Diego, there's a *huge* cockroach in the hut.' She paused to drag oxygen into her lungs—and stared.

Diego was sprawled on top of a mattress that he had unrolled to cover the floor of the Jeep. He was leaning back against a couple of cushions, bare chested, his jeans sitting low on his hips. A kerosene lamp emitted a bright glow that fell on the pages of the book he was reading and cast a pool of light on his torso, highlighting the golden hairs on his chest. With his tousled blond hair and the blond stubble on his jaw, he reminded Clare of a lion: sleek, muscular and supremely powerful.

'Unlikely,' he drawled in his laid-back manner that gave the impression he took nothing in life too seriously.

'There *is*. I know what a cockroach looks like.'

'I meant it's unlikely there's only one. Cockroaches like company and they like to hide in small spaces. There is probably a nest of them behind the headboard of the bed.'

Clare shuddered. 'I can't sleep in the hut with a family of cockroaches.' She screamed as she felt something touch her foot. *'There's a snake on me.* It's running up my leg!'

'Snakes don't run.' Diego held up the lamp so that it shone on the ground where Clare was standing. 'It's just a harmless lizard,' he told her as he brushed the vivid green creature from her leg. 'It's probably far more scared of you than you are of it.'

'I wouldn't bank on it,' Clare muttered as she scrambled into the Jeep, unaware that as she did so the hem of her chemise slid up to reveal several inches of her bare thighs. She pushed her mane of long auburn hair out of her eyes and looked pleadingly at Diego. 'Please can I sleep in here tonight?'

He did not reply and she wondered why he was staring at her as if she had grown another head. 'What's wrong?' she said shakily. 'Do I have another lizard on me?'

'I thought nuns had to cut their hair short.'

Idiot, Clare silently berated herself. She had forgotten that she wasn't wearing her nun's habit and veil. Her hair had dried quickly after her shower, but the humidity and the fact that she did not have her straighteners had resulted in a wild tangle of curls tumbling halfway down her back. She tensed as Diego reached out and wound a curl around his fingers.

'It feels like silk,' he murmured. 'And it's such an amazing colour. It reminds me of the conkers I saw children collecting in England when I was there one autumn.' His eyes narrowed on Clare's flushed face. 'It's a pity to hide such beautiful hair beneath a veil.'

She sensed he was waiting for an explanation and searched her mind for one. 'I'm a novice, which is why I wear a white veil instead of a black one. I don't have to cut my hair until I take my final vows.'

'When will you do that?'

'Soon,' she assured him quickly.

Diego shut the door of the Jeep and resumed his position stretched out on the mattress with his shoulders propped against a pile of cushions. He tucked his hands behind his head and the action drew Clare's gaze to his bare chest and superb muscle definition.

'So you are not yet absolutely committed to your cause?' he said softly. 'You could change your mind?'

The speculative gleam in his light grey eyes sent a quiver along her spine as she became aware of the sexual chemistry fizzing in the close confines of the Jeep. Clare realised she had swapped one danger for another. She had felt unsafe in the hut, but her intense awareness of Diego could prove to be a greater threat to her peace of mind, especially when his gaze lingered quite blatantly on her breasts that were inadequately covered by her cotton chemise.

She remembered Becky and the vital reason why she needed to get to Torrente. 'Nothing will deter me from the path I have chosen.'

His mouth curved into a sexy smile that should be illegal in front of susceptible females. 'You don't think you could be tempted to choose a different path?'

Heaven help her. She wished he would stop looking at her as if he was imagining stripping her naked and having his wicked way with her. She glanced rather desperately around the Jeep for something to cover herself with. 'Could I borrow a sleeping bag?'

'Help yourself.'

She unzipped the bag and gave it a thorough inspection for tarantulas before she got into it and pulled the zip up to her chin. Immediately her temperature soared but at least her body was hidden from Diego's gaze. 'Temptation is the work of the devil,' she said primly.

'Are you telling me you have never been tempted by desire, which is a perfectly natural human instinct?'

His voice was like molten syrup sliding sensuously over her body, inciting all sorts of shocking images in her head. She was fiercely attracted to Diego but she certainly wasn't going to admit it. 'If I did ever feel tempted…I would pray until those feelings passed.'

The Jeep was suddenly plunged into blackness as Diego switched off the lamp. Clare heard him moving. He was obviously trying to get comfortable but his height meant that he had to lie diagonally across the Jeep.

'While you're praying to be delivered from temptation, maybe you could say one for me, Sister,' he muttered. 'You'd better pray real hard because I keep picturing you in your cotton nightdress and I'll be honest, I've never been so tempted by a woman in my life.'

If the devil *did* exist and was waiting to receive sinners into the fires of hell, he was toast, Diego thought to himself. He was burning up with desire to unzip Sister Clare's sleeping bag and remove the tantalising, almost see-through garment she was wearing. If he had ever given a thought to what nuns wore in bed he would have guessed something demure and ankle-length, not a sexy little slip that left little to his imagination.

'I'm sorry I interrupted you when you were reading,' she said quietly. Her voice was as soft as the velvet darkness surrounding them. 'You told me you had a poor education, so when did you discover an appreciation of classic and contemporary literature? I noticed you have a collection of books by a wide range of authors.'

The question took Diego back almost two decades to when he and Cruz had been employed by Earl Bancroft. His first instinct was to tell Sister Clare to mind her own business, but he needed something to distract his thoughts from his damnable desire for her.

'I once worked at a diamond mine in Brazil which was owned by an English earl. My friend was dating the Earl's daughter, and I used to go to the ranch house with him and chat up the housekeeper.' He grinned. 'Lucia was a few years older than me and she taught me a lot.'

'About literature?' Clare asked disbelievingly.

'Well, no. I admit I was more interested in her physical attributes than her mind. But she used to let me borrow books from the Earl's library while he was away.'

Diego remembered he had been blown away by the number of books to choose from. When he had been in prison, Father Vincenzi had taught him English and encouraged him to read, and he had developed a love of well-written stories—anything from classic literature to political thrillers. After his release he had gone to work at the diamond mine at Montez Claros and had spent his free time in Earl Bancroft's library, glad to escape his life of hard physical labour while he was absorbed in a book.

'What happened to your friend who was dating the Earl's daughter?' Clare asked curiously.

'He married her, eventually, and now they have twin boys.'

'Wouldn't you like to get married like your friend?'

'Nope.'

'Why not?'

Diego gave a contemplative sigh. 'I had a girlfriend once who liked me to buy her boxes of chocolates, but because she was watching her weight she only ate the strawberry creams and left the other flavours. To me, marriage is like only enjoying your favourite chocolate in a selection box and ignoring all the other flavours, which to my way of thinking is a waste,' he explained laconically.

Clare made a choked sound. 'That is the most chauvinistic statement I have ever heard. You are...' she struggled to find an adjective that conveyed her disgust '...astonishing.'

'You're not the first woman to think so.'

Clare could not see his expression in the dark Jeep but she pictured his sexy grin. 'I didn't mean it in a good way,' she muttered.

'I still think that how I choose to live my life is more understandable than your decision to deny yourself the pleasures of physical intimacy,' he drawled. 'How can you be certain you won't want to marry in the future if you have never had a relationship with a man? Wouldn't it be a good idea to at least date a few guys before you make your final vows?'

'As a matter of fact I did have a relationship, with a two-timing compulsive liar and cheater.' She could not disguise the bitterness in her voice when she thought of Mark.

'Ah.' Diego's response was laden with meaning.

Clare frowned. 'What do you mean, "Ah"?'

'My theory is that it is possible, likely even, that your decision to become a nun was the result of having your heart broken by the guy who cheated on you.' Diego sounded satisfied that he had resolved a question that had been niggling him. 'You were hurt once and you have decided to hide away from life so that you don't risk getting hurt again.'

Clare was tempted to tell Mr Know-It-All what he could do with his theory but, although she hated to admit it to herself, there *was* a grain of truth in Diego's words. Her break-up with Mark had not made her turn to a religious life, but she had become a bit of a hermit for the past year.

'What was your ex-boyfriend, apart from a jerk? I mean, what job does he do?' Diego reworded his question.

'His name is Mark Penry, which I expect means nothing to you as you spend most of your time living away from civilisation, but he is a very successful male model. He recently appeared in an advertising campaign for the famous Lux brand of underwear. Pictures of Mark wearing just a pair of designer boxer shorts featured on billboards in just about every major city around the world.'

'You mean you broke your heart over a pretty boy who advertises pants?' Diego said sardonically.

'He's not a pretty boy… Well, actually he is,' Clare conceded, remembering how she'd found it irritating when Mark had checked his appearance in every mirror he passed. 'The point is that he let me believe we had a future together. I felt such a fool when I discovered that he was sleeping with another model, especially as many of the other staff at A-Star PR knew, but they didn't tell me because they didn't want to hurt my feelings.'

It was odd that in all other aspects of her life she was sensible to the point of boring, Clare mused, but her good sense seemed to desert her when it came to picking men. She remembered when she was seventeen she'd fallen for a boy at college and had believed Tony returned her feelings. But she'd been devastated when she discovered that he had only asked her out because he'd made a bet with his mates that he could get her into bed. Clare recalled the advice Aunt Edith had given her.

'Don't be in a rush to have sex. One day you will meet the right man, who you will love with all your heart and soul and who will love you.'

Aunt Edith's rather brusque manner had hidden a kind heart. She had understood that Clare had felt second-best when she was a child because her parents had lavished most of their attention on Becky. Clare had taken her aunt's words to heart, and all through university she had dated guys but had never been tempted to take the relationships further. When she'd met Mark she had thought that he was 'the one.' But finding out that he was a liar and cheater had shattered her illusions, especially when Mark had said he'd been forced to get sex elsewhere because of Clare's insistence on waiting until she felt ready to give her virginity to him.

But Mark was a saint compared to Diego Cazorra! She would never be able to look at a box of chocolates again without being reminded of his outrageous attitude towards women. She wished she was brave enough to go and sleep in the hut. It seemed impossible that she would be able to fall asleep when she was supremely conscious of Diego's half-naked body squashed up against her with only her sleeping bag to separate them.

It was her last conscious thought. When she opened her eyes again she saw through the window that the sky had lightened to pearly grey tinged with the palest pink as the sun rose above the tree tops.

Something had disturbed her. She vaguely remembered hearing a harsh voice and realised that Diego was speaking in what she assumed was Portuguese. She unzipped the sleeping bag so that she could sit up, and turned to find him muttering in his sleep. Heaven knew what he was dreaming about. His features were drawn into an expression of terrible anguish and he was tossing his head restlessly from side to side.

'*Assassino!*' He shouted the word and then covered his face with his forearm and gave a groan that sounded as if it had been ripped from his soul.

'Diego!' She called his name several times but could not wake him. He groaned again as if he was in agony. Was he ill? In desperation, Clare shook his shoulder. 'Diego. Diego. *Mr Cazorra*, wake up.'

He moved so quickly that she was taken off guard when he slid his hand behind her neck and threaded his fingers into her hair.

'Do you remember what I said I would do if you called me Mr Cazorra?' he drawled.

CHAPTER FOUR

DIEGO'S SILVER WOLF'S eyes gleamed with a feral hunger as he drew Clare's face down to his and angled his mouth over her lips. His kiss was like no other she had ever experienced—deeply sensual and so utterly irresistible that she did not stand a chance against his skilful seduction.

Still half-dazed with sleep, but more dazzled by him, her lips parted of their own volition when his mouth exerted subtle pressure. Like a connoisseur of fine wine, he tasted her slowly and unhurriedly, yet with such bone-shaking eroticism that she melted against him.

The sense of unreality she had felt since she'd arrived in Brazil increased, and she sank into a dreamlike state where she was only conscious of the strength of Diego's arms around her, the divine smell of him, and the taste of him when she dipped her tongue into his mouth. He overwhelmed her and the feel of his hand smoothing up and down her spine evoked a languorous warmth in her veins.

It seemed perfectly natural when he rolled her on to her back so that she was lying beneath him. His weight crushed her and she felt the slight abrasion of his chest hairs brush against the upper swell of her breasts above the neckline of her chemise.

He deepened the kiss, and the languorous feeling
was replaced with a fierce pull of desire in the pit of
her stomach so that she lifted her hips, unconsciously
seeking to assuage the ache inside her. She sensed a new
urgency in Diego, a barely controlled savagery as he
ravished her mouth with his intoxicating mastery, taking everything she offered him and demanding more.

Molten heat pooled between Clare's legs when she
felt the hard ridge of Diego's arousal straining beneath
his jeans and pushing insistently into the cradle of her
hips. She heard him mutter something indistinct and the
sexy huskiness in his voice scraped her sensitive nerve
endings. He was so *male*, hard against her softness, his
passion without frills, without subtlety, a primal hunger that threatened to consume her in its fiery flame.

She lifted her hand and touched the blond stubble
on his jaw. It was not rough as she had expected, but
felt silky beneath her fingertips. Utterly engrossed, she
moved her hand higher to stroke his hair back from his
cheek—and froze.

The top of his right ear was missing.

In an instant she was hurtled back to reality as she
thought of Becky and the ghastly contents of the box
the kidnappers had sent her. Shame engulfed her as she
realised that while Diego had been kissing her she had
forgotten about her sister's plight.

Diego's jaw hardened when he saw her shocked expression and he flicked his head so that his hair fell forwards to cover his mutilated ear. What did it mean? Clare
wondered numbly. Why did he have the same injury
that the kidnappers might have inflicted on her sister?

She pushed against his chest and when he rolled off

her she snatched a breath and groped for her sanity in a world that had gone mad.

'You were having a nightmare and I was trying to wake you.' She bit her lip as she remembered the indescribable horror in his voice when he'd shouted out. 'What was your dream about? You sounded like you were being tortured.' Her own voice shook and she was incapable of making light of what had happened.

'I don't remember dreaming about anything.' Diego swore silently. He knew what his dream had been about because it was always the same dream. The other inmates had called it the initiation, when new prisoners were beaten until they were a bloodied pulp and the prison guards looked the other way, or sometimes joined in. His horrific nightmares were a legacy of when he had been in prison and, although it was many years since he had been released from what had been a living hell, time had not erased the memories.

'You spoke in your sleep but I couldn't understand you.' Sister Clare's lovely face looked troubled. 'I wonder if something traumatic happened in your past that you relive in your dreams.'

She was too close to the truth for Diego's comfort. He shrugged. 'You may be right,' he drawled. 'I was deeply traumatised when Brazil lost the football World Cup.'

'I was being serious.' She firmed her lips that moments ago had softened when Diego had kissed her. He dragged his eyes from the temptation of her lush mouth and opened the door of the Jeep, pausing to grab his rucksack containing his wash kit before he jumped down and walked away.

His nightmares were the reason why he had never spent an entire night with a woman before, Diego brooded as he strode through the tribal village. When he visited his mistresses in Rio he always left them after sex and went home to sleep alone. During daytime hours he could control his mind and suppress his memories, but while he slept the demons inside him tortured his subconscious so that sometimes he woke up believing he was back in the prison cell he had shared with ten or more other men. The cell had been so small that the inmates had been forced to take it in turns to lie down on the floor to snatch an hour of sleep if they were lucky.

The experience had left him with an irrational fear of confined spaces which made him come out in a cold sweat whenever he rode in an elevator. Even being in the Jeep sometimes made him feel claustrophobic, and he kept the windows open so that he could feel fresh air on his face. He was sweating now, partly from his nightmare and partly because, as the sun burned through the mist, the humidity in the air rose rapidly. He walked through the trees to where a tributary of the river made a natural pool, which was safe to swim in.

Why the hell had he kissed Sister Clare like that? He had only intended to tease her and brush his lips lightly over hers, but when she had opened her mouth for him and he'd felt her ardent response, he had been powerless to resist her. It had never happened to him before. He was *always* in control.

Diego's jaw clenched. He had just proved that his self-discipline was not infallible and the discovery that he could be tempted to act without restraint shook him badly. If he could succumb to passion, he might just as easily succumb to anger and violence, like he had done when he was seventeen.

He stripped and dived into the pool, relishing the cool water washing over his heated skin. He felt more at home in the rainforest than he did in a city. Here, he was free to live his life on his terms without the need to bow to social conventions. Compared to the *favela* where he had spent his childhood, and prison where he had lost his soul, the tropical wilderness, although dangerous in its own way, provided him with a sense of peace. He would not allow a novice nun with the face of an angel and the body of Aphrodite to disturb his sanctuary, he assured himself.

He looked up at the sky and watched a bank of clouds roll in above the tree tops. Experience told him that another day of heavy rain lay ahead, and flooding would make the road from Inua village up to the border virtually impassable. He shrugged. His task was to escort Sister Clare to Torrente so that she could teach at the Sunday school and prepare to make her final vows and, although he felt she was making a mistake by committing her life to the church, it was her choice and none of his business.

Clare was conscious of Diego's brooding gaze as she stepped out of the guest hut and walked over to where he was leaning against the Jeep. She assumed he had swum in the river as his hair was damp, but it was drying quickly in the stifling heat and turning blonder by the minute. At least he was fully clothed, but his tight-fitting white T-shirt clung to the hard ridges of his abdominal muscles and evoked memories of when she had run her hands over his naked torso.

Although she was too hot in her nun's habit, she was glad that her body was hidden from his view, especially when she felt her hard nipples chafe against her bra. She was shocked by her wanton response to Diego and determined to keep her distance from him for the second leg of their journey to Torrente.

As she drew nearer to him he jammed his hat on to his head and pulled the brim down over his eyes, almost as if he wanted to hide his expression from her. If only her veil offered the same protection, she thought ruefully. A large raindrop landed on the dusty path in front of her, followed by another and another. She glanced up at the sullen clouds that had covered up the sun. 'I'm ready to go. I expect you want to get on the road before the weather worsens.'

She expected him to agree, but he did not move, and her intense awareness of him detected his sudden tension.

'Are you sure you want to continue?' Beneath the brim of his hat his eyes gleamed as bright and hard as polished steel. 'It's not too late for you to change your mind…and choose a different path.'

Clare realised he was not talking about her journey to Torrente. For a split second she was tempted to tell him the truth about why she needed to go to the town, but she could not forget the kidnappers' threat to kill her sister if she involved anyone else. She did not know if she could trust Diego. She barely knew anything about him and the few facts he had divulged about himself made him even more of an enigma.

'I am quite sure of the path I must follow,' she said in a low voice, her throat tightening with fear as she faced the prospect of meeting the kidnappers.

'*Deus.* Just because your boyfriend was a jerk, you are going to cut yourself off from life, from love?' Diego forgot his decision not to get involved in Sister Clare's life. 'When we kissed, you were warm and responsive in my arms. What will you do with all your passion and fire when you are shut away in a convent?'

Clare laughed derisively. 'What do you know about love? A man who describes marriage as limiting himself to choosing only one flavour of chocolates from a selection box?'

He stared at her and then shrugged his shoulders. 'You're right. I've never experienced love.' He opened the door of the Jeep and, before Clare had time to realise his intention, he lifted her off her feet and dumped her on the passenger seat. She took a deep breath to steady her racing heart as he climbed in beside her and started the engine.

'Never?' she asked curiously. 'Didn't your parents love you?'

He did not reply while he negotiated a series of deep holes in the road, but after a few minutes he said, 'I never met my father. He abandoned my mother after he got her pregnant with me. The only information she told me about him was that he was an Englishman called Philip Hawke who had come to work as a travel rep at the hotel in Brazil where my mother was a chambermaid. They had an affair, but when she told him she was expecting his child he returned to England and she never heard from him again.'

But Diego had heard from his father's family. Soon after his release from prison he had been contacted by a law firm in England, who had explained that Philip Hawke had died some years earlier but had confided to his own father that he had an illegitimate child in Brazil. Geoffrey Hawke had spent his remaining years searching for his grandson without success. Before Geoffrey died he had instructed the law firm to continue the search, and eventually they had tracked Diego down and gave him the astounding news that his grandfather had left him a fortune in his will.

The money had allowed Diego to become a business partner with his friend Cruz Delgado. They had bought the Old Betsy diamond mine where Cruz's father had found the famous Estrela Vermelha—the Red Star diamond. The discovery in the mine of diamonds worth millions of dollars—including a rare pink diamond, the Estrela Rosa, which Diego had found and kept in his private collection of gems—had made the two men multimillionaires. Recently, another mine that had been abandoned many years ago and was only discovered when Cruz had been given a map of the hidden tunnels by his father-in-law, Earl Bancroft, had been found to contain a huge supply of diamonds, making Diego and Cruz two of the richest men in Brazil.

Wealth certainly had great benefits, Diego mused. But his penthouse apartment in Rio, his various other properties around the world and even his collection of luxury sports cars were simply toys to amuse him. Nothing filled the void inside him or made him forget the poverty and deprivation of his childhood. When he was growing up, what he had wanted more than anything was to feel loved. Love was more precious than gold or glittering gems but, after thirty-seven years without it, his heart had become as hard and unbreakable as the diamonds he mined.

He forced his thoughts back to the present when he realised Sister Clare was speaking. 'It must have been difficult for your mother to be a single parent. Did you spend your childhood in Manaus?'

'I grew up in a *favela* in the city of Belo Horizonte.' Diego gave a cynical laugh. 'The name translates to beautiful horizon, but there was nothing beautiful about the overcrowded and filthy slum where my mother and I lived.'

'Is that why you like being in the rainforest, because it is wild and beautiful and you can be alone?'

Diego glanced at her. 'I'm not alone now,' he drawled. His gut clenched as he watched rosy colour stain her cheeks. She was so beautiful. But perhaps it was the fact that she was out of bounds that made her all the more desirable. It was one of life's ironies that you always wanted what you couldn't have, he mused.

He was surprised by Sister Clare's perceptiveness, and also how easy he found it to talk to her. He was an expert at chat-up lines, but he rarely talked to women, probably because they rarely listened, he thought sardonically.

'I can breathe in the rainforest,' he admitted. 'There is an honesty here that I have never found anywhere else. It's one of the few places on earth where Mother Nature is truly untamed, and that makes her fearsome but fascinating.'

He was an instinctive poet, Clare thought. He wove a pattern with words and revealed his love of the rainforest in his gravelly voice. Who was the real Diego Cazorra? So far she had met the loner gold prospector and the notorious womaniser the Mother Superior had warned her about. But she sensed that Diego rarely allowed anyone to see beyond his outward persona of a laid-back, charismatic charmer.

She remembered the book of poems by the English romantic poet John Keats that she had found in the back of the Jeep.

"*'To one who has been long in city pent, 'Tis very sweet to look into the fair And open face of heaven— to breathe a prayer Full in the smile of the blue firmament,'*" she quoted softly.

Diego glanced at her.

"*'Who is more happy, when, with heart's content, Fatigued he sinks into some pleasant lair Of wavy grass, and reads a debonair A gentle tale of love and languishment?'*" he finished the quote. 'It seems we have one thing in common, at least. Which other poets do you like, apart from Keats?'

'Oh, Wordsworth, Shelley. I love the work of many of the poets of the late eighteenth century. I am an unashamed romantic at heart. How about you?'

'Am I romantic?' He laughed. 'What do you think, Sister Clare?'

'I think you are more than a tough gold prospector.' She hesitated, then felt compelled to ask, 'What happened to your ear?'

'An accident,' he said abruptly. Instantly the connection between them was severed. Clare wished she had suppressed her curiosity, but it was too late to withdraw her question and Diego's answer revealed nothing. She could not tell him her interest was not nosiness, but that she carried with her a box containing what was very possibly a piece of her sister's ear, cut off by the criminals who had kidnapped Becky.

She had only glimpsed Diego's ear, but it had been enough time for her to notice that the top half appeared to have been sliced off. The skin had healed over, as if the injury had not happened recently. Clare had read that a common tactic used by gangs in Brazil to scare families into paying a ransom for their kidnapped relatives was to send them a piece of the victim's ear. There were even cosmetic surgeons who specialised in rebuilding mutilated ears. But Diego had told her that he had grown up in a slum after his father had abandoned his mother, and it seemed unlikely that he had been kidnapped and a ransom demanded for his release.

The mystery surrounding him grew ever deeper. She glanced at him as he concentrated on steering the Jeep around the potholes in the road. He had tipped his hat forwards so that the brim hid his expression, and she sensed that the barriers he had briefly lowered were back in place.

The rain did not stop after an hour or so as it had the previous day, but continued to fall in a relentless torrent that turned the dirt road into a muddy river. Clare lost count of the number of times the Jeep became stuck and she had to get out and help Diego free the wheels from the ochre-coloured soup. By late afternoon she was so tired that she moved on autopilot as she aided him in laying wooden planks beneath the Jeep's front wheels. Diego climbed into the driver's seat and accelerated until slowly, slowly the vehicle inched forwards. He drove into a small clearing in the trees where the ground was covered in a tangle of creeping vines and watched Clare trudge towards him.

'I'll say this, Sister. You are one determined lady.' There was admiration in his voice. 'Most people would have given up by now and asked to turn back, but I haven't heard you complain once about the rain and the damned mud.' He felt a flicker of something that could have been tenderness as he watched her valiantly try to haul herself into the Jeep. She was so tired she could hardly lift her foot on to the step and she did not protest when he lifted her up and deposited her on the seat.

Clare gave him a weary smile. 'I *will* get to Torrente, whatever it takes. A bit of mud won't stop me.'

She leaned her head against the back of the seat and closed her eyes, giving Diego an opportunity to study her without her being aware of his intent scrutiny. Her nun's habit and veil were rain-soaked and her shoes and legs were covered in mud. She was pale with exhaustion so that the golden freckles scattered across her nose and cheeks were noticeable against her creamy complexion.

Desire, as inexplicable as it was inconvenient, tugged in Diego's gut. He liked leggy blondes whose sexual experience matched his own, and he could not understand why it took all his will power to resist covering Sister Clare's mouth with his lips and kissing her until she responded as passionately as she had when he had kissed her that morning.

She lifted her lashes, and Diego stared into the deep blue pools of her eyes. *Deus*, why did he feel an urge to open his heart to her and tell her things about himself that he had never revealed to anyone else?

Cursing his stupidity beneath his breath, he restarted the engine and drove back to the road. 'The rain is easing up and I reckon we'll get to Torrente in a couple more hours.'

When they reached the town he would leave her at the church and never see her again. She had chosen a way of life that prevented her from having a relationship with a man. And he had to face it, Diego mocked himself, he could not have offered her a relationship. All he wanted was to have sex with her, and once he had sated his desire he would no doubt have grown bored of her as quickly as he did with all his mistresses.

'Do you know of a big waterfall near to Torrente?'

He nodded. 'Branco Cachoeirao. The waterfall is three or four miles outside the town.'

'I believe there is a cave nearby, and inside there is a shrine to the Virgin Mary which was carved out of rock by a missionary who was one of the first non-indigenous people to visit Torrente many years ago.'

Diego shrugged. 'I was unaware of a shrine, but I know the cave you mean.'

'Good, because I would like you to take me to it before you drive on to the town. I want to spend the night alone at the shrine in quiet contemplation—' Clare's voice faltered '—and I'll make my own way to Torrente tomorrow.'

'Let me get this straight. You want me to leave you on your own in the rainforest for the night? Sister, you are either crazily brave or just crazy.' Diego shot a glance at her serene face and was tempted to shake some sense into her. He could not comprehend why she was willing to sacrifice her passionate nature for a life of austerity and physical denial, but he was convinced that her broken relationship with her ex-boyfriend who had cheated on her had influenced her decision to become a nun.

The rain finally stopped, which made the driving conditions easier, and as they drew closer to Torrente Diego reminded himself that Clare's decision had nothing to do with him. His gut told him she needed to be saved from making a mistake, but his mind pointed out that he was not the man to save her.

Clare heard the waterfall before she saw it. The thunderous noise of the falls drowned out the sounds of the rainforest that she was starting to recognise: the various calls of hundreds of species of birds, the chatter and shrieks of monkeys and occasionally a deep roar that Diego had told her was a jaguar.

He steered the Jeep down a narrow track where light could barely penetrate through the tangle of trees and vines that formed a living green roof. They emerged into a clearing, and in front was a spectacular sight of white frothing water plunging hundreds of feet over rocks into the river below.

'If I remember rightly, the cave is further on.' Diego inched the Jeep slowly through the dense forest, past giant ferns and plants with leaves that Clare estimated were two metres or more in diameter. A huge cliff of grey rock towered so high that she had to tilt her head to see the top. She peered through the eerie gloom of the jungle and saw a black hole in the rocks. The entrance to the cave was overgrown with vegetation, as if no humans had visited the place for a long time.

Diego stopped the Jeep and jumped out. Clare followed him and gave a startled cry when a wild boar raced out of the cave and disappeared into the undergrowth.

'Do you really intend to spend the night in there?' he asked sardonically as she lingered outside the cave. He obviously sensed her reluctance to step into the blackness. Swallowing hard, she switched on her torch and directed its beam into the dark space before she walked slowly forwards.

'Do you think there could be any other animals in here?' Her voice echoed as it bounced off the cave walls.

'You might find a rock python.'

'Funny,' she muttered, telling herself he was joking. Pythons didn't live in caves, did they? The light from the torch flickered over something that caught her attention. Heart pounding, she moved deeper into the cave and drew a sharp breath when she saw a face. It was not a real person, she quickly realised, but a statue of the Virgin Mary that had been carved into a rock. The figure was about three feet tall and exquisitely detailed, just as the Mother Superior had described it.

There was something incredibly moving about the statue that a priest had painstakingly carved out of the solid rock a century earlier. It must have taken him months to complete and must have been a true labour of devotion. Clare could not explain why a feeling of calm came over her as she touched the figure of Mary, but her tiredness was replaced with a sense of optimism that she would be able to rescue Becky.

She stood by the statue for some time until she became aware of something moving on a rock close to her. She shone the torch in the direction of the rustling sound, and in the light she saw the glint of greeny-brown scales.

Dear heaven, Diego hadn't been joking! Giving a scream loud enough to wake the dead, she ran towards the cave entrance and collided full pelt into him.

'Easy, Sister.' Diego took one look at her white face and, fearing she was about to faint, gripped her by her elbows and held her upright. 'I'm guessing you saw a snake?' When she nodded he said gently, 'Wait here and I'll get rid of it.'

Clare had no intention of following him into the cave and she looked away with a shudder when he walked past her holding a long green snake in his hands. He carried the reptile away from the entrance and came back a few minutes later with some logs and dry twigs that he must have collected from the forest floor.

'What are you doing?'

'Building a fire. It'll burn throughout the night and keep unwanted visitors out of the cave.'

'What about the creatures that have already taken up residence?' Clare gave another shudder as she pictured the python Diego had evicted.

'I took a look around and saw nothing else in the cave. But there is a hole in the roof, which is lucky.'

'Lucky, how? If it rains I'll get wet.'

'It's only a small hole, but rainwater has poured in and made a pool of fresh water that you can drink.' Diego noticed she was still pale from her fright with the python and her eyes looked like dark bruises in her white face. 'Why don't you go and splash some water on your face and freshen up while I get your bags from the Jeep?'

Clare held her torch tightly in her trembling hand and forced herself to walk to the back of the cave. She *had* to spend the night here for Becky's sake, she reminded herself. The kidnappers had instructed her to be at the cave on Sunday but they had not specified at what time. They might arrive at dawn and she could not risk missing them, hence her decision to stay in the rainforest overnight, although she was certain she would not sleep at all. Her nerves were at breaking point but she dared not ask Diego to stay with her in case he was seen by the kidnappers.

She found the small pool where a natural basin that had formed in the rocks had filled with rainwater, and felt marginally better once she had washed her face. But the prospect of meeting the kidnappers the next day filled her with dread. Was Becky still alive? What if the kidnappers took the ransom money and killed both of them? Before she had left England her sister's kidnapping had seemed surreal, but now the danger of the situation was terrifyingly immediate.

A golden glow suddenly flared at the front of the cave and she saw that Diego had lit the fire and also the kerosene lamp, which he had brought from the Jeep. He had been busy, and Clare's heart clenched when she saw that he had spread a sleeping bag on the floor and brought in a few cushions to make her makeshift bed as comfortable as possible.

He glanced at her. 'Sleep close to the fire and you'll be safe from any curious forest creatures. I've brought your bags from the Jeep and also some dried fruit and nuts for breakfast.'

'Thank you.' His gruff concern brought tears to her eyes. 'You are very kind.'

He was standing on the opposite side of the fire to her and his muscular body was silhouetted against the darkening sky outside the cave. His face was shadowed by the brim of his hat but Clare saw the gleam of his white teeth when he grinned. 'I'm no saint, Sister.'

'Perhaps not, but I think you are a better man than you know,' she said seriously.

For several moments he stared at her across the flames that danced between them before he turned abruptly and walked out of the cave, disappearing into the dusk. Seconds later Clare heard the sound of the Jeep's engine, and only then did reality hit her that he had left without saying goodbye and she was alone in the rainforest.

It was what she had planned, she reminded herself. It was vital that Diego was not around when she met the kidnappers tomorrow. So why did she feel numb inside? Why did she feel as if her heart had been torn from her chest? He was a womaniser who made Mark look like boyfriend of the year. But he was also courageous—she remembered how he had captured the python. During the long and arduous journey from Manaus he had proved himself to be patient and dependable, and he had even poured away his beer when she had told him about Aunt Edith being killed by a drunk driver.

The tears she'd managed to hold back before Diego had left now spilled over. She was tired and scared and, to make matters worse, as she huddled close to the fire her damp clothes began to steam. It seemed sensible to at least attempt to sleep, and so she took off the nun's habit and veil and spread them on a rock, hoping they would dry before she had to put them on in the morning.

It was too hot next to the fire for her to get into the sleeping bag but she rearranged the cushions Diego had given her and discovered that he had left behind the book of Keats's poems. His kind gesture undid her completely and she choked back a sob. She felt utterly alone, but a faint noise from outside the cave put her senses on high alert. She strained her ears, hardly daring to breathe. Something or someone was out there and she did not know if she would prefer the intruder to be a wild animal or a kidnapper.

The unmistakable crunch of boots on the gravel floor

at the cave's entrance escalated Clare's terror. Her instinct was to hide but she firmed her jaw, determined not to give in to her fear. If the men who had kidnapped her sister were here it was up to her to deal with them. For Becky's sake she must be brave.

She stood up and hurriedly wrapped the sleeping bag around her. *'Who's there?'*

'It's me, of course.' Diego strolled into the cave and the light from the fire illuminated his big frame. 'Who did you think it could be? No one else is mad enough to spend a night in the jungle.' He threw his sleeping bag down on the floor and tossed his hat on to a rock before raking his fingers through his hair that for some reason was wet although it was not raining outside.

Clare stared at him, hardly able to believe he was real and not a figment of her imagination. He had changed into clean jeans and a denim shirt that was unbuttoned to halfway down his chest, and he looked so ruggedly gorgeous that her heart rate rocketed.

'I…I heard the Jeep and I thought you had driven on to Torrente,' she stammered.

'I noticed the wheels were sinking into the mud, so I moved the Jeep to firmer ground and then took a shower beneath the waterfall.' He stepped around the fire and frowned when he saw tears on her cheeks. 'You didn't really think I would abandon you in the rainforest, did you?'

His sexy smile shattered Clare's tenuous hold on her composure. The terror she had felt a few minutes ago had been needless. Diego was here and for now at least she felt safe. The sleeping bag fell from her shoulders as she gave an inarticulate cry and flew across the few feet separating them to launch herself at his chest.

'I thought you had gone and I would never see you again.' It was a sign of her emotional state that she did not consider how betraying her words were. All she cared about was that Diego had appeared, tall and strong, like a blond Viking. His bare skin revealed by his half-open shirt felt warm beneath her hands as she clung to him.

'Clare?' His voice was deeper than she had ever heard it as his arms came round her and enfolded her. He hesitated for a fraction of a second before he lifted her off her feet and crushed her to him. '*Deus*, do you think I could bear to leave you, *anjinho*?' he murmured against her lips before he claimed her mouth in a searing kiss that plundered her soul.

CHAPTER FIVE

DIEGO BRIEFLY FOUGHT and lost a battle with his conscience. A saint would not be able to resist Clare's passionate response, he told himself, feeling his erection strain against the constriction of his jeans as she parted her lips beneath his.

He was surprised to discover a vulnerable side to her. On the journey from Manaus he had been impressed by her determined spirit and amused by her dry sense of humour. But now she was clearly distraught and he felt her tremble as she burrowed against him like a frightened animal seeking shelter from danger.

She was so tiny. He felt a surge of protectiveness. 'What's the matter, *pequeno*?' Instinctively he felt sure that her tears were not just because she had believed he'd left her alone at the cave.

'I don't know if I am doing the right thing.' Clare's iron control over her nerves crumbled and her fears poured out in a flood of tears. Maybe she should have gone to the police and asked them to find her sister's kidnappers. Maybe she wasn't brave but stupid and naïve to think that she could rescue Becky.

'It's natural for you to have doubts,' Diego said gently as understanding dawned in him. Clare was facing the biggest decision of her life when she would make her final vows and commit herself fully to a nun's life. Perhaps she was having second thoughts about the life she had chosen. His conscience told him he should step away from her and suppress his desire, somehow stifle the sexual chemistry that existed between them, which must add to her confusion about her future. But how could he resist her when she wound her arms around his neck and sought his mouth with hers, initiating a sensual kiss that stirred his body into urgent awareness?

She did not look like a nun. When he had walked into the cave and seen her wearing just a plain white bra and knickers, with her auburn curls tumbling around her shoulders, he'd been stunned by her beauty. She was a petite package of voluptuous curves and he could not stop himself from running his hands over her body, exploring the gentle flare of her hips and the indent of her slender waist.

She tensed when he slid his hands across her ribcage and lightly stroked his fingers over the underside of her breasts. But she did not pull her mouth away from his, and when he deepened the kiss she melted into him and parted her lips to allow him to push his tongue between them.

Diego heard a faint voice inside his head warning him that he must not take advantage of her innocent eagerness. But she had told him she'd had one serious relationship, he reminded himself, so she could not be completely innocent. The way she was kissing him with fiery passion and sliding her hands over his chest was heating his blood and evoking a primal hunger in him that obliterated all rational thoughts from his mind and left only an insistent throb of desire that demanded to be appeased.

* * *

Once again, the situation Clare found herself in seemed surreal. A week ago she had been engrossed in company spreadsheets and wondering what to wear to the Association of Accountants' Christmas dinner. Now she was in a cave in the Amazon rainforest, dreading tomorrow when she would meet her sister's kidnappers, but at this moment she was half-naked and the sexiest man on the planet had laid her down on a sleeping bag and was looking at her with a gleam in his eyes that blazed hotter than the flames of the fire.

Maybe it was all a dream, and if so she did not want to wake up from this part of it. The sensible, circumspect Clare Marchant from England had been transformed by the sultry heat of the Brazilian rainforest into a sensual siren who was burning up with desire. Diego incited in her a need for sexual fulfilment that she had never felt with any other man.

She realised she had been fooling herself by thinking that her decision not to sleep with Mark was because she had wanted to be sure of their relationship. He seemed like a preening, self-obsessed boy compared to Diego's raw masculinity, and the truth was that Mark had not turned her on like Diego did. She had been unaware until now that she was capable of feeling such an intensity of lust. Every word of Aunt Edith's advice about waiting to fall in love before she gave away her virginity was drowned out by the loud drumbeat of desire pounding through her veins.

Diego was kneeling above her, his thighs straddling her hips and his hands resting on the ground on either side of her head so that she was caged by his powerful body. In the firelight his blond hair looked like a golden halo, but he was a fallen angel with a wicked promise in his eyes to fulfil Clare's wildest fantasies.

He bent his head and kissed her mouth again, slower this time, coaxing her lips open so that he could take his pleasure while he increased hers until she moaned softly and curved her arms around his neck. His blatant seduction intoxicated her senses and made her want more, more…

She snatched air into her lungs when he finally released her mouth and trailed his lips down her throat, but the sensation of him sucking the tender skin at the base of her neck where a pulse beat erratically made her catch her breath. The caress was outrageously erotic, but he did not give her time to assimilate the new sensations he was creating, for he was already sliding his lips lower, over the slope of one breast.

Clare felt his warm breath through the material of her bra cup and wished his mouth was on her bare skin. He must have read her thoughts because he slipped his hand beneath her back and, with a deftness that indicated plenty of experience in undressing women, unfastened the clasp and removed her bra.

His silver wolf's eyes gleamed as he rested back on his haunches and stared at her naked breasts. Clare had always felt self-conscious of her curvaceous shape and compared herself unfavourably to her sister who was a model-thin size zero. But the undisguised hunger in Diego's eyes made her glad that her breasts were full and firm, and for the first time in her life she felt proud of her feminine figure.

She did not feel apprehensive when she read the feral intent in his gaze. She felt as though she had been waiting for this, for *him* all her life. Sexual chemistry had sizzled from the moment they'd met and she felt a connection with him on a fundamental level that defied explanation.

'Diego…' She whispered his name like a prayer.

He gave her an oddly crooked smile and held his finger over her lips. 'Don't speak, *anjinho*. Maybe this isn't real, and I don't want to return to reality,' he said softly.

Clare understood exactly what he meant. It was easy to sink into the dream and forget the world beyond the fire-lit cave; easy to sink into bliss as Diego lifted his finger from her lips and traced a feather-light path down her throat to her breast. She sucked in a sharp breath when he touched her nipple and it immediately hardened.

His husky laugh was rough with desire. *'Bela.'* He was still kneeling above her and he cradled her breasts in his hands and flicked his thumb pads across her nipples in a repetitive motion that created such a storm of exquisite sensations in Clare that the pleasure was almost too much to withstand. Diego lowered his blond head and soothed one engorged peak with his tongue before he drew it into his mouth and suckled her until she moaned, and he transferred his lips to her other nipple and lavished the same delicious torment.

She tangled her fingers in his hair and tugged to bring his face close to hers. His smile should come with a government health warning, she thought, but then he claimed her lips in a possessive kiss that emptied her mind of all rational thoughts and left only the certainty that she wanted the kiss to last for ever.

His passion was scorching, yet he tempered his hunger with an unexpected tenderness that infiltrated her heart. When he slipped his hand between her legs it felt perfectly natural for him to caress the silken skin of her inner thighs. Clare's lack of experience meant that this was uncharted territory for her, but she offered no resistance as his fingers skimmed inexorably higher and slipped inside her knickers.

'Open your legs for me, *querida*. That's right,' he murmured his approval when she relaxed her thighs to allow him to gently part her and he discovered the slick wetness of her arousal. The first probing touch of his finger gently easing into her was enough to almost send her over the edge. Her body quivered but instinct told her to try to control the pulsing sensation deep in her core because it was only the start of a journey that she wanted to take with Diego.

To distract herself from her body's response to him she concentrated on his body and undid the last few buttons so that she could pull off his shirt. He had an incredible muscular physique. In the firelight, the satiny skin on his shoulders gleamed like bronze and the hairs covering his chest were pure gold. She ran her hands down over his flat abdomen to the fuzz of hairs visible above his jeans and, after a second's hesitation, she undid the button on the waistband. Her forwardness would have shocked her if she hadn't been in a dreamlike state where anything was possible and nothing was shocking.

He kissed her breasts again, teased each swollen nipple in turn until she moaned and jerked her hips towards the heat and hardness of him in an unconscious betrayal of her need. The gossamer-soft brush of his lips over her stomach elicited a molten warmth between her legs, and when he kissed her *there*, where no other man had ever touched her before, and when she felt his tongue flick across her clitoris, she could not control the pulse waves of pleasure as her body juddered in a swift, intense climax.

She was spinning out of control. It felt as if she was riding a carousel and images and sensations were flashing past her faster and faster. She did not remember when Diego had removed her knickers or the rest of his clothes, and when he stretched out next to her and drew her against his naked body she was too absorbed in sliding her hands over his impressive abdominal muscles to care. He was a work of art and she delighted in tracing her fingertips down his flat stomach and powerful thighs until she came into contact with the solid length of his erection. Her breath left her lungs in a whoosh. He felt big and hard in her hand and she was curious to know what he would feel like inside her.

When she stretched her fingers around him he gave a low groan of primitive sexual need that stirred an equally primitive response in her. He lifted himself over her and it felt perfectly natural to guide the tip of his swollen shaft towards her moist opening. Instinctively she spread her legs wider to allow him to settle his hips between hers, and he slowly eased forwards, entering her inch by careful inch until he possessed her utterly.

Clare caught her breath as she experienced a moment of mild discomfort, but the brief stinging sensation was over before she really registered it. Diego hesitated, but she curved her arms around his back and pulled him down on to her at the same time as she lifted her hips in invitation for him to take her virginity that she offered willingly.

He waited until her breathing had steadied before he moved, slowly at first, pulling back so far that she thought he was actually going to withdraw. He laughed softly when she clutched his shoulders, and pushed forwards again, then drew back, then forwards, increasing his pace with each thrust and going deeper into her so that she was filled by him, overwhelmed by him and felt that he had taken ownership of her body.

In this primal dance of sex he was her master and her tutor. He slid his hands beneath her bottom and tilted her hips, forcing her to accept each devastating thrust of his body into hers. But he countered his strength with gentleness and there was no question of him forcing her to do anything she did not feel ready to experience. She wanted everything he gave her, wanted more, wanted quite desperately the something that hovered frustratingly just out of her reach.

'Easy, *querida*,' his deep voice soothed her. 'Don't be in such a rush. Relax and let it happen.'

She looked into his eyes and saw a familiar glint of amusement at her impatience. But as she watched him make love to her she saw heat and hunger in his predatory wolf's gaze, and she heard the hoarse sound of his breaths coming faster and faster as he increased his pace.

And then it did happen. Suddenly. Spectacularly. He gave a powerful thrust that made her gasp, but before she could drag oxygen into her lungs, the tight knot of tension deep in her pelvis exploded without warning and sent her soaring and sobbing into the stratosphere. Her vaginal muscles contracted and released as wave after wave of intense pleasure swept over her so that she could not breathe or think, could only feel the shattering ecstasy of her orgasm.

Diego waited until she came down before he immediately took her higher again, driving into her with an implacable intent that made her realise he was nearing his own nirvana. She let him ride her fast and hard, instinctively knowing that he needed it like this and the time for gentleness had passed. His passion was raw and elemental. But when he paused and tipped his head back so that the cords on his neck stood out, before giving a harsh groan that sounded as though it had been torn from his soul, Clare was overcome with tenderness for him and pressed her face against his shoulder to hide the tears that inexplicably filled her eyes.

Diego pushed his hat off his face where he'd placed it over his eyes before he'd fallen asleep and was instantly aware of three things. The fire had gone out, the slice of sky that he could see through the cave's entrance was a couple of shades lighter than pitch-black and Sister Clare was lying beside him, as naked as the day she'd been born and, fortunately, fast asleep.

Santa Mãe! He'd found himself in some awkward situations in his life, mostly after he'd drunk more beer than was good for him. But he doubted that all the saints in heaven could help him out of this one. His eyes dropped to the delectable curves of Clare's buttocks and he cursed softly beneath his breath and pulled the sleeping bag over her.

There was no point wasting time in recriminations. He couldn't despise himself any more than he already did anyway, and deflowering a nun simply added another black mark against his name. An image came into his head of the overcrowded prison cell where he had spent two years of his life. His mind flashed back further. He saw the figure of a man sprawled on the floor of his mother's apartment, and a pool of black congealed blood.

Diego swallowed convulsively and forced himself

to look at his hands. There was no blood on them now. He breathed easier. Of course there wasn't; he only saw the blood in his dreams. It had been years ago, and Father Vincenzi had said he hadn't killed the guy. But how could the priest know for sure, Diego brooded, if he had no recollection himself of what had happened the night he had found his mother being beaten up by a drug dealer? The only person who knew the truth was his mother, but the last time he had seen her he'd been seventeen, and she had told the police he was a murderer.

Deus. He snapped a shutter down on his memories and quickly pulled on his jeans, taking care not to disturb Clare. She looked angelic as she slept with her lips slightly parted and her auburn curls spread across her shoulders. But, thanks to him, she was no longer innocent. After she'd mentioned an ex-boyfriend, he had assumed that she wasn't a virgin, and by the time he had discovered her inexperience, he'd been unable to stop himself from making love to her.

Other memories assailed him, not of the distant past but the previous night. He visualised Clare's curvaceous body, her round, creamy breasts topped with pointed, cherry-red nipples that had been ripe for his mouth. The taste of her still lingered on his lips from when he'd kissed her between her thighs and dipped his tongue into the honeydew of her arousal.

He swore beneath his breath and walked out of the cave before he succumbed to the temptation to kiss her awake and instigate an early morning ride. It would be a first for him because he had never spent an entire night with a woman to be able to have sex upon waking. It was curious that he had slept dreamlessly with Clare cuddled up against him, her body all soft and warm like a kitten, he mused. But he had a feeling that in the cold light of day his little cat would reveal her sharp claws and accuse him of seducing her.

Because undoubtedly, and not entirely unfairly, Clare was going to blame him for leading her astray from the life of pious devotion she had chosen. She was unlikely to believe he hadn't intended for things to go so far. But it wasn't all his fault, Diego tried to convince himself. The way she had thrown herself into his arms would have tested a saint, let alone a mortal man.

He tried to dismiss the voice in his head, which said that he should have been stronger and given Clare time to decide if she wanted to give up her life with the church and give her virginity to him. Instead he had lost control and made love to her mindlessly and without a care for the consequences, and it was that which concerned him more than anything else. No other woman had ever made him feel as desperate for sex as Clare had done last night. He didn't do desperate or, God help him, needy. He was a lone wolf without cares or commitments as far as his numerous temporary mistresses were concerned. It was better that way. Safer.

The sky was lightening with the arrival of dawn as Diego followed the path through the trees towards where he had left the Jeep. He rubbed a hand over his rough jaw and decided he needed a shave. Maybe taking a shower beneath the powerful waterfall would help him to think straight and answer a vital question: *What the hell was he going to do with Clare now?*

The answer slipped unexpectedly easily into his head. He would have to take her back to Rio with him. He felt partly responsible that, now that they had slept together, she could not make her final vows to become a nun. But really he had done her a favour. Her uninhibited response to him last night proved she wasn't cut out for a life of chastity. He would set her up in an apartment near to his penthouse overlooking Copacabana beach, and then he would take her shopping. He was looking forward to seeing her dressed in sexy clothes that made the most of her gorgeous figure, instead of her drab grey nun's habit.

His erotic fantasy of watching Clare parade around his bedroom wearing a see-through black negligee came to an abrupt halt when he heard a noise that instantly put him on his guard. The snap of a twig on the floor of the rainforest could have been made by an animal, but Diego knew that only humans moved so clumsily.

He jerked his head in the direction of the noise and saw the dull silver gleam of a gun aimed at him through the trees. His first instinct was to warn Clare she was in imminent danger but, as he gave a shout, he felt something hard hit his skull, followed by searing pain and nothing more.

She hurt everywhere, Clare discovered when she stretched and became aware of a slight soreness between her legs. Her back ached from where she had spent the night lying on the hard floor of the cave and, when she sat up, internal muscles she had never felt before twinged, and she winced as the zip of the sleeping bag grazed her acutely sensitive nipples.

Glancing down, she saw the swollen reddened tips of her breasts and felt a mixture of shame at the memory of her wanton behaviour, coupled with a newly awakened awareness of her sexual needs. Diego had satisfied her last night, but now she felt ready to play again. It seemed that her body was determined to make up for being a late starter in experiencing sensual pleasure.

It was immediately apparent that she was alone. Diego must have dressed—his jeans and shirt were missing—and only her bra and knickers were strewn on the floor where he had thrown them after he had removed them with her willing cooperation.

The pale pink sky outside the cave reassured her that it must be early morning and thankfully it seemed that the kidnappers had not yet arrived. Fear sent a cold chill down her spine and self-disgust churned in her stomach. While she had made love with Diego, Becky had spent another night in terror, held prisoner by the criminal gang who had snatched her.

Feeling guilty that she had temporarily forgotten about her sister, Clare stood up and pulled on her nun's habit, before covering her hair with the veil. Of course she would explain to Diego that she wasn't really a nun and also explain about Becky being kidnapped. He would probably argue when she asked him to leave her alone at the cave, but to save her sister's life she must follow the kidnappers' instructions and meet them on her own.

She picked up her rucksack and the case of money and stepped outside, but there was no sign of Diego or the Jeep. She vaguely remembered that she had been woken by what had sounded like a shout. Unease made her skin prickle. Where was he? She was about to call him, but hesitated. The forest was eerily silent without the usual cacophony of birdsong, and she sensed that she was being watched.

'Senhorita Marchant?'

A man stepped out from the trees to one side of Clare.

She whirled round to face him and inhaled sharply when she saw he was holding a gun. He, and the two men who followed him into the clearing, looked of Hispanic origin, dark-eyed and swarthy-skinned, with an air of menace about them that filled her with dread as she imagined them hurting her sister.

'Where's Becky?'

The man with the gun seemed to be transfixed by her habit and veil. He glanced at the briefcase. 'You have the money?' When she nodded, he held out his hand for her to give him the case.

'I want to see Becky first.' Clare could feel her heart thumping painfully hard in her chest. She had never thought of herself as particularly brave. But her bravery had never been tested when she had lived an ordinary, unexciting life in a leafy north London suburb, she acknowledged. She pictured her father, waiting desperately for news of his daughters, and her fragile mother who was struggling to regain her health after suffering a stroke. Her parents would be devastated if Becky did not return home and Clare knew she was the only person who could secure her sister's release.

She curled her fingers tightly around the handle of the briefcase and stared unflinchingly at the kidnapper when he pointed the gun at her. For some reason she remembered Diego's admiration when she had ignored her exhaustion and helped him dig the Jeep's wheels out of the mud on the road to Torrente. He had made her feel like she was stronger and capable of achieving more than she'd ever realised. Her heart lurched as she wondered where he was and prayed he was safe.

It took all her will power to prevent her hand from shaking as she reached out and calmly pushed the gun away so that it was no longer aimed at her. 'Would you really shoot a nun?'

To her surprise and relief, the kidnapper lowered the weapon to his side and a dull flush mottled his face. 'My apologies, Sister. I was sent here to collect a ransom. I did not realise I would be meeting *uma noiva de Cristo.*'

Clare silently thanked the Mother Superior, who had persuaded her to dress as a nun for her protection. 'I will pay the ransom when my sister is released and transport has been arranged for us to return to England.'

The man shrugged. 'You must come with us,' he said, pointing through the trees to a four-by-four with blacked-out windows parked near the road. He looked at Clare and made the sign of a cross. 'I am sorry, Sister, I just do my job.'

Torrente looked as deprived and rundown as Diego had described it. The main road was busy with street traders selling their goods from the back of carts, and bare-foot children played in the piles of rubbish heaped in the gutters. There was an air of despair about the place, and Clare noticed several young women—some did not look much older than girls—dressed in revealing dresses and towering heels, trying to attract the attention of men who were willing to pay for sex.

The kidnapper who Clare had overheard his companions call Enzo drove through the town and turned up a winding road leading to a huge villa that stood on top of a hill. Whoever lived here was certainly not poor, she thought, as electric gates opened to allow the four-by-four to pass through and closed with an ominous clang behind them. The lush, beautifully manicured grounds were patrolled by armed security guards, and the guards at the front door looked at her closely as she followed Enzo inside.

She had a vague impression of gleaming white marble walls and flashy gold decor, but her heart was beating so fast with fear that she was finding it hard to breathe. They walked along what seemed like miles of corridors before Enzo stopped and opened a door, indicating for Clare to enter the room. She stepped inside and her legs almost buckled with relief when a familiar figure jumped up from a chair and ran towards her.

'*Becky!*' Clare flew across the room and flung her arms around her sister. 'Are you all right? They haven't harmed you?' Another wave of relief surged through her when she saw that Becky's ears, revealed where her long ash-blonde hair was tied back in a ponytail, were perfectly fine. Clare wondered briefly who the severed piece of ear she had been sent by the kidnappers belonged to. But, thankfully, her sister seemed to be unhurt, and in fact looked as beautiful and elegant as she always did, despite having been held captive for a week.

Compared to Becky, Clare knew she must look like a grubby urchin from a Dickensian novel in her crumpled, mud-stained clothes. She realised that her sister was staring at her veil.

'Why are you dressed like that?' Becky pulled the veil from Clare's head and watched her hair tumble around her shoulders. 'Thank goodness you haven't cut your hair short. It's your best feature.'

'It was a disguise. I was helped by some nuns in Manaus and the Mother Superior suggested that I should wear a habit and veil as protection from the criminals in Torrente who are apparently God-fearing, although they don't fear the police.'

Becky gave a shaky laugh. 'I thought for a minute you had actually joined the church. Wearing the veil makes you look like a very realistic nun.' She glanced across the sitting room to a door which led into an adjoining room. 'Don't you think so, Diego?'

Shock robbed Clare of the ability to speak as she spun round and stared at Diego leaning against the door frame, his arms folded across his broad chest and his lips curved into a familiar cynical smile that was not reflected in his hard as steel eyes. 'You certainly convinced me, *Sister* Clare,' he drawled.

CHAPTER SIX

'I WAS GOING to tell you, but I didn't get an opportunity to explain,' Clare muttered. She and Diego were walking along a corridor, following the gang member Enzo, who had ordered them to go with him. Clare hadn't had a chance to replace her veil, and she felt vulnerable now that her guise of a nun had been blown. The way Enzo's eyes had insolently roamed over her made her skin crawl.

She wondered if the person called Rigo, who they were being taken to, was the leader of the kidnappers. She was worried that she'd had to leave Becky in the room where they had briefly been reunited. But hopefully this Rigo would accept the ransom money and allow her and Becky, and Diego, to go free, she told herself.

Diego shot her a scathing glance. 'We had sex, and it wasn't a quickie, over in a couple of minutes. How much *more* of an opportunity did you need to mention that you were only pretending to be a nun?'

He swore with muted savagery, aware that their captor walking just ahead of them could overhear. 'Do you know what a bad time my conscience gave me when I discovered you were…a virgin?' he said harshly.

He was furious with her for making him feel a fool, although her air of innocence hadn't all been an act, he brooded, remembering how she had gasped at the moment of penetration, making him realise, too late, that it was her first time.

'Is that why you had disappeared when I woke up this morning? You felt guilty, so you cleared off.' Clare's initial feeling of relief that Diego had gone from the cave when the kidnappers arrived had gradually turned to anger that he hadn't even woken her to say thanks for their one-night stand, which, of course, was all he had wanted from her.

'I didn't clear off. I was on my way to the waterfall to take a shower when I was ambushed and knocked unconscious.' Diego removed his hat that he'd been wearing with the brim pulled low over his eyes, and Clare made a choked sound when she saw a purple lump on his temple.

'I'm sorry you've been involved. A week ago my sister was snatched while she was on a modelling assignment in Rio, and the kidnappers demanded a ransom for her release. I was instructed to take the money to a cave by a waterfall near to Torrente and was warned that if I went to the police or asked anyone for help Becky would be killed.'

'You should have told me what you were doing.'

'I didn't know if I could trust you.'

'If you didn't trust me, why did you give yourself to me?'

Clare told herself she had imagined a faint note of hurt in Diego's voice. 'It was just sex. It wasn't as if it meant anything to either of us.' She assured herself that her emotions had not been involved, and she was certain it hadn't meant anything to Diego. 'What happened after you were brought here?'

'I must have been knocked out cold and when I came round I was lying on a bed and a beautiful woman, who I've just learned is your sister, was leaning over me.' He grinned. 'For a couple of minutes I thought I'd died and gone to heaven.'

'I doubt you would be allowed in,' Clare muttered, feeling a hot surge of jealousy because Diego thought Becky was beautiful.

'Becky told me she had been kidnapped, but I didn't make the connection between the two of you because I believed your story that you were a nun going to teach at a Sunday school.' His expression hardened. 'You don't look at all like your sister.'

'Which explains why Becky is one of the most photographed models in the world and I'm an accountant,' she muttered.

Enzo halted outside a door and knocked. He looked nervous, and Clare's heart jumped into her throat. 'I wonder who Rigo is,' she whispered.

'His name is Rodrigo Hernandez and he heads the biggest drugs cartel in western Brazil, with smuggling routes across the borders into Colombia and Peru,' Diego explained in a low voice. 'He also operates a huge prostitution racket, has been linked to several high-profile kidnappings and has a reputation for extreme violence.'

'Quiet,' Enzo growled, before he opened the door. 'Rigo will see you now.'

Clare was aware that her life and Becky's depended on the outcome of her meeting with the dangerous man inside the room. She felt sick with fear and her feet seemed to be rooted to the floor so that she could not move. A hand grasped hers and she jerked her eyes to Diego's.

'All right?' he asked softly. He squeezed her fingers when she nodded. 'That's my girl.'

As they walked into Rigo's office, Clare gained an impression of walnut-panelled walls, a richly patterned carpet and heavy velvet curtains that were drawn across the windows and blocked out the daylight. The stark white light from a lamp illuminated the spirals of smoke that rose up from the tip of the cigar that the man sitting behind the desk held clamped between his lips.

Rodrigo Hernandez was dressed in a sober grey suit and tie and looked more like a well-to-do lawyer than a violent drugs lord who was one of the most wanted men in South America. But his black eyes were pitiless, Clare thought, and his cold smile sent a shiver through her.

'Miss Marchant. I see you have brought a friend with you. Take a seat, both of you.'

'Diego agreed to drive me to Torrente, but I didn't tell him the real reason for my trip. He's not involved in any of this and you should let him go.'

'*Should* is not a word I am familiar with,' Rigo said in a pleasant voice that was somehow utterly terrifying. Clare looked into the black holes of his eyes and sat down abruptly before her legs gave way.

'I have the money you asked me to bring.' She put the briefcase on the desk and, at a nod from Rigo, one of his henchmen opened it and took out a number of prayer books. 'Oh.' She had forgotten about the books and blushed at the reminder of how she had deliberately misled Diego into believing she was a nun. She avoided looking at him. 'I meant to deliver them to the Sunday school.' She picked up the book of Keats's poems that she had put into the case for safekeeping and slid it on to her lap.

'Five hundred thousand pounds,' Rigo's assistant confirmed when he finished counting the money.

'Now you know that all the money is there, will you allow my sister to go free as…as was agreed?' Clare's voice faltered when Rigo stood up and walked around the desk. She held her breath as he touched her hair and wound a long auburn curl around his fingers.

'Such a beautiful colour,' he murmured. 'I sense, Miss Marchant, that you have a fiery temperament to match your hair. Men will pay a lot of money to bed a woman with spirit and passion. Your sister is free to leave, but I have decided that you will stay here and work for me.' He tightened his fingers on her shoulder and laughed when she could not repress a shudder. 'I may even decide to keep you for my own pleasure.'

Diego clenched his hand until his knuckles whitened. Rage burned inside him, but he knew he could not slam his fist into the slimeball Rigo's face and force him to take his hands off Clare. In order to protect her he must show no reaction. Act cool—that was what he had learned in prison. He couldn't allow Rigo to know how much he wanted to grab Clare and keep her safe. His only chance of saving her from being forced into prostitution, or forced to become Rigo's mistress, was to offer the drugs lord the thing he prized more than anything else. Money.

'It's my experience that spirited women are more trouble than they're worth,' he drawled. 'Miss Marchant will be more valuable to you if you demand a ransom for her.'

Clare shot him a sideways look. 'My father won't be able to raise enough money to pay another ransom,' she said in a fierce whisper. 'I don't think you're helping, Diego. Let me handle this.'

She looked across the desk at Rigo. 'I came to Brazil in good faith that you would allow me to pay for my sister's freedom and it is only fair that you should let us both go.'

Diego groaned silently when Rigo frowned. He wished Clare would let him deal with the situation but he could not help but admire her bravery and determination to rescue her sister. Most women would have gone to pieces by now, but not Clare. Some of his anger at the way she had lied to him about her identity faded, and he begrudgingly acknowledged that he understood why she had dressed as a nun to protect her from the ruthless men who had kidnapped her sister.

Rigo ignored Clare and spoke to Diego. 'Are you prepared to pay a ransom?'

'I am.'

Clare flashed Diego a rueful smile. 'It's kind of you to offer, but I don't suppose a gold prospector earns much money.'

'That's very funny.' Rigo laughed. 'I recognised you from the media's fascination with your personal life, Mr Cazorra. You are one of the richest men in Brazil and I would do better to demand a ransom for your release.'

Diego shrugged. 'I have no family who care about me, and I do not value my life enough to pay you a *centavo*. On the other hand, I will pay whatever you ask in return for releasing Miss Marchant. Name your price.'

The drugs lord gave him a calculating look. 'The Estrela Rosa.'

Diego did not hesitate. Any life was worth more than a lump of carbon, which was all a diamond was really. He was struck by the startling thought that he would give Rigo every precious gem he'd ever found to secure Clare's freedom. 'All right,' he said calmly, 'we have a deal.'

Clare looked between the two men with a sense that she was going mad. 'I don't understand.'

'The Estrela Rosa, the Rose Star, is the largest pink diamond ever to have been found in Brazil,' Rigo told her, 'estimated to be worth over a million dollars. It was discovered in the Old Betsy diamond mine by one of the mine's owners, Diego Cazorra.'

Not for the first time, Clare wondered if she was dreaming and would wake up in a minute. She stared at Diego's ripped jeans and the battered leather hat hiding his unkempt blond hair. Several days' growth of stubble covered his jaw and he looked tough and sexy and dangerously disreputable. 'You don't look like you own a diamond worth a million dollars.'

Amusement gleamed in his eyes. 'I'm overwhelmed by your flattery,' he said sardonically. He looked back at Rigo. 'Tell your bully boys who took my phone to return it and I'll arrange for the diamond to be flown to Torrente. We'll make the exchange on the airstrip once the girls are safely on board the plane.'

Time passed slowly when there was nothing to do but stare at a clock, Clare discovered. There were a hundred questions she wanted to ask Diego, but she hadn't had an opportunity to talk to him since they had returned to the room where they and Becky were being held prisoners.

'Have you paid the ransom? Can we leave now?'

Becky had asked urgently after Enzo had escorted them back to the room and locked them in.

'We'll be allowed to leave as soon as a few things have been sorted out,' Clare had tried to reassure her sister. But she couldn't have sounded convincing because Becky had burst into tears.

'The kidnappers are going to kill us. I know they are. You shouldn't have come to Brazil and risked your life for me,' she'd sobbed hysterically. The strain of being held captive for a week was clearly getting to her.

'Of course I came for you, and we *will* be freed soon. Diego has arranged for a plane to collect us.' Clare tried to sound more confident than she felt. In truth, she did not understand what was happening. It seemed incredible that Diego owned a diamond mine and had done a deal to effectively buy her freedom from the traitorous double-crosser Rigo in exchange for a valuable pink diamond. It sounded like the plot of a thriller and she did not know who she could trust.

At least she was able to change out of the nun's habit into a pair of khaki shorts and a cotton vest top that she'd brought in her rucksack. She felt cooler in the light-weight clothes, at least until Diego stared at her bare legs with a glint in his eyes that made her blush.

She looked at him sitting in an armchair opposite her, his long legs stretched out in front of him and his hat inevitably pulled down over his eyes so that she thought he was asleep. Her mind flew back to the previous night and she pictured his naked body positioned over hers, the firelight flickering over his powerful musculature. Heat swept through her as she remembered how his rock-hard erection had stretched her when he'd first entered her. The few seconds of pain had quickly dissolved and been replaced with mind-blowing pleasure.

If they made it out of Torrente alive, would she ever see him again? Her common sense told her it was un-likely. She did not even know who he really was—a tough gold prospector who read poetry, or a wealthy diamond tycoon.

She froze when she suddenly realised he was not asleep and was watching her with a glint in his eyes that told her he knew she had been fantasising about him making love to her.

'*Deus*, Clare, I wish we were alone right now,' he said softly.

She snapped her eyes from him and glanced at Becky, who was standing tensely by the window. Per-haps as a reaction to the danger they were in, Clare could recall clearly events from the past, and she pic-tured her sister lying in a hospital bed, attached to nu-merous tubes and wires. It was a miracle that Becky had survived the aggressive form of leukaemia she'd contracted as a child, and Clare was determined her sister's life would not be cut short by a gang of despi-cable criminals.

Last night, a mixture of fear and exhaustion had played havoc with her emotions and led her to succumb to her desire for Diego. For a few blissful hours in his arms she had been distracted from the reason she had come to Brazil, but from now on she must focus on get-ting her sister to safety. 'All I wish is that the kidnappers would release us so that my sister and I can go home to our parents,' she said tautly.

Diego frowned. 'One thing I don't understand is why your family sent you to Brazil to pay the ransom money to the kidnappers. They must have realised the danger you would be in.'

'My father couldn't come because he is caring for my mother who is seriously ill, and I offered to rescue my sister. Dad must be frantic with worry about Becky.'

'I'm sure your father is worried about both of you.' Diego felt a flare of anger towards Clare's parents for the way they had allowed her to feel less loved than her sister. He hoped the Marchants realised how incredibly courageous their older daughter was.

His phone rang and he had a brief conversation in Portuguese. 'Your wish is about to be granted,' he told Clare. 'The plane that will take us to Manaus has landed at Torrente airport.'

It was not a proper airport, just a single runway at the edge of the town, surrounded by dense jungle. As the Jeep driven by Enzo pulled up next to a hangar, Clare saw a sleek private jet sitting on the runway with its engines running. She gripped Becky's hand. 'In a couple of minutes we will be on that plane and your ordeal will be over.'

Becky was white-faced and close to hysteria. 'Something is going to go wrong; I know it is.'

Clare looked at Diego. 'What are we waiting for? I thought the arrangement was for us to board the plane before you give the diamond to Rigo.'

'Rigo got here before us,' he said tensely. 'He's already on the jet. The pilot messaged me to say he's been forced to hand over the diamond.'

'Then we need to get on the jet and be ready to leave.' Clare gave a startled cry when Diego caught hold of her arm and pulled her close to him.

'I want you and Becky to get on to the plane that you can see at the far end of the runway.'

Clare stared in the direction he was pointing and frowned. 'Does it even fly? It looks like a plane from the Second World War.'

'It's a Dakota transport plane which regularly brings supplies to Torrente from Manaus. The pilot is expecting us. Tell him to be ready to take off as soon as I get on board.'

'But why can't we leave on the jet?'

Over Clare's shoulder, Diego watched Rigo walk across the runway and get into a car, leaving behind a group of armed men. *They're unlikely to be waiting to welcome the Marchant sisters on to the jet*, he thought cynically. The situation was becoming more dangerous by the minute and there was no time to explain things to Clare. He looked into her wide blue eyes and saw her fear that she was trying to hide. For reasons he couldn't explain he felt a peculiar tugging sensation in his heart. 'You have to trust me,' he said gruffly. He pushed her towards the Dakota. 'Go. Now.'

You have to trust me.

Diego's words replayed in Clare's head as she peered through the plane's window, hoping to catch sight of him in the deepening twilight. She could not think clearly above the roar of the Dakota's engines and the sound of Becky crying. *'We have to go, we have to go,'* her sister sobbed. 'Please, Clare, tell the pilot to take off before the kidnappers come for us.'

'We must wait for Diego. I'm sure he'll be here any minute.'

Where *was* he? Clare's heart leapt when she saw him

by the hangar. But he wasn't alone. Shock jolted through her when she recognised that the man Diego was talking to was one of the kidnappers who had been with Enzo when she had been taken from the cave in the rainforest. In disbelief she watched Diego and the kidnapper briefly hug each other before the two men started to run towards the plane.

Becky was still crying. *'Please,* Clare, let's go now.'

Clare had a split second to make a decision. Should she tell the pilot to take off, which would ensure her sister's safety? Or should she wait for Diego to board the plane with one of the kidnappers? She felt sick. Was Diego somehow involved with Rigo and his criminal gang?

With a flash of clarity she understood that he must have pretended to make a deal with the drugs lord to buy her freedom. Of course he wouldn't have given away a diamond worth a million dollars to save her. She had been so *stupid* to have been blinded by his handsome face and laid-back, sexy charm.

'Sit down and fasten your seat belt,' she ordered Becky as she ran to the front of the plane and spoke to the pilot. 'We're ready to take off, right now.'

Back on the ground, Diego had breathed easier once he'd watched Clare and Becky board the Dakota. He was fairly certain none of Rigo's men had seen them climb into the transport plane. With luck he would be able to join the girls without being seen and the plane would take off from the airstrip before the gang members realised that their quarry had escaped.

He'd guessed that Rigo had planned to have the three of them killed. The time he'd spent in prison had taught him how ruthless criminals' minds worked, and Rigo was more ruthless than most. He hoped the gathering dusk would hide him as he stepped out from the doorway of the hangar, but a voice speaking in Portuguese stopped him.

'Not so fast. Put your hands in the air.'

Slowly, Diego turned around and did a double take as he recognised a face from the past. 'Miguel?'

'*Santa Mãe! Diego*, is it really you?' The other man lowered his gun. 'The last time I saw you was in prison.'

'Nearly twenty years ago.' Diego pictured two teenage boys being escorted by prison guards to an overcrowded cell, hearing the taunts from the other prisoners, terrified of what would happen to them.

'You saved my life,' Miguel said hoarsely, 'and had your ear cut off by the other prisoners as punishment for protecting me. I've never forgotten.'

Nor had Diego forgotten, despite trying to block out the memories of hell. Like him, Miguel had been on remand and awaiting trial to prove he was innocent of the crime he had been accused of. 'Why are you working for a shit like Rigo?'

Miguel shook his head. 'He threatened my family. But my parents are both dead now and I don't care if Rigo kills me for helping you to escape. I owe you, my friend.'

'Rigo isn't going to kill either of us,' Diego said grimly. 'Come with me.' He swore as he heard the roar of the Dakota's engines. 'Quickly! Our chance to escape is about to take off.'

Clare held her breath as the plane lifted off the runway. Becky was still crying, and she gripped her sister's hand. 'It's all over, Becky. You're safe and we're going home.'

But what about Diego? her conscience asked. She had rescued Becky, but what if she had been wrong to think Diego was involved with Rigo? She had seen him talking to one of the kidnappers, she reminded herself. She'd made the right choice to leave him behind, hadn't she?

'*Deus*, Clare, why didn't you wait for me?'

She gasped, wondering if she had imagined Diego's voice. But as she jumped up from her seat and looked towards the back of the plane, she saw him emerge from the cargo hold, followed by the man she'd seen him talking to on the ground who she knew was a member of Rigo's gang.

Clare's immediate instinct was to protect Becky and she stood in front of her and glared at Diego. 'Keep away from my sister. I know you work for Rigo. And this man—' she indicated the man who had boarded the plane with Diego '—is one of the kidnappers who met me at the cave.'

Diego shook his head. 'Clare, it's all right. Miguel is my friend from many years ago.' He put his hand on her arm and swore when she hit him. He saw genuine fear in her eyes and it hurt him more than it should to realise she was afraid of him.

'You crazy little wildcat,' he growled. 'I kept you safe on the journey to Torrente and spent two days up to my neck in mud. You let me believe you were a nun and made me feel guilty for wanting you. You've cost me a rare diamond worth a fortune. And, worst of all, I haven't drunk a single beer since I had the dubious pleasure of meeting you. But, even after all of that, *you still don't trust me.*'

He threw off his hat and seized her in his arms, holding her wrists behind her back so that she could not fight him as he lowered his face to hers. 'So I guess I have nothing to lose,' he muttered against her lips before he captured her mouth in a punishing kiss that demanded her total subjugation, demanded her soul—and laid claim to her heart.

Clare's common sense told her not to respond to the kiss, but she was outvoted by her body that capitulated with shameful willingness to Diego's mastery. She melted into him, seduced by the hardness of his muscles and sinews and the strength of his whipcord body pressed against hers. He was so much taller than her and, with a muttered oath, he lifted her off her feet to bring her mouth level with his and tangled his hand in her hair to prevent her from trying to escape.

But Clare was burning up in the wildfire heat of Diego's hunger. His mouth was utterly addictive and she wrapped her arms around his neck to allow him to increase the pressure of his lips sliding over hers as he deepened the kiss and coaxed her tongue into an intimate dance.

Reality faded. After everything that had happened in the past few days, Clare no longer knew what reality was. But Diego felt real and solid and nothing else seemed to matter except that he brought her senses alive and made her want to leave behind her safe, sensible life and take a leap into the unknown.

When he tore his mouth from hers and set her back on her feet she stared at him dazedly, slowly becoming aware once more of the rumble of the plane's engines and the realisation that Diego looked furious.

He pushed her down into a seat and leaned over her.

'I swear you would test the patience of a saint. If I hear another word from you for the rest of the flight I'll show you just how *unsaintly* you make me feel, *anjinho*.'

CHAPTER SEVEN

'CLARE, WAKE UP. The helicopter has come for you.'

'What…helicopter?' Struggling to surface through a haze of sleep, Clare forced her eyes open and looked groggily at her sister sitting next to her. She remembered they were on the plane, but the Dakota's engines were silent. 'When did we land? We're at Manaus Airport, I suppose.' Memories of their narrow escape from the kidnappers reminded her that her rescue mission would not be completed until her sister was safely back home. 'I doubt there are direct flights from here to London so we'll have to catch a connecting flight to Rio before we can fly to England.'

'Calm down. We're in Rio,' Becky told her. 'We flew through the night from Torrente and landed a few hours ago. It's morning now. You've slept for twelve hours, but Diego didn't want to disturb you.'

Fat chance, Clare thought sardonically. She found his brand of raw sexual magnetism deeply disturbing. 'Where is Diego, anyway?' She glanced around the empty plane.

'He had to go to his office. Before he left, he arranged for me to fly first class to London. My flight leaves soon, which is why I decided to wake you to say goodbye.'

Clare noted that her sister looked remarkably well after her kidnap ordeal. They had both shed tears of relief as the Dakota had flown away from Torrente and the realisation had sunk in that the danger was over. Becky had kept saying how brave Clare had been, but her praise had increased Clare's sense of guilt that she would never have made it to Torrente without Diego and she *should* have trusted him when he had done so much to protect her.

'Surely Diego has booked us both on to the flight to England?' She remembered his anger when she had accused him of being a member of Rigo's criminal gang. 'Or does he expect me to sit in the luggage hold?'

Becky laughed. 'You must have been in a deep sleep if you don't remember that you'll be staying in Brazil to work for the Cazorra Corporation. Diego told me you are going to run a PR campaign for an associate company he is opening in Rio under the brand name of Delgado Diamonds, which his business partner launched so successfully in Europe.'

'Just a minute…' Clare tried to make sense of her sister's words but Becky carried on talking.

'I told Dad about your plans when I phoned home to let him know we're both safe and he's excited that it will be a fantastic opportunity for A-Star PR. Running an advertising campaign for a huge international company like the Cazorra Corporation will really open doors for the A-Star agency. And it's all down to you, Clare.' Becky gave Clare a hug. 'Dad thinks you're amazing, and so do I. You saved my life and I'm so pleased you're being rewarded with the chance to further your career, as well as spend time with Diego.'

'I'm not…'

'It's all right; you don't have to tell me anything.' Becky misunderstood Clare's attempt to interrupt. 'It was clear from the way Diego kissed you last night that there's something going on between you personally as well as professionally. Just be careful. Diego Cazorra has heartbreaker stamped all over him.'

'*Becky!* Will you listen to me?' Clare's frustration bubbled over. 'There's been a misunderstanding. I'm flying back to England with you.' She searched through her rucksack and in exasperation tipped its contents on to her lap. 'I know my passport was in here.'

'Oh, I gave it to Diego so that he could arrange a permit to allow you to work in Brazil.' Becky stood up. 'It's not surprising you're feeling confused after everything that's happened. I've got to go, or I'll miss my flight. Diego's PA will be able to explain things more clearly.'

By the time Clare had stuffed her belongings back into her rucksack and hurried down the steps of the Dakota, her sister had disappeared into the airport terminal.

'Miss Marchant?' She turned towards the voice and saw an elegant-looking woman with dark hair and an exotic olive complexion. 'My name is Juliana Alvez, Mr Cazorra's personal assistant. If you would like to come with me, Diego has scheduled a meeting with you at twelve o'clock to discuss your new role.'

Clare was conscious that her shorts were creased after she had slept in them and her hair was a wild tangle of untidy curls, in contrast to Juliana's sleek chignon and sophisticated cream skirt and jacket.

How *personal* was Diego's personal assistant? she wondered, hating herself for the hot surge of jealousy that swept through her. Once again she had a sense that her life was spinning out of her control.

'That's good, because I have many questions for Diego,' she told Juliana with an air of calm composure that disguised her anger at the way she had been out-manoeuvred.

A helicopter flight over the city gave Clare spectacular views of the iconic landmarks of Rio de Janeiro, where the coastline was met by steeply sloping hills. Sugarloaf Mountain and the towering peak of Mount Corcovado with its famous statue of Christ the Redeemer dominated the skyline. The chopper swooped over beautiful Copacabana beach before it landed on the helipad at the top of a skyscraper building that looked over the bay.

'Where are we?' Clare asked Diego's PA as she followed her inside what appeared to be a luxurious boutique hotel. The whole beach-facing side of the building was glass so that even the corridors offered views of the sea.

'The helipad has direct access to Diego's private penthouse apartment,' Juliana said. 'He owns the whole skyscraper and the Cazorra Corporation's offices are on the lower floors.' She opened a door and ushered Clare into an enormous suite. 'This is where you will be staying. You have a personal maid, Vitoria, who will look after you, and I will return just before twelve to take you to Diego.'

Clare felt decidedly out of place in her crumpled clothes as she explored the elegant sitting room, huge bedroom and en suite bathroom with a sunken bath the size of a small swimming pool. The decor of muted shades of blue and cream, and dove-grey velvet carpets, was sophisticated but impersonal. She found it hard to imagine Diego living in the penthouse when he had admitted that he loved the wildness of the rainforest.

From the bathroom she heard the sound of the bath filling and headed towards it. The maid, Vitoria, was readying an enticing bubble bath.

'Mr Cazorra said you would like to take a bath,' Vitoria explained as she added fragrant oil to the water and the room became infused with the scent of an English rose garden. The thought of sinking into the fragrant foaming water was too irresistible for Clare to argue and, after she had bathed, she made use of the luxurious body lotion provided and used a hairdryer to tame her auburn curls into glossy waves.

Returning to the bedroom, she found that the maid had laid out a peacock-blue silk dress by a famous European designer. There were shoes to match the dress and exquisite underwear, all in Clare's size, but when she searched the room she could not find her rucksack containing the few items of clothing she had brought to Brazil.

The maid's excellent grasp of English suddenly seemed to desert her when she was asked about the rucksack. 'I do not know where is your bag, but you no need it, because Mr Cazorra has supplied clothes for you to wear during your visit.' Vitoria opened the wardrobe to reveal dozens of outfits, mostly in bright colours that Clare would not have had the confidence to choose for herself, preferring to stick to a safe palette of navy and taupe.

Unless she was prepared to meet Diego wearing a towel, she had no choice but to put on the dress, Clare realised. When she looked in the mirror she was forced to concede that the designer was a genius who had turned a piece of fabric into a garment that was both elegant and sexy in the way it flattered her hourglass figure. The three-inch stiletto-heeled shoes made her appear taller and slimmer, but she firmly reminded herself that she was only borrowing the clothes until she saw Diego and she would insist that her rucksack was returned to her.

He had gone to great lengths to arrange for her to remain in Brazil rather than fly back to England with Becky. The question uppermost in her mind was why. He had been angry that she'd fooled him into believing she was a nun, and understandably furious that she had told the pilot to take off from Torrente without him.

She felt guilty about her behaviour and uncomfortable at the prospect of seeing him again, especially when she remembered them making love in the cave. Colour flooded her cheeks as she recalled her wanton response to him. The time they had spent together in the rainforest seemed like a dream and she had discarded her inhibitions along with her virginity. But now she was back to reality, back to being ordinary Clare Marchant, and she wondered what Diego wanted from her.

His PA could not hide her surprise when she saw Clare's transformed appearance. As she followed Juliana along a corridor to Diego's office, Clare was conscious of the sensual slide of the silk underwear and dress against her skin. Was it because she was no longer a virgin that her senses seemed heightened and she was intensely aware of her femininity?

Juliana opened a door and ushered her into a large modern office. Clare had a vague impression of chrome and black glass furnishings and a stunning view of the ocean, but her attention was riveted by the man standing next to the window, who was familiar and yet almost unrecognisable.

From across the room Clare saw the predatory gleam in Diego's silver-grey eyes that reminded her of the unnerving stare of a wolf stalking its prey. But every other aspect of his appearance was different from the rough, tough gold prospector she'd met in the rainforest.

His jeans and T-shirt had been replaced with a superbly tailored charcoal-grey suit teamed with a crisp white shirt and grey tie. Although his hair was still below collar length and covered his ears, it had been tamed into a sleeker style, and the blond stubble on his jaw was now trimmed close to his skin so that he looked groomed but dangerously sexy.

He waited until his PA had closed the door and watched Clare take a deep breath and walk across the room towards him before he spoke.

'The first time I saw you at the convent I knew there was something not quite right about innocent Sister Clare. I've got it now. It's the sexy wiggle of your hips when you walk.' His voice hardened. 'I should have listened to my instincts that said you were not a nun. But you *are* a liar, like most women.'

She flushed but refused to drop her gaze. 'That's a very sweeping generalisation, and in my case it's *not* true. I am usually honest, but I was persuaded by the Mother Superior to dress like a nun because I hoped the kidnappers would be more willing to release my sister. I didn't expect a…situation to develop between us.'

Clare ignored Diego's snort of derision and sat down on the chair he indicated. She felt as if she was being interviewed when he settled himself in his executive leather chair and surveyed her across his desk.

'I have explained why I couldn't be honest about my identity, but you lied too. You let me think you were a gold prospector.'

'It wasn't a lie. I *am* a gold prospector and I search for gold deposits in the Amazon basin. When I get the opportunity, I still join a team of miners and go into the Old Betsy mine to look for diamonds. For the rest of the time I am here running the Cazorra Corporation. But I get restless after I've been in the city for too long.'

Beneath his designer suit and his veneer of wealth and sophistication was the Diego she had first met, who felt more at home in the rainforest, and who had made love to her and kept her safe in his arms throughout the night. Clare forced her mind away from the evocative memories.

'Why have you brought me here? Why did you tell my sister I will be working for you, and why have you provided me with a wardrobe of designer clothes? I don't know what game you are playing, Diego.' Frustration edged into her voice when his familiar, faintly cynical smile gave no clue to his thoughts. 'I want to go home.'

'You seem to have forgotten something.' Beneath his sardonic drawl Clare heard anger in his voice, and she felt a ripple of unease when she noted that his grey eyes were as hard as steel. 'You seem to have forgotten that I secured your release from Rigo by giving him the Estrela Rosa diamond. In effect, I bought you for one million dollars.'

'Of course I hadn't forgotten.' She bit her lip, thinking of the huge debt. 'As soon as I get home I will make it my priority to work out how I can repay you.'

'It will take you years to earn a million dollars,' he said bluntly. 'I was thinking of a more personal method by which you could repay your debt. By agreeing to be my mistress,' he elucidated when she looked at him blankly.

Clare felt a sharp pain beneath her breastbone, as if she had been stabbed through the heart. She was shocked by how hurt she felt. She *knew* that the night they had spent together in the cave had meant nothing to Diego, and she told herself it meant nothing to her. Anger came to her rescue and made her blink back the stupid tears that she would have rather died than let him see.

'Let me get this straight. You're suggesting that I could pay off my debt by having sex with you? How would that work exactly? Should I draw up a spreadsheet, and every time you have me will mean that I can tick off another few thousand dollars? How much is the going rate for sex?' Her lip curled with disgust. 'Is blackmail the only way you can get a woman? You really *must* be desperate.'

Diego's eyes narrowed. 'Careful of your sharp tongue, *querida*, and you can drop the act of outraged virgin. You gave your virginity to me while you were fooling me that you were a nun. *Deus*—' he slammed his hand down on the desk, making Clare jump '—have you any idea how guilty I felt for leading you astray from what I believed was the chaste life you had chosen?'

She flushed. 'I'm sorry that I lied to you.'

He leaned back in his chair and studied her in silence for several minutes. 'Sex with you was good, I'll grant you, but not so good that you can repay me the value of my diamond by lying on your back a few times,' he said coldly. 'I want more than your body, *anjinho*. I also want your brain—' he gave her a mocking smile '—specifically, your expertise as a PR consultant.'

Despite hating him at that moment, Clare was curious. 'What do you mean?'

'I've looked up reports about A-Star PR, and I'm impressed by the agency and by your leadership. You have run several high-profile PR campaigns for businesses in the UK and I am interested in what you might be able to provide for me. You may have heard of the jewellery company Delgado Diamonds?'

She nodded. 'The London store in Mayfair is always busy, and I believe it was recently granted a Royal warrant.'

'My business partner Cruz Delgado established the business a few years ago when he opened the first store in Paris. Cruz has a family now and wants to cut back on work commitments. He will continue to be CEO of Delgado Diamonds in Europe and I have bought the franchise to open Delgado-Cazorra Diamonds stores in the whole of South America. The first DC Diamonds shop will be launched here in Rio. But there is a problem.'

Diego ran a hand through his hair and saw Clare's eyes dart to his mutilated ear that he had unwittingly exposed. He quickly lowered his hand and his jaw hardened. 'The PR agency I originally hired to plan an advertising strategy has failed to come up with any inspirational ideas, and now the opening of the store is fast approaching but hardly anyone knows about the launch. It's partly my fault for taking my eye off the ball, but I've been distracted…' He trailed off. 'This is an opportunity for a PR expert, possibly you, to impress me by organising an aggressive marketing campaign with the aim of making every household in Brazil aware of DC Diamonds.'

'When is the flagship store due to open?'

'Three weeks from now.'

'Three *weeks*! The kind of multi-strategy campaign you want would take a few months to organise.'

He shrugged. 'If you don't think you can do it, I'm sure I will have no trouble finding a PR agency that will seize the opportunity to represent a globally successful company, which the Cazorra Corporation is.'

'I didn't say that I can't do it,' Clare said quickly. 'It will be a challenge, but it's not impossible.'

'After looking at your portfolio I am confident of your ability to promote DC Diamonds. In the expectation that you would accept the commission I ordered new clothes for you that are more suitable for your role than a pair of shorts, or a habit and veil,' he added drily.

Diego watched rosy colour flare on Clare's cheekbones and pictured her face flushed with sexual arousal when she had lain beneath him in the cave and he had nudged her thighs apart so that he could make love to her. The ache in his gut, which had started when she had walked into his office looking as sexy as sin in a dress that clung to every delectable dip and curve of her body, intensified to a sharp tug of desire.

There was no reason for her to refuse what was, in his opinion, an extremely fair offer that would allow her to repay her debt. Her hesitation fuelled his impatience to conclude their discussion so that he could do what he had wanted to do since she had walked into his office—namely, make love to her on the nearest flat surface, which happened to be his desk.

'Can I assume that you want A-Star PR to be given the commission to run an advertising campaign to promote DC Diamonds?'

'Of course I do. As you pointed out, every PR agency

would seize the chance to work for the Cazorra Corporation.' Clare looked at Diego and hated the way her heart flipped as she watched his mouth curve into a sexy smile. 'But I assume that you will only give me the contract if I agree to *all* your terms and work for you in the bedroom as well as the boardroom?'

'It's a fair deal.'

She stood up and drew herself to her full height, grateful that her high heels gave her a few much-needed extra inches as she struggled to hide her disappointment. It would have been a huge boost to her career and to the reputation of the A-Star agency if she'd secured a commission with the Cazorra Corporation. Her father would have been proud of her, and she would have shown Mark Penry she couldn't care less that he'd cheated the day after he had told her he was in love with her.

With a sudden flash of insight Clare realised she did not need to prove she was worthy of her father's love. Nor did it matter that she didn't share her sister's stunning supermodel looks. The trip into the rainforest had shown her she was capable of more than she'd believed, and nothing, not even the career opportunity Diego had dangled in front of her, was worth sacrificing her self-respect for.

Head held high, she marched across the office and yanked open the door before swinging round to face him. 'You know what you can do with your job offer. I won't take either of the positions, but I *will* find a way to repay you the value of the Rose Star diamond, even if I have to scrub floors and clean toilets to earn extra money. You did not buy me, Diego, because I was not and never will be for sale.'

It was an impressive exit line, she commended herself as she walked out and slammed the door behind her. Unfortunately, she had to spoil it moments later and go back into the room. 'You have my passport and I would like you to return it.'

Even wearing three-inch heels, Clare had to tilt her head to look at Diego's face. She had not expected him to be standing by the door when she opened it and almost collided with him. He was unsettlingly close and her senses quivered as she inhaled an evocative scent of sandalwood cologne mixed with a sensual musk of maleness that was uniquely him.

His expression was unreadable. 'You can have it back once I have confirmation that you are not pregnant.'

Diego waited for a heartbeat and watched the colour drain from Clare's face. 'You were a virgin and therefore I assume you were not prepared for sex any more than I was when we made love in the cave.'

The prospect that she might have conceived his child evoked mixed emotions in him, chiefly anger with himself that he had been so crassly irresponsible. He had never had unprotected sex before, and it was no excuse that the night he had spent with Clare in the rainforest had seemed unreal. The stark reality was that he could have fathered a child with her.

Deus, the idea that he was no better than his own father filled him with shame. But he would not abandon his baby as his father had done. His experiences had shown him that a child needed a father. He thought of Cruz's baby twin boys who were growing up with loving parents, and Diego felt a curious tug on his heart as he imagined himself holding his own son or daughter in his arms. Children were so vulnerable. He had never understood how the man whose genes he carried could have been utterly uninterested in the offspring he had carelessly fathered. One thing was certain, he could not allow Clare to return to England while there was a chance she was carrying his baby.

'I'm sure I'm not pregnant,' she said in a strained voice.

'Are you saying you are on the pill or used some other form of contraception?'

'No. But I'd only finished my period a few days before we had sex.' Clare told herself it was ridiculous to feel embarrassed discussing intimate details about herself when Diego knew her body more intimately than any other man. 'It's a biological fact that women are at their least fertile in the first few days of their monthly cycle.'

'We are not talking about women in general; we're talking about you and the fact that you could have conceived my child,' Diego said bluntly. 'When will you know?'

'In a little less than three weeks.' Her period came regularly every twenty-one days. 'There's no reason why I can't go back to England, and if…if the worst *has* happened, of course I'll phone you.'

'So you would consider being pregnant the worst thing to happen?'

Clare bit her lip. 'I…I don't know how I would feel if I was actually going to have a baby. It's not something I'd thought about at this stage of my life,' she admitted. But now she was forced to think about the full implications of possibly being pregnant—and she realised with a jolt of surprise that being a mother would not be the worst thing to happen. She enjoyed her career and felt proud that her father had put her in charge of A-Star PR. But any job seemed unimportant when she imagined holding her own baby in her arms. Her and Diego's baby, she amended as she glanced up and found him watching her. She wished she knew what he was thinking. 'What I meant was that it wouldn't be great news if I found out I was going to be a single parent.'

'That won't happen. My father abandoned my mother when she was pregnant but I will not allow history to repeat itself. If you are expecting my baby I will support you and the child. I can't allow you to leave Brazil until we know.'

'You can't force me to stay. It's preposterous.' Clare's anger was mixed with panic that Diego was powerful enough to do whatever he wanted. But, deep down, she felt strangely reassured that he had said he would support his child, unlike his own father, who had consigned Diego and his mother to a life of poverty in a *favela*. She reassured herself that statistically the likelihood of conceiving early in her monthly cycle was virtually zero.

'Three weeks is not long, and the time will pass quickly while you are working on the PR contract for DC Diamonds.'

She stared at his chiselled features as if they might give some clue to his thoughts. If he really meant to award her the contract she would be a fool not to accept it. 'I'll be happy to work on the advertising campaign, but that's all. You can't force me to be your mistress.'

His lazy smile caught her off guard. He was altogether too sexy for her own good, she thought darkly. But her traitorous body did not care that he was danger with a capital D. A swift downwards glance revealed the hard points of her nipples jutting beneath her silk dress. She instinctively stepped away from him and found herself with her back against the wall as he moved closer, his wolf's eyes gleaming as he cornered his prey.

'I have never forced a woman in my life and I don't intend to start with you, my little wildcat.' Diego's voice deepened and took on a sensual note that made Clare feel as if thick treacle was trickling over her. He placed his palms flat on the wall on either side of her head and watched the jerky rise and fall of her breasts. 'We both know you will come willingly to my bed whenever I decide to have you.'

'The hell I will.'

His outrageous arrogance fuelled her temper. As he lowered his head and angled his mouth over hers, she stiffened, determined to deny him a response. And she might have succeeded if he had claimed her lips with demanding passion, as she expected him to do. But he did not play fair and took her breath away with a kiss that was as gentle as the brush of a butterfly's wings. He took little sips from her mouth, tasting her, tantalising her. His unexpected tenderness evoked a sensation like a knife being twisted in her stomach and desire flooded through her and pooled, hot and urgent, between her legs.

If she could not fight herself, what chance did she stand against Diego's potent sensuality? Clare thought despairingly. He was not using his superior strength to demand her response, he wasn't even touching any part of her body except for her mouth, but when he deepened the kiss she capitulated and parted her lips to allow him to slide his tongue between them. He continued to kiss her unhurriedly and with such exquisite eroticism that she moaned softly and swayed towards him, longing for him to press his body against hers.

She could have cried with disappointment when he lifted his mouth from her lips and stepped away from her. To give him credit, he did not taunt her for her pathetic weakness, and the sultry glint beneath his half-closed eyelids betrayed his hunger.

'In a moment, Juliana will take you to meet the staff who will assist you with the DC Diamonds PR campaign. If you need to leave the Cazorra building for any reason, whether work related or for personal reasons such as shopping, you will be accompanied at all times by either me or a bodyguard.'

'Is that really necessary? My sister was targeted because she is a famous model and easily recognisable, but kidnappers won't be interested in me.'

'I am not prepared to take the risk. While you are working for me, you are my responsibility.' Diego's firm tone dared her to argue. 'I have assigned Miguel to take care of you.'

'*Miguel!* You've asked one of Rigo's thugs to be my bodyguard?' Clare pictured the man who had come to the cave with the other kidnapper, Enzo. 'I'd prefer to go out alone and take my chances. I know you said Miguel is your friend from years ago, but...'

'But you still don't trust me,' Diego finished her sentence grimly. '*Deus*, without my help, you and Becky would still be trapped in Torrente and at Rigo's mercy. I have asked Miguel to protect you because he is the best person to do so. Many years ago I saved his life. In Brazil it is regarded as a lifelong debt of honour, and Miguel would willingly give his life to keep you safe because I have asked him to.'

Clare wanted to ask him more details of his friendship with Miguel, but Diego changed the subject. 'This evening I am hosting a party at my nightclub and I want you to act as my hostess.' The hard expression in his eyes challenged her to refuse, but she had decided there was no point in arguing with him when he was obviously determined to have his own way.

His brows lifted as if he was surprised by her sudden compliance. He held open his office door, but as she was about to step into the corridor he traced his thumb pad lightly across her swollen, kiss-stung lips. 'I suggest you go to the cloakroom and repair your make-up, unless you want the other members of staff to know that you have been thoroughly kissed by the boss,' he drawled.

Swallowing down a rude retort, she nevertheless deemed it wise to take his advice, and groaned when she saw in the mirror her swollen mouth and dishevelled hair. Diego was right, she looked utterly ravished. Her inability to resist him was humiliating. She *must* not allow him to kiss her again, she told herself sternly. From now on she would be a model of businesslike efficiency, and she was determined to organise a PR campaign for DC Diamonds that would impress Diego with her professionalism.

CHAPTER EIGHT

CLARE RAN HER hand down her gold-sequined dress, relieved to find that the low-cut evening gown with a side-split skirt, which she had worried was too flamboyant and revealing, was a perfect outfit to wear to Diego's nightclub and casino, Kasbah.

The club was a huge venue with numerous bars and dance floors, an enormous gambling suite equipped with poker tables, roulette wheels and slot machines, and in the centre of the club was a revolving stage lit by glittering chandeliers suspended from the marquee-like ceiling. The decor was over-the-top opulent and had been designed to represent a Sultan's harem. Rich purple carpets, gold silk wallpaper and plush velvet seating gave the interior a sensual feel that was enhanced by discreet lighting and the throb of deep bass music.

Diego had arrived at the club before Clare. His PA had explained that he wanted to watch the final rehearsal by the dancers who would be performing during the evening. Juliana had also told her that the party was a fund-raising event for the Future Bright Foundation—a charity set up by Diego and his business partner Cruz Delgado to provide education and college funds for young people living in *favelas*.

It had been left to Miguel to drive Clare to the club. The bodyguard had obviously detected that she felt wary of him and had reiterated Diego's assurance that he would protect her with his life if necessary.

'Diego said you and he were friends many years ago. Where did the two of you meet?' she'd asked, thinking that she might learn more about Diego's past.

But Miguel had given her an odd look and murmured, 'You'll have to ask Diego that question.'

Clare told herself that the mystery surrounding Diego was none of her business. In a few weeks she would go home to England and never see him again. *Unless she was pregnant with his child.* The thought slipped into her mind and she felt a flutter of nerves in her stomach. There was no point worrying about it when the chances that she had conceived were so unlikely, but she couldn't stop wondering if Diego's baby was developing inside her.

She forced her mind back to the present. The guests would be starting to arrive soon and she was wondering what her duties as Diego's hostess would entail. She caught sight of him up on the stage surrounded by a group of exotic female dancers whose costumes comprised of a few strategically placed ostrich feathers.

The girls crowded around Diego, and it wasn't hard to understand why, Clare thought ruefully. He looked amazing in a black dinner suit and white silk shirt, and his tousled, over-long hair and the shadow of blond stubble on his jaw gave him a raw sex appeal that was dangerously attractive.

Although her stiletto heels made no sound on the thick carpet, he turned his head as she approached, as if a sixth sense had alerted him to her presence.

'Clare.' There was a strange huskiness in his voice and the glitter in his silver eyes sent a frisson of sexual awareness down her spine. He did not take his gaze from her as he clapped his hands and the dancers left the stage in a flurry of feathers and a flash of lissom thighs.

'Juliana said I would find you hard at work,' Clare said drily. 'At a rough estimate, I'd guess that you have slept with at least ten of the twenty girls in the dance troupe.'

He grinned. 'But not all at the same time.' The expression in his eyes became feral as he studied her. 'I knew when I picked that dress that you would look stunning in it.'

'How did you know my size?'

'I asked your sister.' He stepped closer and murmured in her ear, 'Besides, I have an excellent memory of your body, *querida.*'

Fortunately the guests began to arrive and Diego moved to greet them, but Clare's hope that she would be able to disappear amongst the crowd was thwarted when he slipped his arm around her waist and kept her clamped to his side.

'Tonight you are my hostess,' he reminded her when she suggested he might want to circulate on his own and chat to the countless beautiful women who watched him hungrily as if they wanted to devour him.

'Why do I get the feeling that you're using me as a shield? Aren't you flattered that you could have just about any woman in the room without even having to try?'

She looked up at his handsome face, expecting to see his mouth curve into an indolent smile, but he trapped her gaze and the heat in his eyes burned her. 'There is only one woman I want but she told me she's not interested,' he said softly.

Clare was aware of the pulse at the base of her throat beating so hard she was afraid it was visible through her skin. She reminded herself that Diego was a womaniser and he was flirting with her because it was second nature to him. But sexual chemistry had sizzled between them in the steamy rainforest and it was no less potent in the semi-dark nightclub with the thudding beat of the music echoing the frantic thud of her heart. She opened her mouth to reiterate what she had told him in his office, that she would not be his mistress at any price. But instead she heard herself murmur, 'I said I wasn't for sale. I never said I wasn't interested.'

What the hell had Clare meant by that? Diego wondered as he watched her walk away from him. He was damned sure she had deliberately made an excuse that she needed to visit the bathroom, and he was tempted to go after her, lock them both in a cubicle and take her up against the wall with all the finesse of a hormone-fuelled teenager.

He raked a hand through his hair, his eyes lingering on the sway of her hips and the taut curves of her bottom beneath her twinkling sequin-covered dress. He couldn't remember when he had wanted a woman as much as he wanted her. But perhaps his inexplicable possessive feeling was because there was a possibility that she was carrying his child, he told himself.

His common sense urged him to put her out of his mind. As she had pointed out, he could take his pick from any of the single females at the party, and probably a few married ones, he thought sardonically. Money was a powerful aphrodisiac, but even before he'd become a multimillionaire women had desired him; strangely, and it was a funny thing, the less he had cared, the more they'd pursued him.

Clare was the only woman who had ever stood up to him. She had even stood up to the ruthless drugs lord, Rigo. He admired her, Diego acknowledged. Hell, he liked her as well as desired her, and he knew, because he always knew with women, that she was halfway to falling in love with him. What troubled him most was the realisation that he did not want to hurt her, which of course he would. He wasn't looking for love. The blank space in his memory of what had happened when he was seventeen hid a truth about himself that he did not want to uncover. It was safer to be a playboy who did not give a damn about anyone.

Across the room he caught the eye of one of his ex-mistresses. Belinda was an attractive blonde, wearing a minuscule dress that showed off her long legs. Like most of his exes, Diego had parted from her on good terms and her body language sent him a message that she was available. He started to walk towards Belinda but then he noticed Clare standing by the bar and scanning the room for him.

The bright lights above the bar danced over her long auburn hair, which fell in rippling waves down her back and shone like silk. *Santa Mãe*, she looked as if she had been poured into the gold dress that hugged her tiny waist and framed her full breasts. She was tying him in knots, Diego acknowledged grimly. The only way to get her out of his system was to get her into his bed.

The finest champagne and exquisite canapés were served to Diego's guests, who had paid hundreds of dollars for tickets to the party, with all the proceeds going to his charity. After the cabaret came the main fund-raising event of the evening, when donated items were auctioned. Earlier, Clare had looked at the variety of items for auction, which included fabulous jewellery, a number of valuable pieces of artwork and, most astonishing of all, a sports car. The only item she considered bidding for was a rare first edition copy of poems by English Romantic poet Lord Byron, but when she saw the starting bid price she realised it would exceed her credit card limit.

In fact, the poetry book was sold for three times the amount expected. 'You looked disappointed that the bidding for Byron's poems was so high,' Diego commented.

'Surprised, but certainly not disappointed because all the money raised at the auction goes to the Future Bright Foundation, doesn't it?'

'Every dollar,' he said with quiet pride. 'The money is put to good use. Cruz and I know from our own experiences growing up in a *favela* that education is the key to escaping poverty.'

Clare looked at him closely. 'You donated the poetry book, didn't you? And then won the bid to buy it back again.'

He shrugged. 'I do the same at every fund-raising auction. When I was a young man and borrowed books from Earl Bancroft's library, reading novels and poetry opened my mind to the realisation that there was a whole world waiting for me beyond working in a mine. I hope to give all deprived children not only a dream of a better life, but the means, by educating them, to turn their dreams into reality.'

His words touched something inside Clare. 'Do you

really not have any family who care about you?' she asked softly, remembering what he had told the drugs lord Rigo. 'You told me that your father abandoned your mother before you were born and you grew up living in a *favela*. Is your mother dead too?'

He shrugged. 'I don't know. I lost contact with her when I was seventeen.'

'Have you never tried to find her?'

'No.' Diego's brusque tone warned her not to ask any more questions.

'Well, here is your book to put back on the shelf in your library,' Clare said when a waiter delivered the leather-bound book to their table.

'Actually, it's yours,' Diego murmured, sliding the book towards her. 'I bid for it on your behalf.'

She shook her head. 'I can't take on any more debt when I already owe you a million dollars for the Rose Star diamond.'

'You don't owe me for the book. It's a present.'

Diego saw Clare's look of surprise and cursed himself. Why was he behaving like a damned fool in love? He was simply wooing her a little so that she would have sex with him, he assured himself as he opened the book at a random page, which happened to be Lord Byron's famous poem, *She Walks in Beauty*.

It was a poem Diego had read many times, and his eyes were drawn to Clare's lovely face as he quoted softly, '"*She walks in beauty, like the night Of cloudless climes and starry skies; And all that's best of dark and bright Meet in her aspect and her eyes...*"'

It was the champagne making her feel light-headed, Clare told herself, not Diego's deep voice seducing her

with Byron's beautiful poetry. The two men had something in common; Byron had been notorious for his
scandalous affairs and Clare had no doubt that Diego's
reputation as a womaniser was well deserved.

But when he asked her to dance with him she found
herself being led on to the dance floor and swept into
his arms. And when their eyes met and his mouth curled
into a lazy smile that stole her breath she gave up trying to resist him.

They danced the night away, and by the time the party
ended and Diego helped Clare into the back of the limousine before sliding in next to her, every nerve ending
in her body felt ultra-sensitive. The brush of his hand
on her bare arm seemed to scorch her skin, and the feel
of his hard thigh pressed up against hers made her recall how thick and hard his erection had been when he
had slowly entered her.

Her awareness of him intensified as they stepped into
the lift, which would take them to the top floor of the
Cazorra skyscraper. The doors closed, and as the lift
began its smooth ascent her eyes were drawn to him.
He had unfastened his bow tie and his streaked blond
hair fell across his brow, adding to his rakish charm.
She wondered why he suddenly looked tense. Maybe
he was irritated because she was staring at him like
countless women at the party had done, she thought
uncomfortably.

The lift suddenly juddered to a standstill and the
lights went out.

'What the hell?' Diego said tersely. The lights flickered and came on again, but the lift did not move.

'Do you think it has broken down?'

'No, I think we're stuck between floors for fun.'

Clare frowned. 'There's no need to be sarcastic.' She studied the control panel. 'There's an emergency button. Should I press it?'

'Deus!' Diego exploded. 'Press the damn thing and tell the maintenance staff to get us out of here right now.'

'Diego…are you okay?' Clare stared at him. His jaw was clenched and he was oddly pale beneath his tan. When he pushed his hair out of his eyes she saw beads of sweat on his brow.

'I dislike lifts.' He caught her questioning look and muttered, 'I have an irrational fear of confined spaces.' Sweat ran down his face. He swore and wrenched off his jacket. A voice speaking in Portuguese sounded over the intercom and Diego answered with a few curt words, and Clare guessed it was lucky she did not understand.

'The concierge says he has called the engineer and the lift will be repaired as soon as possible,' he relayed to her.

She couldn't disguise her shock that he had been fearless in the rainforest, and had even wrestled with a python, but he suffered from claustrophobia. 'How did you spend years working underground in mines if you hate confined spaces?'

He shrugged. 'It was the only way I could earn a living, so I had to do it or starve. Getting into a lift cage packed with men to be taken underground was hell—it still is—but fortunately the mine shafts in the Old Betsy mine are a reasonable size to work in.' He wiped a hand over his sweat-damp face and said with an attempt at humour, 'Anyway, your heart only feels like it's going to burst out of your chest for the first few hours of a shift and, however bad you feel, you just have to get on with the job.'

The discovery that Diego had a vulnerable side to him evoked a curious tug on Clare's heart. 'Do you feel this bad every time you step into a lift? That must be difficult considering you live and work in the Cazorra skyscraper.'

'I don't usually take the lift; I use the stairs.'

'But you live on the thirtieth floor.'

'It keeps me fit,' he muttered.

'So did you only take the lift tonight because of me?'

'I couldn't expect you to climb thirty flights of stairs.'

Clare bit her lip. 'You should have told me. I feel terrible. But probably not as bad as you're feeling,' she conceded, seeing the sheen of sweat on his face. 'Is there anything I can do to help?'

'Not…unless you can come up with a distraction technique to take my mind from the thought that we are trapped in a metal box,' he said through gritted teeth.

An idea came to her, and she acted without pausing to question whether it was wise or not as she stepped closer to him and cupped his face in her hands. 'Perhaps this will distract you,' she murmured before she covered his mouth with hers and kissed him.

She felt the jolt of surprise that ran through him, but he responded instantly and opened his mouth to welcome the gentle probing of her tongue. He was content to follow her lead, and as she continued kissing him she felt the terrible tension that gripped his muscles gradually lessen.

'Is it working?' She finally had to stop and allow them both to breathe.

'I'm not sure,' he said thickly. 'You'd better try again.'

He did not look quite so pale, she thought as she stood on tiptoe so that she could reach his mouth. This time he took control and deepened the kiss until Clare's senses were swamped by the taste of him, the scent of his aftershave, the feel of his strong arms sliding around her waist to pull her even closer to him—so close that she could not mistake the hard ridge of his arousal.

'Something's definitely working,' he drawled, sounding more like the laid-back Diego she knew—and did *not* love. Of course not. It was just a silly saying that had slipped into her mind.

The lift suddenly lurched and then continued its ascent. Clare sprang away from him, hot-faced with embarrassment that in trying to distract him from his phobia she had aroused him, and herself, she acknowledged ruefully as she glanced down at the outline of her nipples jutting beneath her dress.

Moments later the doors opened directly into the penthouse and she heard Diego exhale heavily as he followed her out of the lift. As they walked in silence along the hallway leading to their respective bedrooms she did not know what to think, or what was going to happen next. But she knew with sudden clarity what she wanted to happen. Becky had warned her that Diego was a heartbreaker, but Clare had no intention of letting him anywhere near her heart.

Disappointment swooped in her stomach when he walked straight past the door to his suite without trying to persuade her to sleep with him. Maybe he did not desire her as much as she'd thought.

Her room was next to his. He halted outside the door and casually swung the jacket that he was carrying over his shoulder. But there was nothing casual about the smouldering intensity in his eyes, and his voice was a rough growl that grazed her skin and sent a quiver of excitement down her spine. 'Are you going to invite me in?'

'Yes.' Simple, direct. She was tired of playing games. 'But there is a condition.'

His brows rose in silent query.

'I won't pay off my debt with sex and after tonight I will still owe you a million dollars. I'm inviting you into my bed because I want you. But I won't be your mistress. You will be my…' she had been going to say *lover*, but reminded herself that love was not involved '…stud.'

He gave a husky laugh that evoked a coiling sensation low in her pelvis. 'You are something else, Clare.' There was a curious note that she almost thought was admiration in his voice. He opened her bedroom door, placed his hand at the small of her back and pushed her into the room. 'Be careful what you wish for, *querida*.' He slid his hand down and caressed her bottom, his touch burning her through her dress. 'You want a stud and, as you can feel—' he pressed up against her so that his erection nudged the cleft between her buttocks and their clothes were a frustrating barrier '—I am very willing to oblige.'

Diego knew he was going to have to cool things down. He was fiercely tempted to drag Clare's dress up to her waist, pull her knickers down and bend her over the end of the bed so that he could take her hard and fast, the way his body was aching to do. Adrenaline was still pumping through his veins from when they had been trapped in the lift, but his urgent need to make love to her was more than a primal urge to have sex.

Deus, she had been so sweet when she had kissed him to distract him from his stupid, irrational fear. If she knew the truth of why he hated confined spaces, maybe she would understand that his gut-churning terror of being confined was not irrational. But he had never told any of his mistresses that he had been to prison, so why would he tell Clare?

He realised she was watching him with a faint uncertainty in her eyes that made him dismiss his thoughts and focus all his attention on her. She'd said she wanted a stud, but her only experience of sex was when he had taken her virginity. What she needed from him was patience and tenderness. It occurred to him that he would enjoy teaching her the many and varied pathways of pleasure that she had never experienced with any other man. Diego frowned. This possessive feeling was a new experience for him and not one that he wanted to think about too deeply.

He threaded his fingers into her hair that felt like silk against his skin and lowered his head to claim her lips in a kiss that started out as gentle. But her eager response stoked the fire inside him so that he thrust his tongue into her mouth in an erotic imitation of thrusting his throbbing arousal into her.

She tugged open his shirt buttons and ran her hands feverishly over his bare chest. He gave a half-laugh, half-groan. 'How can I make love to you slowly and gently when you are so damned hot?'

Clare curled her arms around his neck and pulled his mouth down to hers, pressing her curvaceous body up against him so that Diego could feel the hard points of her nipples scrape across his chest. 'I don't want slow and gentle. I don't mind if you are rough,' she whispered against his lips. 'I just want you now, *now*.'

'*Deus*, you will be the death of me, *anjinho*.' He ran

her zip down her spine and tugged the gold dress. She wasn't wearing a bra and her bare breasts spilled into his hands, firm and plump like ripe peaches, and utterly delectable when he kissed the creamy mounds, before he closed his lips around one pouting nipple and then the other.

Her soft moans of delight nearly drove him over the edge, and when she fumbled with the zip on his trousers and her fingers brushed across his arousal he knew he had to take control. He swiftly dragged her dress over her hips so that it slid to the floor, leaving her in just a tiny gold thong and high-heeled strappy gold sandals. Diego knelt and removed her shoes and then scooped her up and deposited her on the bed, but he resisted her attempt to pull him down on top of her.

He stood at the end of the bed and pushed her thighs apart. 'I'll explain how this is going to work, *querida*. I am going to kiss every inch of your body, and I mean *everywhere*,' he warned her softly. 'Now lie back.'

He could not actually mean everywhere, Clare thought as she stretched out on top of the satin bedspread while Diego knelt above her and lowered his head to capture her mouth in a sensual kiss that added fuel to the flame of her desire. He trailed his lips over her throat and breasts, paying special attention to her nipples until she whimpered with pleasure. 'Enough,' she pleaded in a breathy voice she hardly recognised as her own.

'I've barely begun,' he told her as he moved down her body, kissing her stomach and the tops of her thighs. She trembled and instinctively tried to scissor her legs together, but he firmly held them open so that she was utterly exposed to him apart from a fragile strip of gold silk. He pushed her thong aside, and as Clare felt his silky hair brush against her inner thighs she suddenly realised that he really did intend to kiss *every* bit of her.

'I'm not sure…' It seemed like a step too far, too intimate. Yet she was curious, and her body was burning up with need that intensified when she felt his tongue flick across the tight nub of her clitoris. She jerked her hips involuntarily towards his mouth and gasped as he proceeded to lick his way inside her.

Sweet heaven… She clutched the bedspread and held on for dear life as the pressure inside her built with every thrust of his tongue, taking her higher, taking her towards ecstasy. She came so hard that it almost hurt, her vaginal muscles squeezing and contracting with fierce, fast spasms that left her wanting more.

'Please…' Was that really her voice sounding so guttural, so desperate? Clare was shocked by the intensity of her desire. Diego had called her a wildcat, and he turned her into one. With him she became wild and wanton and she practically purred with anticipation as she watched him strip and slide a protective sheath over his awesome erection.

When he dipped his head between her legs again, she made a husky protest. 'No more. I want…' Her voice faded as Diego ripped her thong apart with his teeth.

'I know what you want,' he growled as he lifted himself over her. 'You want this…'

He had tried to be gentle, Diego assured himself, but the combination of his urgency and Clare's eagerness created a simmering chemistry that was about to combust. He looked down at her gorgeous, curvaceous body, her pale thighs spread wide in readiness for him to possess her. Anticipation sharpened his desire to a primitive need he could no longer deny and he thrust into her and drove deep, drawing a gasp of surprise from her as her internal muscles were forced to stretch to accommodate his solid length.

She was so tight, so hot. He paused to give them both time to snatch a breath and felt a curious tightness in his chest when she smiled. *Deus*, she was so beautiful. The sweetness of her smile felt like a punch in his gut. What the hell was happening to him? Diego asked himself grimly. First he had quoted romantic poetry to her, and now he felt emotions surge though him that he did not dare examine.

It was just sex, he reminded himself. He was good at sex, as his numerous ex-mistresses could verify. Clare had told him she wanted a stud and he was confident he wouldn't disappoint her.

He began to move inside her, to thrust and withdraw in a powerful rhythm as he took her stroke by measured stroke while she moaned and writhed beneath him. He could feel his climax building, but he did not falter, driving into her faster, harder until she gave a keening cry and her body shuddered with the intensity of her orgasm.

It was his signal that finally he could take his own pleasure and he surged forwards once more and let himself come. The intensity of his release tore a groan from deep inside him, and in the aftermath, as his heartbeat slowed, he was strangely reluctant to move and disjoin from her.

At last he rolled away and stared up at the ceiling, searching his mind for something banal to say that would shatter the emotionally charged atmosphere. He frowned when Clare snuggled up to him. He did not do snuggling and, however good it felt to have her soft body pressed up against him, her hand resting lightly on his chest, he could not risk falling asleep in her bed. He never knew when his sleep would be disturbed by a nightmare, or what secrets his dreams might reveal.

Her long auburn eyelashes lay on her cheeks and the sound of her even breaths told him she had fallen asleep. He resisted the temptation to wake her and take her again. She would be staying in Brazil for three weeks to work on the PR campaign and that was more than enough time for him to sate his desire for her. No doubt by the time of the DC Diamonds launch he would have grown bored of her. He refused to think of the problems that would lie ahead if she had actually conceived his child.

Taking care not to disturb her, he slid off the bed and draped the bedspread over her before he silently left the room.

Clare watched Diego exit her bedroom with a sense of disbelief that was rapidly turning to anger. She had been drifting off to sleep when she'd felt him move, and at first she had thought he was visiting the bathroom. But as she watched him walk over to the door she realised that he did not intend to spend the night with her.

He'd had what he wanted, she thought bitterly. She had provided him with sex, and presumably he saw no reason to stay in her bed. Why was she surprised? She knew he was a womaniser, but she had conveniently forgotten that fact when he had deliberately seduced her with romantic poetry. She understood now that his motive for giving her the book of Byron's poems had been entirely cynical. But, like an idiot, she had been beguiled by the tender expression in his eyes and, to compound her foolishness, she had been taken in by his apparent panic attack in the lift and his confession that he suffered from an irrational fear of confined spaces. Although when she remembered his clenched jaw and how his skin had turned sickly green, she conceded that he probably hadn't been faking his claustrophobia.

She lay there for a few more minutes, but sleep was now impossible when she felt so churned up inside. Muttering an oath, she swung her feet on to the floor and pulled on Diego's shirt that he'd discarded before he'd taken her to bed.

His room was bigger than hers, she discovered when she padded down the hall and opened his door. Unlike the neutral decor of the other rooms in the penthouse, the walls of Diego's bedroom were covered in prints of the Amazon rainforest. But Clare's attention was focused on the enormous bed where he was sprawled, his broad shoulders propped against a pile of pillows. He was reading, but looked up from his book and frowned when he saw her.

'I'm surprised you didn't leave a handful of dollars on my bedside table in payment for my services,' she said tautly. 'But then I remembered that you believe I should pay off my debt to you with sex. Let's see. There's three weeks until the DC Diamonds launch. That's twenty-one nights, divided into one million dollars, which means it just cost you approximately fifty thousand dollars to have sex with me.' To her annoyance she could not prevent her voice from trembling. 'I hope I was worth it.'

'Clare...' Diego swore beneath his breath when he noticed the glimmer of tears in her eyes. He hated that she was clearly hurt, and he was responsible. *'Querida...'*

'Don't *querida* me,' she said fiercely. 'I'm not your darling. I'm your whore. You made it perfectly obvious when you left my bed that all you want from me is sex.' She tried to swallow her tears and choked. 'You made me feel cheap.'

'Deus,' Diego growled as he leapt out of bed and strode over to her. 'That was not my intention. I thought you had fallen asleep, and I didn't want to disturb you.' He caught hold of her arm to prevent her from rushing out of the door. 'I don't sleep well, and I usually read for several hours during the night.'

'What are you doing?' Clare had tried not to stare at Diego's naked body when he'd got out of bed, but she couldn't ignore his erection that was jabbing into her thigh. She tried to move away from him, but he swept her up into his arms and held her tight against his big chest. 'I can walk back to my room,' she muttered as he carried her into her bedroom and placed her on the bed. 'Leave me alone.' She tried to turn her head away as he slanted his mouth over hers, but he cradled her cheek in his hand and smothered her protest with a sensual, evocative kiss that tugged on her treacherous heart.

'I think I've made it fairly obvious that I can't leave you alone,' he said drily, but his sardonic tone was laced with something deeper and more urgent. He deftly removed his shirt from her, and his eyes gleamed with feral intent as he ran his hands over her body, caressing her breasts before he moved lower and found that she was wet for him. 'I don't want to hurt you,' he whispered against her mouth as he positioned himself over her.

But he would, she thought with a sudden fearful insight. It wasn't his fault. He had been honest and admitted he only wanted to have a sexual relationship with her. It was her foolish heart that was to blame. If she had any sense she would insulate her emotions against his impossible to resist charisma.

CHAPTER NINE

'CLARE. *DEUS,* YOU sleep like the dead!'

The sound of Diego's impatient voice forced Clare to open her eyes, and she stared at him looming over her. As always, the sight of his handsome face and his blond hair falling across his brow made her heart flip. She noted that he looked wide awake and disgustingly energetic, which was impressive as he had not left her bed until some time around two o'clock. She could not be sure of exactly when, because he always waited until she had fallen asleep before leaving her and returning to his own room.

She had accepted his reason that he never spent the entire night with her because he was a restless sleeper and did not want to disturb her, but she didn't know what caused his insomnia. There were a lot of things she did not know about him, she thought ruefully. Diego was as much of an enigma now as he had been when she had started working on the PR campaign for DC Diamonds three weeks ago.

Their schedule every day had been hectic. She had organised a huge publicity campaign to promote Diego's new business venture, and he had insisted on her accompanying him in his private helicopter to TV and radio stations in cities all across Brazil so that he could give interviews and advertise his new jewellery shop franchise.

She stretched her arms above her head, unaware that the sheet slipped down to reveal her bare breasts, or of the feral gleam that flared in Diego's eyes as he viewed the plump mounds of flesh, each adorned with a dusky pink nipple. 'What time is it?'

'Eight o'clock.'

'Why have you woken me up? You might be able to function on six hours' sleep,' she muttered, 'but I need a full eight hours.'

He gave a husky laugh that stirred Clare's body to instant arousal. 'You need to get up, *anjinho*, because if you don't I will join you in bed, and either way you won't get any more sleep.'

She pretended to consider. 'What will you do to me if I refuse to get up?'

'Don't tempt me.' Beneath his playful tone was a rougher note of raw sexual need. 'Seriously, *querida*, I want to take you out for the day. Cruz and his wife, Sabrina, have arrived from their home in Portugal with their baby twins. They are renting a beachfront villa along the coast and have invited us to spend the day with them.'

Clare sat up and pulled the sheet over her breasts to hide them from Diego's heated gaze. 'But tonight is the launch party for DC Diamonds and I need to be here to oversee final preparations and deal with any problems.'

'There won't be any problems. I've seen the size of your folder of notes regarding arrangements for the party and I'm certain you have everything under control. I have been impressed with the PR campaign you organised over the past three weeks. You should be proud of yourself.'

She shot him a glance and realised he wasn't teasing her. His praise made her feel stupidly happy, but she shoved the thought to the back of her mind, along with the other thought that after tonight there would be no reason for her to remain in Brazil. Unless she was pregnant. Her heart lurched. She was only two days late, she quickly reminded herself, and in fact she felt slightly nauseous, which was usually a sign that her period was about to start.

'It will be good for you to spend the day relaxing before the party,' Diego said persuasively.

'What time are we expected to meet Cruz and Sabrina?'

'I told them we would be over in an hour.'

'Mmm…' She let the sheet slide down her body and slipped her hands under his T-shirt, running her fingertips over the golden hairs that grew thickly on his chest. 'So I can stay in bed for a bit longer. Care to join me?'

'Minx,' he growled, helping her pull his shirt over his head. Clare caught her breath when he cupped her breasts in his palms and flicked his thumbs across her nipples, making them tighten and tingle. Their passion for one another had not lessened in three weeks; in fact it seemed to intensify every time they had sex—and they had sex a lot.

She felt hot all over as she remembered the previous day when Diego had called her into his office to supposedly discuss the PR campaign. She should have guessed his intention when he'd instructed his secretary not to disturb them and locked the door. 'I thought we were meant to be having a meeting,' Clare had reminded him when he'd unbuttoned her blouse.

'We are. My body is going to meet with yours, and I promise you the outcome will be very productive,' he'd told her, and had proceeded to make love to her bent over his desk.

It wasn't just the sex that was amazing. They spent all day every day in each other's company, either working on the campaign or relaxing over dinner at the penthouse or a restaurant, and they made love several times every night. The only downside was that he never stayed all night with her. But perhaps it was a good thing because she knew she was increasingly in danger of falling in love with him. Waking up in an empty bed each morning was a stark reminder that the closeness she felt to Diego was an illusion she would be foolish to believe might become real.

They were only half an hour late to meet their hosts, after Diego had made love to her and then carried her into the shower, where he had been very inventive with a bar of soap.

If Cruz and Sabrina noticed the hectic flush on Clare's face, or Diego's smug smile, they were too polite to say so. Clare liked the couple instantly. Cruz's dark, brooding good looks contrasted with his wife's English rose complexion. Lady Sabrina Bancroft, as she had been before her marriage, was elegant and refined, but she exuded a warmth and friendliness that drew people to her, which was one of the reasons, Clare suspected, that her husband was utterly besotted with her.

The couple's nine-month-old twin boys, Vitor and Henrique—named, Sabrina explained, after their two grandfathers—were adorable. Both babies had dark brown curls and green eyes, and were already displaying signs that they had inherited their father's determined personality.

Watching the little boys crawling across the rug, Clare felt an unexpected tug of maternal longing. She had never given much thought to babies, and had assumed she would have children some time in the future. But for the last few days as she'd waited anxiously for a sign that she had not conceived Diego's child, she'd found herself imagining holding her own baby in her arms.

The two men spent the morning riding jet skis on the sea, while Clare stayed on the beach and helped Sabrina chase after the babies, who were intent on crawling away from the shade of a parasol.

'Which of your godsons do you want to hold?' Cruz asked Diego after they had returned to the house.

'I don't want to show favouritism so you'd better hand me both of them,' Diego replied easily. Watching him with the baby boys, Clare felt another tug on her insides as she pictured him cradling a blond baby who was their son or daughter. *Stop it*, she told herself firmly. She *couldn't* be pregnant. The strange light-headed sensation that had swept over her before lunch, when she'd thought she might faint, had been a sign that she was stressed about tonight's party.

The buffet lunch was a relaxed meal that continued into the afternoon. While the twins napped in their prams there was a chance for the adults to chat.

'How is Earl Bancroft?' Diego asked Sabrina.

She smiled. 'Dad is very well. My father lives in a stately home in England,' she explained to Clare. 'He has opened Eversleigh Hall to the public and he seems to enjoy giving tours of the house.'

Clare suddenly made the connection. She turned to Diego. 'So the English earl who owned a diamond mine that you once worked in is Sabrina's father?'

He nodded. 'Some years after Henry sold the Old Betsy mine, Cruz and I were in a position to buy it. Cruz had earned a fortune as a banker, and I inherited money from my father's family. We decided to gamble and invest in the diamond mine, and luckily the gamble paid off.'

She was puzzled. 'I thought you didn't have any contact with your father.'

'It's true I never met him. He knew my mother had given birth to his child but he wasn't interested in finding me. He died young, but before he passed away he told his father that he had an illegitimate child in Brazil. It was a total shock when Father Vincenzi found me and gave me the news that I was my grandfather's only heir.'

'Who is Father Vincenzi?'

'He is a priest who helped me when I...' He broke off abruptly and Clare knew she had not imagined the sudden awkward silence that fell over the table, or the swift glance that passed between Cruz and Sabrina. 'The holy Father helped me when I was a young man.' Diego did not elaborate on his statement. Instead he stood up and spoke curtly to Clare. 'It's time we were leaving. I expect you'll want plenty of time to get ready for the party.'

Diego had demanded something spectacular for the launch party of DC Diamonds and, with an unlimited budget to spend, Clare had chartered one of the world's largest and most luxurious super-yachts, *Serendipity*, for the party venue.

From the balcony of her stateroom she watched helicopters flying to and fro, bringing guests out to the yacht, which was moored in Copacabana bay. She and Diego had arrived by chopper in the late afternoon, and she had spent a couple of hours checking final details with the team of chefs who were preparing canapés, and the bar staff who had created a special cocktail in honour of DC Diamonds, which they had named 'Bling.'

During the party, champagne fountains would flow with Cristal, which guests could enjoy while they watched a catwalk show. Clare had hired top models to wear jewellery from the DC Diamonds collection. Later in the evening there would be a disco with music provided by a world-famous DJ, and the climax of the night was to be a firework extravaganza viewed from *Serendipity*'s decks.

A glance at her watch revealed that the party was due to start in fifteen minutes. All she could do now was hope that everything went to plan. She felt a flutter of nerves in her stomach that grew stronger when there was a knock on her door and Diego strolled in.

He had been uncommunicative when they'd left Cruz and Sabrina, and Clare had not seen him since they had boarded the yacht. But now her breath caught in her throat at the sight of him in a black tuxedo teamed with a black shirt. With his blond hair falling over his collar and his chiselled jaw shaded with blond stubble, he looked dangerously disreputable and utterly gorgeous.

The lazy curl of his smile told her that he had got over his earlier bad mood, and she warned herself to be on her guard against his sinfully sexy charm. But the expression in his eyes was harder to decipher as he said in an oddly rough voice, 'I have never seen you look as beautiful as you do tonight.'

Clare spun round to the mirror to hide the fact that she suddenly felt ridiculously self-conscious. 'It's a beautiful dress. I have to say, you have very good taste in dressing women,' she said, needing to remind herself that he probably had plenty of experience in choosing clothes for his mistresses and had not made a special effort when he'd picked a dress for her to wear to the party.

The sapphire-blue velvet gown with off-the-shoulder straps was a fishtail style, tight-fitting over her bust and hips to show off her curvaceous figure, and the lower part of the skirt flared out into a small train at the back. She had piled her hair into a loose knot on top of her head with a few tendrils framing her face. A coat of mascara on her eyelashes and a slick of pink lipgloss completed her look. She certainly did not need to wear blusher, she thought ruefully when she saw the flush on her cheeks as Diego came to stand behind her.

'You look beautiful whatever you are wearing, but my personal preference is for you to wear nothing at all,' he murmured, bending his head to feather kisses along her collarbone.

'Mmm, not very practical for the party...' She managed to keep her tone light to hide the fierce sexual excitement that made her breasts tingle.

Diego gave a sigh that sounded more like a wolfish growl. 'I can't wait until the party is over and I can have you to myself. Shall I tell you what I plan to do to you when we are alone, *anjinho*?'

'You had better not!' She laughed breathlessly and stepped away from him. It was hard to resist his charisma and sexual teasing. 'You need to go down to the main deck to greet the guests.'

He slid his arm around her waist and led her towards the door. 'I suppose so,' he said regretfully, 'but I insist that my favourite PR expert stays by my side all evening.'

Clare told herself not to read too much into Diego's words, or his attentiveness during the party. True to his word, he kept her close to him as they strolled around the yacht's ballroom and chatted with the guests. Clare sampled a couple of delicious canapés but opted for sparkling water rather than champagne, explaining that she was on duty and wanted to keep a clear head.

There was a buzz of excitement as the jewellery show was about to begin and guests took their seats on either side of the catwalk. She and Diego had front row seats with a perfect view of the models as they sauntered down the runway. The female models wore identical black full length gowns and the men were dressed in black suits so that the audience focused on the fabulous diamond necklaces, earrings and watches being showcased by the models. But Clare's attention was caught by one model in particular. *'Mark?'*

'I get the feeling you wouldn't pay me any attention even if I was butt naked.'

Diego registered the sarcasm in the female voice and he flicked an impatient glance at the woman standing next to him. He had a vague idea that Tiffany Delany was the daughter of a diplomat, and an even vaguer memory that he might have slept with her once. She was attractive and blonde—which were his only requirements, he thought self-derisively. At least, they used to be. He

looked back to the dance floor, where Clare was dancing with one of the male models. Diego's eyes roamed
over her petite figure in the blue dress that hugged her
curves and her auburn hair, gleaming like burnished gold
beneath the disco lights, and he acknowledged that she
was the only woman he wanted.

'Who'd have guessed that Diego Cazorra would suffer
from woman trouble?' Tiffany drawled. 'Your little red-
head must be something special—you haven't stopped
staring at her. Someone ought to warn the guy dancing
with her that you look like you want to kill him.'

'Don't be ridiculous.' As he strode away from the
blonde he knew he should apologise for his curtness, but
Tiffany had touched a nerve. Watching Clare dance with
her supposedly ex-boyfriend had stirred a violent jealous
rage inside Diego. *But was it a murderous rage?* He was
seriously tempted to rearrange Mark Penry's pretty-boy
features, but what if he had actually punched the model
and seriously injured him, or worse? Was that what he
had done when he was seventeen and tried to protect his
mother from the man who'd been beating her? Had he
punched the man with such force that he'd killed him,
which is what his mother had told the police?

Although *Serendipity* was a huge yacht, it was packed
with party guests and Diego felt a tightness in his chest
as he pushed his way through the crowd. Memories of
an overcrowded prison cell flashed into his mind. Violent, desperate men, the stench of sweat in the hot, air-
less cell. *He couldn't breathe.*

He ran up the stairs to the top deck, burst into his
stateroom and opened the sliding glass door so that he
could step on to a private deck area that was only acces-
sible from his suite and Clare's room next door. Fresh

sea air filled his lungs as he leaned against the balcony railing and fought to control the panic attack. *Deus*, was he capable of murder? Tonight had exposed the blackness in his soul.

Clare had disappeared immediately after the jewellery show and Diego had scoured the yacht for her before he'd seen her dancing with a handsome model—Mark Penry, he had learned from one of the guests. He'd instantly recognised the name as the guy who Clare had said had broken her heart. The way she had snuggled up to Penry suggested that she was still keen on her ex, and Diego had come close to striding across the dance floor and snatching her into his arms.

This was why he had never become emotionally involved with any of his mistresses. He could not risk feeling strong emotions like love or hate, jealousy or anger. Especially anger. He was afraid of what he might do if he was pushed too far. The blinding rage that had swept through him when he'd seen Clare with Mark Penry had shocked him. She meant nothing to him, he reminded himself. Sure, she was fun to be with, and the sex was good. The sex was amazing. But it meant *nothing*.

He stiffened at the sound of footsteps crossing the deck. A delicate fragrance of roses assailed his senses and Clare's soft voice made his gut twist.

'I was looking for you. The fireworks are about to start.' She came to stand beside him and Diego was bitterly aware of the immediate effect she had on his body as he felt himself harden. 'Mind you, we probably have the best view from here.'

'That's the reason I came up here,' he lied. 'You looked as though you were having fun dancing. I didn't know you had hired your ex-boyfriend for the catwalk show.' Diego despised himself for sounding like he cared, but Clare didn't appear to notice his strained tone.

'I didn't. I was shocked when I saw Mark, but he explained that he replaced Tom Vaughn, another model from A-Star PR, who should have been on the assignment but broke his ankle a few days ago.'

Some of Diego's tension eased. At least Clare had not arranged for Penry to come to Brazil. 'So, are you tempted to get back with a guy who models underwear for a living?' he said lazily.

She laughed. 'No. I realised during the one dance I had with him that he is completely self-obsessed. He spent most of the time discussing his hair. To be honest, I don't know why I got so upset over him. I think I was flattered that he showed an interest in me.' She hesitated. 'But now that the DC Diamonds campaign is finished I have decided to fly back to England with the models. It will be company for me during the flight and give me an opportunity to catch up on what has been happening at A-Star PR while I've been away.'

Diego felt his gut give another twist. 'Do you know for certain that you are not pregnant?'

'I'm ninety-nine per cent sure. My breasts feel really sensitive, which is usually a sign my monthly period is about to start. I expect I'll be able to confirm the news you are hoping for tomorrow.'

Of course he hoped she hadn't conceived his child, Diego thought, but oddly he did not feel like jumping for joy. It was good that Clare would be going home, he assured himself. He hadn't grown bored of her yet, as he'd assumed he would, but he was confident he would have no trouble finding another woman to replace her. Meanwhile, he still had tonight with Clare. Overhead a firework exploded in a starburst of silver and gold that lit up the night sky, but he was more concerned about the imminent explosion he could feel building inside him.

'Your breasts are always sensitive,' he murmured as he pulled her unresisting body towards him and reached behind her to run her zip down her spine. Her dress fell forwards, spilling her ripe breasts into his hands. Her nipples were already taut and he heard her breath catch when he rubbed his thumbs over them before he lowered his head and captured one reddened peak between his lips.

He loved how she was so responsive. Her little moans of pleasure drove him crazy, and with a groan he swept her up in his arms and carried her into her bedroom.

'Are you going to tell me now what you plan to do with me?' she asked innocently.

Diego dropped her on to the bed and stripped with more haste than grace. He gave a rough laugh when her eyes widened as she watched him slide a sheath over his massive erection. 'I think a personal demonstration is necessary, *querida*.'

Clare heard a voice shouting in her dream. The shouts grew louder and more urgent, forcing her to wake up, and she realised that she hadn't been dreaming. Diego was lying beside her in her bed. Light filtering through the blinds made her realise it was morning. He must have spent all night with her, or what had been left of the night after they had made love numerous times until she had slumped back on the pillows, unable to keep her eyes open a moment longer.

'Diego...' She tentatively shook his shoulder but, wherever hellish place his mind was, he was in too deep for her to reach him. He groaned as if he was in pain and it hurt her to see him so tormented. 'Diego, wake up.'

His eyes opened and he sat bolt upright, his chest heaving with the force of his harsh breaths. He stared at her as if he did not recognise her.

'It's all right,' she told him softly. 'You're dreaming, that's all.'

'Clare.' He swallowed and raked his hair back, revealing his disfigured ear for a few seconds before he remembered and shook his hair forwards again.

'What was your nightmare about?'

He shrugged. 'I don't know. Nothing much.' His tone was dismissive but Clare heard a rawness in his voice that she sensed he was desperate to hide.

'It didn't sound like *nothing much*. Why won't you talk about it?' She could not contain her frustration. 'Why do you have so many secrets? Why won't Miguel tell me where the two of you met? Who cut off the top of your ear? *Why do you always shut me out?*'

The silence following her outburst simmered with tension as Diego's shocked expression turned to anger. Clare swallowed, trying to fight the feeling that she was going to be sick. But the sensation of nausea grew worse and, with a gasp, she leapt out of bed, grabbed her robe and ran into the bathroom. She did not have time to lock the door.

Oh, God, could anything be more undignified? she thought when she had finished vomiting and sat down weakly on a chair. The one and only time Diego had spent the night with her would be unforgettable for all the wrong reasons.

'Go away, please,' she muttered when he followed

her into the bathroom. He ignored her and sponged her face with a damp flannel.

'Feeling better?'

She nodded, hoping he would leave. She was sure he would not answer any of her questions, and she felt emotionally as well as physically drained.

Diego hunkered down in front of her and put his hands on the arms of the chair, effectively imprisoning her. 'Good, because I've got some questions for you. Why did you buy a pregnancy test if you are so sure you're not pregnant? And for how long have you been suffering from morning sickness?'

'It's not morning sickness.' She bit her lip. 'I get sea-sick.'

He gave her a sardonic look. 'The yacht is anchored and the sea is as flat as a pond. Have you been sick before this morning?'

'No. But I've felt nauseous the last few mornings,' Clare admitted. 'I've been telling myself it was because my period is about to start. I bought the test just…just to be sure.' She looked down at the pregnancy test that Diego had picked up from the vanity unit and dropped into her lap.

'Let's be sure then,' he said grimly.

CHAPTER TEN

SHE COULDN'T BE PREGNANT. *But she was.* Clare stared at the two lines on the test kit and reread the instruction leaflet. Two lines indicated a positive result. Maybe the test was wrong? She knew she was clutching at straws and gripped the edge of the vanity unit as her legs almost gave way.

Diego rapped on the door, which she had locked before she had performed the test. 'Well?'

She did not answer, needing a few more minutes on her own to absorb the implications of the result. *A baby. She was pregnant with Diego's baby.* Clare studied her reflection in the mirror, surprised that she still looked the same, apart from her pallor following the bout of sickness. Of course there would not be any visible signs yet of the miracle taking place inside her body. She put her hand on her flat stomach and tried to imagine her belly swollen with her growing child.

Her emotions see-sawed between panic and an unexpected sense of elation and excitement. In a few months from now she would hold her child in her arms, and she felt a fierce sense of maternal protectiveness and determination that her child would never doubt that he or she was loved by its parents, as she had done when she was growing up and her parents had paid more attention to her sister. But how would Diego react to the news that he was going to be a father? Three weeks ago he had said he would support her if she was pregnant, but even if he was prepared to offer financial assistance she could not make him love his child, Clare acknowledged.

'Clare, are you all right?'

She could not put off opening the door any longer. Diego looked tense, no sign of his usual nonchalance on his chiselled features. 'Well?' he demanded again.

'It's…positive.' Her voice sounded rusty. 'I'm…pregnant.' She handed him the test. He looked at it wordlessly and his jaw clenched. Clare swallowed. 'I can't believe it. Some couples try for months, years, even, to have a baby.' Her voice wobbled as the enormity of the situation hit her. She wished Diego would say something, give her some clue as to what he was thinking.

Diego walked over to the window and for a second he could not understand why he was surrounded by the sea, before he remembered that they were on board the super-yacht *Serendipity*. Memories of the DC Diamonds launch party flashed into his mind, but another memory—of the violent anger that had swept through him when he'd watched Clare dancing with her ex-boyfriend—tormented him.

Clare was expecting his child. The words ricocheted in his brain. Like his father before him, he had behaved with crass irresponsibility when he'd had unprotected sex, and the result was that Clare had conceived his baby.

He looked across the room at her sitting on the end of the bed. Her face was so white that the golden freckles on her cheeks and nose were starkly apparent.

'I assume from your silence that you are not pleased by the news,' she said flatly.

Diego turned his head away from her searching blue gaze. He had a feeling she could sense his panic, which made him want to run as fast and far away as he could. It occurred to him that he had been running away all his life.

'It makes no difference whether I am pleased or not. You are pregnant and it is my duty to support you and the child.' He could not bring himself to say *my child*, nor could he say he was pleased. His overriding feeling was of anger with himself, but he also realised that he must reassure Clare. 'I promise you won't have to deal with this alone.'

She went even paler, if that was possible. 'Deal with it? I'm not sure exactly what you mean by that but, make no mistake, I intend to go ahead with this pregnancy and have my baby.'

'Of course.' He stiffened when he realised she had misunderstood him. 'It did not cross my mind that you wouldn't have the child.' The idea made him shudder, and he wondered if his mother had considered aborting him after his father had abandoned her when she was pregnant.

'Look…' He ran a hand through his hair and abruptly dropped his arm to his side when he saw her stare at his disfigured ear. He remembered the questions she had bombarded him with, which he had no intention of answering. 'We need to talk, but we both need some time to come to terms with what has happened. I'm due to give a press interview following last night's party. I suggest we meet back at the penthouse this evening for dinner and to discuss the future.'

* * *

Throughout the day Clare felt a sense of unreality. She went to her office, but there was little for her to do now that the PR campaign had finished. She had been expecting to book her flight back to England, but instead she was expecting Diego's baby. And until they had the discussion he had mentioned she had to remain in Brazil, not least because he still had her passport in his possession.

There was no reason for her to feel nervous, she told herself that evening when she stepped on to the balcony leading from the dining room. She and Diego had often had dinner alfresco over the past weeks and she was glad he had opted for them to eat informally tonight, sitting at the table with views of Copacabana beach.

Diego was standing looking at the view but turned his head when he heard her footsteps. He was wearing sun-bleached jeans that hugged his lean hips and a white T-shirt, through which Clare could see the delineation of his six-pack. Desire unfurled in the pit of her stomach and she avoided his gaze as she sat down on the chair he had pulled out for her. She shook her head as he was about to pour her a glass of sparkling white wine that she usually drank with dinner.

'I'll have water, thanks. I won't be able to drink wine for the next few months.'

'I'm sorry, I'd forgotten. Not about you being pregnant,' he said tersely when her brows rose. 'I guess we are both going to have to get used to a lot of changes, but you especially.'

She did not reply while the maid served dinner. Stew was a popular Brazilian dish, and the aroma given off by the casserole of white beans and sausage stirred Clare's taste buds. If she ate for two for the next eight months she would be the size of a house, she thought ruefully.

They ate in silence for a few minutes, before Diego opened the folder that was lying on the table and took out a document. 'I need you to sign some paperwork, specifically this form, which is to register our intent to marry.'

Clare's heart gave a jolt. She put down her fork and stared at him across the table. 'Marry?'

'Of course. It is the obvious thing to do.'

'It's not obvious to me.' Her appetite had disappeared. 'It's the twenty-first century and we do not have to get married because I'm pregnant.'

'My child will have my name,' he said in an uncompromising voice that matched the hard expression in his eyes. 'In reality, my child will have my mother's family name, Cazorra. I only discovered my father's surname was Hawke after his death. But he did not marry my mother and give me his name. I grew up wondering how a man could create a child but take no interest in his offspring. I won't allow the child we have created to feel compelled to search the faces of strangers, looking for some similarity of features and hoping to one day find the man whose blood runs through their veins.'

Clare swallowed the lump in her throat. Diego's poignant description of how he must have felt growing up without his father touched her deeply. *But marriage!*

She stood up and walked over to lean against the balcony rail. The sky was streaked pink and gold as the sun sank below the horizon. As dusk fell, the lights of the street lamps and from the skyscrapers that ringed the bay cast a silver gleam over the sea. Down on the ground the glow from car headlamps formed an unbroken line as traffic snaked along the main highway.

Rio was a vibrant, exciting city and Copacabana bay was undeniably beautiful, but Clare felt a long way from her home in a quiet north London suburb and from her family and friends.

'I understand how important it is to you that your child will know you as their father and bear your name. But expecting me to become your wife and live thousands of miles away from my parents is asking a lot.' Especially as he did not seem at all enthusiastic about marrying her. It was lucky she hadn't hoped for a romantic marriage proposal, Clare thought ruefully. Indeed, she had not considered marriage as an option. But if Diego were to take her in his arms and ask her to be his wife she would be tempted to say yes. And it was not only for the sake of their baby.

'I don't expect you to live in Brazil.' He stood up and came to join her at the railing, although she noted that he kept a distance between them. 'The marriage will be purely in the interests of the child. Being married will give us equal parental rights, and legally give my child my name, but I will agree to you and the baby living in England in a house that I will buy, and I will provide for you both financially.'

Clare gave him a puzzled look. 'Won't it be difficult to run the Cazorra Corporation and your various other businesses if you move to England?'

'I will continue to live in Brazil.'

The sharp pain beneath her breastbone was the sensation of her foolish dreams being torn to shreds. 'How do you propose to be a father if you are living on the opposite side of the world from your son or daughter?'

'I'll visit regularly, and often. The child will know that I…care about them,' Diego said tersely. Clare watched him curl his hand around the railing so that his knuckles whitened. She sensed he would rather be anywhere than here, having this discussion with her, but *too bad*, she thought grimly. They had both made this baby and she was furious that Diego seemed to think he could fulfil his responsibilities as a parent by throwing money at the problem.

'So your idea of being a good father is to turn up every couple of months, no doubt with an expensive present, take your kid to the zoo for an afternoon and then disappear again with a clear conscience?' She ignored his simmering look. 'Believe me, no amount of presents and occasional trips out could make your child believe you love them. I know because when I was a child, being taken to see a show once a year or being given the latest piece of technology did not reassure me that my parents loved me.'

Tears stung Clare's eyes as she imagined her child feeling the same sense of abandonment she had felt. Of course she would do her best to make up for the fact that Diego would be a mainly absent father, just as Aunt Edith had tried to be a substitute parent. But in her opinion a child needed both its parents, and Diego's idea of good parenting fell far short of ideal.

The condemnation in Clare's voice scraped Diego's conscience raw, and he spun away from her and strode into the penthouse to evade the accusation in her sapphire-blue eyes. Ever since the helicopter had brought them back to the Cazorra skyscraper, he had debated with himself what would be best for his child.

He grimaced as he acknowledged the bitter truth that the best way he could protect his child was to send

them to live as far away from him as possible. All afternoon, while he'd given a series of press interviews
about the DC Diamonds launch, his mind had flashed
back to when he had watched Clare dancing with her
ex-boyfriend at the party. His searing, jealous rage that
had made him want to smash his fist into Mark Penry's
handsome face.

He did not know what he was capable of if he lost his
temper and he did not want to look into the darkness of
his soul to find out. Since he had been released from
prison he had avoided situations that might make him
angry. He had perfected a persona of a laid-back, im-
perturbable playboy so successfully that he had started
to believe it. But last night his jealous reaction to seeing
Clare with Penry had shattered his illusions about himself and proved that although he had suppressed his emotions for nearly twenty years he had not eliminated them.

'Do you have a better suggestion?' he demanded as
Clare followed him into the lounge.

'As a matter of fact, I do.'

Diego noticed her gaze dart to his rucksack and old
leather hat that he'd left by the door, and he saw a question forming on her lips. He folded his arms across his
chest. 'So, what is it?' he drawled.

'I suggest that we get married for real. You want to
give your child your name, but what a child needs most
is a sense of belonging and of knowing that they are
loved unconditionally, ideally by growing up with both
their parents. That isn't always possible for some people,
but why don't we at least try to make a go of marriage
for our baby's sake? Instead of being a part-time parent,
why not be the father you wished your father had been
when he left you to grow up in a slum?'

Emotions he had fought against for so long flooded through Diego. It was as if a tidal wave inside him had burst through the barricades he had painstakingly built. He hated himself when he saw a flash of hurt in Clare's eyes as he shook his head in a silent negative answer. He realised how much it must have cost her to ask if they could have a proper marriage. She was proud, but she had sacrificed her pride for what she believed would be the best for their child, and Diego admired her even more than when she had risked her life to rescue her sister.

But he couldn't do what she had asked. He could not take the risk. What if they argued and he lost his temper with Clare? What if, God forbid, he lost his temper with his child? The thought filled him with icy fear. The only way he could ensure their safety was to live away from them, and when he visited England he would make sure he was never alone with his child.

'You know my feelings about marriage.' He managed to strike his usual tone of sardonic amusement. He swung his rucksack over his shoulder and jammed his hat on his head, pulling the brim low over his eyes. 'I don't share your idealised belief that the only thing a child needs is love. Try telling that to the thousands of children who live in extreme poverty and don't even have the basic requirements of food and shelter, let alone access to education that would help them escape the *favelas*.'

He walked over to the door and glanced back at Clare. Was it his imagination or did her breasts look slightly fuller beneath the cream silk dress she was wearing? Her auburn hair tumbled in silky waves around her shoulders. *Deus*, would he ever escape the spell she had cast on him that made him think of her all the time, and want to be with her day and night?

'I will provide you and the child with an excellent standard of living. You will want for nothing. There will be no need for you to work, unless you choose to resume your career at some point.' He hesitated. 'I realise that you are young and attractive and might want to have a personal relationship...with a man,' he elaborated when Clare looked puzzled.

'Are you suggesting I could have an affair?'

'As long as you were discreet for the child's sake.' The idea of Clare with a lover caused bile to burn like acid in Diego's throat and he gripped the door handle as he fought the temptation to stride across the room and pull her into his arms.

'Are you *leaving*?'

He heard disbelief in her voice and could not bring himself to look at her. 'I have to fly up to Boa Vista to carry out a geological survey of a potential gold mine site in the rainforest. Before I go I'll submit our registration of marriage form. We are legally required to give twenty days' notice prior to getting married. We will marry when I return to Rio, and after the ceremony I will arrange for you to fly back to England.'

'Go then.' Clare gave a contemptuous laugh. 'Run away, Diego. When you helped Becky and me to escape from Rigo and his henchmen I believed you were the bravest man I'd ever met. But I see now that you are a coward. It makes no difference how much money or material possessions you give to our child, because if you won't even try to be a proper father you are no better than the man who fathered and abandoned you.'

Her words stabbed Diego through his heart. Clare

was right; he *was* no better than his father. But it was not cowardice that had led to his decision to live apart from his child. Clare did not understand that he was trying to protect their baby and her.

He groaned and slumped against the door. 'I *can't* be the husband you want me to be, or the kind of father I wished for when I was a boy,' he said harshly. 'There are things about me that you don't know.'

'So tell me.' Her voice was no longer contemptuous, but soft and clear as a mountain stream, and the scent of roses filled Diego's senses when she walked over to him and placed her hand lightly on his shoulder. 'Help me to understand your demons, because the child we created so carelessly will need both of us to be part of their life.'

Diego turned round and stared down at her. She was so petite next to his tall frame, so fragile compared to his muscular build. The knowledge that he could easily hurt her terrified him. He was certain that if he told her the truth about himself she would insist on taking their child to live far away from him, away from the danger he represented. But where did he start? He remembered the questions she had asked that morning when she had woken him from his nightmare.

'You had better sit down,' he said roughly. When she did so, he sat on the sofa opposite her and took off his hat, twisting the brim between his fingers.

'I met Miguel in prison. We shared a cell—' he grimaced as memories of the terrible conditions flooded his mind '—along with ten other prisoners.' He looked up and saw Clare's startled expression. 'We were both on remand. Miguel had been accused, wrongly, of fraud, and I was waiting to be tried…for murder.'

She drew a sharp breath. 'Were you wrongly accused like Miguel? Or…had you actually…killed someone?'

'I don't know.' Diego looked away from the horror he could see in Clare's eyes. 'I don't remember.'

'I don't understand.' Clare's voice shook as she tried to absorb Diego's astounding revelation. 'How can you not remember whether you murdered a person? Surely it's not something you'd forget.'

Diego saw her place her hand on her stomach, as if she was instinctively seeking to protect the fragile new life developing inside her. Protect their child from him, he thought grimly. But, strangely, now that he'd started to talk he wanted to continue. He couldn't run away from himself any more, he acknowledged, feeling a bone-aching weariness from twenty years of running and hiding from his past. Clare was clearly shocked, but she was still here, waiting for him to explain.

'My mother was a drug addict,' he said emotionlessly. 'Dealers often used our one room in the tenement as a base where they sold drugs, and most nights I slept on the streets and searched for food in bins.'

Clare pictured Diego as a little boy, roaming the dark and dangerous alleyways of a slum, searching for a place to shelter for the night. Learning that she was pregnant made his description of his childhood even more poignant.

'By the time I was a teenager I'd seen things no child should see, and from necessity I'd learned how to take care of myself. I was hot-tempered and often involved in fights.' Diego twisted his hat in his hands. 'One night it was raining hard and I had nowhere to go but home. When I arrived, I found my mother bleeding and crying while her dealer beat her because she could not pay for her next fix.'

He swallowed convulsively. 'She was only little, about the same height as you, and defenceless.' He took a deep breath. 'I lost my temper and punched the guy. Hard. I wanted to kill him.'

'But did you?' Clare said shakily.

'I honestly don't know. The guy retaliated and we fought. The last I remember was his fist coming towards my face. The next thing I knew was when I opened my eyes and saw the man lying on the floor and a pool of blood round his head.' Diego's voice was hoarse. 'It was obvious he was dead. The police had arrived and my mother told them…' He fell silent.

'What did your mother tell the police?' Clare prompted.

'She said I'd gone crazy and kept punching the guy even after he'd collapsed to the floor. According to my mother, I had been in a manic rage and she had been unable to stop me from hitting the man. It was as if I had suffered some kind of fit that made me act with uncontrolled violence, until eventually I passed out.'

Diego forced himself to look at Clare. She was obviously shocked by what he had told her but, to his surprise, there was no hint of revulsion in her blue eyes.

'The police arrested me and charged me with murder,' he continued. 'At seventeen I should have been sent to a juvenile detention centre, but it was full so I was locked up in an adult prison to await trial. But I couldn't afford a lawyer and the only witness to what had happened was my mother, who had disappeared.'

'You must have been scared. How long were you held in prison?'

'Two hellish years. It's where I lost the top of my ear.' He brushed his hair back to reveal his disfigured ear. 'I saved Miguel from a beating by some of the other prisoners, and as punishment they held me down and sliced off part of my ear with a razor blade.'

'Dear God,' Clare whispered. 'No wonder you have nightmares.'

'I was befriended by the prison chaplain, Father Vincenzi.' Diego's strained features softened into a smile. 'The priest is a truly good man. He believed I was innocent and fought to have the charges against me dropped due to a lack of evidence.'

Diego recalled the mixed emotions he had felt on the day he had walked out of prison: relief that he was free, but also a terrible uncertainty that perhaps he was guilty of murder, which he still felt two decades later.

'After I was released I went to stay with Cruz and his family and we both worked in Earl Bancroft's diamond mine. A few years later, Father Vincenzi was contacted by a lawyer in England who was trying to find me to give me the news that I was the heir of the lawyer's deceased client, a man called Geoffrey Hawke. He was my grandfather and he'd left me a sizeable fortune in his will, which enabled me to buy the Old Betsy diamond mine with Cruz.'

'Why did the priest believe you were innocent?' Clare asked.

'There were inconsistencies in the statement my mother gave to the police. Also, forensic evidence indicated that the man had died from a blow to the back of his head by something heavy. But I have no recollection of using a weapon. Father Vincenzi thought that my mother may have lied about what actually happened.'

Diego shook his head. 'But she knew I would go to prison. Why would my own mother lie to the police about me?'

'I don't know.' Clare frowned. 'Have you ever tried to find her to ask her?'

'I searched for my mother for years and I believe she is still alive, simply because if she were dead her death would have been registered. A couple of times there were promising leads, and a year ago I received information that she was being treated in a hospital. But I had no response when I tried to contact her and since then she has disappeared again. I came to the conclusion that she doesn't want to see me, and I stopped looking for her.'

'Why wouldn't she want to see her only son,' Clare mused, 'unless she has something to hide? It suggests that she *might* have lied to the police.'

Diego rubbed his hand across his brow. 'It suggests to me that my mother witnessed me turn into a violent murderer and she is scared to meet me,' he said grimly. 'Don't you see, Clare? *I don't know if I lost my temper and killed a man.* Perhaps I was gripped by a manic rage, as my mother said, and I can't take the risk of it happening again in front of my child. *I dare not be a proper father when there is a chance I am a murderer.*'

He dropped his hand down from his face, and Clare's heart turned over when she saw a betraying glimmer of moisture in his eyes. She thought of how he had protected her in the rainforest and helped her to rescue her sister from the kidnappers. Feeling an instinctive need to comfort him, she got up from the sofa and knelt in front of him.

'Diego, you were a boy of seventeen, and you were trying to protect your mother from being beaten,' she said gently. 'Even if you did punch the man who was hitting your mother, it wasn't a premeditated attack. I don't believe you would have intended to kill him, and I don't think a judge would have believed it either. Father Vincenzi obviously didn't believe you were a murderer, or he wouldn't have worked to secure your release from prison.'

He looked unconvinced, and his jaw clenched. 'I won't risk our child's safety, or yours, when I don't know if I can trust myself to control my temper.' His throat worked as he swallowed hard. 'Last night I had proof that I still have a hot temper. When I saw you dancing with Penry, I wanted to throw him over the side of the yacht and I hoped he'd drown.'

Clare's eyes widened. 'Why did you feel like that?'

'I was jealous,' Diego grated. 'It's not an emotion I am familiar with,' he added, sounding more like his old, cynical self.

He had been jealous because she'd danced with Mark! Clare forced her mind back to Diego's harrowing story of his past. 'You might have wanted to throw Mark overboard, but you *didn't* act on those feelings, which shows that you can trust yourself to control your temper.'

His hand was resting on his knee, and she linked her fingers with his. 'You don't know if you were unwittingly responsible for a man's death, but I *do* know that you saved my life and my sister's life when you arranged our escape from Rigo. I'm sorry I accused you of being a coward,' she said in a choked voice. 'It must have taken a lot of courage to tell me the reason why you feel you can't be a proper father.'

She looked into his eyes. 'In Torrente you asked me

to trust you, and I am ashamed that at the time I didn't. But I do now. I trust you completely, and I want to help. It seems to me that the only way for you to come to terms with your past and move forwards with your life is if you make another attempt to find your mother and discover the truth about what really happened when you were seventeen.'

Diego looked down at their linked fingers and felt as if his heart was being squeezed in a vice. Clare was as fierce as a tigress and he was touched by her determination to help him. But her faith in him and her refusal to judge him strengthened his resolve to protect her and their child from himself if necessary.

'If I find my mother, are you prepared to learn the truth about me, whatever it might be?'

She held his gaze steadily. 'Nothing your mother might say will make me lose my trust in you.'

CHAPTER ELEVEN

HOSPITALS ALWAYS SMELLED of disinfectant, Clare thought as she walked with Diego into a hospice in the city of Belo Horizonte. She recalled the private hospital in Rio, where a week ago she and Diego had had an appointment at the antenatal unit for her ultrasound scan. The scan had confirmed that she was now twelve weeks pregnant.

She had been surprised at how clear the image of the baby was when the sonographer had pointed out on the screen the infant's head and chest and a tiny beating heart. Tears had filled Clare's eyes at this first sight of the child developing inside her, and when she had glanced at Diego and had seen his jaw clench she knew he was trying to hide his emotions.

Since his revelation that he might have killed a man twenty years ago, they had both been living in a strange sort of limbo. Clare had insisted that they wait until she was safely past the three-month stage of her pregnancy before they discussed marriage. She had suffered badly from morning sickness, and the constant nausea plus the pregnancy hormones zooming around her body had made her desperately tired so that she was often in bed by early evening.

She had felt quite relieved that Diego hadn't suggested they resume a sexual relationship. Her wan complexion and the fact that she had to rush to the bathroom all the time was probably not a turn-on for him, she thought ruefully. But, with sex off the agenda, a different relationship had developed between them and they had become good friends. To Clare's surprise, Diego talked openly about his deprived childhood and the terrible two years he had spent in prison, and speaking about his horrifying experiences seemed to be cathartic for him.

He had asked Clare to work on ideas for a publicity campaign to raise money for the Future Bright Foundation, and she had been glad of something to do to take her mind off feeling sick. The charity project was also the reason she had given her father to explain why she could not return to England and resume her role as head of A-Star PR. She had decided not to tell her parents about her pregnancy until she had some idea of what would happen between her and Diego. Rory Marchant had sounded happier than he had for a long time as he'd explained that her mother's health had improved significantly and he was now able to go back to running the agency.

Another surprise had been the news that Brazil's most wanted criminal, Rodrigo Hernandez, known as Rigo, had been arrested for drug trafficking. A few days ago the Estrela Rosa, the Rose Star Diamond, had been returned to Diego. But Clare knew he was not thinking of the diamond as they walked through the hospice where, he had learned two days ago, his mother was a patient.

He had hired a team of private detectives to search for his mother but, as the weeks had gone by, Clare had secretly begun to despair that Shayla Cazorra would ever be found, and Diego would never discover what had really happened when he had been a teenager. Whatever had taken place that night twenty years ago would not alter her belief that Diego had been a victim of circumstance, a boy who had been trying to protect his mother. She trusted the man who had protected her since she had come to Brazil, and she could no longer deny to herself that she loved him.

She pulled her mind back to the present as a nurse stepped out of a room and greeted them. 'Your mother is awake, Mr Cazorra, and she is anxious to see you.'

Clare gave his arm a gentle squeeze. 'I'll go and sit in the waiting room while you talk to your mother.'

'I'd like you to meet her.' His jaw was rigid. 'I intend to tell her about the baby and this is perhaps the only chance for her to see you.' He glanced at the nurse, who gave a nod of confirmation.

'Your mother's cancer is very advanced and I am sorry to have to tell you that she does not have long to live.'

They went into the room. The woman lying in the bed was desperately thin and her dark hair was streaked with grey. Clare could see no resemblance between her and Diego, but Shayla Cazorra held out her bony hand to her son, who she had not seen for two decades.

'Diego, *meu filho. Me perdoe*,' she whispered.

'*Mãe.*' Diego did not know how he had expected to feel when he met his mother after so many years. He had thought of her so often, especially while he was in prison, and he'd felt angry that she had disappeared when he'd needed her. But hearing her call him *my son* evoked an ache in his chest. He would not have recognised the husk of a woman who looked so frail lying on the pillows. Instinctively he knew she had days rather than weeks to live.

'*Mãe*, this is Clare.' He spoke in Portuguese, guessing that his mother had not learned to speak English since he'd last seen her. 'We are going to have a baby.'

Shayla's face crumpled. *'Me perdoe,'* she said again, tears sliding down her cheeks.

Diego could feel his heart thudding beneath his ribs. '*Me perdoe* means *forgive me*,' he translated quietly for Clare. He took his mother's hand in his and felt her bones beneath her papery skin. 'Why do you want me to forgive you?' he asked her gently.

Instead of replying, she lifted up her other hand from the bed and gave him a piece of paper which he saw was a handwritten letter. For a moment he hesitated, afraid to read it. Would he finally learn the truth about himself? He felt sick. What if his mother's letter confirmed that he had killed a man years ago? A small hand slipped into his and he glanced at Clare and thought, as he often did, that he could drown in her deep blue eyes.

'I think your mother wants you to read the letter,' she urged softly.

Taking a deep breath, Diego skimmed the words his mother had written, once, twice. *'Deus...'* His voice was choked with emotion.

'What does it say?' Clare asked tautly.

'She killed him.' He read the letter a third time. 'While I was fighting with the man I'd found beating my mother, she hit him on the back of his head with a chair leg. She realised he was dead. I was unconscious from the punch he'd landed on me just before she attacked him. Someone had called the police, and she panicked and

told them I had killed the guy while I'd been in a manic rage.' He exhaled heavily. 'She explains in the letter that she thought I would be sent to a youth detention centre, but she knew she would spend the rest of her life in prison and she was scared of being locked up in a cell.'

Diego's throat ached and he felt an unfamiliar sting of tears in his eyes. For twenty years he had been haunted by the idea that he could be a murderer, and all the time he had been innocent. Tears were sliding down his mother's face and his gut clenched. She hadn't been much of a mother, but she hadn't had much of a life after his father had seduced her and abandoned her when she fell pregnant, Diego thought. He looked into his heart and found no anger, just pity.

'*Mãe...*' He took a tissue from the bedside cabinet and wiped away her tears. '*Eu perdoô voce.*' *I forgive you.*

He did not see Clare wipe tears from her eyes as she quietly left the room.

The flight from Belo Horizonte back to Rio took an hour, and it was late afternoon when the limousine that had collected them from the airport drew up outside the Cazorra skyscraper. 'Are you sure you didn't want to stay at the hospice with your mother?' Clare asked as they walked across the foyer.

Diego shook his head. 'We both said everything we needed to say.' His mother had fallen asleep while he'd sat with her, and the nurse had assured him that Shayla was sleeping peacefully for the first time since she had been admitted to the hospice.

'You don't have to come in the lift with me,' Clare said as he followed her into the elevator. 'I know you prefer to take the stairs.'

The lift door closed and Diego waited to feel the familiar tightness in his chest, the sensation that he couldn't breathe. But nothing happened. He could breathe normally. He thought of the time Clare had helped him cope with his claustrophobia by kissing him. Her distraction method had certainly worked, and the memory of the passion that had blazed between them had a predictable effect on his body.

They had not made love for over two months while she had been suffering with sickness caused by her pregnancy. He had felt guilty that it was his fault she was so pale and fragile, but in the last few days the nausea had lessened and now she looked radiant. There was colour in her cheeks again and her auburn hair shone like silk. To anyone else her pregnancy was not yet visible, but Diego noted that her breasts were fuller and there was a new voluptuousness to her body that made him long to undress her and explore her lush curves.

'How do you feel?' she asked innocently.

Deus, he wasn't going to admit he was so turned on by his fantasies of having sex with her that he was surprised she did not notice the bulge of his erection beneath his trousers.

'You must feel relieved now your mother has told you the truth, that you didn't kill a man.'

'I'm still stunned,' Diego admitted. 'For twenty years I was afraid that I was capable of extreme violence, and I avoided close relationships because I didn't trust myself. Now it's as though a huge weight has been lifted off me and I feel free.' Life suddenly seemed full of possibilities and for the first time in his life he was excited by the future, Diego realised.

As he looked at Clare, he was aware of a strange con-

striction in his chest that was not caused by his claustrophobia. His gaze lowered to the very faint swell of
her stomach and the ache in his heart intensified as he
visualised the scan image of their baby that he had seen
on the ultrasound screen a week ago.

Emotions flooded through him, but he had spent
twenty years suppressing his emotions and he was almost afraid of the strength of his feelings. He needed to
regain control of himself and take charge of the future.

'We need to talk, and make plans,' he said gruffly.
'First off, you need to sign the document so that we can
register our intent to marry.' He frowned as the lift halted
unexpectedly at the eighth floor, which was where the
Cazorra Corporation's offices were. The doors opened
and a huge cheer went up from the dozens of members
of staff who were crowded around the lift entrance.

'What's going on?' Diego demanded as his PA
stepped forwards.

'The figures for DC Diamonds' first two months of
trading have been issued, and profits are double what
they were predicted to be,' Juliana explained. 'I'm sure
you haven't forgotten that you had arranged for all the
staff to be paid a bonus today. Everyone wanted to say
thank you.' She had to raise her voice above the loud
cheer that went up from the crowd.

Diego glanced at the sheet of figures Juliana had
given him and grinned. 'The profits made by the Cazorra
Corporation's newest venture are certainly something
to celebrate with champagne.'

The staff gave another cheer, someone was blowing
into a *vuvuzela*—a long plastic trumpet more usually
heard at football matches. Champagne corks shot into
the air and Diego was pulled into the party.

Clare was left alone in the lift. She watched Diego chatting with Juliana before he was mobbed by some of the dancers from his nightclub, who crowded round him. The sound of his laughter was audible above the babble of voices and he looked more relaxed and happier than Clare had ever seen him. But moments ago he had been frowning when he'd mentioned the marriage application document, which she had yet to sign.

She pressed a button to close the doors, and as the lift ascended to the top floor she pictured Diego surrounded by his staff who clearly adored him. He had looked as if a weight really had been lifted from him. For the first time since he had been freed from prison he was truly free.

Diego sipped his champagne and looked around the open-plan office for Clare. He smiled as he watched his staff enjoying the impromptu party, but he could not see her auburn hair amid the crowd, and when he asked his PA if she'd seen her, Juliana shook her head.

He wanted to celebrate DC Diamonds' success with her. After all, it was Clare's brilliant PR campaign to promote the jewellery shop that was responsible for the excellent profits. He owed her so much. Without her support he would not have made another attempt to find his mother and he would have spent the rest of his life believing he had once acted with such violence that he had killed a man.

He understood now that he had deliberately avoided close relationships because he had been afraid of hurting someone he cared about if he ever lost his temper. But now that fear had gone, just as his irrational fear of confined spaces had disappeared. When he had told

Clare he felt free, he hadn't fully realised the implications of his newfound freedom. He did now. He was free to admit to the emotions surging through him, free to open his heart to love.

The lift took him swiftly up to the penthouse and he checked in the lounge and library before he hurried down the hallway to Clare's bedroom. His heart was pounding with a mixture of nerves and hopeful anticipation, but when he knocked on the door and entered her room he felt a jolt of surprise that turned to unease as he saw her rucksack on the bed.

She walked through from her sitting room and Diego's confusion deepened at the sight of her in the khaki shorts and T-shirt that she had been wearing when they had escaped from Torrente. His gaze zoomed to her passport that she was holding and he guessed from her pink-rimmed eyes that she had been crying. That shocked him the most. He had never seen her cry before, even when she had been scared by the python in the rainforest and terrified by the far more dangerous snake Rigo.

He wanted to stride across the room and pull her into his arms, but two decades of hiding his feelings was a hard habit to break, and he leaned nonchalantly against the door frame and folded his arms over his chest. 'I see you found your passport in my room, although I don't know why you need it. I'm also curious about why you are wearing your old clothes. Are we going to take another trip through the rainforest? I'll get my hat.'

She walked over to the bed and dropped her passport into her bag, taking care, Diego noted, to avoid looking directly at him. '*We* are not going anywhere,' she said flatly. 'I've decided to fly home to England. I don't want to tell my parents about the baby over the phone.'

'Fine, we'll go together so that I can meet your family before we get married. We can even have our wedding in England if you want.'

'I don't. I…I'm not going to marry you.'

'*Deus*, Clare.' Diego's iron grip on his emotions snapped. 'What the hell is the matter? You agreed we would get married once you had passed the first three months of your pregnancy.' He strode over to her and caught hold of her shoulder, spinning her round to face him. She was pale, and the sight of faint tear streaks on her cheeks made his gut clench. 'Do you feel ill? I thought the sickness was getting better.'

'I feel fine.' She dropped her head but Diego slid his hand beneath her chin and tilted her face upwards. She was so beautiful. He breathed in the fragrant rose perfume she always wore and felt a flare of panic when he realised how tense she was. Was she afraid of him?

'You know that my mother admitted she killed the guy, not me,' he said hoarsely. He remembered his mother had written her confession in Portuguese. 'If you don't believe me, I'll give you the letter and you can have it translated.'

'I do believe you.'

He wasn't convinced. 'You have nothing to fear from me, *querida*. I would never hurt you or our child.'

'I know you wouldn't.' Clare bit her lip. This was even more difficult than she had expected. But she knew she was doing the right thing, and her resolve hardened. 'We don't have to be married for our baby to take your name. When he or she is born we can simply register them with the name Cazorra. Nor do we have to be married to be parents to our child. I am willing to move to Brazil so that we can live near each other and take an equal share of parenting. Many families have arrangements that aren't conventional, and if we both try we can make the arrangement I've described work for us and, more importantly, for our child.'

A cold hand of fear curled around Diego's heart when he saw Clare's determined expression. 'When we first found out about your pregnancy, I told you I couldn't be a proper husband and father because I was afraid that I might be a murderer and I could not put you or our child at risk of my temper. But now I know the truth and I am free of that worry.'

'Exactly,' Clare said huskily. 'You are finally free, Diego. You spent two years in prison but twenty years imprisoned in your mind for a crime you didn't commit. Do you think I haven't worked out that you shunned relationships and never allowed yourself to fall in love because you were afraid of yourself, and afraid that you might be a manic killer? That must have been an unbearable burden to carry.'

She had to be brave, even though she could feel her heart breaking, Clare told herself. 'I conceived your baby as a result of a moment of madness. I refuse to sentence you to be imprisoned in a marriage of convenience because you feel it is your duty to your child. For the first time in your life you are free to fall in love and choose the woman you want to spend the rest of your life with.'

Wild and uncontrollable emotions were storming through Diego, smashing down the last of his barriers and making him feel exposed and vulnerable in a way he had never felt before. He thought he understood what Clare was doing, why she seemed to be pushing him away. But he could be wrong and if he was, and she really did not want to marry him, then the future looked unbearably bleak.

'And what if I choose you as the woman I want to spend my life with?' he said roughly. 'What if I told you I love you? Would you agree to marry me then?'

She shook her head and Diego stared into the abyss.

'It's a little too convenient for you to suddenly decide you are in love with me.' There was a catch in her voice. 'I know why you said it. I know you want to be a devoted father like you wish your father had been. I promise I will never come between you and your child.' A single tear slipped down her cheek and she hastily wiped it away. 'You will be a wonderful father,' she choked out, but Diego did not appear to be listening.

'*Convenient!* There is nothing convenient about loving you, *anjinho.* I knew when I first saw you, a picture of innocence in your nun's habit and veil, that you were trouble,' he growled. 'I wanted to do all sorts of unholy things to you, and when we made love in the cave I was willing to pay for my sin of desiring you by spending the rest of my life in purgatory—because that night was the most beautiful night of my life.'

He cradled her face in his hands and gently wiped another tear from her cheek with his thumb. 'I should have been furious when I discovered you had tricked me and were not committed to a life of religious devotion, but all I could think of was that you were free to come to my bed.' His eyes darkened with remembered shadows. 'But I wasn't free to follow my heart and fall in love with you. I had to protect you from the monster I believed was inside me.'

'Oh, Diego, it breaks my heart to think of all the

years you spent alone, fearing to love anyone,' Clare whispered.

He breathed deeply and prayed for the first time in his life. 'The truth is that I never met any woman who touched my heart until I met you, *meu amor*.' His voice deepened. 'I love you, Clare. Not because it is convenient and not because you are carrying my child. I love you because you are the bravest, craziest, most beautiful, sexiest woman I have ever met. When you told me you trusted me, you made me feel like I could conquer the world. But I don't want the world, all I want is you. Our baby will be a wonderful bonus. But I am asking you, *querida*, I am begging you to marry me, because you are everything to me and without you I am nothing.'

The look in Diego's eyes was love, Clare realised dazedly. His words had chipped away at her defences, but the raw emotion blazing in his silver gaze made her believe him.

'When I said I wouldn't marry you, I was trying to be noble,' she explained shakily. 'You could have any woman you choose…'

'I choose you,' he said fiercely. 'I don't want you to be noble, I want you to love me.'

She heard the boy beneath the man, the poet who had read words of love but never heard them spoken to him. Clare reached up and stroked her fingers across the blond stubble on his jaw, traced his beautiful mouth with her fingertips.

'I do love you, with all my heart and all my soul. You are the other half of me, my hero, my protector, my lover and my husband—I hope,' she added tremulously.

'Try and stop me,' Diego whispered against her lips, before he claimed her mouth and kissed her with all the passion and tenderness and love that he had kept locked inside him for so long, until Clare had unlocked his heart and set him free.

Six months later baby Rose Cazorra entered the world and promptly stole her parents' hearts.

'You wouldn't believe such a tiny baby could have such a loud cry,' Diego said as he cradled his daughter in his arms. 'I think Rose has inherited your fiery temperament, as well as your red hair and blue eyes,' he told Clare.

She smiled. 'You could be right. Mum says I had a very loud cry when I was a baby. I can't wait for my parents to arrive tomorrow to visit their new granddaughter. We haven't seen them since our wedding.'

They had married in England five months earlier in a simple but intensely moving ceremony at Clare's parish church. She had worn a white dress decorated with tiny crystals, and white rosebuds in her hair. Diego had looked eye-catchingly handsome in a light grey suit, but his eyes had been focused on his new wife as they had stood on the steps of the church and he'd swept her into his arms and kissed her.

'Te adoro,' he had whispered to her on their wedding day, and he repeated those words now, first to his baby daughter as he placed her in her crib, and then to Clare when he lay down beside her on their bed and drew her into his arms. 'You are my world, you and Rose, and I will take care of you and protect you and love you every day of my life,' he vowed.

'Only every day?' She pretended to pout. 'Will you love me every night, too? Starting with tonight.'

Diego felt his body stir as desire heated his blood

when Clare tugged the straps of her negligee down and her breasts spilled into his hands. 'It's only a few weeks since you gave birth to Rose. Do you feel ready for me to make love to you, *querida*?'

'I always want you to love me,' she whispered, tugging him down on top of her.

'I always will, *anjinho*.'

* * * * *

FALLING FOR THE SINGLE DAD SURGEON

CHARLOTTE HAWKES

To Zena

You keep calling, even when I've got lost inside my own head (or book) and forgotten to call back for the umpteenth time – I have no idea how I got lucky enough to have you!

Sing with me now: 'Thank you for being a friend…' xx

CHAPTER ONE

THIS WOMAN WAS surely going to be his undoing.

The premonition walloped into Jake Cooper as he stared across the throng of well-heeled guests attending the welcome gala dinner for the summer programme at Brazil's renowned Hospital Universitário Paulista.

He knew it, and still he stared. And despite the colleagues jostling to talk to him, he found he couldn't draw his gaze from one agitated figure.

Flávia Maura. Or, as she was more colloquially known, the *selvagem* woman.

Wild. Savage. The jungle woman.

And there was no doubt in Jake's mind that she posed a setback to his own sanity.

She was standing in a trio of women; yet, for him, the other two had blurred into muted shades of grey around Flávia. Just as everyone else in the vast, elegant room had done, the moment he'd laid eyes on this one woman. He might have thought that there was something abruptly wrong with his vision, but for the fact that he was so focused on the image of her, in glorious high definition.

He was supposed to be here for the training programme. A summer of top medical experts from around the world all meeting in one place both to learn, and also to teach, new cutting-edge skills to each other. Not least demonstrating the clinical trial he himself was part of, where he was using a scorpion-venom-based toxin to highlight cancer cells—effectively showing up as a fluorescent tumour paint when put under near-infrared light, within a patient on the operating table.

And Flávia Maura had been one of the researchers who had worked on the toxin he was using for his particular trial.

Only, it wasn't her professional skills which currently had his eyes devouring every inch of her, from the top of her rich, glossy hair right down to the sexy high heels in which she appeared to be trying to balance, and everything in between. Not least the long, figure-hugging metallic gown in some deep green, which seemed to shimmer to black as she moved. Everything about it teased him. The way it clung so lovingly to her body, but the shimmers tricked the eye; the way the neckline offered a mouthwatering taste—but no more—of sexy cleavage; the way the side slit, which tantalised glimpses of endlessly long legs, but never once veered into dangerous territory.

Like the merest whisper of a promise of something more.

It was ridiculous that he—who had known plenty of beautiful women during his assuredly bachelor life— should be so easily ensnared. Yet here he was, like a fish dangling helplessly from a fisherman's hook.

She looked sophisticated yet sexy. Elegant yet slightly devilish. And utterly, and completely, terrified. It wasn't just the way her eyes were darting about the room however hard she kept trying to look her colleagues in the eye. It wasn't simply how her hands kept toying with her dress, her earrings, her shoes, as if she felt completely out of her comfort zone. It wasn't even her confident smile, which froze in place just once or twice.

It was the way she kept subconsciously edging behind the shoulder of one of the other two women, as though they could somehow provide a barrier between her and the colleagues who were clearly edging to talk to her—the woman whose work as a naturalist and researcher were helping to change the face of contemporary cancer treatment.

It should have acted as a warning that he could read her—a relative stranger—so well.

It should have worried him even more that it didn't.

But then, it wasn't the first warning he'd had, was it? He'd known it three days ago, in the middle of an operation, with the guy who'd been the closest thing to a best mate for the better part of a decade.

The memory played out in his head, as if reliving that conversation could somehow help to steel him against the pull of the woman standing no more than thirty metres from him right now.

As if it could help him resist this odd lure of striding across the room and claiming her for his own all night.

Like some kind of Neanderthal that he'd never been before. Like the guy he'd sworn only three days ago that he wasn't.

'So,' his mate and neurosurgeon colleague had demanded good-naturedly partway through their joint operation. 'Who did you sleep with in order to get on to this year's summer teaching programme at Paulista's?'

'Funny, Oz.' He'd grinned but he hadn't even bothered looking up from the surgery.

His eyes had been trained on the brain of his patient as his colleague, neurosurgeon Oscar Wright, had worked to reveal a tumour. They'd made the first incision and had been drilling the bone flap as close to the tumour site as possible.

Once they were ready to start the resection, they would wake the patient and begin brain mapping. Normally, Jake wasn't in on these operations, his area of expertise being vascular oncology, but the tumour paint was *his* clinical trial. Added to that was the fact that the particular young lad in question had always been particularly jumpy and Jake had been working with him long enough to have built up a rapport that would help during the awake part of the surgery.

But in that moment, the lad was still anaesthetised and the banter he and Oz shared often made critical operations like those seem easier.

'Besides, that's more your style than mine, isn't it?'

'You think I didn't try?' Oz had shaken his head. 'I pulled out all the stops last year when they were choosing surgeons to go to Brazil, lot of good that did me. Not that it was a hardship, you understand.'

'I bet it wasn't,' Jake had retorted dryly. 'Though I imagine that high-profile case you have coming might have something to do with it.'

They had both known Oz's name would have been right up there with his if it hadn't been for the fact that Oz needed to stay in London this winter, which was summer below the equator in Brazil.

The guy's reputation as a playboy preceded him, but he was also one of the best neurosurgeons Jake had known. *Work hard, play harder*—that was Oz's single rule for life, just as it had been his own up until ten months ago.

Right up until Brady had appeared in his life.

'When does it start, next week?' Oz had asked. And then, the killer question. 'Did you know that Flávia Maura is scheduled to be talking on Paulista's lecture programme?'

Even then, in that moment, something had kicked, sharp and unexpected, low in Jake's gut. He'd tried valiantly to ignore it, but now he knew that had been nothing compared the maelstrom tumbling around inside him now.

'You know who she is, don't you?' Oz had continued, oblivious. 'She worked on the chlorotoxin you're using in these trials for a while, though I read an article a few months ago that said she's now switched to working on a venom from some species of bushmaster viper that might be able to break down cancer cells without damaging healthy cells. I'd have thought it would have been right up your street. Isn't it a step on from this scorpion-venom-based toxin we're using here?'

'Yes, I know what it is,' Jake had bitten out at length.

Just as he'd known who Flávia was.

And yet, he'd stayed silent. Oz had had other ideas.

'So you've heard of this Flávia, then?'

There had been nothing else for it.

'As it happens, I caught a lecture of hers by accident a little while ago.'

'Really? Is she as wackadoodle as they say?'

There had been no reason for him to bristle on her behalf. No reason at all. And even now, half a world away from that OR and only metres away from Flávia, he felt… not *protectiveness*, obviously, but *something*…even more strongly.

'She's…quirky,' he had admitted reluctantly.

'Quirky? I guess that's one word for it.' Oz had snorted. 'But then, I suppose you have to have something different about you to want to work with an animal, or whatever, that could kill you in a matter of hours. And that's after it has induced vomiting and dizziness, severe internal bleeding and organs shutting down.'

'She loves what she does.' He had shrugged, remembering the passion in her voice as she'd talked about how important the snakes were, and how it was a shame that the only way she could save them from man was proving to man that the snakes could ultimately provide the key to curing cancer.

'And she's highly intelligent.'

'Right.'

'She's hot, too. I've seen a photo. Hence hoping I'd be in Brazil for their summer programme.'

He hadn't liked the way Oz had been eyeing him so astutely. His mate wasn't stupid, and one wrong answer would have given the game away. Jake had known he needed to watch what he'd said next, especially with the anaesthesiologist pretending to be preoccupied and the scrub nurses hanging off their conversation. At least it was a team he trusted.

But still.

'Didn't particularly notice.'

It hadn't been so much a lie, but more a whole tightening around his chest, as though the air was being squeezed out of his lungs. It was ridiculous, and yet he hadn't seemed able to stop it; this woman—this stranger—had such an effect on him.

The effect her presence was having on him even now.

Him.

Jake Cooper. Bowled over by a woman he hadn't even spoken to. Bowled over by *any* woman, full stop. It just didn't happen.

'Really?' Oz had looked sceptical. 'I'd have thought she'd have been just your type.'

'I didn't know I had a type.'

'Smart, stunning and single-minded when it comes to career? You've got a type, all right.'

'You mean as opposed to you.' Jake didn't know how he had managed to force the light, wry note into his tone. 'You just go for female, attractive and up for a good time.'

And Oz had laughed. As though it had been just another version of the conversation they'd been having for years.

'Nothing wrong with that. As long as we're all consenting adults and all that.'

'Yeah, well, I just attended her lecture. Don't really recall anything else.'

And if it was an outright lie, then Jake had consoled

himself with the lie that at least he was the only one who had known.

Still, Oz had eyed him critically.

'Bull. I don't buy that. You definitely would have noticed her,' he had countered. 'Oh, wait, did you sleep with her and never tell me?'

Jake remembered the way the accusation had riled him. Odd, since it never had done in the past. And even then, as he'd scrabbled about for a deflection, he'd known he was in trouble. Even if he hadn't realised how deeply.

'Listen, that lecture was a couple of months after Helen's death. After Brady.'

At least that bit hadn't been a lie.

'Ah, say no more.' Oz had backed off instantly. 'How is the champ?'

Jake remembered pausing. Exhaling deeply. He hadn't liked using Brady to change the conversation like that, but at least there was something of a poetic truth to it. Plus, his nephew catapulting into his life as a seven-year-old orphan was when Oz had proved their friendship of almost a decade was built on more than just nights out after hard operations.

Not every best mate would have been thrilled with a seven-year-old kid bursting in on their bachelor lifestyles, but Oz—the oldest of four brothers—had taken it in his stride, able to relate to Brady in a way Jake himself still hadn't managed.

His nephew was still a complete mystery to him. And it shamed him, angered him and frustrated him, all at once. He wasn't a man accustomed to failure. He had never failed. At anything.

But he'd failed at being a brother to Helen and now he was failing at being an uncle, and sole guardian, to Brady.

And he hated himself for it.

'No idea how he's going to take to Brazil,' Jake had

begun. Then, 'No idea how he's going to like it with only me to talk to.'

'You'll cope.'

If only he felt half as confident as Oz.

He could deal with tumours, dying patients, grieving families. But he was at a complete loss when it came to talking to one grieving seven-year-old boy.

'I suggested going to a water park when I have a free weekend,' he'd told his mate.

'And?'

'He agreed.' Jake grimaced at the memory just as he had done when recounting it to his friend. 'But he wasn't exactly jumping up and down like most seven-year-old kids would.'

'That's because Brady isn't most seven-year-olds.' Oz had shrugged, like it was obvious. 'Did you offer to take him into the rainforest? *That* would have him leaping around like a maniac. In fact, you'd probably get home to find he'd packed both your suitcases. They wouldn't contain anything you needed, of course, but he'd have his test tubes, his sample pots and his magnifying camera for every insect or arachnid you could possibly find.'

'I considered it. But you really think taking a young kid into the rainforest is a responsible thing to do? I couldn't guarantee keeping him safe.'

'*You* wouldn't,' Oz had scoffed. 'You and I are city guys through and through. But you can get guided tours, some especially geared up for kids.'

'How the hell do you know that?'

'Brady told me.' Oz had sounded surprised. 'He didn't tell you?'

No. He hadn't. Because the fact was that Brady barely exchanged a word with him, if he didn't have to. Which told him altogether too much about the kind of absent uncle he'd been—and he didn't like it.

'Okay, that's the next step done.' Oz had confirmed his

focus squarely back on the patient—not that it had ever really left—and Jake was grateful for the change of topic. 'Just one more and you can finally show me this tumour paint close-up. Man, I'd have killed to get this clinical trial of yours.'

'What can I say? They only choose the best.'

'You'd think you'd won awards for your research or something…' Oz had stopped abruptly, his entire demeanour changing in an instant. 'Ah, wait, is that it?'

He'd moved aside to give Jake room.

'Kill the lights, please,' Jake had instructed, all trace of their former banter gone as they'd focused on the task in hand.

The operating room had turned eerily dark, with only the light from the monitors casting out around the area. Then he'd shone a near-infrared light over the patient's brain and a pink-purplish glow had lit up.

'That's it,' Jake had confirmed with satisfaction. 'That's the chlorotoxin we injected last night.'

The chlorotoxin that Flávia Maura had worked on.

The thought had rattled through Jake's brain before he could stop it, proving that, even before tonight, with the vision of her in front of him, the woman had been positively haunting him. And no matter how many times he told himself it was purely professional interest, a part of him knew there was more to it.

'It's lit the tumour up like Christmas lights in a grotto.' Oz had shaken his head. 'I've seen it on footage but never in person like this. She's quite the beauty.'

'Remarkable, isn't it?' Jake had concurred, staring at the tumour. 'The engineered toxin fluoresces every cancer cell, yet leaves every single healthy cell around dark.'

'My God, it shows me every last bit of the tumour which I'd need to remove without worrying about margins and without fear of leaving anything behind, causing a recurrence. The only question will be whether it also interferes with the centres of the lad's brain responsible for speech or motor control.'

'That's your call.' Jake had nodded. 'How about get it out so that my patient can get his life back.'

'Okay, you're ready for the brain mapping? Can we go ahead and wake the patient, please?'

For the next hour or so, Jake had worked with the neurologist, using flash cards, asking questions and just generally keeping his patient talking whilst Oz had sent light electrical currents down the nerves to stimulate each part of the brain, then worked on removing the tumour.

And then Oz had given the signal that it was time to anaesthetise the patient again so that they could close up.

'Okay, mate,' Jake had told his patient. 'Next time you wake up, you'll be out of surgery.'

'You'll be with me?' the lad had managed.

'I'll come and see you as soon as I can and we'll talk you through how it's all gone,' Jake had confirmed, moving back to allow the anaesthetist to take over.

'Want to see?' Oz had offered when he was confident the lad was out again, but Jake had already been making his way around the table.

'I don't see any fluoresced areas.' He'd frowned in disbelief. 'You were actually able to get all of it?'

'Every last bit.' Triumph had reverberated through his mate's voice. 'Your patient might have to relearn his grade-two flute from when he was a kid, but if any tumour recurs in this guy, then it won't be because of anything I had to leave behind. You need to complete these clinical trials so we can get our hands on this stuff for every patient.'

'I'm working on it,' Jake had replied grimly. 'You know how long these things take.'

'Yeah, too long, when we've got patients to try to save.

You'd better ask Ms Maura what else she has up her sleeve. And how long.'

And he'd filed it away as though professional interest was the only reason he was planning on talking to Flávia Maura.

They'd worked carefully, precisely, for a little longer.

'Now bone flap.'

Using plates and wires, they had secured the segment of skull they had removed in order to access the patient's brain. And then the surgery had been completed, and Flávia Maura had still been in residence in Jake's head.

'Nice,' Jake had congratulated as he and Oz left the OR together, trying to shake her, though not too hard. 'Good going.'

'Yeah, well, when you see the delectable Ms Maura, don't go doing anything I wouldn't do.'

'Apart from the fact that leaves pretty much everything on the table—' Jake remembered ignoring the jolt of anticipation which shot through him '—Brady will be with me. So my interactions will be strictly professional.'

Yet now, only three days later, and watching the woman agitatedly shift her weight from one foot to the other before finally taking her leave from the other women, he realised that his intentions towards Flávia Maura were far from strictly professional.

This he admitted as he strode forward and cut a slick path through the crowd to Isabella Sanchez—the woman running the gala evening's slick operation.

Three more nights, Flávia Maura chanted silently to herself as she took her leave from her colleagues, Doctors Krysta Simpson and Amy Woodell, and edged her way through the crowded ballroom with something approaching relief.

Three more nights of awkward social hospital events

and then she could be out of the city and back to the rain-forest, where she felt most at home.

It wasn't that she didn't like Krysta or Amy—far from it. She admired both women, who were incredibly accomplished in their careers and who seemed as kind as they were successful. She'd simply never been very good with crowds.

Animals were fine, but people…? Not so much. In fact, not only had her six- and nine-year-old nieces spent the previous weekend trying to give her a crash course in superficial conversation, but their mother—her own sister—had spent two hours this afternoon primping and preening her like some fun pet project.

Typical bossy Maria, Flávia thought fondly even as she anxiously tried to keep her balance in the unfamiliar skyscraper heels, and smoothed down her long gown. Her sister had practically bullied her into this dress tonight, and although it would undoubtedly look sleek and sophisticated on any other woman, it was all such a far cry from her usual uniform of trusty hiking boots and sensible, light grey cargo pants with a black tee that she felt like she might as well have been wearing little more than a scantily clad, samba carnival dancer.

Either that or like a little girl trying on her mother's clothes and high heels and lipstick, as her nieces had taken to doing with Maria's clothes. Flávia grinned to herself at the image of them playing princesses, even as an uncharacteristically melancholic pang shot through her. She loved the two little girls with all her heart, but sometimes—just occasionally—their lives reminded her of all that she and Maria had missed in their own childhoods. Not least the fact that their own mother had never stuck around long enough to give the sisters time to grow up and start to play dress-up in *her* clothes.

No. Their beloved *papai*, Eduardo, had raised them single-handedly, usually under the canopy of the Amazon or Atlantic rainforests, with explorer clothes instead of princess gowns, and animals for company rather than people. And Flávia had never regretted a moment of it.

Except when it came to taking life lessons from her nieces and then walking in on her sister stuffing condoms into her purse just before the taxi had arrived this evening, with an encouraging, *If you meet a cute doctor, why not try having a little fun for once in your life, Livvy?*

But she didn't want to *have a little fun*. She was here because her boss demanded it, not because she had any desire to be; the sooner the night was over, the better.

She'd take a deadly bushmaster viper, a Brazilian wandering spider or a poison dart frog over trying to make conversation with a normal human being any day of the week. So between the hospital's packed social calendars, it was proving to be a particularly tense week.

Still moving—or rather, teetering—Flávia desperately scanned the ballroom, telling herself that she didn't need an escape route but searching for one all the same. Before her eyes alighted on the doors at the far end and a sense of consolation poured through her.

The botanical gardens were quite busy during the day, but at this time of evening they would probably be closed. If she could sneak in, it would give her a much-needed chance to regroup, and to quell the unfamiliar sensation of champagne bubbles up her nose from the glass she'd been trying to drink for the past hour.

She turned direction sharply, almost straight into one of her least favourite surgeons.

'The hospital should be more careful of their reputation,' the condescending tones of Dr Silvio Delgado—clearly pitched to be heard by as many luminaries as possible, as though by denigrating everyone else he somehow elevated himself—reached her ears. 'First they hire the crazy *sel-*

vagem woman, then the gigolo, and to add insult to injury, they then bring some frump in to lecture. This one looks like a street person.'

A better person, a stronger person, would have carried on walking, not letting that interminably pompous man get under their skin. But Flávia froze, shame momentarily rendering her immobile before eventually allowing her to twist herself around uncomfortably, a scowl pulling her features taut despite her best efforts not to react.

Selvagem—jungle woman.

It wasn't the term itself—she'd been called *selvagem* plenty of times and it didn't usually bother her—so much as the utter contempt in this particular man's tone. The pejorative way he spat out the word—*selvagem*—as if she was as feral as the animals found in the rainforest. Or was that just because Delgado had said as much to her face, many times in the past?

Perhaps that was why Flávia tried telling herself it was the fact that he was also insulting a new colleague—a visitor to Paulista's—which rattled her most.

Frump.

As though what Krysta wore mattered more than the fact that the woman was a focused, driven individual, already a leader in the combined fields of otolaryngology and facial reconstruction.

Flávia felt as though she ought to say something. She wished she could. Then again, what was to be gained from drawing attention to something half the crowd mercifully hadn't understood, anyway, given that Delgado had spoken in Portuguese? Anyway, he'd only laugh her off, and she would probably let him.

All the more reason to get to the gardens and be alone.

Flávia gritted her teeth and gingerly lifted her foot, hoping she wasn't about to do something as stupid as catching the heel in the hem.

'Is that guy always such an abhorrent boor?'

Perhaps it was the clear-cut English accent which gave away the fact that the speaker was Dr Jacob Cooper. Or it could have been the rich, utterly masculine timbre, suggesting a barely restrained dynamism. Or maybe it was the fact that she remembered that voice only too well. It had featured in her pitiful dreams several times over the past eight months—and in those it wasn't just asking that one question after her lecture.

Whatever the truth, sensations skittered this way and that, like interlopers, inside Flávia's chest. The mere sound of his voice ignited every inch of her nerve endings, leaving her feeling as though her entire body was…*itching. On fire.*

An effect that no one had ever had on her before. Not even Enrico, the man who she had once called her fiancé.

Holding herself steady, Flávia spun slowly back around to face the speaker.

And promptly wished she hadn't.

CHAPTER TWO

THE MAN WAS—her brain faltered, flailing to understand what her eyes were seeing—simply extraordinary.

Last time she'd seen him, he'd been one figure in a sea of faces, every one of them clad in work suits, and yet, to her, he'd stood out. Now, he wore the same impeccable tuxedo as every other man. His hair the same, neat style as every other man. He was well groomed, with intelligent eyes the same blue as roughly three hundred million other human beings in the world. And yet…he wasn't the same as them.

There was nothing *the same* about Jacob Cooper, whatsoever. Indeed, far from her memory making more of the man than had ever really been, Flávia now realised, to her horror, that her brain hadn't *nearly* recalled quite how magnetic he was.

Flávia couldn't quite put her finger on it and yet it was there, nonetheless. Maybe it was that he seemed infinitely leaner, taller, more powerful, than any other man she'd ever known. Perhaps it was the way those eyes—as blue as a morpho butterfly—rooted her to the wooden dance floor. And yet simultaneously made her feel as though she was floating a good foot or so above it. Or possibly, it was the fact that the air around her seemed to be heating up, as if flowing right from this stranger's body straight into hers.

Like nothing she'd ever experienced before.

She eyed the empty champagne glass accusingly. Evidently, the alcohol had allowed her sister's ridiculous *have a little fun* instruction to get into her head, and now it was running riot, upending the customarily neatly arranged compartments in her brain.

Vaguely, she recalled that he'd levelled a question at her, although for the life of her she couldn't remember what that question had been.

Ah, something to do with Delgado being a boor.

She really ought to speak, but how could her brain form words when it couldn't even think straight? Flávia slid a discreet tongue over her teeth, unsticking them from her suddenly parched lips, and forced her vocal cords back into operation. And if her tone was a touch huskier than usual, well, was he really to know? From one lecture?

'You speak Portuguese?'

'A little.'

'That's unusual.'

He didn't so much as shrug to give the semblance of it.

'I made it my business to learn the language when I got the invitation to this summer's teaching programme and I knew that your man over there was head of the oncology department.'

Interesting.

'Why do that?' she couldn't help but ask. 'There are so many countries attending these annual summer teaching programmes that the common language is generally English, anyway.'

For a moment she wasn't sure he was going to answer her. His eyes bored into her and she felt something unfurl from her toes right the way up. Then, suddenly, he spoke.

'Let's just say that I make it my business to understand the nature of the people with whom I'll be working closely over the next few months. I like to know their character and I like to know their mettle.'

He smiled. Or, at least, he bared his teeth into something which could equally have been a smile, or a grimace. And Flávia couldn't have said why it made her think that she pitied anyone who tried to stir things up with this man.

It also made her more open with him than she might otherwise have intended.

'Dr Silvio Delgado's grandfather was one of the founding contributors to this hospital.' As the man was all too fond of telling people at every opportunity. 'He believes that gives him an inalienable right to insult whoever he pleases.'

Like calling her 'jungle woman' and turning it into an insult.

Then again, was it surprising she was sensitive to it? A childhood of being mocked by the other kids—her sister leaping in to fight her battles—had left more of a scar than Flávia would have liked. Yet she suspected, right at this moment, that it was the idea of *Jacob Cooper* thinking she was a bit...*odd* that bothered her more than anything that idiot Delgado could ever say.

'Indeed,' he offered in a tone so neutral that Flávia couldn't ascertain anything from it.

It irritated her that she was trying.

Why should she care what this stranger thought?

'Jacob Cooper,' he introduced himself, his words like the sweetest caramel moving through her veins.

'Yes, of course.'

'Of course?' he echoed, a hint of a smile toying with his altogether too-mesmerising mouth. 'I didn't think we'd met.'

Flávia blinked, heat rushing to her cheeks. She could only hope that her colouring, and the light levels, concealed her embarrassment.

'Well, I mean...*of course* I know the name. After all,

who, with any connection to the oncology world, doesn't?' She was babbling, but for the life of herself she couldn't stop. 'Dr Jacob Cooper…that is, *you*…have a reputation for pushing boundaries. Running clinical trials that others were too afraid to touch, like the scorpion-venom-based fluorescent dye which lights up cancer cells like some kind of personal beacon. Making Hail Marys look like a proverbial walk in the park.'

Oh, Lord, now she sounded like she was fangirling. *This* was why she hated people. She really had no idea how to talk to them without coming across as either aloof, or a bit of a fool. A *bobo*.

'Well, I'm flattered.' His voice sounded all the richer, and more luxurious, and Flávia wasn't sure she cared for the effect it was having on her.

Turning her into even more of an *idiota*.

She didn't want to shake his hand. She feared what that contact might do to her given the effect the mere sight of him had. Yet she watched her arm reach out nonetheless, as if under some form of energy other than her own muscles.

When he enveloped her not-exactly-petite hand in his much bigger one, making it seem more delicate than it ever had before in her life, her heart stopped. Hanging there for a beat, or ten—sensations raining down on her like she'd charged into the ocean splashing spray high into the air and was letting it land on her skin—before pounding back into life like a thousand horses galloping in her chest.

'Flávia Maura,' she bit out by way of introduction. And only after what felt like an eternity.

His eyes glinted, but still she couldn't read them.

'I know,' he answered evenly. 'If we're going for a mutual love-in, then I feel duty-bound to point out that you're one of today's foremost authorities in the field of venom-based medicine. I caught your lecture on the application of a cancer-targeting toxin in Brazilian wasp venom some months ago.'

'Oh…' she offered, hoping that her scorching cheeks didn't give her away. 'Right.'

She could hardly admit that she recognised him from one question out of the raft of them she'd had that day, could she? Hardly tell him that his face had invaded her dreams ever since, like she was exactly the kind of weirdo Silvio Delgado would love the world to believe. Hardly confess that she'd looked for him after that lecture, wanting to ask *him* questions of her own.

So, instead, she fell back on her usual safety net. Discussing facts like they were the only conversation she knew how to have.

'Polybia-MP1. It exploits the unusual make-up of lipids and fats within cancer-cell membranes and essentially creates holes in the latter. These gaps can be wide enough to let molecules like proteins escape, and since the cancer cells can't function without them, the toxin ultimately acts as an anticancer therapy.'

She stopped abruptly, aware that this time his mouth was more than twitching with amusement.

'As I said. I caught the whole lecture.'

'Yes…well…there you go.'

With more effort than she cared to admit, Flávia attempted to propel herself forward again, away from this mesmerising man, needing the quiet respite now more than ever.

'So what are you working on now?'

She stopped.

'I… Well… I'm pretty much living my dream. Working as a naturalist and researcher, splitting my time between caring for pit vipers in a sanctuary in the rainforest, and my work at Paulista's.'

'I heard you were looking for ways to use venom to halt

the metastasising of cancer cells in humans? Amazing to think that what had started as a passion for the wildlife of the Amazon rainforest can now enable you to save human and snake lives, alike.'

Flávia froze, her body practically shaking.

'You've read my recent interview?' Her voice cracked with shock.

'Indeed.'

'In Portuguese,' she added weakly.

That slow, sexy grin of his was going to be her undoing. She was sure of it.

'So I noticed.'

It stood to reason that he would know of VenomSci's work. But the fact that he'd read a piece on her life, and her naturalist goals, *and then quoted them back at her*…? Well, that was doing insane things to her insides.

She needed to get away. *Now.* Before she did something as ridiculous as her sister had suggested.

Turning sharply, Flávia lurched off. It was only when she was a metre or so away that she realised he was falling into step beside her.

'Where are we heading?'

'We?' she managed. '*We* are not heading anywhere. *I* was heading to the gardens.'

He moved with an enviable ease and confidence. A self-awareness as though he expected people—the world—to make way for him. Then again, it probably did, given the way people were hastily repositioning themselves to make way for him.

'That desperate to escape already, huh?' His voice actually seemed to rumble through her. 'Well, sorry to be the bearer of bad news, but the gardens are locked now.'

'They are?' She snapped her head around. 'How do you know?'

He hesitated. So fleeting that anyone else may not have

noticed it. But Flávia wasn't *anybody*. She hadn't avoided being bitten by the fast, deadly vipers she had come to love by failing to miss tiny, telltale signs. It piqued her curiosity in an instant, although Jacob had apparently already shrugged the moment off.

'I tried earlier,' he answered smoothly. 'They told me it was closed for the night.'

'I see.'

There was something else. Something more. She'd lay a bet on it.

'May I recommend the bar instead? That far end looks pretty quiet.'

She ought to decline.

Her mind was still racing. Trying to fill in that missing moment. And then she shocked herself again by flashing a dazzling smile, which her sister was always telling her to use more often with people other than merely her beloved nieces.

'Why not? I'm sure we can have quite the party of our own.'

She ought to tell him she wasn't interested in a party *of their own*. She ought to be mingling, the way her boss had told her to do. She ought to draw more people into the conversation—she could see a couple of other medical and surgical oncology team members hovering for a chance to talk to the highly respected Dr Cooper.

Yet she didn't say any of those things, and by the time she reached the bar, Flávia found herself alone with a man who made her body fizz disconcertingly, and an empty countertop.

Then, with nothing more discernible than a diplomatic hand gesture, two fresh drinks materialised in front of them. A glass of champagne for her and, she hazarded a guess from the deep amber colour of the liquid swirling in the tumbler, a top-drawer whiskey or cognac for him. And suddenly, inexplicably, it all felt slightly too…intimate.

Flávia opened her mouth to refuse the drink and take her leave—not that she really believed her single glass of champagne was to blame for this…*thing* that hummed between them, but why take any chances? And then he thanked the bartender.

She had no idea what it was about the simple gesture, so understated yet so polite, and so unlike too many of the doctors in this room who thought themselves too good for something as apparently irrelevant as good manners.

She turned her head to look at him again and, once again, her heart slammed into her chest for no apparent reason. Was breath truly seeping from her lungs like a popped balloon or was she just imagining it? And never mind the dress feeling constricting and small, right now it was her very skin which seemed to be too tight for her own body.

Flávia couldn't help it—her eyes scanned over him. Quickly. Then slowly. Like they didn't know where to start. Or maybe where to stop. And still she stood there. Still. Ensnared.

No man had ever got under her skin like this. Ever. She told herself it meant nothing. That she must just be feeling out of her depth at this welcome gala, and vulnerable after Delgado's dig.

'Dr Cooper—' she began.

'Jacob,' he interjected.

She sucked in a breath. 'Jacob,' she began, then paused. As ridiculous as it was, his name sounded altogether too intimate on her tongue. She tried again. 'Jacob…'

'But you can call me Jake,' he interrupted, and this time she knew she didn't mistake the amused rumble in his tone. 'And for the record, you really shouldn't let oafs like Delgado get to you.'

'I don't,' she denied hotly, then cursed herself for sounding so defensive.

'I beg to differ. It was clear from the way you reacted that he had rattled you. And you have to know that's only going to encourage him all the more. Bullies like him thrive off making others feel small.'

'I'm well aware of that.' She bristled, despite her attempts not to. 'But it was the doctor he called a frump who I was most concerned about.'

'Who? Krysta Simpson? I'm running a case with her at the moment… Actually, it would interest you—the patient has oral cancer and I'll be using the scorpion-venom-based fluorescent contrast agent when I remove the tumour in their jaw. But the point is, there's no need for you to worry about Krysta. She's more than secure enough in herself not to let such a comment get to her.'

Yes, that much was clear. Flávia couldn't help thinking that if she had a fraction of Krysta's confidence then she, too, could be wearing a dress which—if she had to be entirely honest—might not be the most flattering, but in which Krysta looked entirely comfortable.

What must it be like to be so cool and self-assured when chatting with these people?

Instead here she was, feeling utterly self-conscious in a figure-hugging dress and statement shoes, both of which her far more fashion-forward sister had insisted on foisting on her for tonight's event. Yet all Flávia could think was that one couldn't make a silk purse out of a sow's ear— and she most definitely felt like a sow's ear. And no matter the shocked compliments she'd been receiving all night.

Hastily, she told herself that she felt nothing at Jacob's… Jake's…apparent appreciation. Assuming that was what this was, of course. And if he did appreciate her, then it was the dress he admired—her *sister's* dress—not *her*, per se.

Only, she wasn't sure she believed that. Or, more pertinently, *wanted* to believe it.

Admittedly, she adored the colour—a forest green which shimmered to inky black as she moved, the stunning colour so like another of her beloved snakes—but other than that, she was too plagued with self-doubt to relax. Was the neckline too low? The slit in the skirt too high? Did it cling to her a little too much when she moved?

Her only consolation was that if she *had* looked as *on display* as she'd feared, then Silvio Delgado would surely have taken great delight in mocking her clothes, as well as her choice of career.

So maybe it was more that the clothes mirrored her environment and how she felt about her state of mind? Out in the forest, in her bush gear, she felt strong, powerful, in control. She spent practically twenty-three hours out of twenty-four in blissful solitude, with the glorious orchestra of the rainforest pleasing her senses. Here in this ballroom, in this city, harsh sounds assailed her from every side.

Some people loved the city with its shimmering lights, vibrant sounds and bustling life—her sister and brother-in-law being prime examples—but Flávia had never been able to understand its allure. Whether it was the light pollution, the noise pollution, the air pollution, Flávia couldn't be sure.

She felt out of her depth, like she was suffocating.

At least, she *had* felt that way, right up until a few minutes ago—ever since Jacob Cooper. Now, the butterflies were still there, but instead of flutterings of fear and discomfort, she could swear they were flutterings of…awareness? Anticipation? Not least because he was looking at her as though he thought she was the only woman in the room.

And then she hated herself, because her goose-bumping body seemed to find that rather too thrilling.

'Did you want to speak to me about anything in particular?' The question came out sharper than she'd intended.

'Frankly, Flávia Maura, I find myself curious about many things right now,' he answered, and she couldn't have said why but she wasn't sure he'd intended it to have quite the huskiness that it did. 'But how about we start with your antivenom therapy, and how you think your snakes can change the face of cancer treatment today?'

She could see the inherent danger in responding to Jake's question—the effect he was having on her just from a few minutes in his company. Yet, like a frog attracted to the sweet-scented nectar in a tropical pitcher plant, Flávia couldn't resist the open invitation to talk about her work—her true passion.

Even as she knew that, like the pitcher plant, a man like Jake would eat her up in a heartbeat.

Worse, the naughtiness of such an idea was almost deliciously thrilling.

She shook her head. It didn't completely rid her head of the uninvited images, and that made her feel more combative than she knew she should.

'You say it as though I'm suggesting the awful hoax remedies they call "snake oil."'

'On the contrary,' Jake answered easily. 'I'm well aware of the difference between "snake oil" and very real medicine. A recent study listed six groups of venom-based drugs which have gained FDA approval in the last thirty-five to forty years.'

Flávia didn't know whether to be impressed by his knowledge or irritated that it wasn't helping her to be any less attracted to him. She gritted her teeth.

'I'm guessing that you also know that captopril, an ACE inhibitor used to treat high blood pressure, some types of congestive heart failure and kidney problems caused by diabetes, is derived from snake venom?'

'I do know that, given that it's used by around forty million people worldwide.' Jake nodded.

'Well, did you know that it comes from *bothrops ja-raraca*, which is another of the Brazilian pit vipers I deal with?'

'That part I didn't know,' he conceded, and Flávia didn't like that it gave her such a punch of triumph.

Was she really trying to impress this man that much?

'Plus, clinical testing for venom-based drugs began in 1968 with an anticoagulant derived from a Malayan pit viper venom.'

'I didn't know that, either,' he acknowledged with a grin that revealed straight, white teeth. As though he knew exactly what she was trying to do.

'So, *jungle woman*,' he asked softly in a way that didn't make the term sound like an insult whatsoever, 'what makes pit vipers so special?'

'Because of disintegrins,' she declared firmly, unable to help herself. 'Which is a group of proteins found in bushmaster venom. Furthermore…'

The low reverberation of a gong cut her words short, and Flávia spun around as Isabella stepped forward to announce that the dinner was about to be served.

'Shall we?'

Dropping her eyes, Flávia took in the sight of Jake's proffered arm and strove unsuccessfully to quash another bout of shimmering nerves.

She bit back the stuttering words which suddenly cluttered up her throat and swallowed once, *twice*, until she was sure she could answer with confidence, even if she didn't feel it.

'I don't believe we're sitting at the same table so you should probably ask one of the women at your table. There's a seating chart by the entrance.'

'Actually, I believe we are.' His voice rumbled around her, skimming over her skin and making it prickle like

she'd somehow missed a joke she hadn't realised someone had told.

'Oh. Right.' Her voice sounded odd, but she couldn't
help that.

It was the way he was watching her so curiously. So intently. His eyes holding hers and preventing her from dragging her gaze away, however hard she tried. And she did
try. Because the longer he held the contact, the more certain she was that he could see into her, far deeper than her
mere soul. Right down to that dark, unwelcome pit inside
her, and every embarrassing secret that she'd long since
buried within.

'Very well, then.'

Squaring her shoulders, Flávia raised her arm and linked
with Jake, but still she couldn't steel herself enough against
the thrill that rippled through her at the contact.

It was only as they moved to the entrance and past the
board that she sneaked a glance at the chart; as she'd suspected, Jake—it still felt odd not thinking of him as Dr
Jacob Cooper—wasn't supposed to be at her table. Yet when
he walked her to her seat—through the round tables, with
their pale damask cloths and stunning flower-covered to-
piaries—there was his name, at the place setting right next
to hers.

And she was far too pleased about it for her own liking.
Not that she had to let him see that. She pulled her face
into a disapproving frown.

'Did you sneak in here and change this around?'

'Are you accusing me of schoolboy tactics?'

Another grin, and another glimpse of that perfect mouth,
which she couldn't stop imagining against her skin. At the
hollow of her neck, or trailing down her body. This time,
there was no pushing the images away. So, instead, she
focused on the rules. The regulations. The things which
couldn't get her into trouble.

'You can't just move things around on a whim. How did you even get in here? You realise these doors were locked for a reason?' She was rattling off too many questions, but she couldn't seem to stop herself. 'Months and months of planning went into this. Besides, you're meant to be on one of the VIP tables, with Silvio Delgado. Experts in your field. How do you think he's going to react to someone from my table being bumped up to take your place at his table?'

Despite her rambling, Jake looked as composed as ever. He flashed her another even smile, and Flávia told herself she didn't feel it rushing through her, right down to her very toes. The thing was, no matter how Dr Delgado reacted to Jake's stunt, she couldn't imagine it intimidating the man standing in front of her right now.

Honestly, she couldn't imagine *anyone* intimidating this man.

'I imagine Silvio will be rather irked.' Jake shrugged, proving the point. 'But then, I imagine if it wasn't me inconveniencing him, then it would be someone else, so that's no great issue. Besides, do you not think that you're as much an expert in your field as he is in his, Flávia?'

'Yes, well…' Heat flushed her at the compliment. 'You still can't go around moving people *quer queira ou não*.'

'I don't see why not.' He laughed, a deep, rich sound which…*did things* to her.

'Dr—'

'Fine.' He cut her off with another dazzling smile. 'Would it settle you to know that *I* didn't change the place settings?'

'Really?' Flávia raised her eyebrows sceptically. 'Then who did?'

'Isabella Sanchez,' he answered slowly, flicking his arm out to where Isabella was leading another guest—presumably the guest originally intended to sit at their table—to Silvio Delgado's table—as if playing his trump card.

Then again, he *was* playing it.

Isabella was ultimately responsible for organising this entire programme. She wasn't a surgeon, or even a doctor, but she practically ran Hospital Universitário Paulista single-handedly. There wasn't a single thing which went on within the brick, glass and metal walls that Isabella didn't know about, and she controlled the floors with an iron fist clad in the most silken, smooth glove. She truly was a woman so formidable that even Silvio Delgado would be taking his life into his hands going up against her.

'Why would she do that?' Flávia shook her head.

'Because I asked her to.'

'Why?'

It still didn't seem to make any sense.

'Because I wanted to meet you properly.' He lowered his voice until she had to lean in to hear him, so that she was no longer sure if they were talking medicine, or not, and it suddenly felt entirely too intimate.

'I wanted a chance to talk to you.'

Flávia didn't answer.

She couldn't.

For the longest time she just watched him, his eyes snagging hers and refusing to let her look away. And she had the oddest sense that she was telling him entirely too much even though she wasn't saying even a word. That he was reading the truths she preferred to keep securely hidden.

Oh, boy, she really was in so much trouble.

CHAPTER THREE

'BUT IF A BITE from these vipers could kill a human within hours, or even minutes,' a Spanish doctor was asking Flávia, 'surely you can't cure cancer by injecting the venom without killing them? Not unless you're reverse-engineering a synthetic version.'

Jake took a spoonful of his dessert, a velvety crème brûlée which he barely even tasted, and tried to work out what the hell he thought he was doing.

Flirting with Flávia Maura?

The way he'd been doing for the past two hours. From even before she'd turned her mesmerising eyes on him and her smooth, lilting voice, which could surely have charmed arboreal snakes from the trees, had wound through him like a boa around its prey.

Business, he reminded himself, savagely turning his attention back the conversation which had all the table joining in.

'Well, that all depends on the snake, the make-up of its venom and even its delivery method. And, of course, it also depends on what we're trying to achieve.' Flávia leaned forward.

There was no doubting that her career truly drove her on, and he couldn't help but find it an exceptionally attractive quality. She was even more focused than he was—which was saying something.

'You'll know, I'm sure, that snake venom is a cocktail of hundreds of different components, including minerals and proteins, peptides and enzymes,' continued Flávia. 'Our goal is to isolate and then repurpose certain toxins within this venom, which would ultimately kill cancer cells whilst leaving healthy cells intact.

'There's an Australian researcher, Pouliot, who has been working on venom which will stop metastasis in breast cancer. He has been able to reverse-engineer venom from *bothrops alternatus*, which is a different bushmaster to the one I work with, and lab clone an inhibitor. However, he has still been unable to reverse-engineer and clone an inhibitor from the *microvipera lebtina*, so for that study he still needs live venom on hand.'

'Given how aggressive these deadly serpents are, you must be more than keen to reverse-engineer it to isolate and lab clone the toxins you need,' another of the diners declared. 'So that you won't need live snakes so much any more.'

Jake found himself pausing, his spoon halfway to his mouth. Was it only him who noticed the way her body stiffened ever so slightly? The way her back pulled that little bit tenser?

And then Flávia turned that hot, caramel gaze on him and his whole body kicked up a notch.

Business, he roared silently again. *Not pleasure.*

He suspected he was fighting a losing battle.

Twelve months ago, he would have willingly blended the two. If the chemistry that arced and sparked between them was anything to go off, he could only imagine how glorious the sex would be. Although his mind was doing a sterling job of painting a picture.

Grinding his teeth together, Jake shook his head, as if

that could somehow free his mind from the grip of too many deliciously tempting images. But as he'd told Oz—was it really only three days ago?—that wasn't who he was. Not any more.

Not since Helen's death, and Brady's appearance. Not since this whole past horrific year.

'Actually, quite the opposite.'

He was vaguely aware of Flávia's response. Albeit through a slight haze.

'Bushmasters are actually very gentle, sensitive and fragile animals. If you approach them correctly, then they rarely harm. But their backs are like glass, and if you don't handle them with care they can, quite literally, break their spines twisting away from you. It has always devastated me to think that in the herpetologist Raymond Ditmar's books from the 1920s and '30s, the suggested method of catching snakes was to noose them from a safe distance. But for the delicate bushmaster, this will actually snap their backbones.'

A couple of the diners frowned.

'Nonetheless,' one of them persisted, 'lab cloning must be preferable, on the basis that even mishandling the tiny pot of venom extracted from these vipers of yours could kill you, even by simply getting a splash on your skin.'

'Let me tell you a not-so-secret fact about me.' Flávia smiled, and Jake thought that perhaps it was only him who could tell that it was just a little too tight at the corners of her mouth to be as genuine and open as everyone else seemed to think. 'My whole reason for moving into the venom-therapy world of cancer cures was not to save humans, but to save snakes.'

'I don't follow?' another diner pressed, clearly as enthralled as the rest.

And who could blame them—he wasn't far behind them. For all his self-recriminations.

'Don't misunderstand me,' Flávia pressed on. 'I love the thought of being able to come up with a solution that halts the metastasis in cancers. But what *truly* drives me is the knowledge that the bushmasters and others are now listed as vulnerable, because as we humans decimate their natural habitats in the Atlantic Forest, their populations have plummeted.'

'Surely, all the more reason to reverse-engineer a synthetic toxin?'

Flávia's smile brightened even further, and once again, Jake was convinced that only he felt its sharpness cutting through the air.

'Or perhaps an opportunity to educate people to take more care of these snakes. It might not be perfect that we have to prove these animals could save human lives in order for humans to start trying to save the animals in turn, but it's a good place to start.'

And it was in that moment that Jake grasped the depth of his peril. Because Flávia Maura and her obsession for her work was well and truly under his skin. Where it simply couldn't be.

Where he couldn't let *it be.*

He had no room in his life for anything but Brady and his career. Not that it was love—he knew that wasn't possible, though perhaps he might have better understood such an emotion if his own parents had set any kind of example of a caring, loving marriage. No, his parents had ensured that emotions weren't an affliction from which he was ever likely to suffer. But he had responsibilities nonetheless. Like work, and his nephew. He had to get them both back on track. This inconvenient attraction to Flávia Maura couldn't get in the way of that. It wouldn't. He refused to allow it.

'You look a million miles away.' Her gentle voice tugged him back into the room. And he had no idea for how long he'd been distracted, but her previously enraptured audience was now, finally, engaging in conversations of their own.

'Or are you only six thousand miles away?' she added. 'Back in London, perhaps? A girlfriend?'

What did it say about him that he was already searching her tone for something approaching...disappointment?

He shouldn't bite. It made no difference.

'No girlfriend.' He told himself he wasn't still searching for her reaction.

Good thing, too, since she kept her tone excruciatingly neutral.

'Ah. You just seemed distracted. Or bored.' Her expression pulled suddenly tight, and her cheeks flushed a dark pink. '*Meu Deus*, have I been rambling too much about the rainforest? Everyone tells me I do that.'

'No.' He reached to place his hand on hers before he could stop himself, his whole body jarring as though from a jolt of electricity at the contact. And by the way Flávia was staring down at it, her entire body now stiff, she was equally shocked. 'Absolutely not. Talking to you has been even more interesting than I had imagined it would be.'

He should stop there. Anything more wasn't her business. It wasn't *anybody's* business, ever. But especially not when they were at a table with ten of their colleagues, even if those colleagues were beginning to move around now that the meal was over, all engrossed in their own conversations.

'But... I really ought to go and check on something. Will you excuse me?'

Setting his napkin on the table, Jake stood abruptly. He really did need to go and check on Brady, even if it was just a phone call to Patricia, the retired nurse the hospital had engaged as a quasi nanny for this teaching programme, back in the accommodation the hospital had also provided.

Yet, more than that, Jake needed a reason to put a bit of distance between himself and Flávia Maura.

The woman was like no one else he'd ever met in his life, he thought as he strode across the room, deftly avoiding calls from other colleagues to come and join their conversations. The woman drew him in, slowly, inexorably, until suddenly he'd found himself about to tell her personal details he would never willingly share with anyone else; it was altogether too...*disquieting.*

He'd known he was attracted to her ever since he'd seen her give that lecture. But he hadn't been prepared for this. The way she made the air sparkle around her.

Around *him.*

If he'd thought her career drive and passion, her ability to shape the medical landscape with every project she undertook, was intriguing, then it was only exceeded by her captivating voice, her Delphian smile, her mesmerising body. Flávia Maura was utterly intoxicating.

And he was already captivated.

Reaching the lobby now, Jake slid his mobile out of his pocket. Once he'd ensured that Brady was all right, he would go back and find Flávia. He still had a plethora of questions for her, but this time he was prepared for her.

This time he wouldn't allow her to slide into his head.

'I was beginning to think you'd left.'

Flávia spun around with a low gasp. She'd thought she'd be alone here, in the botanical gardens, where no one else was likely to want to venture at this hour. Especially since, as Jake had told her earlier, they had indeed been locked up and she'd had to bribe the hotel's concierge to let her sneak in for a few moments.

Sometimes, it seemed, being the infamously mad *jungle woman* did have its merits.

'You startled me.'

'My apologies,' he offered. Only, he didn't seem remotely repentant.

Much the same way that he'd refused to apologise for
having Isabella change the seating arrangements last minute.

She told herself not to feel so flattered.

'I've spoken to Isabella,' she told him before she could
stop herself. 'She confirmed that you asked her to change
the table plans for the sole reason of talking to me.'

'You needed confirmation?' He looked unperturbed,
and she flushed slightly.

Still, she was determined to stand her ground.

'She also told me that you declined her offer to bump
me up to your original table.'

He didn't answer, though he lifted his shoulders—yet
somehow it was too gentlemanly to be a crude shrug.

'You didn't want Silvio Delgado causing a scene and
making me feel uncomfortable.'

It was a stab in the dark, not even an educated guess,
but when after the briefest pause Jake dipped his head, she
knew she was right.

That he should have been so considerate to her roared
through her like a battle cry, screaming at her to fight this
insane attraction to a man she barely knew.

Even if her years of following his work made it feel like
otherwise.

'How did you know I was in here, anyway?' She tried
to pull the conversation back onto safer ground.

'I've been looking for you for the past half hour when I
remembered you were heading for here earlier to hide out
after that first incident with Delgado. What are you doing
in here alone?'

'I'm not hiding out,' she snapped, a little too sharply.

His mouth pulled at the corners and, too late, she realised
he'd been baiting her and she'd fallen for it.

'Anyway, why were you looking for me? I thought you were meeting someone?'

It was such an obvious attempt to change the topic and yet, despite his attempt to give himself space and regroup, for some inexplicable reason Jake heard himself replying to Flávia.

'Not meeting, just checking on.'

'Doesn't sound remotely stalkerish.' She arched her eyebrows.

Although—even if she hadn't heard the stories about the perennial bachelor Jake Cooper—she could never have imagined him chasing after any woman.

'I'll bear that in mind.' His tone was dry, but clearly he wasn't about to elaborate.

She told herself there was no reason to feel disappointed. Yet still, she did.

Well, what did you expect? she berated herself silently. *That wanting to talk shop with you over dinner meant you're suddenly the man's confidante?*

And then he shocked her by continuing.

'I went to check on Brady. My nephew. He's seven and he's being looked after by one of Paulista's retired paediatric nurses. Still, he's in a strange country and a strange room, and I didn't want him to wake up and be disorientated.'

She wasn't sure which part of the admission hit her hardest. There were plenty of stories about Jake Cooper the supersurgeon, and just as many about Jake Cooper the stag.

But there were absolutely none about Jake Cooper the doting uncle.

'You have a…nephew?' She blinked abruptly, and he paused, but then continued.

'Yes. My late sister's son.'

Flávia opened her mouth, then closed it again. She thought of her sister, and her brother-in-law. And then she thought of her young nieces. When she spoke again her tone wasn't shocked, or gushing. It was just as honest and sincere as she felt.

'I'm so sorry for your loss. Was it recent?'

It felt like a lifetime that she thought he wasn't going to engage with her. And then...he did.

'Ten months,' he bit out.

'Was it sudden?' she pressed gently. 'Or was there some warning? Not that it's ever enough.'

Another long beat of silence swirled around them before he answered. Each admission drawn out from him as though he didn't want to, but as though he couldn't stop himself. Because Jake wanted to talk? Or because he wanted to talk to *her*?

Flávia wasn't sure. She told herself it didn't matter either way.

'Oesophageal cancer,' he growled. 'Apparently, she went to her local hospital with stomach pains and they told her they suspected gallstones and sent her home telling her they'd send a follow-up appointment within weeks.'

She could hear the gruffness to his voice and she knew he was trying to eradicate it. Didn't it speak volumes about the man's compassion that he couldn't quite manage to do so?

'She told me she took painkillers and missed the appointment because Brady had some recital she couldn't miss. Something about being a single mum.'

'I can understand that,' Flávia murmured quietly.

'By the time things got so bad that she had to call an ambulance, they diagnosed advanced oesophageal cancer and she finally called me to come up from London. We weren't exactly close the last ten years, the odd phone call once or twice a year.' She could hear the bitter notes he was trying too hard to conceal, and her heart ached for him. 'But we led different lives. Anyway, by then there was nothing they could do but move her to a hospice. She died six days later. Ironic, wouldn't you say?'

She cocked her head, studying him.

'Why?' she asked at last, the infinite sadness in his voice seeming to draw some invisible band tight—almost too tight—around her chest. 'Because you think you should somehow have been able to save her?'

'I'm an oncologist.'

'Can you save everyone who walks through your door? Especially when they come to you so late?'

He didn't like it—she could tell even as she ignored the part of her brain wondering *how* she could tell.

'She was my sister,' he ground out. 'And she was the only parent that seven-year-old boy had. I should have been able to do…something.'

His voice cracked suddenly. Unexpectedly.

Flávia didn't think, she just moved. Closing the gap between them and placing her hand on his forearm as though it could somehow offer him a comfort that no words could. And even when he lowered his head stiffly and stared down at it, as if wondering where the contact had come from, she didn't move.

Neither did Jake.

'And now you're doing the only thing you can. You're his legal guardian.'

'Yeah.' His voice hardened to a grim, self-deprecating edge. 'Jake Cooper, the guy with the reputation as an emotionally detached workaholic.'

'But clearly, your sister thought you were the right choice.'

'Not really. I was just the only choice Helen had.'

'I can't imagine…' Flávia trailed off. 'So your parents are…have passed away?'

The silence eked out between them. So long and so

heavy that Flávia began to wonder if she could say some-thing else until, finally, he spoke.

'This isn't a conversation you should be burdened with.' He was too clipped, too crisp.

Clearly, he didn't *want* to be having the conversation with her. But not wanting to and not *needing* to were two different things. That was something she knew for herself all too well.

'We should go back,' he rasped. Still not moving.

And Flávia didn't answer, yet it was disconcerting the way those deep, dark cacao depths of hers seemed to pierce right through him. It felt as if she could see right through to his very soul.

So she slid her hand gently down his arm, covering his hand with hers, and she waited for him to pull away and head for the door.

But he didn't move. And he didn't pull away.

'I have a sister,' Flávia murmured at last when she thought he'd passed up enough chances to shut things down for good. 'Her name is Maria, and she has two daughters. Julianna is nine and Marcie is six, and I love being the fun aunt. We've always been a close family.'

'I've never been the *fun* uncle.' She suspected that the words were out before he could bite them back.

'I can't even begin to think how I would feel if anything happened to any of them,' Flávia continued softly. 'I have an apartment in the city for when I'm not at the sanctuary. But most of the time I end up staying at their home, Maria and Luis's—that's my brother-in-law. Their guest room seems to have become my personal bedroom and I always get at least one of the girls sneaking in for a sleepover.'

She laughed and even to her own ears the love and warmth of the sound seemed to reverberate around the room. Like it was too big to be contained in this space.

Which was how it always felt to her.

However, Jake wasn't smiling. He was grimacing. He pulled his hand free and rubbed his eyes wearily.

'I'm pretty sure Brady couldn't care less whether I was around or not.'

'And yet, you just left this gala to make sure he was okay,' she pointed out.

'I made a phone call. I hardly dashed across the city.'

'Why even call, then?' she challenged softly, though a part of her already knew the answer.

He glowered at her for a moment before reluctantly conceding. 'I just wanted to call and make sure he hadn't woken up and panicked or become disoriented in the unfamiliar surroundings.'

'Does he often wake?'

'Pretty much never. At least, not any more.'

He didn't need to voice the words for her to imagine how different things would have been straight after his mother's death.

'And he hadn't woken tonight?'

'No.' Jake raked his hand through his hair in such a disarmingly boyish gesture. 'It seems Patricia has it all in hand.'

She couldn't pinpoint exactly why she sensed a slight undercurrent. She eyed him speculatively.

'Surely, that's a good thing?'

'Of course it is.' He bobbed his head as though the action could emphasise things even as his words failed to.

'Then why do you look as though something about it bothers you?' she pressed softly.

They were so close she could feel his breath on her cheek. Blowing over her eyelashes, and sizzling through her body.

An ache stole through her, settling in all the places it shouldn't. Heating her from the inside out.

Jake opened his mouth to tell her she was wrong, she

was sure of it, but then he simply closed it again. Closing his eyes for a moment, like he was working out whether to answer or not.

'It doesn't bother me,' he denied eventually, his gaze snagging hers, and revealing all the things his lips were concealing.

Like the fact that his denial was a lie and there was nothing she could do about it. There was no way to help him. She didn't even understand why she so desperately wanted to. Or why she so badly wanted those lips to drop down to meet hers.

It made her feel out of control, and she told herself that couldn't be a good thing.

'I… I think I ought to head home.'

'During a welcome dinner?' He stopped abruptly and she told herself that it was fanciful to believe he was disappointed.

'The dinner is over,' she pointed out. 'I've done my duty. I've attended it and I've spoken to more people than I can remember tonight. I think I can safely sneak out without getting it in the neck from Isabella. Besides, I have a lecture to give soon. I can say I'm prepping for that.'

'You haven't prepared it?' One eyebrow rose in a perfect arch, and Flávia had to clench her hand in a fist not to reach up and trace the curve. 'I'd have thought you were the kind of person to have written it months ago, only needing to slip in new data as it emerged.'

Which was another way of saying he thought she was predictable, and nerdy. And though that was probably true, she suddenly, inexplicably, felt like doing something out of character. Something that would take this man, who seemed to think he had the measure of her, by surprise.

It made no sense, but Flávia didn't care. She told herself it was the wine talking, or her sister's well-intentioned advice, but deep down she knew neither were true.

And yet she found herself tilting her head back, meeting those piercing blue depths, and any last remaining voices in her head were silenced as she rolled up onto her toes and pressed her mouth to his.

Need punched through her in an instant—even before Jake angled his head and deepened the kiss. The slide of his tongue over hers making her blood tingle in her veins and a thrill zip around her body as his hands gripped her shoulders, pulling her in tighter.

She thought it would never end—she wished it could never end. Right up until the botanical gardens sprinkler system kicked into its nightly routine and showered them both. And even then, she didn't notice immediately.

It was the kind of fine downpour that looked as though it couldn't possibly even wet a leaf, but which ultimately soaked a person right through to the skin.

Flávia wasn't sure who broke the kiss first, her or Jake. She only knew that it had been with great reluctance. And that his hands were still holding her shoulders, just as hers were pressed against his chest.

One of them had to speak, even if she had no idea what to say next.

'So what now?' She choked out a half-nervous, half-amused laugh.

Deus, but she could so easily lose herself in those electric-blue pools of his when he looked at her like that.

'We are in a hotel,' he managed thickly, at last.

Her heart practically launched itself at her ribs, hammering so loudly it was impossible to believe he couldn't hear it. It was exciting. Thrilling. *Her*, the woman who hadn't had a fling in her life, taking her sister up on the teasing dare to *have a little fun*.

And with Jake she felt naughty, and daring, and not at all like her usual buttoned-down self.

The sense of freedom was heady.

'We are indeed,' she agreed, barely recognising the desire in her own voice.

This time, Jake didn't reply. Instead he took her hand, enveloped in his, and tucked her into his side as he hurried her across the floor and out of a hidden staff door to the side.

And all Flávia could do was follow. They were like two tree frogs hurrying to the shelter of a bark hollow to seek safety from a deluge.

CHAPTER FOUR

As THEY STEPPED through the bedroom door, Jake deliberately ignored that part of him demanding to know what the hell he thought he was playing at.

He had no idea how he'd managed to slow things down. He only knew that he needed to give her—and himself—time to think.

How had he let himself kiss her? More than that, when the sprinklers had started and they'd finally pulled apart, why had he decided the next best step was to usher her to the reception desk and book a suite upstairs for them?

As if he couldn't help himself. As if he hadn't risked any one of their colleagues walking out and seeing them. As if he wasn't now responsible to a little boy across the other side of town.

So much for not letting Flávia Maura slide under his skin.

He didn't know what had compelled him to book a suite for them, any more than he understood why he'd started to tell her things—like anything about Helen, and his irrational sense of guilt—that he'd never told anyone else in his life. Not even Oz.

Or, more to the point, he did know. He was just trying to pretend that he was still in control of himself—and not just the fact that he'd barely been able to keep his hands off her in the lift, enduring what had to be the longest elevator ride of his life.

This was the craziest thing he'd done in ten months—longer, really—and yet he couldn't bring himself to feel guilty. Was it really so much to crave one night with a woman who made him feel...*something* again? Was it too much to want to feel normal again, instead of feeling as though he was constantly on the brink of drowning in the responsibility of a seven-year-old boy who barely liked him, let alone wanted him around?

And, of course, Brady didn't want him. The poor kid just wanted his mother—and that was just one more thing for which Jake felt as though he'd failed his nephew.

Tonight.

One night.

With a woman who made him feel *alive*.

Closing the door behind them and leaning his head on the cool wood for a moment, he tried to make himself think. Only when he thought he finally had a grip on his uncharacteristically out-of-control libido did he finally turn.

Only to see Flávia clad in nothing more than the sexiest lace bra-and-panties set he could swear he'd ever seen in his life. And hold-ups, which practically stopped his heart in his chest. Her shimmering gown lay in a puddle around her sinfully high heels. Jake tried to force himself to think straight, but it wasn't easy when the woman had the kind of eyes that pinned him to the spot, the thickest and glossiest curtain of chestnut curls and a body which ought to be illegal, it was so dangerous.

There was no doubt about it: Flávia was some kind of goddess that no red-blooded male could ever hope to resist.

Or want to.

Yet for all that, her hands were clutched almost self-consciously to her front, over the apex of her slender, tanned legs that seemed to go on for ever and, despite his best intentions, made him imagine hooking them over this shoulders as he engaged in far more carnal pursuits.

A fresh lick of attraction wound its way over his body—hardly helping matters. Blood pooled in the hardest part of him. She made him feel hotter, greedier, more alive, than he'd ever felt in his life.

Worse, he didn't mind feeling so out of control—yet he surely should have minded.

Instead, all he could think of was how her skin would feel, right there in that inviting hollow of her neck, how those dark nipples—which were announcing themselves so proudly through the scrappy lace—might scrape the middle of his palms or under the pads of his thumbs, or how sweet she would taste if he crossed the room right now, lifted the hem of his tee and buried his face right there between those long, tanned thighs.

He snapped his eyes back up to hers, aware that he'd let them trail over her in a way to which she would no doubt object. But as those amber depths locked with his, his heart jolted. Because he didn't see censure, or displeasure, in her gaze; instead, he saw something far more primal. Something far more like a mirror.

The proof that, just like down in the gardens, she ached for him just as much. It was all he could do not to give in to this raw *need* which scraped away inside him. And then she pulled her lower lip in with her teeth.

'Is this…okay?'

It was incredible that she actually sounded uncertain. As if he might have, for some wholly ludicrous reason, changed his mind. Jake couldn't hold himself back any longer.

He closed the gap between them in an instant.

Fresh attraction arced between them, so bright and so electrifying that for a split second he was astounded that it didn't shock him where he stood. But then he was moving, gathering Flávia to him as he bent his mouth and tasted those honeyed lips for only the second time ever.

Yet as her body moulded all too willingly against his, Jake felt as if she'd been handcrafted just to fit him, and she was winding her arms around his neck as if hanging on for her life. And those small, needy sounds she was making in the back of her throat were doing nothing to help him regain any last scrap of self-control.

He'd put his life on hold for Brady for the past ten months, and he hadn't resented it even if he'd struggled to see how he was the best person for the task. And tomorrow he would go back to sacrificing for his nephew, because that was what Brady deserved.

But tonight?

Tonight was his. And Flávia's. To indulge and to be free. And he'd be damned if he wasn't going to enjoy every last second of it.

The instant before he claimed her mouth with his, Flávia had been telling herself that she was being silly. That practically stripping for the man was insane. That she needed to get back into her dress and get out of there and back home before she did anything else totally out of character.

But all of that had happened before Jake Cooper had lowered his head and taken her mouth, so purposefully and so expertly, with his own.

And suddenly she was on fire, and all she could do was try to match him, flame for flame.

She might not have taken Maria's suggestion to *have fun* seriously this afternoon, but she had every intention of following it to the letter right now. After all, when would she ever come across another guy like Jake, who had made her feel fluttery in her chest—and, all right, a damned sight lower—just from a first look?

Even after that horrid Silvio Delgado's *jungle woman*

jibe. In fact, Jake had been the one to turn it around and make her feel as though the work she did was the *only* thing he was interested in, in a room full of top-flight medical colleagues.

No, she wasn't about to give him reason to suddenly wonder what he was doing up here with her now, when he could be with someone a little more cultured. So she gave herself up to every last sensation. Dancing in the flames of the same scalding hot desire that had been licking at her ever since that first moment in the bar. But now they weren't merely licking at her, they were consuming her.

And Flávia never wanted the fire to die down. She lifted her hands and flattened them against the solid wall of his chest, revelling in the hard ridges and contours which seemed so opposed and yet perfectly paired to her soft palms.

It wasn't mere heat. It was scorching. Tearing right through her like a blaze through dry tinder. The slow drag of his mouth over hers, the decadent tease of his tongue, the gentle pull of his teeth on her plump lower lip.

She gave herself over to every second of it. Meeting him and matching him. When he was done, she felt almost bereft, but then he repeated it, a little faster this time, a little harder, a little naughtier.

And then again. Each time angling his head a different way, causing new sensations and leaving her begging for more. Over and over, as if he was every bit as lost in the moment, as incandescent, as she was.

It still wasn't enough. It should have scared her how much she wanted Jake, yet it didn't.

Instead, with every kiss she felt surer of herself, and of what she wanted, than ever before. He swept his hands up and down her spine, then to the sides, as though he was learning every contour. And taking his sweet time doing so. When she wasn't sure she could take any more, Flávia rolled onto the balls of her feet, lifting herself a fraction higher and pressing her body to his, moving a fraction closer. Wanting more but not knowing how to ask for it.

It was inexplicable.

She was hardly some untried virgin, but never had any of her few relationships ever made her feel this *urgent*, this *greedy*, this *wanton*. Not even Enrico. When Jake lifted up her arms to skim his fingers down her sides, her eyes locked with his and she revelled in the way his pupils darkened and his breathing sounded that little more ragged. Then he slowly, deliberately, lowered his head and took one up-turned nipple deep into the heat of his mouth. Not even moving the fabric of her bra aside to do so.

Sensations exploded through Flávia.

Her back arched and she let her head fall back, losing herself in the magic of it. The way he toyed with her, teased her, sucking on her nipple, then grazing his teeth over it—pain and pleasure rolled into one. At some point, she realised he had deftly removed her bra, because when he lifted his mouth, cool air swirled around her nipple moments before he drew tiny whorls with his tongue. And all Flávia could do was gasp and run her fingers though his hair in a silent plea for him never to stop.

When he did, it was only to turn his attentions to her other breast, and repeat the whole glorious process all over again, those sensations in her core winding more and more taut. Fraught with need.

She had no idea how long they stayed like that, lost as she was in the moment. But suddenly he was lifting her up to wrap her legs around his waist, to nestle her softness against the hardest part of him, and as she heard the soft moan escape her lips she wondered how much longer she could hold out.

If at all.

'Bed,' Jake commanded brusquely, as if reading her mind.

She nodded, even as he was already on the move. Lifting her up and carrying her across the room like some kind of infinitely romantic gesture, before depositing her on the bed. She realised then that she was wearing nothing more than a skimpy metallic black scrap of material, whilst he was still in his full tuxedo.

She ought to feel embarrassed. She wasn't the kind of woman who had been especially comfortable parading around in front of her—albeit it two—serious boyfriends in such a scanty bit of lace. Yet with Jake she felt bold. Even naughty.

'I feel you're a little overdressed,' she managed huskily.

He looked down as if he hadn't even realised, then cast that rich gaze over her, all over again.

'Perhaps that's something you should remedy.'

An instruction, a command. And she'd never been so happy to obey.

Sitting up, she reached forward and hooked her fingers into his waistband, tugging him forward, not that he put up much resistance, and concentrated on undoing each button of his shirt. Her fingers actually shaking with anticipation as she pushed the sides open.

My God, he is glorious.

Hard ridges and sculpted contours drew her hands, and Flávia imagined she could spend a whole lifetime acquainting herself with the ever-delicious delineation. And another tasting it. She dipped her head and ran her tongue over one defined line and sensations burst in her mouth.

Salt and fire, and everything in between.

Jake.

She wanted more. As he concentrated on shucking off his top half, Flávia dipped her head and she traced more of him, learning the relief of his chest with her mouth and her hands, moving lower. And lower again. Until she was at the top of the deep V that led her tantalisingly down until it disappeared below the waistband of his trousers.

Her hands were shaking even more as she tried to work the zip, but she was determined not to let him see it. Not to let him realise how little experience she actually had. She had heard the rumours about Jake Cooper, and whilst he wasn't exactly a playboy, she knew he'd had at least a couple of high-profile…*partners* over the years.

For one night only, she was going to have that same kind of fun.

Pushing his trousers down with renewed confidence, she cradled his straining boxers and finally released him from his material cage. Yet nothing had quite prepared her for precisely how *impressive* the man was.

So hard, so velvety and so very, very hot. She wanted to touch him, to feel him, to *taste* him. But before she could do any of it, he was taking a step back.

'I don't have any protection,' he gritted out as though it was all only just occurring to him.

'Sorry…' Her head was swimming, not quite following.

'Condoms,' he bit out. 'I don't have any.'

Later, she would consider that it was a good sign that he hadn't been prepared for her or anyone else that night. Later. But not in that moment.

'In my clutch.' The words surfaced hazily. 'Over there.'

His eyes flickered but he turned with a harsh, 'Don't move.'

Not that she had any intention of moving.

'Do you always go around carrying so many condoms with you?' he demanded a few moments later as he unfolded them from the little purse like a magician producing ream after ream of coloured silk.

She flushed. 'Does it matter?

'Call it male ego,' he quipped, but she was sure there was an edge to his tone.

'My sister put them there,' Flávia managed.

'Ah…' His face cleared and, however fanciful it seemed, she felt it was like the sun coming out on a grey day.

'She might have been a touch overenthusiastic.'

'Yeah, well—' he discarded his remaining clothes and approached the bed '—I, for one, am pretty grateful right now.'

Anything else she might have said was chased from her head as he reached down and took her bottom, pulling it towards him until she was lying on her back, her hips raised whilst he removed the triangle of lace. And then he was alongside her, his mouth catching hers, demanding, and imprinting.

The kind of kiss her sister had waxed lyrical over but that she herself had never—until now—actually believed existed. It made her whole body sing. Soar. And when his hand skimmed over her belly, everything clenched and fizzled inside her.

He took his time, just like before. Only, this time, Flávia didn't think she could wait. She already knew the muscled chest, and the corded neck. She had acquainted herself with those strong arms. But now she needed more.

So much more.

Reaching down between them she took hold of him, her fingers curling around his thickness. Surely, she had never felt anything so silken steel.

The man was incomparable.

'Slow down, *jungle woman*,' he teased, trailing kisses down her neck and to the sensitive hollow where she shivered with desire. But his voice was thick and, somehow, just like before, he made the name sound utterly sexy and not at all insulting when it dropped from his lips. 'I'm not sure I can hold out for long if you touch me like that.'

Flávia had no idea what took her over in that moment, yet suddenly she felt a boldness she'd never known before.

'That's what I'm counting on.'

A low, infinitely feral sound rumbled from his chest. Flávia felt it low in her belly. It pooled between her legs.

'Is that so?' he demanded gruffly, shifting position before she could answer.

Then his fingers were moving, travelling down her body. Over her stomach, and her lower abdomen, then lower still, until he was dancing long, clever fingers where the lace had recently covered, before dipping into her wet heat.

'Jake...' A whisper and an exaltation all at once. She arched her back, and moved against his hand.

'Patience,' he instructed, playing with her.

Teasing her entrance, slowly at first, like he had all night and he intended to take his time. She wanted to tell him she needed more, but the words didn't materialise. Instead she moved against him, letting him build the rhythm inside her. A little faster now, dipping in once. Twice. Then returning to play with the core of her need.

And all the while, his lips were still paying homage to her mouth, her neck, her breasts. Like an exquisite assault from every direction.

She wasn't sure when it went from fire building to a blaze. It was as though it had been glowing for so long that she hadn't realised how close she was to combusting. Like starting a fire in the bush from a couple of sticks and a fluff of wool. One moment it's merely smouldering, and the next moment it's bursting into flames.

A yearning rushed her. Flávia shifted and jerked, raising up to meet his hand, knowing he was catapulting her to the edge and helpless to do anything but let him. She slid her hand up and under the pillows above her head. She was close. So close. And it was the most carnal thing she'd ever known. Then he flicked his wrist and slid two fingers inside her without letting up the pressure of his thumb caressing the centre of her need.

Flávia shattered.

She heard herself cry out, felt her whole body react, tensing, releasing and then tingling. From the top of her head right down to her toes, which were actually curling into the down cover, which they hadn't even bothered to remove.

Who knew that wasn't just a myth? she thought in wonder as she floated somewhere out there where no one had ever taken her before. She had no idea how long she stayed there, but when she came back to herself, Jake had moved. Settled over her, but propped up so that he wasn't crushing her.

She wanted to say something, but she couldn't. She could only take her hands from above her head and wind them around his neck, pulling him closer again. Right up until she felt him right *there*. Hot and ready, the hardest part of him against the softest part of her.

'Ready, Flávia?' he muttered, and for the first time she realised quite how hard Jake was fighting to stay in control.

It made her feel good. More than good.

'I don't know,' she teased. 'You might have to give me a bit longer to recover.'

'You don't have any longer,' he growled, and whatever else she was going to say to tease him was torn from her mouth as he flexed against her, his blunt tip nudging at her. A plethora of emotions cascaded through her all over again.

As he slid inside her, slowly and carefully at first, giving her a chance to shift, to accommodate him, a tenseness coiled itself around her belly again. So many sensations that she couldn't begin to identify them.

He began to move faster then. Sliding in, then out. Then in, and out. Stoking the fire that she now realised had only been lying dormant. She could barely move, barely even breathe. All she could do was wrap her legs around him, her fingers biting into those strong shoulders, and match him, stroke for incredible stroke.

Faster and deeper. Until she was grazing her hands down his back to clutch at him, and pull him in deeper.

'Flávia…' he groaned her name, her unexpected action making him jerk and thrust that little bit harder.

And sending Flávia that bit closer to the edge.

She repeated it with the same effect. All that bright sensation so close now she could almost touch it.

'Don't stop,' she muttered, her hands gripping him tightly, her bottom raising up to meet him, to match him.

She heard the guttural groan as he slid his way home for the last time, sending her soaring just like before.

And this time, when she fell off the edge, Jake went with her.

CHAPTER FIVE

'LIGHTS, PLEASE,' instructed Jake Cooper.

The operating room went dark, almost eerily so, with only the glow of the large operating monitors lighting up the space. And then Jake shone the near-infrared light over his patient's mouth.

One solid area glowed a purplish hue, with a tiny purplish dot slightly to the side. His patient's squamous cell carcinoma.

'There's our villain,' Jake announced to the gallery of residents watching this surgery to learn.

Once his team had removed it, along with part of the patient's jaw, he would pass the surgery on to Krysta Simpson, for her team to start reconstructing a new jaw based off a titanium plate.

All in all, it would be a circa ten-hour, multidisciplinary operation, but if he was honest with himself, he was relieved to be able to concentrate on something other than Flávia Maura.

Memories of that night had haunted him all week, and only his surgeries—demonstrating his clinical trial for residents and esteemed colleagues alike—gave him something else for his focus. So much for his promise to himself of one night, and then his entire focus would be on his responsibility for Brady.

He couldn't get Flávia out of his head. He even dreamed about her.

It was insanity.

Ejecting the thoughts from his head, Jake focused on the patient in front of him. It was an operation he'd performed many times in the past, but still he never stopped respecting what could happen with any patient on that operating table.

'That smaller dot there, that's where the tumour has started to metastasise?' one of the residents noted via the intercom from the gallery.

'Right.' Jake nodded. 'Too small to show up on any MRIs or CTs pre-op, if we didn't have the fluorescent contrast agent to light it up, we wouldn't have known it was there. We'd have resected assuming margins, and then had to wait for the pathology to come back to tell us if those margins were clear. At best, we'd have taken more than we needed, leaving our patient here with more of his jaw missing. At worst, we'd have taken too little and left some tumour in there, and we'd have only found out when the cancer recurred.'

'So that's it?' someone else asked. 'That tumour dye shows up exactly where the SCC is, and if we take everything that glows, we've got it? No need for margins?'

'That, ladies and gents, is what we're in this clinical study to determine,' Jake agreed. 'But so far, it's looking good. Anybody know what the national figures are for positive resections following surgery in head and neck squamous cell carcinomas?'

The intercom clicked a few times and then a female voice spoke.

'I read it was somewhere between fifteen and thirty percent with poor outcomes, ultimately necessitating some form or another of additional therapy.'

'Gold star, that woman,' Jake confirmed. 'So to combat that, we take greater margins and leave the patient with more disfigurement leading to a lowering of quality of life. Now, hopefully, we won't need to. We can see exactly what we're doing.'

'And leave the oral and maxillofacial reconstruction team with more to play with?' the female added.

'Right. We'll be doing a segmental mandibulectomy with a modified radical neck dissection on the left side of the mandibular structure. The reconstruction team are intending to use a plate reconstruction, so our goal is to leave them as much as possible.'

'Osseointegrated dental implants?' someone asked.

'Again, that'll be up to the OMS team. However, in this case, resection will likely result in significant loss of mandibular support to the teeth—though with this dye showing us exactly where the tumour is, we'll be able to really keep that to a minimum. Nevertheless, I think we can expect to lose all but one, maybe two molars, and a couple of root stumps, so conventional dental solutions will be unfeasible.'

Jake worked steadily for hours, careful to take all the tumour but leave as much healthy tissue as he could, and ensuring he stayed away from any major nerves which, if damaged, could leave the patient with facial paralysis, and finally he was on the last bit, and Krysta and her team were entering the OR ready for handover.

'How's it going?' Krysta asked.

'It's gone well,' Jake confirmed. 'We're completing a type-L modified neck dissection. The patient has remained stable throughout and there have been no complications. I've concentrated on areas here, and here, which is where the contrast agent highlighted areas outside of the normal scans.'

'Nice,' Krysta approved.

'I've left as much of the ascending ramus and condyle as possible.'

'Excellent.' She nodded. 'That gives me more than I was expecting to work with.'

Running through the remaining points, Jake finished up his team's part of the operation and moved to clean up. If he was quick, he realised, he could probably catch Brady for lunch.

And if that was another means of occupying his attention and avoiding Flávia, then he pretended he didn't notice.

It was only once he found himself scanning the cafeteria that he realised he was looking for Flávia.

As he always did.

Everywhere he went in this place, it seemed that he was scanning for her, listening for her, disenchanted when he didn't see her. It was foolish. Added to that, it was dangerous. This wanting…*more*.

He never wanted more. Not from any woman.

He wouldn't have categorised himself as a playboy by any standards, but he never went in for long-term relationships. When did he ever have time? Even before, when he'd been a so-called carefree bachelor. And certainly not now that he had to be responsible for his nephew.

Yet he searched for Flávia, all the same. Like he wanted their one night together to be something that it wasn't.

It was insane.

He'd even tried telling himself that the unexpected intensity of the attraction was because, since he'd become sole guardian to Brady, he hadn't had any women in his personal life, at all. The poor kid had been through enough turmoil without having his uncle bringing random women home.

Yet the other night, he'd gone and booked a suite just so he could take Flávia, a virtual stranger, to bed.

As if he hadn't been able to help himself.

He gripped his cup, willing the memories away. This attraction had to stop now. For Brady's sake, if nothing else.

As if to consolidate the idea, his nephew chose that very

moment to walk through the cafeteria doors, but there were too many people milling around and Brady didn't see him. Jake stood, ready to wave, but then he saw his nephew stop dead, his attention clearly arrested by someone or something.

Standing resolutely, Jake picked up his coffee cup and strode across to the tray corral. He could still just about see Brady but now, to his surprise, the characteristically serious, silent nephew was chatting—somewhat animatedly. Jake watched, but it was next to impossible to spot people from this distance. Even so, his stomach dipped oddly when he caught sight of the back of a head sporting long, glossy waves just like Flávia's. He craned his neck for a better glimpse, but there were too many people and he still couldn't tell who the boy was talking to.

He was seeing ghosts, he reprimanded himself sharply. He'd been thinking about Flávia and so his imagination had conjured her up.

But he was here for Brady. Not her.

He would not just stay here, hoping that this woman would walk through the door any moment. He would attend her lecture, like every other doctor there using the summer programme as a chance to broaden their knowledge base and keep up to date. But other than that, he wasn't interested in seeing Flávia Maura again.

Then, tossing his rubbish into the bins, Jake weaved his way through the tables.

Flávia had been scanning through her lecture notes in the cafeteria when the young voice had penetrated her concentration.

'Did you know that the terms *venom*, *poison* and *toxin* aren't synonyms?'

She had looked up slowly, taking in a young kid with an English accent who was wearing cargo pants and *A Bug's*

Life tee, which probably explained his opening question. She had followed his gaze as it flickered onto her laptop case, the VenomSci logo emblazoned on the pristine black material, then she'd glanced back at him.

Even in that moment, her traitorous heart had begun to pound a little faster. Surely, there was no one else this kid could be but Jake's nephew? Which meant Jake couldn't be far behind. She had tried in vain to stop her eyes from darting around the room, bouncing off every wall and every person, as they looked for Jake.

She'd ignored the dip of her stomach when they finally confirmed what some intuitive part of her already knew— that he wasn't there. He couldn't be. Still, the hairs on her neck had stood up with some kind of awareness.

Time to calm down, she had remonstrated herself. *Seeing Jake's nephew here was pure coincidence, nothing more.*

Except that she'd known that was a lie. There was only one reason that she had frequented Paula's Café more times in the last week than she had probably used it in the last twelve months, and that reason was about six foot two, with dark hair, and almost as serious and earnest as the boy standing at her table.

However, it was the haunted expression which had poked its way into her, scraping at her. The brief story that Jake had told her about the boy's mother had echoed painfully around her chest. Oesophageal cancer. So sudden and unpredictable. How easily could that be Julianna or Marcie?

Deus, it didn't bear thinking about.

'As it happens, I do know the difference between poison and venom,' she had acknowledged gently. 'But why don't you tell me what you think?'

The boy—Brady, if she remembered Jake rightly—had dipped his head in acknowledgement, maintaining direct eye contact but without a hint of a smile. All business.

'Both poison and venom are toxins, but it's the method

of delivery that changes. Venom is injected whilst poison is secreted.'

He had delivered the facts quite animatedly, with such an intensity in his gaze that it had been like looking into a mirror to the past. For a moment, it had taken her quite aback.

Now, tugged back into the present, something slammed inside Flávia's chest. How much of her own childhood had she spent lost in knowledge, and facts, and learning, in a way that her peers simply hadn't understood? Greedily soaking up information and devouring books about anything and everything, but especially the natural world?

It had made for a rather lonely childhood, craving someone who would share her knowledge and her passion, but more often than not being thought of as a bit nerdy. Or, more likely, plain *weird*. Not least by her younger, social-butterfly sister, who had loved her but never understood how Flávia could have preferred ants over boys. Then again, if it hadn't been for Maria dragging her to every party and social event going, maybe she would have turned out a lot more…introverted than she actually felt. At least now, in social situations, she could fool people around into thinking she was more confident than was actually the case.

Something twisted in her chest, but she pushed it aside. She wasn't that weird kid any more. She'd come out the other side a long time ago and now her life was everything she could ever have dreamed it would be. An internationally respected, cutting-edge research scientist by day, and a loved and admired best aunt in the world to her two gloriously fun nieces by evening. The perfect life. But this poor kid still wouldn't be there for about another ten years or more.

If that was, indeed, his path. Folding her hands in her lap, she cocked her head to one side. How like the seven-year-old Flávia was this boy? Did he get adults dismissing him the same way that she used to? Would he respond to someone who treated him as more than just a kid, and could talk to him on his level?

'Nice. So, do you want to give me some examples?'

A sense of victory punched through her as she saw that closed expression relax a fraction. Then he edged closer to her.

'Bees, scorpions, spiders, ants, snakes—they all deliver toxins through their bite or sting, so that's *venom*. Rough-skinned newts, poison dart frogs, cane toads—all secrete, so they're poisonous. That's also why we say food *poisoning*, not food *venoming*.'

'I'm impressed.' She smiled widely. 'Okay, here's a bigger test. What about the Asian tiger snake?'

He narrowed his eyes.

'That's not a bigger test. It's venomous, like I said. Snakes inject through their bite.'

'Actually, as well as fangs to deliver venom, the Asian tiger snake has defensive glands on the back of its neck which deliver poison that it stores from eating poison toads, making it the only snake which is poisonous as well as venomous.'

It was a gamble, Flávia knew that. She wasn't intending to trap him or belittle him, although she knew other kids might have felt that way. But this kid was different, and she suspected that as long as she was feeding him more information, he wouldn't care about being wrong. He'd just store the knowledge for the future.

Still, she didn't realise she'd been holding her breath until the boy's eyes widened and he edged forward again.

'What else do you know that I don't?' he demanded, almost breathless with excitement.

'I'm willing to bet lots.' Flávia grinned, relieved when he smiled back. 'But first, how about we find who you're here with?'

She couldn't bring herself to say Jake, but when he

backed up almost imperceptibly, and his little face shuttered down, she could have kicked herself for not thinking faster.

'My mummy died last year.'

'I'm sorry, Brady. It is Brady, isn't it?'

He nodded.

'I know you're here with your uncle. I just meant, who is looking after you now? A hospital nurse?'

'Patricia,' he confirmed after a moment, jerking to an older woman paying for something at the counter. 'She's getting me a meal. Then Uncle Jake will meet me here.'

'Soon?'

'Whenever he finishes.' He shrugged, that sadness swirling around him again.

He might as well have slammed her in the chest. Flávia fought to breathe. It was all she could do to stay composed.

'I see,' she managed.

The silence moved around them, and then Brady narrowed his eyes—eyes which must have been identical to his mother's given how closely they resembled Jake's blue depths.

'Why do you work for a company called VenomSci? Do you use animal venom? Do you hurt them?'

It was the distraction she needed.

'Quite the opposite,' she assured him. 'I've worked with wasp venom, scorpion venom and snake venom. But whatever project I work on for pharmaceutical companies, my personal goal remains the same, and that's finding ways to protect and save as many animals as possible.'

He eyed her suspiciously.

'Why would I believe you?'

'I don't know. But I have a nine-year-old niece and a six-year-old niece, and we often go exploring the forest together to see what we can find, and which animals we can help.'

Although she never let the girls go near anything that could possibly harm them.

He scrutinised her for a little longer.

'Promise?'

'I promise.'

They eyed each other for a few moments, and she knew he was assessing her. Evaluating. Just the way that she would have done at that age.

'Brady? *Brady?* Why aren't you with Patricia? What are you doing here?'

It was the moment she told herself she'd been dreading. It took everything she had not to spin around in her chair, but instead she waited for him to draw level with her table.

'Jake.' She inclined her head as professionally as she could. 'I already checked where Patricia was, and she's right over there by the counter.'

'I was coming to sit down when we...' Brady paused, looking to her.

'Flávia,' she supplied helpfully.

'Flávia and I started taking about venom and poison.'

'Is that so?' Jake bit out, eyeing her as if she had somehow engineered the situation.

Evidently, he'd had no intention of seeking her out after their night together, and probably would have been more than happy if their paths hadn't crossed for the remainder of his stay in Brazil.

She told herself she didn't care, that she'd known the parameters of their...*encounter* the night of the party. But the way her throat was closing, and the shameful stinging behind her eyes, told her a different story.

Idiot that she was.

'How did you get talking, anyway?'

'Because she knows about nature, too.' The kid looked at his uncle as though the answer was surely obvious.

Clearly, Jake wasn't convinced.

'He spotted my laptop case.' She gestured to the bright logo. 'It caught his interest.'

'Ah…' Jake surveyed the case, and if he didn't actually roll his eyes, then he at least gave the impression of dismissal. 'That would have done it. He's obsessed with everything from ants to cheetahs. How they live, how they feed, how they defend themselves.'

'Fascinated,' Flávia corrected automatically, unable to help herself.

'Sorry?'

'He's *fascinated*. Not *obsessed*. There's a difference.'

It was like a mini stand-off, but Flávia couldn't bring herself to regret it. She told herself she was just looking out for the child. She suspected a part of her was also trying to help Jake make that connection he hadn't been able to bring himself to outright admit to her was lacking.

'The difference is called *hyperfocus*,' he told her, his tone clipped.

She glanced at Brady, and this time it was her turn to do a little assessing. He stared right back at her with intelligent—if sad—eyes, a slightly cheeky set to his mouth and a vaguely mutinous look to his stance.

She didn't see *hyperfocus*, or any other issue that she imagined people might have thrown at Jake over the past ten months. She just saw a bright little boy, grieving for his mother, possibly too bright for his own good, probably considered cheeky or disruptive in school and misunderstood by the adults around him.

She saw herself.

But where she'd had her father, always there to encourage her curiosity and teach her new experiences, she wasn't sure Brady had the same level of support. Though, it was clear that he had an uncle trying desperately to do his best.

She could shut her mouth and stay out of it, or she could try helping both Brady and Jake, all the while knowing that she risked Jake believing she was using his nephew to wedge herself into their lives after what had been, for all intents and purposes, a one-night stand.

Finally, decision made, she turned back to Jake.

'Maybe,' she answered coolly, even though her heart was now threatening to beat right out of her chest. Though not necessarily for the same reasons as before. 'But I don't think so.'

He could see the fury in Jake, in the tight set of his jaw, and the tiny pulse flickering in his neck, though he reined it in admirably.

'Brady,' he addressed his nephew in an eerily calm voice. 'Please join Patricia for a moment.'

'But I wanted to ask Flávia some more questions.' The boy frowned, apparently oblivious to Jake's anger.

'*Now*, Brady,' Jake instructed. 'Please.'

He waited until his nephew was an adequate distance away before he turned his gaze back to her. The fury in his gaze almost blistering her skin everywhere it fell, though regrettably not for the same reasons as the other night.

'Listen—'

'Not here,' he cut her off harshly, leaving her no choice but to grab her bag and stand.

No sooner had he done so than he took hold of her elbow—not roughly, but not with the tenderness of the other night, either—and ushered her out of the room, down a corridor and into the first unoccupied room he could.

And Flávia steeled herself for the inevitable onslaught.

'What the hell do you think you're playing at?'

CHAPTER SIX

HE COULD SEE the flinty look in Flávia's eyes as he challenged her. A part of him even admired her for it.

But not when she was pulling Brady into some game.

Rage coursed through him…and something else. Something it took him a while to recognise.

Disappointment, he realised darkly. He was disappointed in Flávia.

He couldn't explain why, since one night of sex hardly equated to a deep knowledge of another person, but that simply wasn't the way he would ever have expected Flávia to behave.

'I'm not playing at anything, Jake.' Her honey-hued eyes gleamed. 'I'm trying to look out for a little boy.'

'You believe that I'm *not*?' he barked.

'I don't believe I commented on you, whatsoever,' she answered evenly, though he could see the hectic racing of her pulse at her neck.

'You don't know the first thing about Brady, and yet you feel you have the right to judge him. Why? Because we slept together once? I have news for you, Flávia—I have had a fair few one-night stands in my life, and they tried many things to draw more of a relationship out of it, but none of them acted so low as to bring a seven-year-old boy into it.'

He'd intended to throw the verbal punch, but when it hit home, when she recoiled, he felt...*remorse. Regret.*

Then, to his surprise, she straightened herself and faced him boldly.

'I dare say that's because you only took responsibility for Brady ten months ago. If he'd been around when those kinds of women had tried to ingratiate themselves into your life, then I imagine some of them might have thought he was fair game.'

He inhaled sharply but then, astonishingly, she held her hand up to silence him.

'I, however, do not think he's *fair game.* But for what it's worth, I know more about boys like Brady than you might think.'

'Is that so?'

'There's something special about Brady.' She smiled, a soft smile which inexplicably made Jake feel as though he was intruding on her personal memories. 'And I'm willing to bet that it doesn't fit with whatever you've been told about him being a difficult kid in school. I think you know it, too.'

Jake faltered. Her words made more sense than he'd have liked to admit. Before he could answer, she had started talking again.

'And, for the record, I have no interest in drawing out *anything* with you.'

She was lying. He knew it as surely as he knew his own name. He knew it in the way her pupils dilated when she looked at him, the way her pulse still raced and the way her cheeks flushed slightly.

And he knew it in the way his entire body reacted to her.

One night hadn't sated the extraordinary attraction between them. If anything, it had only made their chemistry stronger.

It was baffling. Yet here he was, drawn in, compelled

to hear whatever else Flávia had to say. Though, whether
it was for Brady's sake, or simply his own selfish desire to
prolong any contact with her, Jake couldn't be sure.

'What do you think you know about kids like Brady?'
He gritted his teeth. 'Or is it just because he happens to
have this damned obsession with venom, or snakes, or
whatever?'

She actually snorted at him—even if he heard a faint
shake behind the sound.

'Sorry—a *fascination*,' he corrected, remembering her
earlier words. 'As if it makes that much difference.'

She sucked in a breath, composing herself.

'It does make a difference,' she insisted. 'Listen, I can
see that you care for your nephew, and that you're trying to
do your best in a really horrible situation. But labels matter. Attitudes matter. And how you help Brady matters.'

'I appreciate your attempt to help…' He really wanted to
say something else, but decided it wasn't the best idea. Her
words echoed Oz's only too closely, if a little more forth-
rightly, and it hit him again how little he knew about kids—
any kids—but especially about his little nephew. 'But you
really don't know what you're talking about.'

'I *know*.' She scowled.

'How?' he pressed, uncertain why it mattered. Was he
asking for Brady? Or was there a part of him that was hungry to know Flávia better? 'How do you know?'

'It isn't relevant.'

He could feel his patience fraying and snagging at the
edges. He just wasn't sure why.

'When you're standing here telling me I'm not doing the
best thing for my nephew, and that you believe the things
I've been told are wrong, believe me, it matters. So, I'll ask
you one more time, Flávia—how do you know?'

She glared at him, her teeth bared in something of a

snarl, and he got the sense that she wanted something said without actually wanting to utter the words.

Just when he thought she was going to concede the argument, or discussion, or whatever it was that they were even having, she squared up to him and spoke.

'Because I *was* a Brady.'

The words hung there, between them, shimmering like a curtain.

'What do you mean, *you were a Brady*? What is *a Brady*? He's just a normal kid retreating into a subject that he's decided has caught his interest, because his mother is dead.'

He nearly choked on the words. Nearly choked on the guilt that had followed him around like a dark cloud ever since he'd failed to save his sister's life.

'I don't think so.' She shook her head.

'Then what?'

'I don't think it's *hyperfocus*, ADD, ADHD or whatever else schoolteachers, doctors, other professionals may have told you—and don't get me wrong, I know those conditions are very real for some kids, but not for Brady.'

'So what, in your professional opinion, is it?'

He heard the edge of sarcasm in his tone, just as he heard the edge of desperation and hope.

'It's nothing.' She shrugged. 'At least, not like you're thinking. But you don't have to take my word for it. How about when you have a free moment today, maybe between operations, you bring him to VenomSci's visitor centre and we'll find out?'

'Music, please,' Jake requested, making the first incision as the first song on his playlist filled the operating room.

At least with this, his first teaching operation instead of just lecture room talks and video presentations, he finally had something to really get his teeth into, and switch his head off from Silvio Delgado's most recent shenanigans.

And from more run-ins with Flávia.

Why the heck had he gone at her so hard in the cafeteria? He could pretend it had been about protecting Brady, but he knew that wasn't it.

No, he'd been making a point of proving to her—and, more pertinently, himself—that their night together had been a one-off. That he harboured no lingering desires.

He knew it was a lie. Still, he wasn't certain how taking Brady to VenomSci's visitor centre was designed to help, but there was a part of him which welcomed the opportunity just to change the dialogue between them.

'I realise you've been thrown in at the deep end on this case and haven't had a chance to do surgical rounds on the patients in my clinical trial.' He glanced up at the new surgical intern, after a while. 'But it will be a great learning opportunity for you. So talk me through what you *do* know about this patient.'

It wasn't the intern's fault that Delgado had stirred things up by claiming the intern, who had been shadowing Jake for the past week, for a surgery of his own this afternoon. Typical Delgado, still smarting from Jake's perceived snub at the Welcome Gala, and trying to stamp his authority all over the hospital.

'The patient is a thirty-five-year-old female. She has *dermatofibrosarcoma protuberans*—a rare type of soft-tissue sarcoma developing in the deep layers of the skin.'

'So how would you normally expect to operate on the patient?' Jake asked, his eyes on the patient and the image on the monitors.

'Resect the tumour by cutting a two-centre margin around the sarcoma. If they come back negative, then you've cleared the tumour and there's a very low chance that the cancer should return.'

'Good,' Jake confirmed, continuing his work until he was satisfied. 'Now what we're actually going to do is this...lights, please.'

As the OR went dark, the familiar glow could be seen on the patient's body. As Jake had anticipated, the dye showed the sarcoma to clearly be larger than images had been able to identify, reaching out in multiple directions and travelling from the dermis, quite deeply down.

'So there it is.'

The intern peered in.

'It's like our own personal markers,' he breathed.

'Right. No guesswork needed. No taking healthy tissue unnecessarily as part of the margins. But more significantly, no inadvertently leaving behind unidentified tumour, thinking that we've actually got it all. DFSP is one of those sarcomas where local recurrence is particularly common if the resection is incomplete.'

'So no intraoperative freezing to cut sections for biopsy?'

'We'll still do that as we resect the tumour, then we'll close with a skin graft, and follow up with vacuum sealing negative pressure drainage.'

Flávia watched Jake usher Brady through the doors of the centre and told herself that she didn't really feel her pulse hammering through her veins like air in the old radiator system of her first city apartment.

Especially pretending that she didn't feel it pulsing at her neck, her nipples, her core.

Part of her hadn't really thought he'd come, though she'd wanted him to.

For the kid's sake, she reminded herself hastily.

But she plastered a smile on her face and crossed the room.

'Jake, Brady, I'm so glad you came. This way, please.'

'What is it you want to prove?' Jake muttered as they followed her through the centre and to the area she wanted them to see.

But Flávia was already paying attention to Brady, at the way his eyes widened, beamed and then focused as he glanced around the space. A Ferris wheel spun slowly, with a projection behind, showing different rainforest animals and their habitats and prey. There was an interactive area with knowledge-based quizzes, games showing mimicry in nature and challenging the player to tell one from the other and an arcade-style machine for the life cycle of a butterfly.

And Brady was utterly fascinated.

'What exactly is the point of this?' Jake demanded after ten minutes or so.

'Give it time and you'll find out,' she instructed him. 'Now, go to the gallery over there, get a coffee, sit down and just watch.'

She could feel his eyes boring into her as she deliberately turned her back on him, and the barely suppressed fury. Yet he obeyed. Clearly, despite the way he had presented the facts in the past, his nephew meant more to him than just a responsibility his sister had left on him.

Flávia filed that away for later.

Then, she watched as Brady made his way into the interactive area, taking in each game and experiment and weighing each of them up as he decided which one to look at first. Evidently torn.

'This one is all about mimicry in nature.' She tried to help him, selecting one of the games and taking a few steps towards it, to see if Brady followed her. 'Do you recognise any of them?'

He practically skipped behind her.

'That pair is a viceroy butterfly and a monarch butterfly—the viceroy mimics the monarch, which tastes horrible to predators because of its milkweed diet as a caterpillar.

That pair is a bushveld lizard and an oogpister beetle, and the beetle tastes horrible to predators because of the formic acid due to its diet of army ants. And that pair is a wasp spider and a wasp, which it kind of self-explanatory.'

'Good.' Flávia nodded. 'Although the viceroy and monarch butterflies are now thought to show mutual mimicry, as the viceroy can release its own toxins when stressed, which makes it equally unpalatable to predators.'

'Really?' Brady stared at her in wonder.

'Sure. Look, if you press that button you can start the game and learn more.'

The boy didn't need any more encouragement, and Flávia backed off to let him have his head.

For over an hour she accompanied him around the room, letting him choose what to try next, only giving guidance to information when Brady invited it. Nonetheless, it was a good hour later before he finally showed signs of becoming saturated, and she called him for a short break, watching as he enjoyed his slushie, his eyes still roaming the room, from the activities he'd enjoyed the most to those he evidently still wanted to try.

And then, unexpectedly, he turned his serious eyes on her.

'Are you Uncle Jake's girlfriend?'

'I…no.' Flávia fought against getting flustered. 'I'm just a colleague.'

'Oh.'

There was no mistaking the disappointment in his tone, and despite everything in her screaming to leave it alone, Flávia couldn't help herself.

'Does your uncle have lots of girlfriends, then?'

'No.' Brady took another sip of his drink. 'Mummy told me that he might do, before she died. But he hasn't. Not until you.'

He was so calm, so collected, but Flávia hadn't missed

the way he'd steeled himself before he'd spoken. Jake had told her that Brady didn't seem to want to grieve at all for his mother, but she suspected that wasn't right.

'You must miss your mummy a lot.'

The little boy stopped drinking. He stared at his glass. 'I miss her all the time.'

'Do you talk about her, with your uncle?' she asked quietly, even though she already knew what Jake had told her. 'No.'

'Why not?' she pressed gently.

'I think it makes him sad.' He sucked in a breath. 'It makes me sad, too, sometimes. But it also makes me happy to remember her. I don't think it makes Uncle Jake happy to remember Mummy. I think he would prefer to forget her.'

Her heart almost broke for the little boy. Brady *did* grieve for his mother. He just held it in, keeping it away from Jake because he didn't want to hurt his uncle. The way she had done with her father when her mother had walked out on the family.

Only, she'd been lucky. She'd had her sister to talk to.

'Oh, Brady, I don't think that's true. I think your uncle would hate to know you felt you couldn't talk about your mummy to him. I don't think he'd want you to forget her.'

'I won't forget her. I have a memory box. Mummy and I made it together when I was a kid.'

'Does it have photos?'

She didn't like to point out that, at seven years old, he still was a kid.

'Lots and lots of photos.' He nodded. 'And flowers we picked on picnics, the programme for a football game we went to, cinema tickets, museum tickets, tickets to our favourite film…' He trailed off. 'It's in England, though. So I can't show you.'

'And you've never shown your uncle?'

'No, but I nearly showed Oz once.'

'Who's Oz?'

'He's Uncle Jake's best friend. He's kinda cool and he *does* have a lot of girlfriends. I talk to him about Mummy sometimes, but not always. I don't want Uncle Jake to hear and be upset.'

'What about you? Do you have a best friend? In school, maybe?'

'Not really.' He shook his head. 'I did have one at my old school, but I had to leave it because Uncle Jake works in London, and they're not as friendly in my new school. Sometimes they crawl under the table when the teacher is out of the room and slap my legs. And they play games I don't know, or won't let me join in because in my old school we had different rules. I bet you had a lot of best friends when you were in school.'

'I'll let you into a little secret,' Flávia whispered, wishing with every fibre of her being that she could haul the little boy into her arms and cuddle all his unhappiness away. But she couldn't bring back his mum, and that was the one thing he would really want. 'I didn't have many friends in school, either.'

'So, what did you do?'

'I was lucky. I had my sister,' she admitted. 'And when I came home I had *papai* and *vovô*. My dad and my grand-dad.'

'I have a granddad. And a grandma. But I only met them once. Mummy didn't like them. She said that they weren't unkind but that they were very cold, and they didn't know how to show love. She told me that was why she wanted me to live with Uncle Jake.'

'Because he knew how to show love?' Flávia managed, her heart breaking all over again.

'She said he could learn, but my granddad and grandma never could. She said Uncle Jake was a good brother when they were little, they had just gone different ways when they grew older. She told me it was going to be my job to teach him how to love. Because she thought he could, he just doesn't know how to. But I don't know how to teach him.' He looked up at her abruptly, his eyes swimming. 'He isn't like Mummy and I don't know what I'm supposed to do.'

She glanced up to where Jake was in the gallery, but he wasn't there. Hoping against hope he was on his way down, Flávia didn't think twice. She moved around the table, her arms going around the tiny, shaking body, her mouth pressed to his head, her voice low and soothing. And if it was a little choked up, she prayed that Brady couldn't tell.

'You're not supposed to do anything, sweetheart. You're doing everything right, trust me. I know your uncle loves you, very much. I just don't think he knows how to show it, but I think you can teach him. Just like your mummy believed you could.'

'You have to help me,' he whispered fiercely.

She wasn't sure that she was the best person to teach anybody about love. Sure, she loved her family with everything she had, but she didn't know how to love anybody else. Hadn't Enrico taught her that much? Hadn't he pointed out how selfish she was when he called off their engagement? How wrong she was for being unwilling to sacrifice the dangers of her career for a life with him?

He'd made her choose between risking her life with her deadly snakes, and marrying him and having a family. And she'd wished she could choose him. She'd wished she could be the kind of person who would *want* to choose love.

But she'd had to accept the fact that she wasn't that kind of person. When it had come down to it, she'd been afraid that she would end up resenting him for making the ultimatum and so, in the end, she'd chosen her snakes.

So how was she the right kind of person to help Brady teach Jake *anything* about self-sacrificing love?

Besides, there was no question that Jake would hate her inserting herself into their lives. Into *his* life.

But how could she refuse when Brady was asking so desperately? When he was clinging to her as though she was his life raft in his own personal storm? When she could feel his wet tears soaking into her cotton tee?

'It's okay, sweetheart. I'll help you as much as I can.'

CHAPTER SEVEN

JAKE HAMMERED THE punchbag, over and over and over again. Anything to get rid of this suffocating emotion which had come over him in that visitor centre when he'd watched Flávia with his nephew. When he'd heard Brady taking to her, spilling his heart to her, connecting with her, in a way Brady hadn't done, even once, in their ten months together.

He'd left the gallery partway through Brady's confession, intent on coming in and setting the record straight. Telling his nephew that he would never have avoided conversation about Helen if he'd realised that Brady wanted to talk about his mother.

But as he'd stood in the doorway and watched Flávia cradle the little boy in her arms, he had frozen. A thousand self-recriminations chasing through his head.

What the hell did he even say to the boy?

The simple fact was that he should have *known* that Brady would want—*need*—to talk about his mother. He hadn't avoided the topic purely out of respect for Brady's space—the kid was only seven. *No*, he'd used that as an excuse to help *himself* avoid conversation which might include things as complicated, as *icky*, as feelings.

Helen had been right in that their own parents hadn't prepared them for or taught them about love. But she had been wrong thinking that he had the capacity to learn it now.

So what use was he to Brady?

He, who had never failed at anything in his life before?

And so, he'd stood there at the door, watching a relative stranger give his nephew the kind of love and comfort he himself had no idea how to show. He'd tried to force his legs to move, to carry him inside, to say any one of the caring things that tripped easily off his tongue when dealing with frightened cancer patients and their even more terrified families. But his body and brain had refused to work. He'd been immobile. Numb. Until suddenly, he'd found himself moving again. Only, he hadn't been heading into the room with his nephew; instead, he'd been halfway across the hospital grounds, calling Patricia to let her know where to collect Brady for their usual afternoon session, whilst he'd thrown himself into his next operation.

Ironic how residents and colleagues thanked him for his quiet, efficient teaching style, whilst the one person he couldn't teach, or even talk to, was a seven-year-old kid who needed him most.

And so, after the operation, he'd wound up here, in the gym complex within the hospital guest accommodations. People were out there in the main area, on treadmills, or rowing machines, or whatever, but in this small side room, with the boxing equipment, he felt as though he was in his own little world. He could belt seven shades out of a punch-bag and hope to hell he could simultaneously beat some sense into himself.

He kept seeing Flávia's face, hearing her words, but it wasn't her whom he was mad with. It was himself. And his own inabilities.

Of all the people with whom to have left her infinitely precious son, Helen had chosen him. Not for the first time, Jake seriously doubted the rationale of his sister's decision.

Who would ever have considered him, so famously

detached for all his life, to take up the role of a surrogate father?

Surely, even his parents—Brady's grandparents—would have been a better choice?

In spite of everything.

Jake slammed his gloved fists into the bag again.

He was going to mess it all up. Mess Brady up. He didn't have a clue how to care for the boy properly; today had taught him that much. He'd been too quick to accept all the explanations that people had given him. Whether it was to blame Brady's wild actions on the fact that his mother had died ten months ago, or to blame his refusal to communicate with others on a genuine physical and mental inability to do so.

Flávia had come along, and in one afternoon she'd turned all of that on its head.

She'd shown him a bright, engaged and engaging seven-year-old. A *normal* kid who was obviously grieving over the death of his mother, but who wasn't irreparably damaged.

She had seen all that. And he'd seen nothing. So he had to ask himself if that would still be the case in another year—in six months, even—of Brady being in his care.

Again and again, he slammed his fists into the bag. But none of it did any good. None of it changed anything. Until, suddenly something lifted. And he knew, in that instant, that he was no longer alone. Flávia had walked into the gym.

Jake stopped. Not turning around. Just waiting.

'So this is where you went.'

She didn't even bother to disguise the accusation in her voice and he didn't blame her. Even as he lied.

'I had a teaching operation to get to,' he said over his shoulder, still not turning.

'You heard our conversation, didn't you.' It was phrased

as a question but it was more of a statement. 'From the gallery.'

He exhaled deeply.

'I heard most of it.'

'You heard him say that he never talked about his mother because he was upset that it hurt you too much.'

The admission had walloped into him hard enough when he'd heard it come out of his nephew's mouth. Coming out of Flávia's mouth, it lacerated just as much.

'I heard,' he managed thickly.

'And?'

'*And?*' he managed incredulously, finally turning around.

'Yes.' She gazed at him evenly. 'And…?'

'How do you think it feels?' he growled.

'Why don't you try telling me?'

All of a sudden he realised what she was doing. He snorted. Loudly.

'You really think me telling you how guilty, how bad, I feel will suddenly put me in touch with feelings we both know I don't have?'

'Don't you think it might be a start?' she challenged. And suddenly, he couldn't argue with her.

Or maybe you don't want *to argue with her?*

'Fine,' he shot at her. 'I feel like crap. I just had to listen to my seven-year-old nephew say that he has been hiding a box of memories of his mummy because he was trying to protect me. When *I'm* the one who is supposed to be protecting *him*.'

'So talk to him about it.'

'You don't think I've tried? I can't—I think that much should be obvious to you by now.'

'Didn't your parents teach you never to believe in that word *can't*?'

'My parents didn't teach me much at all. They expected

the private school Helen and I attended to do that. But sure, I never believed in that word up to ten months ago, only now I do. If you hadn't been there today, I still wouldn't know any of those things he said. So, I can't talk to Brady. I don't know how to.'

'Then learn,' she bit out. 'You're bright—heck, you're a top oncologist. You can learn if you want to, and that little boy needs you to learn. He needs you to take care of him.'

'And I will. Materially, anyway.'

She snorted, throwing her hands up in the air.

'He needs more than that. He needs your love, Jake.'

'And I can't do that. Helen knew that, but she entrusted Brady to me, anyway.'

'She also believed in you enough to think that you could learn.'

'She was wrong.'

'Is this because of your parents? Is what Brady said about them true?'

He didn't want to answer her—it wasn't any of her business. But the closer Flávia got, the more she pushed, the less wound up he seemed to feel. She had an uncanny knack of highlighting his shortcomings, yet simultaneously make him feel as though she could help solve them.

It made no sense.

'They did their duty by us. Neither Helen nor I were ever hurt or mistreated by them.'

'That's basically what Brady said. But it doesn't fully answer the question, does it?'

'It isn't relevant,' he deflected.

'We both know that it is. Unless you're happy with your relationship with your nephew, that is. And we both know that you aren't.'

'Well, talking about it isn't going to change that, is it?'

Jake didn't know what he expected her to say, but it wasn't what she came out with.

'You're right. I can't *tell* you how to treat Brady, how to connect with him. But maybe I can show you.'

'Show me?' he echoed sceptically.

'He loves animals, and the natural world. Why not let me take you both into the rainforest for a day or two? Doing something new like that, something he loves but with which he has no residual memories of his mother, might help the two of you connect. Build some memories of your own.'

'I don't think so.' The refusal was out before he'd even engaged his brain.

'Why not? Brady would love it!'

Jake opened his mouth to reply, but couldn't bring himself to tell her that he'd heard the rumours about the way she risked her life. He didn't want to say that he was worried she would risk Brady's.

He found he didn't want to hurt her.

So what did that say?

'I'm not exactly an authority on the rainforest. I wouldn't know how to keep myself safe, so how can I keep a seven-year-old safe?'

She wrinkled her nose and, without warning, looked awkward, and he would have given anything to know what she was thinking in that instant.

'Then why not try smaller?' she suggested after a moment.

'Smaller?'

'My sister is having a barbecue at the weekend. There'll be lots of people there, but especially my family. My nieces. Brady said he didn't have many friends at his new school and I wonder how much is Brady's lack of confidence. Julianna and Marcie are sweet, and funny, and friendly. They would love Brady, and you can help him to get out of himself, and start building new, positive experiences with you. It might even take some of the pressure off you so that you can find a way to let the kid in.'

'You're inviting me to a family barbecue?'

She huffed as though she was irritated, but he could see her level of discomfort grow.

'From everything I said, *that*'s the point you're hung up on?'

'I'm just trying to establish exactly what it is you're suggesting.'

'I'm trying to help your nephew,' she snapped, a little too tightly.

He should refuse. They'd had a one-night stand; he wasn't looking to make some kind of relationship out of it. And yet, the idea of going was more appealing than it ought to be.

'I'm not using Brady to try to score points with you,' she added, bristling.

'I know,' he replied, and the odd thing was that he did know.

The more worrying point was that he found he was slightly disappointed that she wasn't looking for some kind of excuse, though.

As Jake leaned against the wall, the cool of the concrete seeping through to his shoulder, and watched Brady trailing happily around the garden with Flávia's nieces, Julianna and Marcie, it wasn't all that hard to admit that Flávia had been right.

Watching Brady relax, and gain acceptance with his peers, did somehow help him to feel more relaxed. Less pressured. And all the trio were doing was wandering around the garden, their heads pressed tightly together.

Brady would listen avidly as they taught him the Portuguese names of different plants and insects, then he would teach the girls the Latin names where he knew them. Otherwise, all three children would huddle around the phone he had lent them as they looked up the missing, vital information.

Emotions tumbled through him, almost too fast to separate them, but for the first time he was beginning to think he could see a way to connect with his nephew. At long last. He sighed to himself. It was a complicated business, looking after a child. The struggles he'd had with Brady these past ten months had given him a new appreciation for all his sister had contended with, all these years as a single mother. And it augmented his sense of guilt that he should have reached out to her more over the past few years.

Was it self-deceptive to think if he had done that, Helen might still be alive today?

Possibly. But it didn't stop the thought from lurking there, in the back of his head.

'He looks happy.'

Jake turned at the sound of Maria's voice. Her voice was so similar to Flávia's, with basically identical intonations and emphases, and yet even from a distance he knew instantly who was talking in any given conversation. As though his whole being was programmed to tune into Flávia and no one else.

Already.

Which might have sounded alarm bells if he hadn't pretended to ignore it.

'Yes, he does.' Jake turned back to watch his nephew. 'Thanks again for inviting us here. I know Patricia does her best to entertain him, but it's not the same.'

With a soft smile, Maria leaned on the concrete pillar opposite his and took a sip of wine.

'I don't doubt it. And, as for the invitation, that was all Livvy,' she confessed, and he loved the affection in the nickname Maria had for her sister.

The woman paused as though thinking twice about something, then seemed to decide to say it, anyway.

'I think Brady reminds her of herself.'

Jake frowned.

'She said something like that before, but I didn't understand it.'

He didn't realise he was waiting, almost on edge, hoping for more than this unexpected scrap of information relating to Flávia, until Maria shrugged almost dismissively.

'It's hard to describe. It isn't anything I could put my finger on, just the little things. The things that make her stand out from the average person now were the things which made it hard for her to make friends in school. I suspect you know what I mean, though.'

It didn't even begin to answer all the questions he realised he had about Flávia. But he told himself that was no bad thing. He shouldn't care, anyway. That one night had been…extraordinary. To match the unique Flávia. But it had to remain a one-off. It couldn't happen again.

For Brady's sake, he wouldn't allow it.

Just for Brady? a voice needled. But Jake ignored it.

'That said,' Maria continued, 'I don't see him having any trouble with my girls.'

'No, they're getting along really well,' he acknowledged, surprised. 'I think coming here has been the best move I could have made for Brady.'

'I take it you didn't want to?' Maria asked. 'Livvy strong-armed you?'

'Maybe a little.' Although a part of him had been only too happy to let her. 'Turns out she was right, though.'

'Yeah, she has a maddening ability to do that.' The quiet laugh filled the air around them. So like Flávia's, and yet it didn't crawl inside him the way her laughter did. As though it was filling him from the inside out.

'Was she always so maddening?' he asked.

'You'd better believe it.' Maria laughed. 'The scrapes I had to get her out of when we were kids. She was so intolerant of others, saying exactly what she thought with no filter. Papai told me that it was my role to be her protector and so I did. She never thanked me for it.'

'I bet.'

He was soaking up the information with a thirst that shouldn't quite fit, but he couldn't stop himself. He wanted to know more about Flávia. As if it could somehow sate that ache inside him.

The...*yearning* he hadn't been able to quench ever since that night in his suite.

'Brady gets into fights in school,' he made himself say, as if reminding himself why he was supposed to be at Flávia's family's house in the first place. 'I thought it was a result of the trauma he has gone through with his mother's death, and having to move schools, and be in London with me. But it turns out he always had some problems, even at his old school. Nothing serious, you understand. And it isn't as though he can't make any friends.'

'He's just intolerant of so-called *idiots* in his class?' Maria guessed. 'Those who don't want to learn and so disrupt the class?'

'To the extent where he stands up and tries to give them punishments, as though he's the teacher.'

Maria threw her head back and emitted a happy, infectious laugh.

'Yeah, that's just like Livvy.'

'She offered to take Brady into the rainforest, you know.' The words were out before Jake could second-guess himself. 'With me, of course.'

'I think Brady would really like that.'

'I know.'

'But...?' Maria prompted lightly when he didn't elaborate. 'You clearly have reservations.'

Jake stared across the garden. This was arguably dangerous ground; he risked offending Maria, and ultimately

Flávia. But he had to ask. This was potentially his nephew's safety at stake.

'I've heard the stories—' he pulled a face '—that Flávia can be reckless.'

'I see.'

'I don't like rumours. But if it's true that she spent a year handling vipers even when she knew there wasn't enough antivenom on hand in the event that she got bitten, how can it be responsible of me to let her take us into that kind of environment?'

He didn't realise how badly he'd wanted to hear Maria laugh and declare it to be absolute rubbish until she stayed silent, the air thickening around them with every passing moment.

Suddenly, his shoulder felt like a block of ice, frozen tightly to the cold, concrete pillar. He, who was rarely wrong about anything in his life, had never wished he could be more wrong than he did in this instant.

'So it's also true that she ended up getting bitten?'

The silence seemed to grow heavier somehow. And louder. Or perhaps that was just his own blood, thundering through his veins.

And then, at last, Maria spoke.

'You really should speak to Livvy about that.'

Silence weaved around him for a moment. Then he offered a tight nod.

'I'm the closest thing Brady has to a father right now. And you have two kids of your own. So I'm asking you.'

Another beat. Then Maria scrunched up her face.

'I can tell you this,' she told him firmly. 'My sister is passionate, and focused, and driven. And maybe she does take occasional risks when it comes to her own life out there. But she has never, *ever* taken a risk with someone else's life.'

'I don't know that it helps,' Jake began, finding he had to fight to try to get his head around Maria's words.

'Then maybe this will. I know what Livvy does can be dangerous. A matter of life and death, even. And sometimes I do look out at the jungle when I know she's in there, wondering if she's going to come back safely. But I've never once felt that way when she's been out there with one of my girls.'

'She takes Julianna and Marcie?'

'She does,' Maria declared. 'She and Papai have taken the girls out there at least twice this past year. And on those occasions, I never looked out over that rainforest and wondered if they were okay. Because I knew that she would take care of my daughters in a way she never thinks to take care of herself.'

'I see.' He nodded slowly. 'I just didn't think of it that way. Flávia told me that she was *the fun aunt*. I guess I assumed that also meant...'

'That she wasn't entirely responsible with them?'

He eyed her sharply but there was no judgement in Maria's expression.

'I suppose.'

'I understand why,' she continued. 'But no, that isn't what Livvy is like at all. That's what Enrico couldn't seem to get his head around.'

'Enrico?'

'Her ex-fiancé.' Maria rolled her eyes. 'Idiot man.'

It was irrational. And insane. But jealousy swept through him like a tsunami, and even though he tried to pull himself up, it was too late. He'd waded in too deep and now he couldn't get out.

'Who's an idiot man?'

They both swung around at the sound of Flávia's voice.

'Boy, do you both look guilty.' She tried for a laugh when they didn't answer. 'Never mind. You don't have to tell me.'

'I wasn't going to.' Maria laughed at last as she turned around to leave, dropping a kiss on her sister's cheek as she did so. 'I think I'll leave you to it while I go and find my husband.'

'Luis has his chef's cap on. He looks set for the night.'

'Great. That means I can grab another wine and find somewhere else to hide before he drags me in to help him.'

'Yeah, good luck with that,' joked Flávia, watching her sister go.

Just as Jake, in turn, was watching Flávia.

As though he had no choice in it. Because he seemed to have very little control over himself when it came to Flávia Maura.

And then they were alone, and he found himself fighting some inexplicably primal urge to grab and kiss her, and make her his—over and over—when she started to speak.

CHAPTER EIGHT

'WHY WERE YOU talking about Enrico?' she asked carefully.

'You heard that, huh?'

If she'd hoped to decipher anything from his tone, then she realised she was out of luck. She had to force herself to keep her own voice deliberately even.

'I heard Maria tell you he was my ex-fiancé.'

'Was it recent?'

Was he asking out of simple curiosity? Or something more?

'We broke up two years ago.' She shrugged. 'Dated for eight years before that.'

He cocked one eyebrow.

'And since then…?'

'There's been no one but you,' she confirmed, her eyes locked with his, almost daring him to comment.

But he didn't.

'How did it end?'

She scowled at him like it was none of his business. Yet she answered him, anyway. It was like a compulsion. He'd asked and she had to answer. Though she'd never talked about Enrico to anyone but her family.

Then again, she'd been experiencing a plethora of firsts ever since Jake had approached her at that Welcome Gala.

'He gave me an ultimatum. Him or the sanctuary.'

'You chose your snakes,' he guessed.

'I shouldn't have had to choose.' She frowned, willing him to understand. As though his opinion mattered to her. 'There was no need.'

'He cared about you. He didn't want you to get bitten again. I can see where your ex was coming from.'

He sounded almost...*angry* about it. But that didn't make sense.

'I've been bitten plenty of times over the years.' She narrowed her eyes. 'It's a hazard of my career.'

'Maybe, but have you always risked a bite when there's been no antivenom on hand?'

She watched him in silence, not sure why he sounded so accusatory.

'It happened years ago,' she spoke at last.

'Sorry?'

'The incident people talk about. It happened years ago,' she repeated, as coolly and calmly as she could. 'There *were* actually some vials of antivenom, though admittedly not enough.

'The government had received a complaint from some high-ranking official whose condo backed onto the sanctuary's land.' She leaned sideways and flopped her shoulder against the concrete pillar opposite his. 'I believe the guy wanted to build an extension, but he couldn't build that close to his boundary so he decided the solution was to acquire sanctuary land. But the sanctuary is struggling for more land as it is, without losing any.'

'So you risked your life over *land*?'

Something swirled between them—dark and tight—but she couldn't work it out.

'The government revoked the licence for eight months, maybe nine. But without it, Cesar and Therese only had about four vials of antivenom remaining and they couldn't acquire any more venom.'

'Someone told me that a nature programme presenter got bitten once and needed nineteen vials to keep him alive,' he bit out incredulously. 'Is that true?'

'Yes.'

'So then, how far did you really think four vials would go?'

'We didn't think about it,' she told him evenly. 'There was no choice, so we just got on with it.'

'You could have died.'

He doesn't care, she reminded herself urgently. *Don't read too much into it.*

'We could have.' She bowed her head, making no attempt to deny it. 'But we've all been bitten before—we build a little immunity. And, like I said, we had no choice.'

'You had a choice, Flávia. You all had a choice. You could have just kept yourself safe. Fought it in court and then gone back to the snakes when the government reissued the licences, or permits, or whatever.'

'To hundreds of dead or ill snakes? We had a responsibility to them, Jake. We weren't about to just abandon them.'

'You have a responsibility to yourself as well. And those who love you.'

'Now you really do sound like Enrico.'

She could actually feel the air around her turning frosty. Taut.

'Is that so?'

His tone was silky, and quiet. But she knew she didn't mistake the edge to it. And still she kept pushing the invisible boundaries.

'He didn't like me putting myself in danger, either. He always wanted me to give up the sanctuary part of my life and focus on working full-time from the research lab. As if the lab isn't the bit of my job that I endure until I can get back to the forest and escape the city.'

'Sounds very much as though he loved you,' he gritted out, scowling at her for so long that Flávia wondered if time had stood still.

'Maybe you're right,' she offered at length. 'At the time I didn't think so. I thought that if he really loved me, then he could never have asked me to choose.'

'And now you realised he cared and you regret your decision,' he scorned.

'No.' She pulled her lips together ruefully. And the way Jake's eyes followed the movement heated up her whole body. 'I guess the truth is that I just didn't love him back. At least not enough to want to give up my life for him.'

Something flickered across those morpho-blue pools. Too fast for her to follow.

'Maybe you just haven't met the right person yet,' he suggested.

'Is that an offer?' The wry question slipped off her lips before she could bite it back.

'That night was a one-off,' he answered hastily. 'I have Brady. My career is in the UK…'

'Relax.' She forced a laugh, and prayed it didn't sound as hollow to Jake's ears. 'I know you're not in the market for a relationship.'

'Evidently, neither are you.'

He paused, as though waiting to hear her response.

'No,' she answered, quelling the voice inside which taunted otherwise. Assuring herself that the voice was wrong.

'I love my job. It's who I am. Surely, if someone loved me enough, he wouldn't ask me to change that?'

Jake didn't answer, though she wanted him to. More than she would have cared to admit.

She could imagine he was thinking about Brady, and how much the boy had already lost. And then, though she tried to pretend otherwise, she tried to imagine how he might feel if she and Jake were together and something happened to her.

And suddenly, she wondered if he'd lost more than he'd realised when Helen had died. She knew the rumours. She knew he'd always had a reputation for avoiding relationships, but now she'd gleaned the little she had about his parents, she couldn't help wondering if it had been a means of self-defence rather than anything else.

And had his sister's death affected him more than even he had realised?

'Perhaps you're right,' he murmured, as if feeling he ought to put an end to the conversation, but was unable to. 'But you're working on a venom-based therapy that could stop cancer cells from metastasising. That's incredible, Flávia. And you can still have that. You can still save all those lives. But do you have to be the one at the sanctuary risking your life to do it?'

'Yes,' she answered.

'Why?'

'Because, for me, it isn't just about the research to save human lives, Jake. It's about the protected habitats we're creating to save the snakes. It's about education for people not to club them to death—which you can understand when they know the snake could kill their kid within hours.'

Neither of them looked at each other, both of them appearing equally distracted by the to-ing and fro-ing of the barbecue guests. She wondered if his was as much of an act as hers.

'I need those snakes, Jake. I need to see them grow older, bigger, healthier, instead of seeing their numbers dwindle year on year. It's the only tangible reward I receive. I don't get to see the results in a patient, right there in front of me, telling me how I've changed their life.'

'But they're out there. More and more as each trial is successful.'

'Yes, and *you* get that. But I don't. I work in a lab and I work in the sanctuary. So the snakes are *my* patients. I shouldn't be told to give them up because it doesn't fit with someone else's idea of what I should reasonably do. How would you like it if someone told you that you couldn't be a surgeon any more?'

Jake opened his mouth to tell her it was completely different, but suddenly something stopped him. He wanted to argue, but he found that he could see what she was getting at.

Perhaps understand it. To a degree.

Even now, he still got a kick of satisfaction from being able to give a patient their life back. He got to see them, and their families, at that moment when they all realised that something he had done had given them the most precious gift of all.

The gift of time.

But Flávia, and others like her, never got that. Even though, without them, he couldn't do what he did.

So if she considered the snakes to be her patients, then he could understand why.

'You're right,' he answered eventually. 'I wouldn't like it if anyone asked me to give up what I do. Why should it be any different for you?'

She didn't answer out loud. Instead, she turned her head to look at him, scrutinise him, trying to decide whether he really meant it.

Then, after what felt like an age, she smiled. That soft, quirky smile of hers which seemed to have the knack of reverberating right through his gut and all the way along his sex.

One step and he could reach her, sweep her up against him and carry her back into the house without any of the guests seeing.

God, what is wrong with me?

Gripping his drink tighter, he made himself take a long, deep swig.

'I've been watching Brady with Papai. And with the girls,' Flávia told him a few moments later. Oblivious to the battle he was waging with himself.

'Yeah?'

'The hospital isn't going to help Brady settle, you know. However lovely Patricia is, and whatever clubs they've laid on for the few kids who have come with their parents for this summer programme, it won't work for a boy like him. He won't be mentally and physically stimulated. He won't be happy.'

'No, I realise that. But I'll find a solution.'

'You could always bring him here for days out with Papai, or Maria, and even me. The girls like spending time with Brady.'

'That's incredibly thoughtful of you, but…'

'It's a longer commute for you, of course. But Luis makes it every day and he can show you the best routes.'

'I'm not bothered about me…but the imposition.'

'Papai loves taking the girls for walks and teaching them new stuff. I know he'd love Brady's eagerness for learning.'

'That's incredibly kind, but you don't even know what your father or sister would think.'

'Of course I do,' Flávia scoffed immediately. 'Whose idea did you actually think it was?'

He didn't know what it was, but he couldn't help grinning. He might have known Flávia would push the credit onto someone else. Although, it was still ridiculously generous of her family to agree.

'It's really very—'

'Before you turn me down,' Flávia cut in, 'I should say that this has nothing to do with the other night. That was a one-off. Never to be repeated. It doesn't suit you because of Brady and it doesn't suit me because, frankly, I filled my fun quota for the year with you. Maria can't hassle me again for at least twelve months.'

Jake laughed.

It was amazing how he could have spent ten months not wanting to laugh at a single thing, and then Flávia had come along and in two encounters had brought light—*air*—back to his dark world.

'One more thing.' She finally pushed herself off the wall where she'd been lounging and spun around to face him.

It took everything he had not to haul her to him and take up where they'd left off a week ago.

'And what's that?' he asked, feigning an air of resignation.

'Before you decide, remember that this isn't about you, or me. This is about Brady. And what works best for that seven-year-old boy.'

Her amber eyes pierced through him. Pinning him down. So intelligent and so caring. But he thought he preferred them best when they were glazed over and spilling with need.

'I know this is about Brady.' Jake wasn't sure how he pulled himself together.

This staying away from her business wasn't really working. If anything, he thought it was making him want her more.

Maybe it was time for a differential diagnosis.

'I tell you what,' he answered thoughtfully, at last. 'I'll bring Brady here if you agree to come and watch a medical procedure with me.'

He saw her eyes flicker with interest before she even spoke.

'What kind of procedure?'

'The kind where I use one of the antivenoms we're trialling for VenomSci. One of the antivenoms that you helped to create.'

'You know, I have never actually seen one of those for real. Only footage afterwards. And I've followed case studies, of course.'

'You've never seen what we do close-up?'

'I worked tumour paint in the lab, but I was only a small part of that team, and then I moved on to my own project trying to find this application of snake venom to stop tumours from metastasising.'

'Nonetheless, you were still an integral part of the team that developed VenomSci's fluorescent dye. Want to see how you've helped to reshape the face of surgical oncology for me today?'

'You'd do that for me?'

'Why not?'

He knew he couldn't claim his offer was for entirely altruistic reasons. But when she looked at him like that, he didn't even care.

CHAPTER NINE

'THE FIRST THING I want to teach you is how to set up your camp correctly.'

'The first thing?' Jake answered dryly. 'You took my rucksack from me back at the house to give me one of your own instead. Then we spent the last few hours hacking our route through the jungle—and that was only after you instilled in me how crucial it is to have a machete and know how to wield it.'

Jake was glad his nephew was safe with Flávia's family. Only the prospect of a sleepover with his two new best friends, and the promise of a day on an adventure trail with Eduardo, had stopped Brady from kicking up a fuss about not accompanying Jake and Flávia into the Atlantic Forest.

'Are you pining for your luxury city life already, *urbanista*?' Flávia teased, the way she'd been doing more and more, ever since they'd left the city.

As though the rainforest was bringing out the real her, and she was more relaxed and contented than he'd ever known her. As though he was seeing the real Flávia, which very few others outside her family would ever see.

He found that he liked the sensation. Most likely a little too much. He could picture how it might be if this was the life he and Brady could lead for good. And then it worried him that it was all so easy to imagine.

No woman had ever made him think of the future before, not to mention that 'having fun for one night only' Flávia Maura certainly shouldn't be the one to break that pattern.

He had no room in his life for her. For any woman. He'd do well to remember that.

'You'd better believe I am. I simply don't see how you can prefer tramping through undergrowth, with no idea what lurks within, and eating corned beef hash out of a tin tray to the convenience of a hot power shower, climate control and a beautifully prepared meal.'

'Is that so?' She shook her head, smiling. 'Listen, Jake. Tell me what you hear.'

Jake listened, uncharacteristically obedient. This was her show. Her party.

'Nothing. I hear absolutely nothing,' he announced at length. 'No city buzz, no verve. No hooting of cars letting you know the place is full of energy. Alive.'

'Listen again.' She practically twirled round in bliss, and he found his eyes drawn to the way her cargo pants perfectly cupped her pert backside.

You're in the jungle, for pity's sake.

'You can't hear all that you just described, it's true,' she continued, oblivious. 'But who wants to? All that noise pollution drowning out what really matters? You might not hear the loud city cacophony, Jake, but you can't say you can't hear anything. This place is practically teeming with life.'

He tore his gaze away and tried to listen again, a part of him loving the way her brow pulled taut in frustration at his admissions, making her look all the more adorable.

And tempting.

'The jungle is full of animals, and insects, all coming together in a harmonious concerto of sounds. Listen.' She closed her eyes and held her finger up as if to emphasise her point. And he tried. He really tried. 'I can hear birds, and frogs, and insects—all chirping, croaking, humming. I can even hear howler monkeys. And take in the scent of all that vegetation. Soil, wood, flowers, trees. It's as though the jungle is dancing with our every sense. Seducing them.'

Whatever innocent picture Flávia had succeeded in painting in his head shattered at that final comment.

All he could think about was a different kind of seduction. The images in his head were all about Flávia, with that shimmering green dress of hers pooling at her feet, and that look of pure pleasure playing over her features. But Jake kept that to himself.

His body tightened at the memory, but he kept that to himself, too.

Instead, she continued.

'The reason I exchanged the rucksack you'd brought for one I'd packed myself is pretty much for this very reason.' There was almost a merriness to her tone. 'Bush craft is all about preparation. Working smart and planning out beforehand, so that ultimately you don't have to work harder than necessary. Especially out in the jungle when everything can be so unpredictable.'

'Go on, then, *jungle woman*,' he said softly. 'Give me your first lesson.'

She studied him sharply, but he could read that pulse flickering in her neck, and it didn't help his attempts to stay on topic.

She cleared her throat.

'When I'm setting up a temporary camp, I like the KISS approach…' She flushed but rushed on. 'As in, Keep It Simple.'

'Should I remind you that *kiss* is spelt with a double *S*?' he asked huskily, unable to empty his head of the image of his lips claiming hers.

'Fine.' Flávia glowered at him, but he noticed the way she swallowed. Hard. 'Keep It Simple, Stupid.'

And what did it say about him that he liked how easily he could provoke her?

'In the top of your rucksack, you'll find a tarpaulin to shelter yourself from the rain, and a hammock to keep you off the jungle floor, each bound up with paracord. Get the tarp first…it's the camouflage one. Good. Wait—what are you doing?'

He stopped, looked.

'Don't leave your rucksack on the jungle floor like that—you'll get all manner of things trying to crawl in there and hitch a ride. Let me just tie this off…okay, you can hang it on that hook.'

The woman had a system for everything. And her bossiness was oddly compelling. He couldn't hardly help himself. What if he crossed the divide between them, his hands sliding around her waist, turning her to him?

'What about Raoul and Fabio?' he bit out.

'Don't worry about them,' Flávia answered merrily, her back still to him. 'They're over there making their own shelters from scratch. When you're done here, get them to show you how they strip vines to make ropes, and saplings like little joists.'

He looked around. Far away, but not far enough.

'They're building a damned house,' he exclaimed.

'More of a tree house, but I agree it's pretty impressive. Now, I chose this because it's a good spot. You have two fairly straight trees a decent distance apart over there, and two more just here. You're taller than me, so you take that pair over there.'

Dutifully, Jake ignored the protestations of his taut body and moved out to the farther set of trees, taking the bound-up tarp with him. He watched her smoothly unravel the cord from her own and began to copy. It didn't unravel quite so smoothly. Which might have been his lack of technique, or it might have been the fact that his mind was still elsewhere.

'Sorry.' She didn't make much of an effort to conceal her amusement. 'I tried to make it idiot-proof, but I guess I should have made it *urbanoid*-proof, too.'

'I'm glad I entertain you,' he remarked wryly.

'Okay, so loop it around one tree, as high up as you can reach, and tie it off using those knots we were practising with Brady the other night.' She deftly tied one of hers down to demonstrate, then stretched the line out and tied the other end off on the other tree.

Now, watching Flávia tie off another knot on another tree, Jake copied, possibly a little bit clumsily, yet bizarrely he wasn't hating the experience half as much as he'd feared he would. Especially when she crossed over to him to check his handiwork; the coconut scent of her hair, piled up on her head for practicality, pervaded his nostrils. His body went into overdrive yet again.

Good God, what the heck is it about this woman?

'Not bad.' She nodded. 'Not bad at all. Now, you need to open out the basher—the roof—and tie it off on some other trees. I have extra cord if you're missing a tree on one side and need me to make an extension.'

He looked around, trying to get a feel for it in his head, then set to work. Oddly, he was beginning to enjoy it. Whether it was because he could imagine teaching these skills to Brady or, more selfishly, because he enjoyed shaking Flávia's image of him as a city slicker, he didn't care to evaluate too deeply.

'Done,' he declared, looking up proudly. Where he had a roof—albeit a good one—she had a whole system in place, including a mosquito net, and what looked to be a hanging line for all her gear. 'My God, have you finished already?'

'I've been doing this a long time.' She laughed. 'Come on, we'll work together. You take one end of the mosquito net and I'll take the other. They can go below the tie-offs for the roof, but when you tie the tape ends of the hammock around the trees, they'll need to go above the cord for your net and your roof. Got it?'

'Got it,' he agreed.

It was incredible watching Flávia work. Like poetry. And he, who was accustomed to all manner of dexterous operations, might as well have been putting up his sleeping system with his thumbs and his toes.

But then, suddenly, it was done. A roof, a mosquito net and a hammock, all complete.

'Okay, here's some extra cord. You can tie that off up near the apex of your tarp, but inside the mosquito net, then you can hang your gear off that during the night and nothing will get in there. And whilst you do that, I'm going to try and find some dry firewood so that we can light a fire.'

'Using what? Two sticks?' he teased.

Flávia arched her eyebrows at him.

'I can, if I really need to. But I'm usually more organised than that, urbanoid. I carry a lighter and a few strips of rubber. That gets a fire started pretty nicely, even if the firewood is wet, as it so often is in the forest.'

'Then what?'

'Then you cook me dinner,' she told him happily, grabbing her machete and heading into the jungle.

He lifted his head.

'What are we supposed to eat?'

'Rat,' she called over her shoulder. 'I'll hunt them, you'll cook.'

And he was left staring at her in disbelief as she plunged into the undergrowth, her sexy posterior practically wiggling at him as she moved.

In the end, she had lit a fire, taken a small pan from out of her rucksack and a couple of sealed ration packs, and they'd eaten a pre-prepared meal. But it had occurred to Jake that this prank-style Flávia was a different Flávia again from either the one with her family, or the one at the hospital.

And it had sent a bizarre sense of possessiveness through him that he seemed to be the only person—at least outside of her family—to see this side of her. Another layer to his fierce, strong *selvagem*.

The real Flávia Maura.

And when she looked at him, and laughed as though he was the only man in the world, he'd had to contend with a great fire roaring through his veins, proclaiming things it had no right to as he looked at her.

Mine. Only mine.

And telling himself it was sheer insanity did nothing to dampen the flames. They'd only been fanned the more she'd opened up her world to him. As though letting him in to another universe inside of her that no one else ever got to experience.

It felt inevitable that something more would happen— needed to happen—between them. He felt the inexorable draw and, rather than fight it, he found himself welcoming it.

Flávia was like no one else he'd ever known. Even here, and now, he knew he'd never meet anyone like her ever again.

They'd even been onto Fabio and Raoul's tree house with Raoul's high-tech camera and seen some of the jungle's nocturnal creatures, including a crab-eating fox, a prehensile-tailed porcupine and a fight between a wandering spider and a raid of army ants.

'Brady would go mad for this,' Jake had said in awe.

And so Flávia had given such vivid detail to each and every one of them, things that he could pass on to his sponge-like nephew, that he'd found himself lost in her passion. More and more, he could see what she saw in Brady that he had missed all these months.

It didn't make him feel good.

Now, lying in his hammock, in the relative dark with nothing but the sounds of the jungle around them, and the crackling of the fire, it felt almost intimate. Raoul and Fabio were close enough for safety but not so close that they could hear any conversation he and Flávia might have.

And right now, he was glad of it, because he was still grappling with the questions running around his head.

'A penny for your thoughts,' she said softly. 'I think that's the phrase?'

He shouldn't answer, and yet Jake found himself opening his mouth. As if he was the kind of man who found it that easy to talk.

Except, with Flávia, he was turning into that man. And he couldn't help but think that it wasn't a bad thing.

'I think I'm beginning to understand Brady's obsess... *fascination*,' he corrected, 'for this stuff. Just like you.'

'Just like me,' she concurred quietly.

'I wouldn't have seen it, if you hadn't come along.'

He knew he would never have made the admission back in so-called real life. But here, now, he could say it to the stunning, starry night sky—a sky like none he'd ever seen before. The lack of light pollution, just as Flávia had said.

And he could say it to Flávia.

'I think you would have.' He could hear the soft smile even in her voice. 'It just might have taken you a bit longer, and you wouldn't have known what you were looking for.'

'I want to believe it. But I'm afraid, in this, that view affords me too much credit.'

'Then look at it this way. You'll never have to find out because, fortunately, you *do* know. Even better, you're acting on it.'

'I still don't know whether to bring him out here.'

'He'd love it,' Flávia laughed softly.

'Oh, he would. No question. But I still don't know if

it's responsible to bring a seven-year-old into the Atlantic Forest.'

The air went silent, though not still, as Flávia appeared to ponder his question.

'Many kids, maybe not,' she offered eventually. 'Although, they do run mini expeditions from the city and there are kids under ten. But Brady is different. He would really soak it all in.'

'I know, but—'

'You're not his father, but you're wholly responsible for him,' she supplied. 'Which makes the decision that much harder.'

He blew out a deep breath and time passed, but he didn't know how long.

Maybe a lifetime.

He'd never voiced these fears to anyone before. He didn't even know he was going to voice them to Flávia, until he heard them coming out of his mouth.

'I don't know about any of that. I just know that I made a promise to Helen that I would take care of Brady, and I would never break that promise. But... I can't reach Brady. I can't connect with him. He doesn't seem to notice whether I'm there or not and I don't know that I'm the right person to bring out the best in another human being.'

He didn't mention the fact that *love* wasn't even an emotion he was sure he possessed. At least, not in that all-consuming way that parents had for their kids. Or even couples had for each other. Because the fact was that the more time he and Brady spent with Flávia and her family, the more he began to wonder if maybe he *could* learn to love after all.

The way Helen had believed he would. And the way Flávia had told him he could.

'I know he was close with his mother. He was Helen's little prince. But I can't seem to build a relationship with him and I feel he is withdrawing every month that goes by. Then I try to make amends by letting him get away with behaviour that I know school would pull him up over. I don't want to be so poor of a guardian to my nephew that I actually end up somehow damaging him.'

He didn't know what he expected Flávia to say; he certainly wasn't expecting her to say something which would make him feel instantly better. So why was he so compelled to talk to her?

Either way, she was silent for so long that Jake began to regret voicing the plaguing doubts.

'It's an impossible balance,' she conceded. 'Maria makes it look so easy, but it isn't. Kids do need boundaries, though. They have to know their limits. But have you talked to Brady about his mother since that day in the visitor centre?'

'I tried…' Jake thought back. 'I asked him if he missed her, but he didn't respond.'

Certainly not the way he had with Flávia when he'd broken down in her arms. And he hadn't pushed. Who would *want* to make a child cry, anyway?

She tilted her head. 'Maybe there's another way to approach it.'

'Go on,' he encouraged when she fell quiet. The crackling of the fire was almost a comforting sound in the noises of the jungle.

'Maybe instead of asking him about his feelings, you should tell him about yours, first.'

'Talk to him about my…*feelings*?' Jake blew out sharply.

'It isn't a dirty word,' she chided gently.

'I know that. I just… What would I even say?'

'I don't know—tell him some of the good things you remember about his mother.'

'I didn't even know Helen these last ten years. What would I tell Brady?'

'Then tell him about your memories of her as a kid. She

told Brady you were once a good big brother to her—can't you talk about that?'

'I don't even know how I was a good brother.' Jake shook his head in the darkness, and he wondered if she could hear the same ring of anger to it that he could. 'I guess I was just...*there*...someone to talk to about what was going on in our lives. Not that we did all that much, but God knows our parents *never* talked to us about anything other than homework, or school, or something equally educational.'

'You once said they did their duty by you?'

And Jake didn't expect himself to answer; this was far too personal for his liking. Yet he heard himself speak, all the same.

'They were academic surgeons. High-achieving, focused, but detached. If they weren't learning on a practical level, they were writing medical papers, securing research funding, travelling the world for conferences. They sent Helen and me to good schools, dressed us in new clothes and kept a clean, albeit old-fashioned home. They believed there was nothing my sister and I couldn't learn from books.'

She didn't answer, but he knew she was listening. Absorbing it all.

'They provided for us well, but they were detached. Cold. You could go to them for practical, medicinal care if you were ill, but forget a show of affection, or a word of love. That wasn't who they were.'

'I can't imagine that,' Flávia said quietly, and he could well believe it having met her sister and her father, who had given him an exuberant bear hug the first time he'd met him at that family barbecue.

'You've seen how I am.' Jake shrugged. 'I never really thought anything was lacking. Until Brady came along.'

'I think you did,' Flávia countered after a moment. 'You

just didn't have any reason to tackle it. But his mother wasn't like that, clearly.'

'No,' he agreed. 'Somehow, Helen managed to change things for herself. For Brady. I don't know how.'

'Why did you fall out?'

'We didn't.' He shrugged, scarcely able to believe he was still talking. Still confiding about things he had barely even let himself *think* about in the past. 'We just…drifted apart when we went to uni.'

'To study medicine,' Flávia finished, more as if she was thinking out loud than actually talking to him.

'What is it you want to know?' he asked astutely.

'I suppose—' her answer was slow, thoughtful '—that a part of me wonders why you followed them into medicine. Given how they were.'

As though she knew him better than anyone else ever had.

'Not just medicine. Surgery. They didn't want doctors for kids… They insisted we both became surgeons.'

'Insisted?' He could actually hear the smile in her voice, could imagine it hovering on her lips, as if she didn't fully believe him.

He didn't blame her.

'There was no option. They made it clear from as early an age as I can remember that they would never accept anything else from either of us but becoming surgeons.'

'Oh.'

'Actually, I didn't want to,' he shocked himself by saying. 'I spent most of my childhood and teenage years dreaming of becoming an engineer.'

It was a confession he'd never told a living soul.

The moment seemed to hang between them.

'It should surprise me more,' she murmured after a while. 'You're such a skilled, driven, compassionate surgeon, it's no wonder you were sought out to run clinical trials. But the truth is that it doesn't surprise me that much at all.'

'I don't know if that's a compliment.'

'It is,' she laughed softly. 'So you and your sister are… were…both surgeons.'

'I am. Well, you know that, of course. But although Helen studied medicine at uni, it was partway through her third year that she fell pregnant with Brady.'

'I can't imagine that went down well, from everything you've said.'

'It didn't,' he acknowledged. 'They didn't shout, or yell—that wasn't their style. But they told her that she was too young, that a baby would ruin her career at this stage and that the logical solution was to terminate.'

He could remember it now. The cool, firm statement made as they'd all sat around the table in a restaurant for a typically uptight *family meal*. There had been no scene in any real sense of the word.

'What happened?' Flávia asked tentatively, drawing him back to the present.

'Helen wiped her mouth with her napkin, set it to one side and quietly told them that she would be keeping her baby. Then she got up and discreetly walked out of the restaurant.'

Not that her parents had ever made any attempt to stop her.

'And that was it?'

'That was it. They went back to their lives, I went back to uni and Helen did her own thing. We didn't see her again for about six years. So, you see, I wasn't much of a brother to her at all.'

'What about the father? If you don't mind me asking.'

And the fact was that he didn't. He had no idea why he was still talking—maybe it was the intimacy the rainforest created—but it was somehow cathartic.

'Helen never told us who he was. The first and only time

I met Brady he was five, and I did ask her about the father. But she simply said that she'd told him she was pregnant and given him the choice of how involved he wanted to be. Apparently, she'd never heard from him again, but her son was her world.'

'I can tell that. She was a good mum.'

'She was,' Jake agreed. 'I've no idea how, given the example we had set for us. I just know that whatever she had, I don't have it in me. But I'm trying, thanks to you, and I should be grateful for that much.'

He'd possibly intended the conversation to end there, but he heard the light creaking of the tree and could imagine she was flipping onto her side on her hammock. When she spoke, her sweet, gentle voice seemed that little bit closer.

Or perhaps that was just his wishful thinking.

'It's up to you, Jake. You can be as close as you want to. The question of whether you bring him into the jungle or not is more about the symptom than the cure. If you want that connection, then yes, you just need to approach Brady like he's more than a seven-year-old kid. And yes, you need to talk to him, ask him what he wants. But more than that, I should imagine, you need to talk to him about his mother. Because you're the only connection he has left to her now.'

'Maybe you're right—when we get back to the city, I'll take him out for something to eat and we'll talk.'

'One more night after this one and then you talk. *Really* talk,' Flávia added fiercely, the second greatest champion Brady had ever had.

As though she truly cares, Jake thought as he stared past the confines of his shelter roof, and to the vast night sky beyond.

CHAPTER TEN

FLÁVIA HURRIED INTO Maria and Luis's pool house, and froze.

She'd intended to drop off large towels whilst Jake was filling Brady in on the two days of their short jungle expedition. Either that, or Brady would have been filling Jake in on his first ever sleepover in her sister's mad household.

She hadn't expected to be faced with the sheer mouth-watering sight of Jake standing in the kitchen with only a tiny towel around his waist, his dark hair still slick from the shower.

'Where's Brady?' she managed, her tongue suddenly too thick for her mouth.

'Maria took them all out for ice cream. Apparently, she'd promised them this morning and she hadn't expected us back until much later.'

'Oh. Right.'

'She made a point of telling me that they wouldn't be back for a few hours.'

'Oh,' Flávia repeated. Then, as the import of his words sank in, she felt the flush creep up her body. *'Oh.'*

'She isn't the most subtle, your sister.' Jake grinned suddenly.

'No. Not at all. Anyway, I… I thought you might need

these,' she offered redundantly, edging forward to slide the towels onto a bar stool before edging backwards again.

But only a few steps, her body resisting all instructions from her brain to turn around and leave.

The revelations of two nights ago had been more than she'd expected, and at times she'd even convinced herself that there was something arcing between them again. She'd even been waiting—hoping—for something to happen out there. A loaded glance, maybe. Or even a stolen kiss. But ultimately, nothing had happened.

She'd told herself it was for the best. That her…dalliance with Jake had been over after that one night together and now she was just trying to be a good friend to him. And to Brady. But right now Jake was standing metres from her, practically naked, his lightly tanned skin shimmering from the water. Worse, with a hungry gleam in his eye that seemed to perfectly match the roar inside her.

Try as she might, it was impossible to stop her eyes from skimming their way down his body. From the sharp lines of his jaw, over the impossibly contoured ridges of his abdomen and to the deep V which disappeared tantalisingly below the fluffy, white material.

She didn't want to be his friend. She wanted more than that.

And she wanted it too much.

Flávia swallowed. Once. Twice. Dragged her eyes back up to where they ought to be. But they didn't quite make it, and instead she found herself staring at some point around his collarbone, forcing her mouth into more mundane conversation.

'I thought you'd still be telling Brady about your *jungle adventure*, as he calls it.'

'Brady said he'd rather hear about it when you're there.' The wry smile was almost her undoing. 'He thinks I might miss important fauna details.'

Flávia tried to laugh, but it came out slightly choked. Her heartbeat was frantic. Her skin felt like it was too tight for her own body, and between her legs was molten.

'You *will* need to get the details right.'

'Don't I know it?' He flashed her a smile which felt like it was shot through with lust, and the air thickened in the room around them.

She ought to leave. The door was right behind her. But she still couldn't seem to get her feet moving.

'Do you want a drink?' She didn't even realise she'd started moving again until she found herself in the kitchen area. 'There should be something in the fridge.'

Then she was standing in front of him, so close that she could imagine reaching her hands out to flatten them against those oh-so-appealing abdominal muscles. Her palms prickled with the effort of resisting. And then she lifted her head, their gazes colliding, his eyes hot, and almost black with desire.

It was like a catalyst.

Jake slid one hand into her hair—still wet from her own shower—and hauled her to him, his head bowing so that his mouth could claim hers and at last—*at last*—they were kissing again.

Only, Jake didn't merely kiss her, he dominated her. Deliciously and devastatingly so. Even better than she remembered.

His mouth claimed hers with such complete authority, just as electrifying as she remembered. She could feel it deep in her core.

A heat bloomed right through Flávia.

She pressed her body against his, her hands gliding over him and revelling in every ridge and every dip, as though she couldn't get enough. Her entire body shivered when he dipped his fingers into the waistband of her jeans and hooked around her fitted white tee, pulling it up and over her head.

Then Jake unhooked her bra and removed that, too, her nipples proud as they strained against his chest. The slide of her bare skin over his was almost too delicious, and as he kissed a trail along her jawline and down her neck, his hand skimmed over her to cup one heavy, aching breast.

Gentle and demanding all at once, driving the sense of anticipation up even further.

Almost too much to stand.

He toyed with her, played with her, then let his hands smooth over her skin as if reacquainting himself with every inch of her. From the ridges of her spine to the soft curve of her waist. Only, unlike last time, this felt less urgent.

More indulgent.

Without thinking, Flávia reached out and hooked one finger into the waistband of his towel and it fell away with one flick.

Her mouth went dry in an instant. She hadn't overplayed her memories of last time as she'd begun to fear she might have, because he was every bit as hard, ready and uncompromisingly masculine as she recalled.

She didn't realise he'd swept her into his arms, high against his chest, until he started carrying her through to the bedroom, and all she could do was cling tightly and gaze at him, lost in those impossibly blue depths.

A thrill coursed through Flávia as he laid her on the bed, and stripped her down with ruthless efficiency. She sank back, expecting him to move alongside her, to cover her body with his own, but suddenly she felt his hands slide under her backside and pull her forward.

When she looked up, he had already settled himself between her legs, a wicked curve to his lips, and her heart slammed against her ribs.

'Jake…'

'Brace yourself, my *selvagem*. Now it's time for me to dole out the lessons.'

Before she could answer, he lowered his head and used his tongue to trace the line up the inside of her raised thigh only to stop a breath short of her core. Then he tracked his way back down the other thigh.

It was the sweetest torment she thought she'd ever known.

Again and again he teased her, stoking her desire, making her lift her hips in anticipation each time, only for him to skim over where she needed him most. She threaded her fingers through his hair, unable to help herself.

'Anyone would think you didn't know how to hit your mark,' she grumbled breathlessly on his third time over.

'Oh, I know how to hit my mark,' he muttered, his mouth never leaving her skin. So close that she could feel the curve of his wicked smile. 'You just don't know how to ask for it nicely.'

She lifted her head to glare at him, but this time, when he reached the top, he paused, and looked at her.

'Still, maybe I should prove it to you.'

Then he dipped his head and licked his way into her. Jettisoning her into pure sensation.

He tasted her, over and over, using his tongue like the most exquisite weapon against her. Licking her, sucking her and making that hot thing in her belly pull tighter, more hectic.

She rode them out for as long as she could, these desperately perfect sensations. And when she didn't think she could bear it any longer, he sucked harder and slid one finger deep inside her.

Flávia broke apart. Splintering into a million tiny fragments which she didn't think she'd ever be able to put back together. No one had ever made her feel like this. So wanton. So alive.

By the time Flávia came back to herself, it was to find Jake lying next to her, propped on one arm and watching her, his expression entirely too self-satisfied for her liking. She'd been entirely too lost in the moment and she felt the flush of embarrassment creeping over her.

'That was hardly balanced.' She was going for prim, but her raspy voice fell far too short of the mark.

'You aren't really complaining.'

Less of a question, more of a statement.

Unable to answer, she merely reached for him, pulling him onto her. Letting him haul her into his arms beneath him, and settling himself between her legs like he was meant to be there.

And, so help her, that yearning in her swirled around all the more. Coiling tighter every time he nudged against her entrance, making her want to lose herself all over again. Not that she could, surely? Not so soon?'

Flávia shifted her hips, trying to find out, and a low sound escaped the back of Jake's throat.

'Careful, Flávia,' he warned.

Could it be that he wasn't as in control as he was pretending to be?

The realisation stirred through her. She tried it again with the same result. Lifting her legs, Flávia wrapped them, with deliberate ease, around Jake's hips and wriggled around him.

'If you keep doing that, I'm not going to be responsible, my *selvagem*,' he growled.

She felt heady, too close to the edge. Again. Already.

'Who says I want you to?' she murmured, meeting his eyes as he looked at her.

Then he held her gaze as he thrust into her. Long, and slow, and deep, as her lungs expelled every last bit of air in a soft, juddering sigh, before drawing back out again.

'Again,' she choked out, her arms looped around his neck

and her legs still locked around his waist. And he complied with devastating control once. Twice.

Each time, she could feel herself adjust to him, tighten around him, and then he started to set the pace. Steadily at first, but building quickly, the fire raging wildly under every inch of her skin. And Flávia, already halfway there from what he'd already done with her oh-so-compliant body, clutched tightly and surrendered to him.

In. Out. Faster and faster, taking her higher than she'd ever been, until he was driving her straight to the edge, and her body was shaking as she begged him not to stop.

Never to stop.

So good that she could almost cry.

When he slid his hand down between them, it was like a ball of flames shooting straight through her veins, and he finally took her over the edge.

For one long moment, she felt herself floating there, and there was nothing but a white heat rushing headlong towards her. And then it hit, and she started falling—spinning and somersaulting over and over as she tumbled into the blissful abyss, calling Jake's name.

And as he followed her, this time he called her name, too.

By the time she woke, several hours later, she was alone in the bed.

She glanced around for Jake, even listening out for the sound of him moving around in the main lounge, but it was silent out there. Of course, he would have had to take Brady home. She'd lost track of time, but he couldn't afford to. Their lives were so very different.

Sitting up, Flávia threw her feet over the edge of the bed and moved gingerly forward. Her body ached in places which hadn't ached for too long; they'd been intimate twice more after that first time. But, crucially, it was her heart which ached the most.

She glanced tentatively around the bedroom—the supposed scene of the crime—but even though she had no idea how Jake was going to treat her the next time she saw him, she couldn't say that she regretted what had happened.

Scanning further, she'd been surprised, even touched, to see her clothes folded over the chair in the corner of the room rather than dropped around the place as they'd left them. But then it occurred to her that he hadn't done it for her, but to ensure than Brady didn't see anything when they'd all returned home after their ice-cream trip.

Quickly, she grabbed a shower—Jake had thought to place the towels she'd brought in the bathroom—and dressed, before hurrying out to the main house. And straight into her sister, who eyed her knowingly.

'Good afternoon?'

'Great,' Flávia replied loftily. 'And yours?'

'Well, I got honeycomb ice cream, so I can't complain.'

Flávia waited for Maria to say anything more. Unreasonably disappointed when she didn't.

'Did you...um...see Jake before he left?'

'Well, now that you come to mention it, I do believe I did.'

Another pause. It seemed that her sister was going to make her fish for every detail.

'And did he say anything?'

Maria cocked her head speculatively.

'Livvy...'

'Uh-oh.' Flávia forced herself to grin. 'I know that tone—it's never a good one.'

'No.' Maria shook her head. 'It's not like that.'

'Then what?'

'You're not falling for this guy, are you?'

'Of course not,' Flávia scoffed. But even to her own ears her voice was too bright. Too high.

'Oh, *Livvy*.'

'I'm not.'

'This is all my fault.' Maria shook her head, her hand reaching out to stroke Flávia's cheek.

Flávia pulled away sharply. 'I'm *not* falling for Jake. You told me to have a little fun, that night of the gala, remember? So that's what I'm doing. I'm having a little fun.'

'You're falling for him.'

'No,' Flávia denied.

Only in that instant she realised, with blinding clarity, that she was lying.

'You can't fall for him, Livvy. He's leaving. In a matter of weeks,' Maria pointed out forcefully.

'I know that.'

So why did it now press so heavily on her chest that she felt as though she was suffocating?'

'Do you? Because I've never seen you like…*this* before, Livvy.' Maria swirled her arm in Flávia's general direction. 'Not even with Enrico. And if I'm right, then you're setting yourself up for the hardest fall of your life.'

'You're wrong.' Flávia crossed her arms obstinately. 'I know the situation. Jake is going back to England, and I'm going back to the jungle.'

'And he *will* be going, Livvy.'

'I know, Maria.' Flávia rolled her eyes. 'Look, it was only supposed to be a bit of fun that night. But then this happened—and do I need to remind you that *you're* the one who encouraged it, with your "we won't be back for hours" comment? But that's it now.'

'I encouraged you before I realised you were in so deep,' Maria censored.

'Well, I'm not. Look, I've had fun, but now it's done. I doubt I'll even see Jake again before the closing dinner.'

'Is that right?' Her sister pulled a suspicious face.

'It is,' Flávia concluded firmly.

'Well, you won't care that he asked you to meet him tomorrow, then.'

As bait went, it was a powerful one. Flávia felt her heart stop. Then lurch. She glared at Maria, who looked equally defiant.

'Meet where?' she demanded.

'What does it matter?'

'Maria?'

Okay, so she was in deeper than even she had realised. But she knew there was a deadline to their relationship.

Jake *would* be leaving. And as long as she remembered that, she could certainly handle anything else.

'Where does he want me to meet him, Maria?'

Maria pursed her lips and then finally relented.

'For breakfast, at the café opposite Paulista's.'

'When?'

'About seven.'

Flávia drew in a breath and tried to rein in the galloping in her chest.

'Thank you,' she told her sister at last.

'Livvy—'

'I know,' she cut her sister off, moderating it with as gentle a smile as she could manage. 'I'll be careful.'

Only, Flávia had a feeling she was already further gone than she would ever have wanted to be. Yet, she couldn't bring herself to care.

CHAPTER ELEVEN

'DID YOU TELL your uncle what you saw on the adventure trail yesterday?' Flávia asked Brady as he finished his eggs and sat back, replete.

Brady wrinkled his nose.

'Uncle Jake isn't like us. He doesn't like animals—he only likes his hospital work.'

There was no animosity in the boy's tone, no making a point, just a simple statement of fact. Which arguably made it all the more damning an indictment, as though for every three steps forward he seemed to be making with his nephew, they then took two steps backwards.

But before Jake could say anything, Flávia cut in, her voice light and encouraging.

'I think he'd be really interested to hear about the otter Maria told me you saw, though.'

Brady didn't look convinced. He just turned his head, and Jake could only categorise his expression as *wary*. It cut, deeper than Jake might have thought.

Over Brady's head, Flávia was dipping her head, clearly suggesting he say something. Jake wasn't certain what that something was, so he took a guess.

'I really would like to hear,' he managed, and her rewarding smile really shouldn't have made him feel quite so proud. Like a kid in class getting a coveted gold star from the teacher. Nonetheless, it emboldened him. 'Mate?'

Jake wasn't sure what he'd expected. Whether he'd thought perhaps that Brady would see right through his feeble attempt to connect, and scorn him for it. Or had he just thought that Brady would refuse to respond?

Too little, too late.

Either way, it wasn't the flash of pleasure which shot through the boy's eyes, dissipating the first little bit of wariness.

'Really?'

'Sure.' He made himself smile at his nephew. It wasn't that hard.

'Okay, we saw a neotropical otter—or *lontra longicaudis*.'

'Wow.' Jake nodded enthusiastically, hoping it was the appropriate response.

A triumphant grin pushed a little more of the wariness off Brady's face.

'It's amazing, isn't it? The neotropical otter is on the "threatened" list in the *Red List* of endangered Brazilian fauna.'

'I did not know that,' Jake answered, relieved that he hadn't simply offered to take Jake to the zoo the moment they got home to see the otters there.

'They usually avoid areas with high human traffic—it disturbs them.' Brady was warming up to the topic now. 'But they like high riverbanks to avoid floor issues, and lots of vegetation to provide coverage and protection.'

'I see.'

Was his chest actually swelling at hearing the happiness in his nephew's voice? The passion? The way that Flávia did when she talked about the rainforest. Or the way that he felt about his own career.

How had he missed this in Brady before? How had he dismissed the boy as a kid who had nothing really relevant to say? No wonder he hadn't been able to connect with Brady.

If it hadn't been for Flávia, he might never have seen a possible way to do so now.

If it wasn't too late.

He could imagine his sister talking to Brady one to one. Taking him on her own version of Eduardo's adventure trail. Helen had always been more like Flávia's family than like their own detached parents. Than like himself.

'Want to know what we saw in the jungle?' Flávia opened her eyes wide, her voice already painting a picture that had Brady spinning around in anticipation.

'What?'

And then his nephew's gaze turned on him as Flávia glanced over Brady's head expectantly, and Jake felt lost all over again.

'What did you see?' Brady repeated.

'We saw a Brazilian wandering spider.'

'Wow!' Brady breathed, awestruck.

'But there's something even more incredible, isn't there, Jake?'

Realisation hit him. Hard.

'Oh, no,' he balked. 'I really don't think a seven-year-old—'

'I do,' Flávia cut in firmly. 'I *really* do. Trust me, he's a boy. But first, Brady, can you tell me anything about the Brazilian wandering spider?'

'Well.' He frowned, deep in thought. 'They're quite big spiders. Brown and hairy, and they're called wandering spiders because they don't build webs like other spiders, but they hide under logs and stuff in the day, and then at night they come out and wander the jungle floor looking for prey.'

'Do you know what they eat?' she asked.

'Um…insects? Mice? Maybe other spiders?'

'Right.' Flávia nodded. 'Know what other insects come

out at night? I'll give you a clue—they build living fortresses, known as bivouacs.'

'Army ants!' Brady shouted out.

'Well done, mate,' Jake praised as Flávia gesticulated wildly over his head. 'So, did you know that army ants send out thousands of ants at a time to hunt prey?'

'Yes.' Brady eyed him, unimpressed. 'They're called raids. And by the way, there are about two hundred subspecies of army ants.'

'Well, we saw army ants and a wandering spider come face-to-face.'

'Wow!' Jake had hoped to capture Brady's interest, but he hadn't been prepared for the level of attention his nephew was now directing at him. 'Did they battle? Who won? Was it incredible?'

'Ultimately, the spider—'

'We'd love to hear who you think might win a battle like that,' Flávia cut in swiftly, and belatedly Jake realized he needed to prolong the moment, and get himself and Brady to engage with each other on a level that his nephew would love.

'Hmm.' Brady knitted his forehead together. 'Well, I think that the army ants are fearless and fierce. They can inject venom to paralyse their prey using a stinger, and they have sharp mandibles which cut insects and crush them. They could tear the legs off the spider.'

'Yeah, we saw how ruthless they are.' Jake nodded, trusting that Flávia knew what she was doing and it wasn't going to give Brady nightmares.

Then again, with everything he'd been learning about the boy lately, he was beginning to realise that whilst the human world may hold painful experiences for his nephew, Brady could cope far better with the concept of survival in the natural world.

'The wandering spider has the most potent venom of

any spider, though. It even kills humans. The spider would have to win over the ants, wouldn't it?'

'Yeah, I thought that, too,' Jake agreed. 'But actually, when we watched, we saw the sheer number of ants overcome the spider, and they ended up taking it down within minutes.'

'That's so cool,' Brady enthused. 'I wish I could have seen that. Can you take me into the jungle next time, Uncle Jake? Please? I know Flávia will look after us.'

Jake hesitated. He wanted to agree, especially because he was starting to understand why it meant so much to the kid. But he needed time. He wouldn't be rushed into it. The objective was to bond with Brady, true; it had to be the responsible thing to do. And right now, he couldn't be certain that agreeing wasn't just him leaping at the opportunity to spend more time with Flávia.

With each day that passed, his return to London got closer, and yet with each moment spent with Flávia, it was getting harder and harder to imagine his old life back in the UK.

He didn't *want* to imagine it. And he knew, without Brady even having to say a word, that his nephew felt the same. Which was, ironically, some sort of progress.

But Jake couldn't shake the ridiculous notion that progress meant nothing without that one, unique woman.

He felt tied up in one of her friction hitch knots. He knew there was an easy release, but if he pulled the wrong way he'd end up bound tighter than ever.

'I honestly don't know, mate,' he answered, and this time, it didn't feel so odd using the nickname. 'I can't promise you that we will, but I can promise you that I will seriously think about it.'

And even though Brady sulked, he realised that he didn't feel as guilty, or as lost, as he might have done in the past.

He was setting appropriate boundaries and he was sticking with them, the way Flávia had told him he ought to do.

He noticed that Flávia was deliberately staying out of it, and he was grateful for her tact, even if a part of him wondered if she would have handled it differently.

But then, to Jake's surprise, Brady's sulk lasted only a few seconds before he bit his lip and seemed to pull himself together.

'I'm sorry, Uncle Jake,' he managed, delving into his bag and pulling out a sheet of paper. 'Vovô Eduardo says he doesn't like sulking. And Julianna says that I look like a baby. So I want to give you this.'

He looked down and saw the bird picture and it was as though someone had sat on his chest. It felt tight. Or full. Or both. Brady had never given him anything before, let alone one of his precious wildlife drawings.

This one was yellow and black, and whilst it might not be artist quality, it was nonetheless an impressive representation.

'It's a saffron-cowled blackbird,' Brady qualified.

'It's really…very beautiful,' Jake managed.

He tried to add something more but suddenly found it was impossible. His chest was swelling even more, and there was an unfamiliar ball lodged in his throat. It was almost a relief that Brady was turning to Flávia, his cheeks suddenly flushed, looking apologetic.

'I was going to draw it for you,' he mumbled an apology. 'But I just thought that Uncle Jake might like it… Maybe for his office?'

'I think it's a really lovely gesture,' she assured him, taking Brady's chin in her hand and dazzling him with her brightest, most beautiful smile.

And Jake thought he was the only one who heard the slight thickness to her voice.

'I'll hang it on the wall for all my patients to see,' Jake

managed brightly at last, his chest now constricted, as though it couldn't make up its mind how to feel.

Whatever he'd expected from this summer programme in Brazil, however he'd imagined it going medical-wise, he had never, in his wildest dreams, thought that it might improve his fractured relationship with his nephew. And he knew he had Flávia to thank for that.

'Come out with me,' he announced abruptly, the moment Brady had left to look for something—Jake realised belatedly that he hadn't even been paying attention.

'Sorry?'

Startled amber eyes flickered to his and something deep inside Jake shifted, and burned.

He had no idea what he was doing. In a couple of weeks, he and Brady would be gone. Back to England. Back to normal life. And yet here he was, proposing dates as though any relationship between him and Flávia actually had a future.

It was nonsensical. And still, he waited impatiently for her answer.

'You're taking me to the Theatro Municipal de São Paulo?' she guessed the moment he ushered her off the subway.

'I am,' he confirmed. 'You were born in this city, yet Maria told me that you haven't been since you were about six.'

'It wasn't the rainforest,' she quipped. 'So you can hold your shock.'

She hadn't intended to sound so sharp, but it was almost touching that he'd planned this out. Certainly, it was more than she'd been expecting, as if this...non-thing between them was more than just sex, and more than just Brady.

Just like yesterday morning, sitting in that café sharing breakfast with Jake and Brady. He was sharing more and more with her, first offering her glimpses of the secrets he held inside his head, and then almost inviting her in.

It was intoxicating to feel as though she was some kind of confidante to him. The *only* confidante he'd ever had. And it all felt so remarkably right. So easy.

Yet, wasn't that what made it all the more dangerous?

It made her let her own guard down, and let him in. It made her forget that he would be leaving soon, but when she remembered, pain slammed into her, hard and painful. And given that she'd known the situation from the start, it had no right to do so.

No right whatsoever, a voice shouted loudly inside her head.

Only, it didn't sound as angry as it was trying to. It just sounded frightened and lost, which made no sense. Everything should just go back to the way it had been before they met. Except that a part of her couldn't even remember what that had been.

Didn't want to.

'I'm sorry,' she apologised. 'I didn't mean it like that. It's a lovely thought for a date. Really.'

Jake didn't answer; instead he brushed a stray hair from her face and tucked it behind her ear. Excruciatingly tenderly. It was all she could do not to tilt her head and lean her cheek into the warmth of his palm.

'I think you'll love it, so trust me, okay?'

She nodded wordlessly. The insane part was that she did trust him.

Then, taking her hand in what felt like a ridiculously intimate gesture, he pulled her body into his and they walked along the street together until they turned the corner and the stone steps and glorious pillars of the *theatro* came into view.

They stood for a moment, drinking in the stunning architecture, until Flávia turned and realised he had been studying her instead.

'Did I tell you how beautiful you look tonight?'

'Thank you.'

She lowered her head, knowing she was blushing, but hardly even caring. With any other man, she might have been wary that it was a line. A thing to say. But she was quickly realising that, with Jake, he was too serious and too direct to feed a person lines.

If he told her she looked beautiful, it was because he thought she did. And because he said it, she didn't let herself worry that she looked like some wild jungle creature. She simply believed him.

It should have rung an orchestra of alarm bells in her head. The summer programme was nearly over and he would be leaving soon. Letting herself get attached could only end in heartache. And yet, she was letting herself do precisely that.

Just as if a part of her hoped she might be able to change the inevitable by sheer power of thought.

If she had any sense, she would turn around and tell Jake Cooper that she was happy to be his colleague, his friend, but that this date could never lead anywhere.

Better still, she would make her excuses, turn around and leave. Back to her family, and her career, and all the things she could depend on.

'Ready?' he asked, holding out his arm.

And then, because she'd always been drawn to the most dangerous flames, Flávia turned her head to cast him her brightest smile, and she took his arm.

'I loved that,' Flávia exclaimed a couple of hours later as they exited their floor of the *theatro* and headed down one side of the sweeping, double staircase. 'I didn't think I would, but I did. So thank you.'

'Such faith.' Jake shook his head. 'This way.'

'Where are we going now?'

'Another surprise,' he told her. 'I'm glad you liked the theatre. Maria told me you used to love this place when you all came here as a family. I guess I hoped it would bring back those happy memories.'

'I don't know about that, but I know it has created new happy memories, which stand strong all on their own.'

'Are they that sad?' he asked abruptly, the odd expression on her face gnawing into him. 'Is that how you knew I needed to create positive memories with Brady so that he had some which didn't all involve Helen?'

'It's slightly different.' She shot him a smile, but it was too bright, too brittle, for Jake's liking. 'His mum died.'

'As did yours.' He frowned.

Flávia stopped. She twisted her head around to look at him.

'What made you think that?'

'You told me you understood exactly how he felt. You said that.'

'I said I understood how he felt with regards to his passion for nature, and science. I never said my mum died.'

'But she did, didn't she?'

The silence was so leaden, so oppressive, that Jake was sure he'd stopped even breathing.

'My mum didn't die,' Flávia gritted out when he'd almost given up hope of her speaking. 'She walked out. Leaving my father to pick up the pieces for two devastated little girls.'

A complication of emotions twisted their way across her lovely face at that moment, and Jake wished he could take back every word. To have never reminded her of such pain. For the conversation never to have started.

But it had, and he needed to find a way through it.

'Do you want to talk?'

'No.' Then, 'Maybe.

'My mother had never wanted to be a mother. She was a nurse, but I think she'd always wished she could have been a doctor.'

'Why wasn't she?'

'I don't know. I don't think she ever wanted to have children, but then she met my father, fell pregnant and got married. She became a wife and mother and that was what her family expected of her. And as long as she moulded to those rules, everything was acceptable. The fact that she made a terrible mother seemed to be something everyone was prepared to overlook.'

He couldn't explain what it was that made him want to...to *be there* for her.

'Terrible, how?'

She wrinkled her nose and pulled her lips together as though she didn't want to be telling him any of this, and yet somehow couldn't help herself.

'You once told me that your parents didn't neglect you. They gave you time—as long as it was the topics they deemed important—but they didn't show you emotion. Well, my mother *did* neglect us.'

'You and Maria?' Jake asked gently as Flávia swallowed.

'Right. My...our...mother only ever really acknowledged us if it gave her a way to blow off some steam, you know, vent her frustrations? And I gave her plenty of excuses to do so.'

'You?'

Flávia shrugged, as though trying to ward off the terrible memories.

'My sister told you I got into fights in school, right? Ironically, I hated the fights at home so I would constantly sneak out of the house. I'd just creep into the edges of the forest so that I could see the animals, and I'd stay there for hours watching them. It infuriated my mother.'

'Could she perhaps have been concerned?' Jake asked carefully. He, of all people, knew better than to sit in judgement. 'Frightened for you?'

Flávia's mouth twisted into a hollow smile that tugged at his chest.

'A part of me wishes that were true. But no, her only concern was for the hassle that I brought. She would shout at me. *Scream* at me. Always saying how much she hated me.'

'Flávia...' He couldn't imagine anyone hating someone as bright, and interested, and sweet, as her.

'She was always telling me that I made her life difficult,' Flávia continued, clearly trying to keep her voice level. Even succeeding at times. 'That I was impossible. And I believed it, for years. It was only when I grew up that I realised my transgressions were just excuses for her to shout at me. The real truth was that she hated me for existing in the first place. Maria, too.'

'Flávia, I'm so sorry. I had no idea. But you know that was more about her than about you. You understand that now, don't you? She isn't worth your time or your heart now.'

'I know that,' she agreed, her eyes locking with his, searching them. And when some of the tension eased from her face, he couldn't help but wonder if that was because of him. 'Although, Maria did track her down a few years ago. I didn't want anything to do with her, but Maria had just had Julianna and Marcie and she needed to understand what had driven our mother to be the way she was.'

'Why?'

Flávia twisted her face again.

'I don't know. My best guess is that she was afraid of turning out like her. She wanted to be sure.'

This time it was more of a grimace, and Jake felt his heart fracture at the expression. He didn't know what to say, or what to do.

'The worst thing about it was that she had remarried, only a couple of years after she'd walked out on us. And despite everything she'd said, she'd had another family with him.'

'Flávia,' he muttered, pulling her to him and cradling her in his arms.

He stroked her hair as if that single action could somehow make all her pain go away.

It was beginning to explain a lot. Like why she loved escaping into the rainforest, or how she focused on her work. Even why she kept people at bay.

Except for Brady.

And maybe himself.

'I swore I would never be like her, Jake. I promised myself I wouldn't make those mistakes. I wouldn't drag a family into the kind of life that I lead. Yet, I inserted myself into your life, yours and Brady's, and I had no right.'

'And we're both so much better off for you in it.'

Which sounded a hell of a lot like a declaration that he hadn't even known he wanted to make.

It was insane. Preposterous. And it couldn't happen. In a matter of weeks, the summer programme would be over and he and Brady would be flying back to the UK. There was no doubt in Jake's mind that the next sensible action, the reasonable one, would be to start creating some much-needed distance from this quirky, funny, sexy woman who had, incredibly, managed to sneak under his skin.

For his sake, but mainly for Brady's. Because God knew they were both at greater risk than ever of falling for the unique Flávia Maura.

Which only made his next move all the more irrational.

'If that offer to take us into the rainforest is still on, I think when I get my free weekend next week, Brady and I would very much like to take you up on it.'

'You trust me?' She stared up at him, her amber eyes bright, proud. 'With Brady?'

'There's no one else I'd trust more,' he assured her, lowering his head and finally, *finally*, claiming her mouth with his.

CHAPTER TWELVE

'*PARE! OLHE!*'

Raoul stopped abruptly, pointing something out that Flávia had to train her eyes for a moment to see.

'Wait,' she instructed Brady and Jake in turn, then panned with her camera until it caught what Raoul had first spotted. 'Look—there in that glory bush.'

Brady and Jake peered into the image and belatedly, Flávia realised that she had effectively invited Jake to step closer to her. As her thundering heartbeat now heralded.

The past few hours with Jake had been eased by the presence of both Brady and Raoul. She'd used the pair of them almost as a shield to help her create some distance from Jake.

It had to be one of the hardest things she'd ever had to do in her life, but what choice did she have?

Flávia didn't even recognise the woman she'd been last week on their date. She had never opened up to anyone—not even Maria—the way she'd opened up to Jake. It went deeper than the mere secrets she'd shared with him. It was more than just the way his grey-blue eyes had seemed to shine light on the darker corners of her soul, making the things which had once scared her seem less frightening. It had gone beyond the way they'd returned to her city apartment and made love slowly and tenderly. Then hard and illicitly.

And for the first time in her life, her apartment had felt like a home instead of just the crash pad she used when she couldn't get back to the rainforest and it was too late to travel to Maria's.

That entire night with Jake had felt like a surrender.

And it terrified her.

So, she'd gone out of her way to avoid bumping into him ever since. She'd snuck in and out of her lab and avoided all the places in the hospital that she knew he usually frequented. She'd even avoided Brady—which only made her feel guilt on top of all these other tumbling, confusing emotions.

It had been fortunate that the week had also been one of the busiest of the summer training programme and she'd known Jake had practically been in back-to-back teaching operations and seminars, anyway.

So why didn't she feel that fortunate?

But now she was here, in the middle of the Atlantic Forest with Jake, and it was getting harder and harder to pretend things were normal between them. She had no idea what he was thinking, and it was making her crazy.

She was turning herself inside out. Wondering. Imagining. And then, trying to act as though it didn't matter to her.

Impossible.

'Wow...' Brady breathed, drawing her back to the present in an instant.

And as soon as he did, her gaze pulled inexorably to Jake. Just in time to watch as his eyebrows knitted together in disbelief.

Her fingers actually ached to reach out and smooth his brow.

Hopeless!

'What *is* that?' The scepticism leapt from his tone. 'It can't be real.'

'It's real.' Flávia ignored her leaping nerves and tried for a light laugh. 'Even though, I'll agree, it looks like something straight out of a sci-fi movie. Gentlemen, meet *bocydium globulare*—aka the Brazilian treehopper.'

'No, surely not? That's really real?' Jake shook his head.

'What are the balls on its head?' Brady demanded, fascinated.

And she found it was easier to concentrate on Brady and pretend that Jake wasn't there.

'Ah, now, they are spheres of chitin, a fibrous substance and primary component of the exoskeletons of arthropods, as well as the cell walls of fungi.'

Brady touched the screen with his finger, as though it could somehow bring him closer.

'Is it a male?'

'Nice guess—you might think so given how flamboyant the males of species often are compared to their female counterparts,' Flávia congratulated. 'But actually, this ornamentation is found on both sexes of treehopper alike.'

'So what are the spheres for?' Brady asked.

'Honestly, Brady, we're not entirely sure. We think it's possible that they are there to deter predators. It would certainly be harder to catch and eat something like this with all those balls on its head, wouldn't it?'

'Yeah.' Brady nodded vigorously.

'That said,' Flávia hurried on, reminding herself to stay focused on Brady rather than the fact that Jake seemed to have taken a step closer and was now sending her reactions into overdrive, 'these spherical ornaments also sport bristles, so it's possible that they are sensory bristles and the ornamentation also has some tactile function we don't yet understand.'

'That's so cool,' Brady inhaled.

'I like to think so.'

It was all she could do not to snap the camera back into place and leap away from Jake. To try to regain even a fracture of her composure.

Her brain didn't really seem to be functioning well all of a sudden.

'Anyway, come on, the sanctuary is this way.'

'I didn't know we were going to the sanctuary?' Jake frowned, his low voice sending ripples right through her.

'We weren't.' Why was it suddenly so hard to keep her voice light, and breezy? 'But I thought you might like to see it, given the amount I've talked about it.'

And maybe there she could remind herself where her heart, and mind, lay. And help her to get over this obsession with a man who could never exist in her real world.

'Flávia…'

She wanted so badly to stop. To talk to him.

Pretending not to hear, Flávia practically launched herself in front of Raoul. Anything to establish a bit of a gap— however artificial—between her and Jake.

'Come on. I'll lead the way for a bit.'

Cesar stepped into the designated habitat, the large viper coiled on the ground, and Flávia watched him move his homemade staff to the snake's neck. Gentle and accurate, that was Cesar's motto. And much as the two of them adored their beloved snakes, they would never lose respect for what the powerful animals were capable of.

She held her breath, as she always did at these moments. Then Cesar was moving, fast and precise, pinning the bushmaster to the ground before scooping it up, keeping its neck straight and smooth so it couldn't snap its head back and clamping it under his arm.

Flávia moved forward quickly with the film-covered

container, and Cesar lowered the snake until it bit down, its venom sliding into the clear pot.

'I always hate this bit,' he muttered, his accent as heavy as ever. 'But I have to tell myself that every sample is a step closer to finding a solution that will make my country-men realise how valuable these snakes can be and therefore encourage them to cherish the animals instead of merely fearing them.'

Carefully placing the pot in another, sealed container, Flávia exited the cage and handed it off to Raoul, who promptly turned to Brady, who had been waiting outside in safety, with Jake. The passionate little boy appeared to have captured yet another heart.

'Come,' Raoul said to Brady and Jake, 'I show you where this goes now.'

'This is amazing,' the young boy enthused. 'I'm going to make a project as soon as I get back home.'

'To the UK?' Raoul guessed. 'Are you looking forward to it?'

Brady's face darkened instantly.

'No, I don't like it there.'

'Excuse me,' apologised Raoul hastily. 'I was thinking...'

He tailed off but it didn't matter. Brady hadn't taken of-fence. He never did.

'I meant home to where Vovô Eduardo is. And Julianna and Marcie.'

'Ah...' Raoul looked over Brady's head with a knowing smile. 'Flávia's family are being very kind. I, too, am lik-ing them very much.'

'I wish I could stay with them for ever. I don't want to go back to England next week.'

Next week!

As Flávia went hot, then cold, she watched Jake stiffen, and in that moment she would have given anything to know what was going on in his head.

It didn't matter how much she'd been reminding herself of the truth, and schooling herself to keep her distance; the truth sounded that much less palatable when she heard it spoken aloud.

She couldn't speak. Couldn't even breathe. All she could do was stand, motionless, watching as Raoul led Brady and Jake out. Pretending she wasn't standing there, staring at the door long after they'd left, and it had slammed shut behind them.

Why had Jake reacted? Because he didn't want to be leaving in a week's time? Or because, for him, it couldn't come soon enough?

She was desperate to know.

But worse, she was terrified that he might give her the wrong answer.

'Ready to get more samples?' Cesar's voice at her shoulder made her jump.

'Yes.' She snapped sharply back into the present. In this job, there was no time to be distracted. 'Ready.'

For the next half hour they worked quickly and systematically, collecting sample after sample, and packing them away carefully. She fought to focus, using the space as a chance to remind herself what really mattered in her life. Her career, and her snakes. Not some fling who seemed to have got inside her head, however much he felt like more than that.

What really mattered was her work with Cesar. With VenomSci. And slowly, slowly, she managed to calm her racing heart and throw herself into the task she knew so well. They worked steadily, going from enclosure to enclosure and collecting venom from each bushmaster, treating the snakes with care but always respecting them.

By the time they had finished and made their way back through the sanctuary, Jake was sitting at the battered old picnic bench in the staff area and being treated to Raoul's homemade dessert using the most succulent exotic fruits.

'Where's Brady?'

'Fabio took him to look at something snake-related.' Jake shrugged.

'So you guys are leaving next week.' She tried for up-beat and breezy as she slid in opposite Jake.

It had been the little test she'd set for herself as she'd been working. And she'd passed. But now it was getting harder as she sat there whilst Jake studied her for a long moment.

'Brady wouldn't be, if he could get his way. Your sister would be ending up with a third kid all of a sudden. And not the baby she keeps teasing Luis that she's going to have.'

She tried to echo his low laugh, wondering if it was just her imagination that it sounded more forced than usual.

'I honestly don't think Maria would mind. She's rather taken with Brady. They all are.'

'You're very lucky, Flávia. You have an incredible family, and you're so close.'

'Yes.' She swallowed abruptly. 'Well, we've had to be.'

'Because of your mother,' he said softly.

And she hated that he could read her thoughts.

Hated, she repeated firmly. Not *loved* the fact that he seemed to understand her so well.

But that didn't mean she needed to bore Jake with the details of her own childhood sadness. Her mother walking out wasn't exactly in the realms of what had happened to Brady's mum, but it had affected her all the same. It had moulded the person she was—as Enrico had pointed out, *very* categorically.

'Never mind.' She shut down the discussion quickly, her own fault for such a thoughtless comment in the first place, of course.

Still, she shook off the melancholy that seemed to be

hovering; she was where she needed to be now, so she was more than happy with the way her life had turned out.

At least, she had been, until Jake had slammed into it and apparently knocked it off its comfortable little axis. And try as she might, she couldn't seem to restore order.

'So what about you? Are you looking forward to leaving? Getting back to your own hospital and your work?'

He took a fraction longer than necessary responding.

'I *will* enjoy getting back to my own hospital. Maybe implanting some of the lessons learned here.'

It wasn't exactly the answer she'd been hoping for. She plastered the brightest smile on her face and forced out a hollow laugh.

'Lovely. That's fabulous.'

'It is?' he asked softly, not joining in with her brittle laughter.

Yet she couldn't bring herself to stop.

'Well, of course. Isn't it?'

And when he looked at her like he was in that instant, his blue eyes almost silver, it was enough to make her stomach twist itself up into the most perfect Siberian hitch knot.

'I don't know,' he answered softly. 'Can we talk?'

'Talk?' she echoed weakly.

A hundred questions tumbled through her head. A thousand. But all Flávia could do was nod jerkily, before a commotion by the door caught her attention and a few words made their way to her ears.

Government inspection?

'We have to go now,' Cesar confirmed. 'Flávia, are you coming?'

'Coming,' she responded instantly, steadfastly ignoring the regret that washed over her.

This was her job. It had to come first.

She shot an apologetic glance to Jake, who wore a disconcertingly neutral expression. If he was disappointed not to have had that conversation, then he wasn't showing it. Then she followed Cesar out the door.

And if an odd sense of foreboding followed her, then she refused to let it affect her.

Jake knew something was wrong even before anyone uttered the words. Even before people started rushing around in a frenzy.

He couldn't have said how he knew or, more to the point, he didn't want to acknowledge how. That icy wash that poured through his veins with no warning, and for no apparent reason, an hour later.

'*Acidente*. Accident,' Raoul growled as he raced by.

'What kind of accident?' Jake demanded. 'Where's Brady?'

'He's fine—he's with Fabio.' But Jake couldn't shake the sick feeling in his stomach as he fell in behind the running Raoul. 'Flávia?'

He knew.

'Flávia? *Sim.* Flávia is collecting *o veneno*. Venom.'

'She was bitten?' He yanked open the door to the medical room, all but pushing Raoul ahead of him with the medical supplies.

'*Sim.* Yes. The *idiota* government official—he go into enclosure because he see no snake. Flávia, she try to stop him. She get the bites.'

An overwhelming sense of horror swept through him. Filling every last dark corner and jagged crevice inside of him. Snuffing out all the little atoms of light she had begun to leave there.

He'd never known anyone like Flávia. The thought of losing her was almost too much to withstand. Following Raoul, they entered where Cesar had Flávia on a table.

'Is she okay?' His tongue felt too thick for his mouth, his lips numb.

This was why he didn't do emotion. This was why he'd carried on the harsh lessons having parents like his had taught him, and kept himself detached.

Because he had no doubt that he had never felt worse than he did, right at this moment.

'No.' Cesar looked up, his face grim, his eyes flashing with a combination of fear and fury as he took the supplies from Raoul.

Disastrously, it was the fear that seemed to be winning out. Though he knew Cesar would never succumb to it.

'Antivenom,' Cesar demanded urgently, all but snatching the vials that Raoul presented to him. 'I can't stabilise her blood pressure.'

Jake advanced into the room, his eyes trained on Flávia.

'What can I do?'

'I need to administer an initial bolus dose of AVS, and immobilise the affected lower limb.'

'You deal with the limb, I'll get an intravenous catheter for the AVS.' He quickly picked up the kit he needed.

The medical bit was something he could do eyes closed. And it made him feel as though he was *acting* instead of simply watching. Dreading.

Jake efficiently inserted the catheter so the AVS could be administered continually, before checking the bandages Cesar had applied. They were tight, but not so tight that they threatened too-tight arterial compression.

'Good,' he muttered, stepping forward to perform a fresh set of obs.

'We have called *ambulância aérea*?' Cesar asked.

'Air ambulance?' Jake nodded and looked towards Raoul. 'They're on their way?'

'*Sim.*'

That was good, at least.

'You will travel with Flávia?' Cesar asked Jake quietly. He wanted to say yes. He'd never wanted something so much in his life. Flávia looked so small, so fragile, that something in Jake's chest seem to crack wide open. He could hardly bear to see her there. But he had Brady to think about.

Not just in this moment, something nagged at him. *But for life.*

'No,' he ground out. 'You must go. You know more about the snake that bit her. I'll get Raoul and Fabio to lead Brady and me back out.'

He barely waited for Cesar to agree before he resumed his continual monitoring of Flávia—checking her vitals, making sure she was still alive—and with each moment that ticked by, the reality of the situation rammed home inside him and words scraped against the roof of his mouth, paring away at it.

This wasn't something he'd ever thought he could, or would, say to anyone. But he needed to say it. Here. Now.

He covered her smooth hand with his, before sliding his other hand beneath it, too. As though he could protect her from every possible storm, when the real truth was that he couldn't protect her from anything, because Flávia Maura *was* that storm.

And he told her that she was a glorious, wild, terrifying monsoon. And that he...*loved* her for it. If this flawed, terrifying thing he felt could even be called *love*.

Although if it was love, his voice cracked at that point, *how would he even know?*

Abruptly, Cesar's radio crackled into life and a voice alerted him to the fact that the *ambulância aérea* had arrived. And Jake stepped back, waiting for them to come through the doors.

It was just over twelve hours later when Flávia stirred from sleep in her hospital bed as the doctor came in to check on her. Jake's neck was killing him from the awkward position he'd been sleeping in in the wingback chair, but he didn't care.

Maria and Eduardo were still asleep—Maria on the couch, and Eduardo in a similar straight-backed chair. They had only dropped off around three in the morning, and he was loath to wake them, but he knew they wouldn't miss this moment for a second.

He tried to follow as the doctor chatted with Flávia, and from Maria's tearful laugh and vigorous nodding, and Eduardo looking slightly less pale than before, it seemed to be good news. He clenched his hands in his pockets; it had never been this hard to be patient before, but they'd been good enough letting him join them in the room. The least he could do would be to bite his tongue.

Still, it felt like an eternity before the doctor left and his heart lifted a fraction more as he watched Maria and Eduardo hug each other, then Flávia, then each other again. And then they both hugged him.

'We're going for breakfast,' Maria told him, patting his arm. 'Give Flávia a chance to tell you…the news.'

He waited for them to leave before crossing the room. Lowering his head, he stroked her hair and planted a soft kiss on her forehead.

'I take it it's good news, then?'

'There's some localised swelling and oedema, and they want to keep me in a bit longer for observation, but the preliminary assessment is that I am going to be all right.'

'That's good,' he managed. It was impossible to articulate how relieved he felt. Nonetheless, his mind was whirling. 'How is that even possible?'

'They can't say for certain, but there are a few theories. First off, it was a very young bushmaster. Also, it didn't deliver the kind of bite that I know it could have. And because I've been bitten so many times during my career— not just by bushmasters, but by other snakes, by spiders, bullet ants, there's quite a list—my body has built up some immunity to toxins. Enough that, when combined with the antivenom I received, and the fact that it was administered so quickly, I seem to be remarkably *okay*.'

'So there won't be any long-term effects?'

For an instant, he thought she hesitated, as though there was something more to say, but then she smiled. A tight, tired smile, but a smile nonetheless.

It had to be just his edginess which had him seeing things that weren't really there.

'They won't know for certain until all the test results come back,' Flávia told him, and this time he was sure her voice sounded odd. Strained. 'But as I said, preliminary findings look good.'

He wasn't sure he could take her lying to him.

'Is there something you aren't saying?' he bit out.

She hesitated again.

'Is it true that you were in that room with Cesar? That you took charge like it was one of your operations?'

'Anyone would have,' he managed gruffly.

'I remember hearing certain things...' she managed after a while. 'At least, I think I did. It's kind of hazy.'

It took him a moment to realise that it was a question.

'What did you hear?' he demanded, his voice clipped.

She flushed, and he knew what she was going to say.

'Something about me being...a monsoon? And—' she stopped, her cheeks flushing even darker before she dropped her voice to little more than a whisper '—and that you love me?'

'I also said I don't even know what love is,' he rasped. 'And it doesn't matter either way.'

'I think you do,' she began before pausing. Frowning. 'What do you mean it doesn't matter?'

He would have given anything to wipe away the wary look that had just clouded her beautiful features.

Instead, Jake thought of Brady, and he slammed a steel cage shut around his chest. And whatever it was that might, or might not, be inside it.

'It doesn't matter because I can't be with you.'

He heard her sharp intake of breath. Saw her pale. But he couldn't cede. Not now. There was more than just him and her to think about.

'You don't understand…' she began helplessly, but he cut her off.

'I think I do,' he said. 'You once told me that you love your job, that it's who you are. And you said that if a person loved you enough, they wouldn't ask you to change that.'

'I remember,' she managed.

'Well, I'm not asking you to change. I know who you are and I accept that.'

'Jake…'

'But I can't be with you. I can't put Brady through what I went through today. I *won't*.'

He ignored the sharp lance of pain, just as he shut his ears to the taunting voice, needling that maybe it wasn't just Brady he wanted to spare from the pain of today.

That maybe he himself couldn't stand to go through it again.

But he refused to ask her to change who she was. That would be like finding a bird of paradise, only to clip its wings to prevent it from flying. And Flávia deserved to fly.

He just couldn't stand to watch her get too close to the sun.

'I see,' she managed at last.

And he thought the brittleness of her voice might topple him once and for all.

'Well, listen, Jake. Thanks for being here, but you really shouldn't.'

'I don't have to go right this second,' he told her gruffly, a tightness lodged in his throat. A huge part of him madly wanting to claw every word back.

Wishing things were different. And he'd never been the kind of man to wish for things that couldn't be.

'I can stay. Until you're on your feet,' he rasped. 'In fact, right now there's nowhere else I'd rather be.'

For a fraction of a second, her whole face appeared to soften and threatened to crumple. He moved in, on some insane whim, to kiss it smooth, but Flávia turned her head and seemed to steel herself, right before his eyes.

'But there's somewhere else *I* would rather you were.'

'Sorry?' He wasn't sure he was following her.

Again, she hesitated, as if she was having second thoughts. Or perhaps that was just his imagination.

Everything in him was spinning. Sliding this way and that as though it didn't know where it was meant to be.

'This is a time I should have my family around me,' she said firmly. Pointedly. 'And you have your own family to care for.'

He'd hurt her. He hadn't wanted to, but what choice was there? It was her or Brady. Still, it didn't mean he found it that easy to turn his back on her. Not when every fibre of his being was howling at him to change his mind. To find a way to make it work.

'Brady is with Luis,' he managed. 'And Julianna and Marcie.'

'But he should be with *you*,' she answered, and he felt the barb as surely as if she'd jabbed it into his skin.

'You want me to go now,' he realised.

He could hardly blame her after all he'd just said, so this was no time to succumb to this offensive, putrid *thing* sloshing around inside him.

'Message understood.' He stood. Stiffly. Awkwardly. 'I should have thought. I won't disturb you any longer.'

'Jake...' she whispered, looking suddenly pained. 'It's

just…you're right. It wouldn't be fair on Brady, for a start. That kid has been through enough with his mother without having to deal with…*this*.'

She was grasping. Making excuses. He could read her as easily as he could read an X-ray.

My God, does she actually pity me?

'Don't concern yourself,' he managed flatly. 'As you so unambiguously put it, Brady is my family, my responsibility. Not yours.'

Even though he'd made his decision, his heart still cracked when he thought about trying to explain to Brady why he wouldn't be seeing Flávia, or Maria, ever again. To say nothing of Eduardo, or the girls. But Flávia was right—it was better that than his young nephew ever seeing Flávia like this. Or worse.

Jake had managed to whisk Brady home from the forest with the quiet assistance of Fabio without panicking him about what had happened to Flávia. The official line was that she'd been called away for a government inspection and that was it. He could never bear to tell the boy that something had happened to her.

He wasn't sure he would ever be able to bear hearing it himself. Which only seemed to confirm that it wasn't just Brady's heart he was trying to protect.

Not that he cared to dwell on that particular realisation right now.

CHAPTER THIRTEEN

'FOR THE LAST TIME, Livvy, will you just call the guy and tell him how you feel? Before you dust the paint off my favourite vases?'

Miles away, her sister's voice finally penetrated Flávia's subconscious and she looked up from her cleaning task. She lurched forward, knocked a vase, steadied it and stared at Maria loftily.

'I don't know what you're talking about.'

Maria rolled her eyes.

'Of course you do. You've been moping around for the last month. Ever since Jake and Brady left for England.'

So much for thinking that she'd contained her feelings well. Still, Flávia pulled back her shoulders and thrust her head a little higher into the air.

But it was exhausting, trying to pretend that her heart wasn't smashed into a billion tiny fragments.

She should never have sent Jake away. *Never.* But what choice had she had? Once the doctor had told her the news.

'Should I remind you that I got bitten? That I've been unwell? If I have been acting a little oddly, it's because I'm under the weather. Not because I'm *moping*!' She practically spat the word out.

Maria levelled a direct stare at her. 'You've been moping.'

'No, I—'

'You love the guy and he loves you. So why make a drama out of it when all you have to do is call him and tell him you're sorry?' she added archly.

'I don't love him,' Flávia protested—poorly, probably, since this was to her sister. She felt too hot. Too...*tight*. 'But even if I did, Jake Cooper certainly doesn't love me.'

'He loves you. And if you explain why you lied, he may just understand and still love you.'

It was foolish, the spark of hope that danced inside her chest. Moreover, it was dangerous.

'I didn't lie, I just omitted one detail. And only because they still had no idea at that time what would happen, given the bite,' she parroted out the excuse she'd been telling herself ever since that morning.

'You lied,' Maria stated flatly. 'And you know it.'

Flávia began to deny, then thought better. She rubbed her hands over her eyes.

'It's more complicated than that.'

'Only if you make it more complicated.'

'No.' She shook her head at her sister, her shoulders starting to slump as the fight left her. 'You're right. He talked to me about love, but when I got bitten he realised that he couldn't be with me. He couldn't put Brady through that if next time I wasn't as lucky. If next time, the bite is fatal.'

'Couldn't put Brady through it, or himself?' Maria wondered, more to herself than to Flávia.

Either way, Flávia's pulse kicked up a notch. Had she wanted Maria to argue the point? Somehow?

'Turns out Jake isn't so different from Enrico.'

'He's completely different,' her sister refuted instantly. 'And I know you know that, too.'

'How? How is it different, Maria?' cried Flávia. 'They both ultimately needed me to give up my snakes, my career, to be with them.'

'Not your career, just the dangerous part. The same bit that you yourself have talked about giving up ever since you found out about the baby. You need to call Jake, Livvy.'

'Call him and say what?' Flávia lifted her hand and dropped it against her thigh in despair. 'That I'm pregnant, but whilst I seem to be okay, the doctors still have no idea how the bite might have affected the baby?'

'It's a start.'

'Right,' she snorted, but it was more like fear, regret and grief all merging into one harsh sound. 'So, get Jake to drop everything and drag Brady halfway across the world for a baby that might not even survive.'

'I think Jake would rather prefer that to being left in the dark, the way he is now,' Maria pointed out, not unkindly.

'I don't think he would,' Flávia countered defiantly, as if that could somehow quell her jangling nerves.

Frankly, she had no idea what Jake thought. She wasn't sure she had ever really known. Though her sister didn't need to know that.

'I'm telling you, when it comes down to it, there are no differences between Jake and Enrico.'

'There are lots of differences.'

'Go on, then. Give me one of them.'

She hadn't realised how desperately she wanted to make that distinction until she levelled the question at her sister.

'I'll give you two,' Maria replied. 'First, Enrico gave you an ultimatum a year after he'd already asked you to marry him. Mainly because you didn't exactly rush to set a date, and deep down he knew that you weren't as eager to marry him as he was to marry you.'

'I loved him,' Flávia lied.

'No, you didn't, and you know that. You're just being obstinate now. You would never have gone to the lengths for him that you went to for Jake these past few months.'

'I was looking out for Brady, his seven-year-old nephew,' Flávia pointed out hotly as something swelled up inside her.

Something she couldn't—or didn't want to—yet identify.

'You were,' Maria agreed with a delicate lift of one shoulder. 'But you were also doing it for Jake.'

'And the second difference?' Flávia demanded.

For a moment, her sister just watched her. Studied her.

'The second difference is you, Livvy,' she said at last. 'It's how you feel about each man. You could never have contemplated changing any part of what you do for Enrico. But your heart hasn't been in it at all since Jake left. *That's* your main difference.'

'It's my career, my life, and I love what I do.'

She always had loved it. So why didn't it hold quite the same power that it had before?

'I know that,' Maria acknowledged. 'But we both know you're going to change it, anyway. For your baby. Besides, no one is saying give up your career completely.'

'Then, what?' Flávia asked.

Her head was a mess from all the back and forth. If only she knew what she really thought. What Jake really thought.

'You can keep doing your work in the sanctuary, and you can raise awareness. Just give up going into the pits for the collections. You said Cesar was thinking about doing so because he was getting old and his grip was weakening. Isn't that why Fabio and Raoul have been drafted in? To start taking on that side of it? And there are two other employees now, aren't there?'

'Yes.'

'So, there you go. You ease back on the hands-on, just like Cesar is. But no one's asking you to give up the sanctuary altogether, Livvy. We all know it's part of who you are, and what you love.'

And it was odd, wasn't it, that the suggestion didn't fill her with indignation, like it would have even two months ago. But still, something bubbled away inside her. Low yet lethal.

She tried to articulate it, but the words wouldn't come.

'What if I'm not cut out for it?' she settled for instead. 'What if I give it up for him, for the baby, and then I end up resenting him for it?'

'You won't.'

She almost envied Maria her certainty, because her own fears were starting to eat away inside her.

'You can't know that.'

'I can.'

'How?'

And the beat hung between them for such an interminably long moment.

'Because you're not our mother,' Maria said quietly. Angrily.

Everything around Flávia started to spin, and it was impossible to keep the pleading from her voice. All this time, she'd thought Maria hadn't known her deepest fears.

'How can you be so sure?' she whispered.

'Because I am. Because you're a completely different person than her. You're a loyal sister, a loving aunt and a compassionate woman. You love your job, but you didn't put it ahead of your family… Well, sometimes you did, but nothing like the way that she did.'

And despite everything, they both laughed, albeit weakly.

'You're not like *her*, Livvy. You never were. But especially not now.'

Flávia didn't know how long they stood together, whilst she absorbed what her sister was telling her. She might look tough but deep down she wasn't, she never had been, and right now she didn't even feel herself. She felt stripped down, fragile, broken. Just like the delicate back of her beloved bushmasters.

But finally, finally, she lifted her eyes and looked at Maria.

'So I decide to do that…to throttle back on the hands-on work at the sanctuary. Then what?' And there was no way she could keep the shake from her voice.

'Then you call Jake and set out what you've decided, and you tell him that you love him.'

'I don't know. That's a scary idea.'

'Scary?' Maria laughed. 'Telling him you love him is scary? You got bitten, several times over the years, and yet you went back in with those bushmasters of yours each time. Surely, *that's* scary?'

'Not if Jake walks away from me. He already has done once.'

'Because you sent him away.' Maria blew out a deep breath. 'I don't know, that's just my two cents' worth. But ultimately, Flávia, it's down to you.'

And the words echoed through Flávia's head all afternoon and all the way home.

Ultimately, it was down to her.

Jake leaned on his car as the kids were let out of school, waiting at a distance the way that Brady had asked him to do. Still, he didn't miss the march from the building, or the tightly locked jaw.

'How was your day?'

'Three words,' Brady bit out mutinously as he practically threw himself into the vehicle. 'Brazil. Right. Now.'

Each word was punctuated by the little lad counting a finger in mid-air. The worst of it was Jake couldn't agree more. But he couldn't say that; it was his job to make his nephew feel better.

'Listen, mate,' he offered, 'I'm sorry that it was a bad day, but—'

'I want to go home.'

'This *is* home…'

'No. Home was in São Paulo. I miss those weekends in the rainforest,' Brady cut in, his eyes locking with Jake's in challenge. 'I miss Julianna and Marcie, and Vovô Eduardo. And I miss Maria and Luis. Most of all, I miss Flávia.'

'I miss Flávia, too, mate,' Jake answered before he could even stop himself.

Even the closing soirée had been hell, being back in that hotel ballroom. Everything had looked the same, from the same tablecloths to the same people in the same evening clothes.

But it hadn't been anywhere near the same. Because Flávia hadn't been there.

'Then why are we even here?' Brady demanded, yanking Jake back to the present.

That was a good question.

'It isn't as black and white as you think,' Jake began. 'There's your school, my job…'

He stopped, running out of excuses, and Brady narrowed his eyes at him, for all the world looking at least twice his seven years.

'I hate this school, so what does it matter if I go to school out there instead? And if you really wanted to, you could change jobs and work out in Brazil.'

'Me going to work out there isn't that simple.' Jake shook his head, holding on to the only part that he could of what his young nephew had said. 'It's complicated.'

'Mummy always said that's what adults say when they don't want to explain something. I'm not a little kid,' he spat out.

'I know you like to think you're mature and understand life and the world around you,' Jake cut in firmly, shutting the conversation down. 'But that's exactly what you are, Brady—*a kid*. Something you have to understand is that adults know more than you do. And that we know what's best.'

'This is so unfair!' Brady cried, but at least the conversation was over.

So why did he feel so bad about it?

It felt like they'd made such progress in their relationship whilst they'd been in Brazil, but returning home had cost them, had propelled it all backwards.

Far from the engaged, social boy that his nephew had been when Flávia was around, as soon as they'd got home to London, Brady had started locking himself in his room and working on projects alone. No amount of cajoling had brought him out—not even Oz's famous cooking—and all the nature programmes that Jake had sat watching, just so that he could keep connecting with his nephew, was going to waste.

And he needed Flávia. Though not to resolve the problem for Brady...so much as to resolve the problem with himself.

How many times had he replayed that last conversation, trying to read every nuance? Trying to understand the fear which had made him say what he'd said. Words which, in his head, had sounded so logical and well-considered, but which had haunted him as a mistake ever since.

But there was one other thing stuck in his head.

Flávia's expression when she'd been talking to the doctor, and then the way she'd looked at him.

There had been something there—something he'd missed—but no matter how many times he replayed it, Jake couldn't get a handle on it.

His mind was still stuck on it when he pulled the car into the drive and shut off the engine to talk to Brady, but the boy was already snatching at the lever, practically hurling himself out of the vehicle and racing to the front door when he jabbed his finger at the hi-tech security lock.

Jake was fractions of a second away from letting Brady just run away when an image of Flávia popped into his head. A memory of her crouched down in front of the boy, talking to him on the same level, never dismissing his opinions or feelings.

With a sigh, he followed Brady up the stairs. He couldn't give up. He wouldn't.

Jake raked his hand through his hair and stared at the solid piece of wood as though willing it to open in front of his very eyes.

Maybe for Flávia it would have done so. But it didn't open for him.

He lifted his hand, second-guessed himself, and then— at last—he knocked on Brady's door, trying to affect an upbeat tone.

'You okay in there, mate?'

The door opened unexpectedly, nearly making Jake stumble back in surprise. A piece of paper was thrust out.

'I need you to give this to Flávia.'

'Flávia?' Even her name made something leap inside of him. 'You want me to send this to her?'

'No.' Brady clucked his tongue irritably. 'I want you to *give* this to her when you *see* her. It'll mean more.'

Jake raked his hand through his hair.

'I told you, I won't be seeing her again, Brady.'

'Why not?' Brady looked mutinous.

'Because I won't be returning to Brazil.'

There was no reason for his heart to thud so heavily, so leaden, in his chest at the finality of the statement. No reason at all.

'Why can't you be a surgeon out there? They have hospitals, too.'

Jake was sure he could actually hear Flávia's voice in his head, light and happy, telling him to keep cool. He gritted his teeth and tried to sound understanding.

'You know the answer.'

'If you really wanted to, you could change your job.' Brady looked so sad, so lost, that Jake's chest pulled—taut and painful. 'I'd rather be out there than back here.'

The worst of it was that Jake felt the same way. For a long moment, the two of them stood in their respective positions, eyeing each other up.

If he was going to win back the connections they'd started to make in Brazil, then it occurred to him that he was going to have to be a little more truthful with Brady.

'Flávia is incredible. She made an impact on both of us—her whole family did—and I understand why you want to go back there. But I'm trying to protect you. You might not understand now but, trust me, one day you will.'

He sounded like those clichéd films, but what else was he supposed to say to a seven-year-old kid? He could hardly go into detail, could he?

Brady eyed him critically, his small brow furrowing into tight lines.

'Because she got bitten by a snake?'

Jake hesitated. He hadn't thought Brady had known, but he supposed it was too much to think that he hadn't been talking about it with Julianna and Marcie. Typical of Brady to keep it inside all this time, though.

'That's part of it,' he acknowledged at last.

'Were you frightened she might die? Like Mummy?'

God, the kid is too astute for his own good sometimes.

It took him a while to answer.

'Yes, mate. I was.'

'Me, too,' Brady whispered.

Without warning, the boy took a step forward and threw his arms around Jake's waist. Startled, it took Jake a moment to react, but when he did, it felt like the last obstacles between them were starting to crumble away.

And Flávia was somehow at the centre of it all again.

'That's why I don't think it's a good idea to go back out there,' Jake said after he'd carried the boy downstairs and settled him on the couch.

Maybe it was time to do what Flávia had kept suggesting, and talk.

'Why?' Brady pressed, and Jake drew in a steadying breath.

'Well, what if we did? What if we had Flávia in our lives and she got bitten again? And what if she didn't get better this time?'

'You mean, what if she died?' Brady looked at him solemnly.

The thought was sickening, but Jake forced himself to answer.

'Yeah, mate. What if she did?'

His nephew continued to gaze at him, solemn and unblinking.

'What if she didn't?' he asked at last. 'But, what if we stayed here and then you got sick, like Mummy, and you died. Who would look after me then? I don't want to live with Grandma and Granddad. I know I'm not supposed to say it, but I don't like them.'

'Is that what you think about?' Jake demanded.

It made sense, he supposed, given all that the kid had been through. But he hated that he hadn't realised Brady feared it. Hadn't thought about it.

No doubt Flávia had. That was yet another reason why she had been so good for them.

Still, doing it for Brady wasn't a good enough reason to go out to Brazil. If he was going to fight for Flávia, then he'd better be damned sure he was doing it for the right reasons.

And the simple truth was that he was.

Brady was right, of course. He could use Flávia's career as an excuse for anything if it suited him, and it had, because he'd been afraid of the way he felt about her. He'd spent so many years detaching himself from feeling anything that he'd refused to admit what had been staring him in the face.

She'd broken defences he hadn't even known he'd had, and she'd helped him connect with his nephew in a way he would never have managed left to his own devices. She'd mellowed him. More than that, she'd thawed him.

And it had taken Brady's boldness to stop him from being so scared of admitting it.

Carefully, thoughtfully, Jake turned the paper slowly around and looked at it. A frog?

'What is it, anyway?'

'She'll know what it means.'

'Right.' Jake pressed his lips together.

To his surprise, Brady relented slightly.

'It's a strawberry poison dart frog, and it's a super-parent. Just like Flávia.'

'It's perfect for her.' Jake grinned conspiratorially. 'So I guess we'd better book a couple of plane tickets and go and give it to her.'

CHAPTER FOURTEEN

Passport. Tickets. Money. Check.

Flávia lowered her small cabin bag onto the ground and wheeled it out into the corridor. She was locking the door to her apartment when she heard the *ping* of the lift doors opening out of sight. But there was no way she could have anticipated seeing Jake walk around the corner.

Everything stopped. Her legs. Her heart. Her brain.

She had no idea how long she stood there, immobile, just watching him stride up the corridor towards her.

'Going somewhere?'

His dry, sure voice floated in the air, and then everything kick-started inside her again, with a jolt.

'What are you doing back here?' She was running hot, then cold, then hot again, and she barely recognised her own voice.

'I'm back here for you,' he responded simply, and the certain, unequivocal nature of it seemed to steal her breath away.

'Why?' she demanded hoarsely as emotions spiralled through her, too fast and too many to grasp.

But she recognised one of them. *Hope.* Why else would Jake be here, if not for her? Yet, at the same time, she could remember with painful clarity all the things they'd said to each other before he'd left Brazil last time.

And she knew the one thing he didn't. That she was carrying his baby.

'I'm guessing for the same reason you were heading to London.'

It was so simple, so direct, it made her heart stop for a second time in as many moments.

'How do you know?'

He half shrugged.

'I went to your sister's house as soon as I landed, thinking you'd either be in the rainforest or there. She told me.'

Her heart raced. Or stopped. She wasn't sure which.

'What else did she tell you?'

'That she was glad I'd come. That I should leave Brady with her whilst I found you, and that whatever else happened I should know that much.'

'I see,' Flávia managed, for want of anything better to say.

And then he moved closer, the air around them drawing that much thicker, that much tighter.

'I don't think you do see, Flávia,' he rasped. 'Not completely. And that's my fault for not saying it before. For not having the guts to say it before.'

'To say *what* before?'

He didn't answer, leaving her heart to thud. Long and slow and heavy.

'You told me that you couldn't put your desires ahead of Brady's needs,' she pressed on eventually. 'And I understand that. I get it.'

Jake took another step forward, his eyes holding hers so that she couldn't have dragged them away even if she'd wanted to.

'Only, what I feel for you is more than mere *desire*,' he murmured. 'It's much deeper than that.'

She wasn't sure when her soul left her body, but it was almost as though she was floating above the scene. Watching herself having this conversation, but too numb—too wound up with desperate anticipation—to actually feel part of it.

'Then…what?'

'I love you, Flávia Maura,' he told her simply, as if he hadn't just flipped her entire world upside down. Inside out. 'I can't imagine my life without you.'

Heat shot through Flávia's chest, plunging it into fire, like ramming it into a blast furnace. Then, just as quickly, doused it in an icy shower.

'Wait, Jake, before you say anything—'

'No, I waited before when I shouldn't have. I should have told you, because the simple truth is that I love you, but I'm not asking you to give up what you do. I know that makes you who you are. My fears were that something would happen to you, but I've come to see—actually, Brady has helped me to see—that those fears are for me to deal with. Not for you.'

'You don't understand—' she began, until Jake cut her off again.

'I can't subject you to a life where you spend every waking day in a lab, unable to escape into the rainforest, or spend time in that sanctuary which is so precious to you. I won't be the kind of man who does that—that isn't love. Not when I know who you are, and I understand what makes you tick. That is to say, I'm beginning to understand, and I truly can't wait to learn more about you. Every single day.'

'So…what are you saying, Jake?'

'I'm saying that I'm moving to Brazil. I've spoken to the board and we've started the ball rolling on the necessary procedures.'

It was more than she could ever have hoped for. Of course, guilt would have to hold her back. And it wasn't that protective armour she'd pulled around herself for years. It wasn't about her at all. It was about the baby that she hadn't even told him existed.

He might be saying all these things now, but how would he feel when he realised what she'd kept from him? Panic surged through her.

'You can't...' Every syllable quavered. She desperately fought against getting her hopes up, in case he hated her once he knew the truth. 'You said it yourself. Brady has to be your priority.'

'Brady loves you. He has made it unequivocally clear where his heart lies. And, like mine, it's very definitely out here. With you. You connected with him in days, in a way that I never could in almost ten months. He never came close to trusting me the way he trusts you. And Maria and her family, for that matter. You've made me realise that family is more important than anything. A good one, anyway.'

Flávia couldn't take it any more.

'Stop, Jake. Please, you have to stop.' Swinging around, she fumbled with the lock before pushing the door open wide. 'There's something you deserve—need—to know.'

Then, because there was no other way to say it than to be honest with him—finally—Flávia simply blurted it out.

'I'm pregnant.'

If she had slammed him in the gut, he wasn't sure it would have winded him any more than he already was.

He stared at her. Numb. Disbelieving. He waited for the betrayal to kick in, but although there was something there, it never quite kicked in.

'Pregnant?' It was him speaking, but he didn't recognise his voice.

'Yes,' she whispered.

'How? When?'

'You need me to run you through the mechanics of creating a baby?'

She was trying to brazen it out, that much was obvious.

But the quake in her tone betrayed her. He couldn't answer, but his eyes never left hers until, abruptly, she slid her gaze away, her cheeks flushed.

'Possibly from that day we returned from the rainforest that first time. And it was the only time we didn't use protection.'

The time in the pool house, he remembered. Only too vividly. And now he was going to be a father.

Again, if he counted Brady, because for all intents and purposes, he was the closest thing the boy was going to have to a father.

'How long have you known?'

'Ever since the doctor told me in the hospital room that day. It was extremely early days, usually too early to tell, but I guess this little guy or girl was a fighter from the start.'

'I was in the room,' he realised with sudden clarity, and felt a tremor of impatience. But nothing like he might have expected.

That was the moment that had replayed in his head all this time. And then another thought slammed brutally into him.

'The bushmaster bite…?'

'The baby seems fine.' She practically fell over her words. 'I had tests and so far everything has checked out, but they're monitoring it.'

'I have a contact,' he growled, pulling out his mobile and beginning to punch in numbers. 'I met him this summer.'

'It's fine. I have someone already.'

He wasn't prepared for the way she placed her hand out to stop him. The contact seared straight through him.

'Why didn't you tell me? As soon as it happened?'

'I don't know.' She dropped her shoulders, her eyes meeting his imploringly. 'I was going to, but I didn't know how to. And then…'

'And then I told you that I couldn't put Brady through

losing someone else he was close to,' he realised, and Flávia nodded awkwardly.

'But still…'

It was odd, but he couldn't quite decide how he felt. Both about the baby, and about the fact that Flávia had concealed the pregnancy from him.

'I didn't know if the baby was going to be all right at that point. Also, I didn't want you staying out of duty. Then resenting me.'

'I should never have put you in that position,' he rasped, because it was finally starting to sink in.

'You were looking out for Brady. I can understand that.' She shook her head, and he couldn't bring himself to elucidate.

Not yet. Not until he knew exactly what he wanted to say.

'I have to go into Paulista's. There's someone I need to speak to. Fancy a ride?'

She looked at him as though she was about to say something, then changed her mind.

'Sure.' She shrugged. 'They'll be surprised to see me here when I'm meant to be on a plane to London, but they won't complain.'

Jake took her keys, unlocked her door and deposited her cabin bag back inside, trying to make sense of these emotions sloshing around inside him. Was he angry or happy? He couldn't be sure. And until he was, he didn't want to confuse the issue.

He just knew he wanted to find a solution. Quickly.

Flávia left her lab late that evening, her mobile phone in her hand and the text from Jake still illuminating the screen.

She'd spent the day working since Jake had been in with the board all day and, to some degree, it had been a relief. At least it had distracted her from all the worries racing around her head.

Jake hadn't been furious as she might have expected when she'd told him about the baby, and she'd initially taken that to be a good sign.

Now, she wasn't so sure. What if it meant that he didn't care?

Trudging through the corridors, she pushed open the door to the car park and looked for his rental car, her heart nonetheless leaping as she saw him leaning on the bonnet. His impossibly masculine chest was shown off to perfection in a fitted shirt. Had he gone to a hotel room to clean up and change? Because that certainly wasn't what he'd been wearing this morning.

She edged nearer, her low heels tapping on the ground.

'Fruitful day?' he asked, his even tone giving nothing away.

'I guess,' she hedged. 'You?'

'Very.' And she thought she saw a quirk of his lips, but she couldn't be sure.

'Jake, listen, I should have said something this morning. Just so you know. But I knew I wanted this baby from the second I realised I was pregnant.'

'That's good to hear.' He dipped his head.

It wasn't the clearest of signals, but she'd take whatever she could.

'And I know I told you about the rainforest being my life, and the way my mother was, but I don't know if you understand how it relates. I don't know if *I* even understood it before.'

'But you do now?'

'I think I do,' she began. 'I told you that I was always… *different* as a kid, you've heard that before. The rainforest fascinated me from before I could even walk or talk. But when my mother walked out on us, I threw myself into it with everything I had. Maybe I thought fighting for a cause, taking on pet projects, gave me a place in life. I wanted to make a difference. I think I felt it made me relevant. Less disposable. Whatever, it became my life.'

'There's nothing wrong with that. What you do *matters*. You make a difference, Flávia.'

'Yes, and that was who I was. Without it, I feared I was no one. When I met Enrico, I thought my priorities would shift. I'd never give up my career, but I'd embrace being a wife. I'd want a family.'

'But you didn't.' He shrugged. 'That isn't who you are. It doesn't matter, we'll find a solution.'

'No, you don't understand.' She smiled. The realisation that Jake wanted to work through it with her buoyed her more than it had any right to. 'I was afraid that I was like *her*.'

'Your mother?'

She jerked her head in a semblance of a nod, but she couldn't bring herself to say it.

'I hated myself for it, but I couldn't make myself feel any of the things I thought I should. All the things Enrico wanted me to feel. And I thought it was my fault. For two years, I thought it was my fault. And then I met you.'

Jake moved closer to her. She could feel the heat, the energy, coming off him, pouring into her. The most glorious feeling she'd ever had.

'Even from that first night—our attempt at a one-night stand—I started to feel things for you that I'd never once felt for Enrico. But you were on the summer programme, you would be leaving, so I told myself that I was being ridiculous.'

'And do you still think that?' he demanded, his voice thick, a half-smile curving that all-too-tempting mouth of his.

She forced herself to stay focused.

'Who knows? I only know that I was ready to give up

my life here, in order to follow you to the UK, before I even knew you would have me. Before I knew I was pregnant.'

'And now that you're pregnant?'

'Now I don't want to do anything to ever risk my baby, or myself. I love my career, but I want to be a mother, too. A good mother. A loving mother. I don't resent my baby. I can't want to meet it. Him. Her. I don't care.' A giddy laugh escaped her at the mere thought.

'Well, if it's confession time, then I guess I should make one to you,' he surprised her by saying. 'This morning, you told me that I was only looking out for Brady, but the fact is that I was looking out for myself, too. It suited me to hide behind Brady rather than acknowledge this multitude of... *feelings* I have for you.'

'You really do?' she breathed.

He loved that she sounded so breathless. So filled with anticipation.

'I really do,' he confirmed.

'That's good, because I'd almost started to think this morning was a hallucination. Too perfect to be true.'

'You're carrying my baby. Which only means that you belong with me. For ever.'

'For ever,' she echoed softly, almost a question.

And finally, Jake stepped forward and took her face in his hands, an infinitely tender gesture.

Then he lowered his head and kissed her. Slow, deep, intense. And she wrapped her arms around him, held him close and gave herself up to every exquisite second of it.

A second chance she had feared she would never get.

And then, when the kiss finally ended and he set her slightly back from him, Jake moved to the side, gesturing to the small copse of trees in the near distance. Rubber figs, flooded gums, blue gums. And suddenly, in amongst them, she spotted a shadowed area and her eyes narrowed instinctively.

A sleep system, with a basher and hammock, swayed lightly in the breeze. And little lights besides.

'What is this?' she breathed.

'Go and find out,' suggested Jake, so sure, so confident, that it sent a current of electricity pulsing through her veins.

Flávia had no idea how her shaking legs carried her over to the area. She only cared that she got there. And when she did, she realised the lights were tiny, twinkly, solar-powered stars.

'Not that it can ever compare to the canopy of stars in the jungle.'

'When the trees aren't so dense they cover it.' She laughed as best she could when she could barely breathe.

She was nervous, yet she didn't know why. Carefully, she slid to sit on the hammock. More for something to do than anything else.

'Pretty good,' she managed. 'Though there's only room for one.'

'I'm fine here,' he told her, his voice sounding even more strange.

And then he dropped on one knee and she realised he'd pulled a box out in front of her, and her heart stopped. Or raced. She couldn't quite tell.

She'd spent the day thinking he was discussing a patient case, wondering if he'd even remembered she was here. Instead, it seemed he'd been racing around getting changed, buying a ring and setting up this scenario.

As though nothing else had been on his mind but her. It was touching.

'Flávia Maura, you are the most complex, complicated woman I've ever known. And yet, you're also the most genuine and straightforward. You've been stealing your way inside a heart which I didn't even know I had, ever since the first moment. You make me feel things I've never before felt in my life, and now I know what it's like, I can't ever imagine going back.'

'Me, either,' she whispered.

Her head was spinning and twisting so fast it might as well have been on a coaster ride. Everything he was saying was almost too much. Too dreamlike. Too perfect.

'I don't see my life without you in it.' And she loved that it sounded more like a vow. 'And I know for a fact that Brady feels the same. You saved me, Flávia. You saved both of us and I love you. Marry me.'

'I love you, too,' she choked out. 'Yes. Yes, I'll marry you.'

Then, as Jake slid the most stunningly simple ring onto her finger, she realised she had never, ever felt so complete—*so right*—before. This time, when he drew her into his arms and kissed her, she knew it would never end.

This wasn't an end. This was just a beginning. And she couldn't wait to start the rest of her life with the man who had saved her just as much as he told her she had saved him.

They were married a month later in a quiet, closed ceremony in the botanical gardens where they had first got together. Eduardo gave her away, whilst Brady shared the responsibility of best man with an astonished Oz.

Julianna and Marcie were possibly the most excited bridesmaids in the history of weddings, whilst their mother cried enough tears to replenish the Amazon River. They had about thirty guests, including Cesar, Raoul and Fabio, and everyone cried a little, drank some wine and danced a lot.

The Maura-Cooper family welcomed their fourth member six months after that, on a glorious spring morning when the sun couldn't have shone any brighter.

Antonia Maura-Cooper came into the world with a battle cry fit for trailblazer, and Jake took her in his arms and gazed at her with such unadulterated love that Flávia's heart swelled so much she feared it might shatter.

And then he shifted his gaze to her and she felt as though she was the most powerful woman in the world.

* * * * *

AWAKENED BY
HER BROODING
BRAZILIAN

ANN McINTOSH

To all the women and young girls dedicated to STEM subjects and the advancement of science.

Thank you for your brilliance!

CHAPTER ONE

IF THERE WAS one thing beyond his medical specialty of plastic surgery that Dr. Francisco Carvalho knew, it was fashion, and Dr. Krysta Simpson's formal attire made him almost want to cry.

It was not that it was cheap looking. On the contrary, she'd probably paid a pretty penny for the gown, and the design of the dress, with soft draping at the neckline and cinched waist, was impeccable.

No. He could find no fault with the gown itself, even if it were outdated, but on Dr. Simpson it was a micron away from being an abomination.

Firstly, it was at least one size too big, and hung on her like a sack. Secondly, the celadon silk washed out her complexion—which was toasty brown with rich coppery undertones and freckles—making her look sallow.

To cap it all, her shoes would be more suitable for a woman three times her age, with fallen arches and an abiding distain for anything feminine or fashionable.

Who wore clunky flats with a formal dress?

Apparently, Dr. Simpson did.

It didn't help that she was standing beside a beautiful woman wearing a lovely, infinitely flattering teal, one-shouldered gown. Francisco didn't recognize her,

and figured she must be another of the foreign specialists. On her other side was Dr. Flávia Maura, a well-
respected researcher into the use of snake and spider
venom to treat cancer and other diseases. He'd been
surprised when she walked in, since she was in a gorgeous, shimmering green dress, and he'd never seen
her in anything other than cargo pants, boots and a
T-shirt. She looked fashionable and glamorous, especially in contrast to Krysta Simpson.

Yet, Francisco couldn't help admiring Dr. Simpson's
aplomb. She was chatting away with all the insouciance
of a woman wearing a bespoke haute-couture outfit,
completely unaware of the way she stuck out in the
stylishly dressed crowd.

And who could blame her for her confidence? In
Francisco's mind, she was a medical goddess of sorts.
Not even thirty years old and already a leader in her
combined fields of otolaryngology and facial reconstruction, Dr. Krysta Simpson had been making waves
in the medical community for the last five years. More
if you considered the fact that she was the youngest
woman to graduate medical school with those particular specialties. When she'd been picked to work on one
of the finest facial transplant teams in the world, no
one who'd followed her career was surprised. Her research papers were must-reads in the plastic surgery
community, if one wanted to keep current, learn about
new techniques and get a feel for what was coming in
the future.

After hearing her give a talk at a symposium in Lisbon three years ago, Francisco's one wish had been to
speak to her and pick her brain further. When she'd quietly slipped away from the conference and he'd missed
that chance, his disappointment had been acute. So, on

hearing she was traveling to São Paulo as part of Hospital Universitário Paulista's summer lecture program, he'd hardly believed his luck.

Even more exciting was hearing she'd be performing a mandibular reconstruction on the Brazilian billionaire, Enzo Dos Santos, while there, and Francisco being pegged to assist. Being able to see her in action in theater would be the highlight of his career.

He'd been waiting for a chance to approach her since the welcoming soiree started, but was reluctant to interrupt her conversation. Instead of simply marching over there, he'd been casually circling, inching closer in the crowd. If he wasn't careful, the cocktail portion of the evening would come to a close without him even introducing himself.

He was only about five feet away from her now. Sipping the sparkling water he'd gotten from a waiter, he considered how best to approach. It was testament to how much he'd changed over the last few years. In the past, there'd be no hesitation. That younger Francisco had been supremely sure of himself and his place in the world he inhabited, even though much of that bravado was ill deserved, and had caused more problems than anything else.

The older, wiser man was more watchful, wary. All too cognizant of the way people could misconstrue and misinterpret the most innocent or casual action. The last thing he needed was for her to think he was kissing up to her.

It may have been years since the end of his engagement to Mari, but the unfairness of how he'd been treated by the press, and by people he'd thought of as friends, still stung. It had left him isolated, and unwilling to open himself up to others, for fear of being betrayed again.

Leaving Rio had felt like making a fresh start, but unfortunately his was a face, and a name, all too recognizable. His problems had followed him to São Paulo like a phantasm that had decided to haunt him forever. Luckily, work kept him busy and gave him little time to stew on the way his life had turned out. And now, getting to work with Dr. Simpson gave him something tangible to look forward to.

Ah, there. Flávia Maura was walking away, and the woman in the teal dress put her hand on Krysta Simpson's arm, seemingly to take her leave as well. As she stepped away in Flávia's wake, and Francisco was about to move toward where Dr. Simpson still stood, he heard the distinctive, dismissive voice of Dr. Silvio Delgado, oncologist.

"The hospital should be more careful of their reputation. First they hire the crazy *selvagem* woman, then the gigolo, and to add insult to injury, they then bring some frump in to lecture. This one looks like a street person."

Francisco's fingers twitched as he reined in the impulse to plant his fist in the other man's face. The situation's only saving grace, in his estimation, was that Delgado spoke in Portuguese, the comment aimed squarely at Francisco and Flávia, rather than Dr. Simpson. The chances of the visiting doctors understanding the nasty comments were slim.

Even as he had the thought, he saw Flávia stop and look back, her brows coming together in a scowl, no doubt at being called a "jungle woman," and Krysta Simpson turned, too, her dark eyes zeroing in on Delgado. Francisco's heart sank momentarily, thinking Dr.

Simpson actually knew what was said, but there was no hurt or anger on her face, just curiosity.

When Francisco had first starting modeling at the age of fifteen, his manager and mentor, Caro, had told him, "You must practice different looks, Cisco, so you are always ready to give the photographers exactly what they want. Remember, there are no words to tell the viewer what they should feel. The only clue is in your appearance."

He'd heeded her, of course. The money he made with his face and body was the only way he could achieve his dream of being a doctor. It had felt silly at the time, but he'd done as she'd asked, and developed a repertoire of expressions hailed as impressive.

Now, he put that art to good use.

He turned his head and, as expected, found Delgado's beady, malicious gaze trained on him. Looking down his nose at the shorter man, he met that stare squarely, and allowed his face to fall into an expression of such hauteur he might well have been a king.

You are a worm.

Uncouth.

Dust beneath my feet.

Unworthy of even a moment's more consideration.

All this and worse his expression said, and he saw the exact moment Delgado read it aright. Red washed the other man's face, his nostrils flared slightly and his lips all but disappeared as he pressed them together.

Then Francisco slowly turned his head away, knowing the gesture to be the final insulting blow to the man who felt himself above anyone not from his social circle.

The circle Mari was born into, and Francisco had walked away from, knowing it wasn't anywhere he belonged. Or wanted to belong.

There was a muffled curse from Delgado's direction, a titter from someone else in the vicinity, but Francisco paid neither any mind.

Instead, he walked purposefully toward Dr. Simpson, releasing his irritation along with a long, silent exhale through his nose.

Working with Dr. Simpson was a once in a lifetime opportunity, and he'd allow nothing—no one—to interfere with it.

Krysta knew herself to be an overachiever, no matter what intellectual journey she embarked on, a trait her therapist had suggested, ad nauseam, she try to dial back. There'd been no reason to immerse herself in learning Portuguese over the last six months since she'd agreed to come to Brazil, but in her mind, there was also no reason *not* to.

It wasn't as though she had a life outside of work— another issue her therapist encouraged her to try to change.

Now, she was glad she'd turned what one colleague had called her "diabolical focus" on learning the language. Being able to understand what was being said, especially when others didn't know you could, was a handy thing indeed.

While she couldn't understand all of the words, she surmised some of them were aimed at the way she was dressed. She was used to it, and whenever she got a strange look or overheard a comment, it rolled right off her.

There were many things in life she really didn't give a fig about. While she could admire other people's clothes sense, or even beautiful tropical decor like that of the room they were in, it was in a distant, disinterested way. She never became emotionally involved with, nor was she particularly moved by, beauty. She'd stood in the Sistine Chapel and thought more about how the painting had been achieved than about how lovely it was.

And that disinterest carried over to her wardrobe.

The dress she was wearing had been bought in London five years before, when she'd suddenly realized she had nothing to wear to a formal dinner. She'd asked the concierge at the hotel for the name of a boutique, gone there, walked in and grabbed the first dress she'd seen. That had caused considerable consternation among the staff, who'd wanted to advise her or, at the very least, force her to try it on.

Krysta had refused, pulling out her card to pay for it. The woman behind the counter had looked as though she might cry, but valiantly tried one more delaying tactic.

Would madam like a pair of shoes to go with the gown?

No, madam would not.

Not when every pair of shoes she saw scattered about the store had sky-high heels!

So, being ridiculed for her appearance meant less than nothing to her. In fact, there was benefit to looking frumpy. Others took you seriously, rather than focusing on your figure, or the fact you were female. The only area of life that mattered was her work: the research and surgeries she undertook in hopes of helping some of those who needed it.

Those things took all the emotional energy she had to expend.

On top of that, even if she were inclined to take umbrage, there was no mistaking the true target of the comments was the tall, exceedingly handsome fellow the other man had been sneering at. The same man striding across the floor toward her. She believed he'd been referred to as a gigolo...

And his reaction had been *amazing*.

Everyone, doctors in particular, had a look they gave those who were being especially displeasing, dense or obstructionist. Krysta's included a deadpan stare and lifted eyebrow, which usually was effective. But she'd never, ever seen such a steely, arrogant expression of distaste on anyone's face before.

How she wished she could pull that off, the next time someone crossed her!

Then there was no more time for rumination, since the man in question came to an abrupt halt in front of her, surprising her no end, since she'd thought he'd go straight by. She found herself looking up into a strong, almost lupine face with intent light brown eyes, and a *zing* of awareness fired down her spine. Even she, no expert on attractiveness, instinctively knew this man would turn every head wherever he went.

He certainly seemed able to turn hers.

"Dr. Simpson." It wasn't a question, so Krysta just looked up at him silently, noting the steely expression wasn't gone from his gaze, but was merely muted. "My name is Dr. Francisco Carvalho, and it's my great pleasure to meet you."

His deep, accented tones seemed to vibrate into her bones in the most surprising way, but she smiled politely as they shook hands, recognizing the name. He was one of the craniofacial surgeons she'd be working with, but he'd missed the video conference calls they'd had regarding the Dos Santos case. It would have been nice to have warning of his attractiveness before this!

"Nice to meet you, too, Dr. Carvalho."

"I am a great fan of yours," he said. "I saw you in Lisbon, speaking about the use of titanium in three-dimensional printing for facial reconstruction, and had hoped to speak more with you after the lecture. I also recently read, with great interest, your paper on the development of new, lighter polymers for the same purpose."

Now there was a shocker.

"But that paper was released only a couple of days ago."

He shrugged lightly, the tiniest of smiles tipping his lips momentarily. Krysta's heart did a weird, crazy little dip as she noted the way his face softened, even as the wolflike appeal increased.

"Anyone in my line of work who has any sense in his or her head knows that when Dr. Krysta Simpson releases a paper, it is in our best interest to read it, as soon as possible."

Normally, compliments and flattery mattered to her as little as clothes or interior design, but something about his tone said that his words were neither. That Dr. Carvalho was stating what was, to him, a fact, and despite herself, Krysta was pleased by it.

Yet it wasn't in her nature to agree.

"I would think Ferguson or Charpentier would be at the top of the must-read list."

Dr. Carvalho nodded. "*Verdade.* Indeed. But they are, in my opinion, old school in their presentations. You take a more progressive line, allowing us a glimpse into what might be, should research advance sufficiently."

Krysta tilted her head briefly to the side in both acknowledgment of the statement and amusement. "I've been taken to task for 'prognosticating' a number of times."

His expression morphed into arrogant amusement in the blink of an eye. "Yet the journals keep printing your papers, and your demand grows. The last I heard, the French team was trying to woo you away from your current position."

"Mere rumor," she replied, although there had been some overtures. "You shouldn't pay attention to gossip."

He looked anything but chastened. In fact, he smiled. "I would like it very much if we sat together at dinner." He gestured to the empty glass in her hand. "May I get you another drink in the meantime?"

"Yes, thank you. I'm having fruit punch—mango and passion fruit, I think the bartender said."

Taking her glass, he stepped away with a murmured, "I'll return in a moment."

Krysta saw the way others watched him walk across to the bar, amused at how right she'd been. Dr. Francisco Carvalho certainly attracted a lot of attention, from admiring stares to what appeared to be envious ones.

"Dr. Simpson, what pleasure it gave me to learn you would be joining us here at the hospital." Krysta turned to see the man who'd made the nasty comment earlier standing behind her, a sly smile on his lips. "I am Dr. Silvio Delgado, oncologist."

She didn't smile back, but shook his outstretched hand and said, "Dr. Delgado."

Not being pleased to make his acquaintance, she didn't say she was.

"You may not know it, but my grandfather was one of the founding contributors to this hospital," he started, obviously expecting her to be overcome with fascination at this information.

Blah, blah, blah...

She tuned him out, wondering if her assistant back in

New York had had any luck accessing the information she'd requested. Her latest research project was due to start as soon as she got back to the States and, without the proper accumulation of data, might be pushed back.

Then she heard Dr. Carvalho's name, and tuned back in.

"...no doubt, but I have to tell you his reputation isn't particularly stellar. He might have been famous as a model, but the way he treated his ex-fiancée is a disgrace."

Krysta held up her hand, cutting the man off. "But is he a good doctor?"

Delgado blinked, several times, rapidly. "I beg your pardon?"

"Does he do his job in an acceptable way? Is he a good surgeon?" she asked, making her voice slow, as though to make sure he understood.

"Well... I...I suppose so," he replied, and she saw the way his ears reddened.

She shrugged. "That's all I care about."

"Your drink, Dr. Simpson."

Speak of the devil.

"Thank you, Dr. Carvalho," she replied, turning to take the frosty glass from his hand. Had he heard the exchange between herself and the other man? There was nothing at all in his expression or demeanor to give her any clue. This Dr. Carvalho was a master at hiding his thoughts, unless and until he wanted to share them.

"It appears dinner is about to be served," he said, extending his arm toward her as an announcement to that effect came over the PA system. "Shall we go through?"

"Yes, thank you," she replied, laying her fingers on his impressive brachioradialis and strangely having to squelch the urge to squeeze it, just to see if it were as strong as she thought. Then she gave Dr. Delgado a level, straight-faced look and continued, "You will excuse us, won't you? I'm famished."

She saw the exact instant Dr. Delgado realized she'd spoken in Portuguese. His eyes widened, and his face paled. It took everything she had inside not to lose her poker face at his horrified expression.

And she now knew, for a fact, how hard Dr. Carvalho's arm muscle really was, as it tightened to rock beneath her fingers. Glancing up into his startled face, she said, "I hope my accent isn't terrible. I've only been learning the language for a few months."

He blinked, and she saw amusement flood his eyes, causing them to gleam. "Not at all," he replied. "In fact, it is *perfeita*."

CHAPTER TWO

FRANCISCO HURRIED ACROSS the grounds toward the conference and lecture center, glancing at his watch as he went.

Ora bolas! Krysta Simpson's first lecture was supposed to start in less than a minute, and he was only now getting through the door into the building. It had been a busy morning, one that started at 4:00 a.m. with a call from the hospital concerning a victim of a robbery gone wrong; he'd had severe zygomatic and maxillary fractures. They'd taken him straight into surgery, and the delicate procedure of rebuilding his orbital structure hadn't ended until almost nine. Luckily, there didn't appear to be damage to his eye, but ophthalmology had been alerted and a specialist would be along to examine the patient once the swelling had abated.

Francisco had already told his head of department that, whenever time permitted, he wanted to attend as many of Dr. Simpson's lectures as possible, and Dr. Emanuel had readily agreed. Getting her to Paulista's was a coup for the hospital, since it was well-known she rarely lectured, preferring to devote her time to research and major, cutting-edge operations. Having her agree to perform the surgery on Dos Santos, who'd suffered oral cancer, was an added bonus. The patient had

had a segment of his mandible removed, along with his tumor, in London, and specifically wanted her to do the reconstruction.

All the team members were familiar with the technique she would be using, where a piece of the patient's fibula, along with blood vessels and a flap of skin, would be used to reconstruct the piece of mandible removed by the oncologist. Francisco had done several, even a couple where the inferior alveolar nerve running through the jaw to the chin and lower lip had been repaired as well. What Krysta Simpson brought to the table was a newer way of approaching the operation itself, and techniques not used everywhere yet.

Beyond all that, though, Francisco found her even more fascinating than he expected. Before meeting her, his sole focus had been on her work, the advances she'd been a part of in the world of facial reconstruction and the research she spearheaded.

That was before he'd heard her cut Delgado off when the other man was trying to poison her against him. And when she'd spoken in almost-perfect Portuguese... If he were still capable of doing so, he would have fallen for her right there and then. It had been *magnífica*. Just the expression on Delgado's face had been enough to elevate the evening into one of the best Francisco had had in years.

They'd sat at the same table at dinner, and spoke almost exclusively to each other during the meal. He'd found himself avidly watching her face as she spoke, all but drowning in the twinkling brown eyes. It was only after he went home that it struck him why he'd enjoyed the night so much.

Communicating with Krysta Simpson had been easy, without any kind of undertones, or nosy questions. He'd been at ease with her, and found the wall of reticence he'd built up over the years rather thinner around her than it usually was. Perhaps it was because of her direct way of speaking, and how obvious it was she didn't care about his storied past. It had been a long time since he'd felt so comfortable with anyone outside of his family, and had been a very pleasant experience.

Although he could certainly do without the thrill of attraction he felt toward her.

Now, finally getting to the lecture hall, he glanced in through the glass at the top of the door and found everyone already seated, with a few people even standing at the sides and back of the room. Most were students and residents, but there were a few established surgeons seated at the front. Not wanting to cause a disturbance when he expected Dr. Simpson to step out onto the stage at any moment, Francisco turned and headed for the door leading to the room adjacent to the hall. It was where lecturers waited for their audience to assemble, but it also led directly to the wings, via a corridor. His plan was to quietly make his way to the edge of the stage, and listen to her from there.

It would cause much less fuss than walking into the crowded room and perhaps even have one of his residents get up to offer him a seat, which was not outside the realm of possibility. All the young doctors he supervised were ambitious, and keen to make a good impression on the more experienced staff members, in hopes of it giving them a leg up on the competition.

The L-shaped waiting area beside the lecture hall was much like any of the green rooms Francisco had been in during his modeling days. There were a few upholstered chairs, a couch, coffee table, refreshment area and, set into a secluded alcove at the back, a desk.

At first, when he entered, he thought it empty, then he heard what sounded like low mumbling coming from the desk area. Curiosity took him the steps necessary to peer around the corner, and he was taken aback to find Dr. Simpson standing beside the desk.

Her back was to him, her face to the wall, her hands pressed flat against the surface in front of her, the knuckles almost white with the pressure she was exerting on her fingers.

His first instinct was to leave her alone, but something in the stiffness of her posture, the cadence of her voice as she recited something to herself, kept him there.

"Dr. Simpson..."

She turned a pale, sweat-sheened face to him, snapping, "I asked for just a few more minutes." Then she shook her head, as though trying to bring herself back from whatever unhappy place she'd just been.

"My apologies," he said stiffly, annoyed with himself for disturbing her. "I thought perhaps you were unwell."

"Sick," she mumbled. Then her voice rose. "God, I hate public speaking."

She seemed so confident generally it was startling to see her this way, and he said, "But you do it so well. No one would ever believe your aversion."

Krysta gave him a wan look as she reached into the pocket of her oversize jacket and pulled out a handful of tissues. Dabbing her forehead, she replied, "Do you know why you couldn't find me to speak to me in Lisbon after my presentation? Because I was in the bathroom throwing up. At least this time I threw up first."

When he'd mentioned he'd looked for her then, she hadn't commented. Now he understood why.

"If you hate it so much, why do it?" he asked, honestly perplexed. It wasn't as though she needed to raise her profile in the medical world. And if she did, Brazil probably wouldn't be first on the list of places to do so.

"I'd promised myself not to do it again, but over the last couple of years I've been trying to work through some…issues, and my therapist told me I need to face my fears. And she also told me I needed to get out more, experience more of life, since I spend all my time working. Brazil seemed like a good place to kill two birds with one stone."

Francisco was unsure of what to say to that but, before he could reply, the noise level in the lecture hall seemed to rise to a grumbling murmur. Krysta obviously heard it, too, as she straightened, giving her forehead one last pat down with the tissues. To his amazement, all signs of distress and trepidation fell away from her face, and although he saw her swallow hard once, she appeared perfectly collected, if still a little pale.

"Okay," she said, as much to herself as to him. "I'm ready now."

She walked past him with long confident strides, and then paused to glance back at him. "Are you staying for the lecture?"

He gestured to the corridor she was about to walk down. "I'll be watching from the wings."

The smile she gave him made something warm and pleasant bloom in his chest.

"Good. Great."

"And perhaps we can lunch together afterward?" he asked before she disappeared. "Before I do my rounds?" They were getting together that afternoon for a preliminary team meeting regarding the upcoming surgery, but the urge to spend more time with her was unmistakable.

"Sure," was the nonchalant answer.

Then she was gone, and as he followed and saw her step out onto the stage, the applause began.

There were many divides between Krysta and her father, but as she explained to Dr. Carvalho over lunch, she owed her ability to deal with whatever was happening directly to him.

"He's an auto mechanic," she said as she arranged the food on her plate to her specifications: meat at five o'clock, rice at seven and vegetables taking up the rest of the space. No restaurant, or cafeteria like the one here at the hospital, ever got it quite right. "He proudly calls himself a grease monkey, and never really understood why I wanted to go into medicine, yet everything important I know about getting through life I learned from him."

The conversation had started when Francisco had asked how she'd gone from a shaking mess to composed so quickly. Usually, she'd have brushed it off, embarrassed to be seen that way by anyone, but, somehow, she'd minded neither his intrusion nor the question. She felt remarkably comfortable with Francisco Carvalho, once she subdued the rush of awareness she experienced whenever their eyes met.

Seeing the quizzical expression being sent her way, Krysta elaborated. "He always told us, 'Fear and doubt are contagious. If you let others see you're feeling them, they'll catch it, and mirror it back to you tenfold.' In my head, I equate it to when a family gets the flu, and keep passing it back and forth. When you get it the second time, it's usually much worse."

"Ah," he said, nodding. "I see. So you trained yourself to go through the fear and get the job done."

"You have to sometimes," she agreed, while putting

together the perfect forkful of food. "I've gotten out of the habit of pushing myself, outside of my usual work life, but I'm thankful to know that ability to compartmentalize in uncomfortable situations hasn't deserted me."

"I enjoyed your lecture, as I knew I would." He had a direct, unruffled way of speaking she really liked. "The information you're imparting to our staff should prove highly valuable."

She finished chewing and swallowed before she replied. "It's available elsewhere. I just have it put all together in one presentation, because of my research and specialties."

The lecture, the first of three parts, dealt with the ever-widening and exciting world of biomaterials for medical applications. It was a topic she was fascinated by, since new discoveries opened up advanced and improved ways of disease diagnosis, delivery of medications, even tissue generation. In later lectures she'd go into greater detail regarding specific applications, particularly when used for facial reconstruction.

He shook his head, giving her one of his abbreviated smiles.

"The information you have is *not* available to everyone. You must have gotten fifty different permissions just to do this lecture series."

She tried not to smirk, but probably failed. "More like sixty, including being able to talk about and show some of the work that went into the facial transplant I assisted with."

Francisco's eyes widened. "Really?"

"Mmm-hmm," she murmured around another mouthful of food, unreasonably glad to have truly impressed him with that pronouncement. She wasn't sure who at Paulista's pulled the strings, but someone at the hospital had a great deal of clout.

He took a moment to have another bite of his *feijoada*, which reminded her a little of Jamaican stewed peas, although it was made with black beans instead of red kidney beans and had sausage in it, rather than just salted meat. She'd opted for *churrasco* and wasn't disappointed as the tender barbecued beef melted in her mouth, releasing its delicious flavor. Francisco swallowed, and seemed about to say something, when Flávia Maura stopped by their table, tray in hand, and Krysta looked up to smile at the other woman.

"Hi," Flávia said, speaking directly to Krysta after acknowledging Francisco with a terse nod. "I was wondering if you wanted to come over to the sanctuary for a tour sometime while you're here. I can show you the live specimens, and some of the research data I've collected."

An involuntary shiver rustled up Krysta's back.

"I'm really interested in your findings, because I think the possible applications are fascinating, but unfortunately I don't do snakes. Just the thought of being around a lot of them gives me the chills."

"You're not afraid of them, are you?" Flávia seemed both bemused and disappointed. "As a scientist, surely you understand their importance, ecologically and medicinally?" She shook her head, then ran her fingers through her hair. "The amount of time I spend trying to explain that to people…"

"Oh, I understand," Krysta said, not at all offended at being taken to task. She completely related to Flávia's drive and passion. Although their fields were very different, the other woman's intensity mirrored her own.

"I've just never been comfortable with reptiles or amphibians, although I don't mind arachnids."

Flávia's gaze swung toward the door and lingered there for a moment. As a hint of color touched the other woman's face, Krysta glanced that way in time to see the British oncologist Jake Cooper heading for the buffet line. When she looked back at Flávia, it was to see the other woman rubbing one cheek, as though to erase the warmth accumulating there. Then her hand dropped away, and she shook her head slightly, her gaze returning to meet Krysta's.

"Well, if you change your mind, let me know. The invitation is always open." Flávia glanced at Francisco, and added, "You can come, too, if you like."

He dipped his head in acknowledgment. "Thank you for the invitation but, unlike Krysta, I'm leery of spiders, ever since I was bitten by a brown widow as a child."

Flávia made a little sound best described as a snort. "*Latrodectus geometricus.* Did you not check your shoes before putting them on?"

Francisco shook his head, but there was a wry set to his mouth. "More like stuck my hand into somewhere it didn't belong."

Flávia nodded, and gave him a little smile in return. "I've been known to do that myself, from time to time."

Why did Krysta feel there was more to both those stories than met the eye? Her curiosity was definitely piqued. Just as it had been when she noticed how coolly distant Francisco was with everyone. Well, except her.

Then Flávia was taking her leave, striding off to sit at one of the other tables before Krysta even thought to invite her to sit with them.

Francisco gave her one of his noncommittal looks,

and said, "I thought you were on a campaign to over-come your fears. Wouldn't this be a good opportunity?"

Was he being serious, snide or teasing? Krysta nar-rowed her eyes in an attempt to figure it out. Then she noticed the twinkle in his eyes, and decided it was the latter. To date, she'd seen nothing snide in his manner, which was probably why they got along so well. After so many years of, in different situations, being the youn-gest, or only female, or just plain different, she was adept at spotting even a hint of condescension.

Looking down at her plate, she set about arrang-ing another forkful, and replied, "Perhaps I'll go...if you do."

There. When she glanced up, the twinkle in his eyes had definitely deepened, and his lips quirked in amuse-ment. "Hmm, I wouldn't wait around for that if I were you. I have no problem admitting I avoid spiders when-ever I can, and tend to swat the ones I can't elude."

Krysta gave an exaggerated look over her shoulder. "You better not let Flávia hear you say that. You've al-ready moved down a few notches in her estimation, and that would send you straight to Hades, without even a pause in purgatory."

He laughed.

Not just a chuckle, but a full-on deep laugh.

It was such a departure from the contained and con-trolled Dr. Carvalho, Krysta found herself transfixed by the sight.

The way his face lit up. The low, somehow sexy rumble of his merriment. The crinkling of the skin at the corners of his eyes, and slashes, like long dimples, in his cheeks.

Heat washed through her veins, out into every crev-ice and corner of her body, the sensation unlike any she'd experienced before. Instinctively, she looked down, not wanting him to catch her staring, and tried to catch her suddenly nonexistent breath.

The sensation was akin to how she felt before lecturing: scared, a little shaky. Completely sure something unknown and horrible was coming her way.

Frazzled, she shoved the fork into her mouth, even though half the salad had fallen off.

She'd have to try to work it out later, although she had the distinct feeling there was some important data she lacked.

His laughter subsided, but there was still a touch of amusement in his voice as he said, "Would you like to do rounds with me, before the meeting with the surgical team?"

No.

Yes.

No.

Indecision wasn't something Krysta tolerated in others, and despised in herself, yet her brain ping-ponged back and forth in a most annoying manner at his simple question. Then common sense reasserted itself.

"Do you have any patients I could be of particular help to? If not, I need to contact my research assistant and make sure everything is under control before he goes on holiday next week."

The smile stayed on his lips, but she thought she saw a flash of disappointment in his eyes as he replied, "No, not really. But I'm sure the residents would have questions they'd love to ask."

Ah, he was thinking about the residents. That made sense. She shrugged, and concentrated on her plate.

"I'll be available for the next few months. There'll be plenty of time for them."

"Indeed," he replied, but something in his voice made her glance up at him, and now it was she who was disappointed when he wasn't looking at her, so she couldn't see his eyes. "Perhaps, if you're not too busy, we could lunch again tomorrow."

"Perhaps," she replied, trying to remain noncommittal, even as she knew she'd be there.

CHAPTER THREE

LATER THAT EVENING, Krysta made her way down to the indoor pool at the apartment building where she was staying. She'd tried to settle in for the evening, but her whirring brain made her restless, and swimming laps was one surefire way to work off some of her excess energy.

All in all, it had been a constructive day, but the stress of lecturing, coupled with the preoperation group meeting, rendered her unable to relax.

Getting to the pool, she was happy to find it deserted. After she'd shed her robe and slippers, she made her way to the deep end, putting on her goggles as she went.

Then she dove in, automatically counting the strokes it took to get to the opposite end, and then keeping count of the laps. But even so occupied, her brain still had more than enough space left over to go through the day once more.

Yet, surprisingly, considering how stressful it had been, it wasn't the lecture or the upcoming operation she found herself contemplating.

It was Francisco Carvalho, and her completely untoward reactions whenever he was around. Those moments of hesitation—procrastination—when he'd invited her to accompany him on rounds was bad enough but, to make it worse, she'd found herself distracted by him during the meeting with the surgical team.

She'd brought one of the three-dimensional replicas of Mr. Dos Santos's skull with her, showing how it had been prior to the segmental mandibulectomy, along with a 3-D model of his mandible, and recent scans.

"The oncological team used fluorescent contrast preop to locate the cancer cells, and luckily, because of that, we have decent margins to work with. As you know, we'll be performing a vascularized fibula flap transfer, with simultaneous dental-implant placement. We will be using titanium plates specifically crafted for Mr. Dos Santos to hold the transferred bone in place, along with cutting templates to shape the fibula into the exact shape needed."

Francisco leaned closer to get a better look at the 3-D skull, bringing his shoulder into close proximity to hers. Warmth flooded her arm, making her wonder if the heat emanated from him or if her body was spontaneously creating it.

Flummoxed, she was forced to strain to concentrate when one of the residents raised his hand and said, "If I may ask, why wasn't the reconstruction done immediately following the mandibulectomy? Isn't that the standard of care?"

Krysta dragged her mind back to the meeting, but it was Jake Cooper who answered.

"Dr. Simpson wasn't available to perform the operation when I had the mandibulectomy scheduled," he replied. "And Mr. Dos Santos insisted she be the one to head the team."

"Dr. Simpson was in France, assisting with a facial transplant," Francisco interjected. "And some of what the French were able to achieve, she will be sharing with us in her lectures."

That brought another little murmur from the assembled group, which Krysta ignored. Just as she outwardly ignored Francisco's interruption, even as she felt a silly little glow of pride.

Instead of acknowledging his words, she continued. "While it is common practice, none of the data show any difference in outcome if the reconstruction is secondary. And since it affords us an opportunity to make full use of the new technology, we can ensure a shorter, more efficient operation, along with superior function and aesthetic results, long-term. In consultation with both Dr. Cooper and the patient, it was decided the benefits of waiting outweighed the detriments."

Francisco asked, "Could you expound on that a little, Dr. Simpson? I'm interested in how that decision was made."

She'd found herself reluctant to look directly at him, so she let her gaze roam the rest of the people in the room.

"Every patient is different," she began, gathering her thoughts carefully. "In situations such as the one Mr. Dos Santos found himself in, each person has their own concerns and fears. Some just want the cancer removed, no matter what that entails, not thinking past surviving. Others fear the surgery almost as much, if not more, than the disease. In this particular case, on speaking to the patient, I realized he wasn't particularly worried about his prognosis. He truly believed his strength of will would make his recovery all but inevitable. But there was one thing he was deeply worried about, and that was his postoperative appearance and facial functionality."

There was a murmur through the room, and Krysta held up her hand to silence it.

"Mr. Dos Santos isn't just a wealthy businessman, but the face of his company, and of his *futebol* team, Chutegol. Much of his success has come from being 'Senhor Chutegol,' recognized by everyone, parlaying that recognition into bigger and better successes."

At the mention of the well-known soccer team, which was in the prestigious Brasileirão league, the assembled team nodded, and Krysta could see understanding dawning in most of their expressions.

"Once I realized how important the aesthetic result was to him, I then spoke to him about timelines. I explained that if I were to do the reconstruction secondary to the mandibulectomy, I'd want to wait until he'd also finished his radiation treatments, and his recovery time would be extended. He didn't care about that. As most of you know, he'd announced his diagnosis to the media, and was willing to take as long as necessary to recover, as long as he looked almost the same when he finally reemerged. That was when I suggested the CT mapping, and 3-D printing approach.

"And there was one final deciding factor," she continued. "I explained to him that I was committed to coming here for three months, and so would have just a short window prior to my visit to do the surgery. That was when he requested, if possible, that the surgery be done here, in his home country, and be used as a training opportunity."

Once more, murmurs broke out around the room, but there was a decidedly appreciative cadence to them.

"While you all are familiar with the standard fibular free-flap reconstruction, introducing you to some of the newer techniques in presurgical planning, along with the 3-D planned plates and templates, will serve you well in the years to come. It's an exciting and fast-evolving technique in our line of work."

They'd gone on to discuss the operation in detail, but through it all Krysta was supremely aware of Francisco next to her, whether he was contributing to the conversation or not.

Now, as she finished her twenty-fourth lap, she had to admit to herself the patently obvious truth.

She was attracted to him.

That in itself was unusual enough to throw her off her stride. Not that it was the first time she'd found a man attractive, but unlike the other times, there was a stronger pull, a growing need for his company she didn't understand.

Worse was this sense of wanting to do something about it, take it further to see where it might lead. That was very different from the times before, when she'd been content to look and do nothing about her feelings.

Not that she'd know how to go about getting from point A to point B with a man like Francisco Carvalho.

She'd succumbed to curiosity and looked him up on the internet. Francisco Carvalho had lived an exciting life as a model prior to becoming a surgeon. Back then, he was known as Cisco, and there were myriad pictures of him in ads and on catwalks around the world. He'd even been the face of a cologne produced by a designer whose name even Krysta recognized.

And then there were the shots of him at parties and galas, and in many of them he had a gorgeous blonde woman on his arm, described in some of the captions as Mariella Guzman, his fiancée. That wide-eyed beauty had seemed the perfect complement to Francisco's dark, brooding handsomeness. Recalling Dr. Delgado's comments on the night of the reception, she'd been tempted to see if there were any articles saying what happened, but decided against it. She'd seen enough to tell her everything she needed to know.

Francisco Carvalho may be her contemporary in the medical world, but in every other way, he was light-years beyond her.

All her life she'd been an outsider, far younger than any of her classmates or work contemporaries. When her mental contemporaries had been experimenting with love and sex, she'd been focused on her studies or career. And before she'd gotten to the point where perhaps she'd have been open to exploring her own sexuality, she'd been traumatized by an assault.

That wasn't something she'd thought or talked about in years, pushing it away and minimizing it in her head. After all, she told herself, it wasn't as though she'd been raped. There were other young girls who'd been hurt far more severely than she had.

It wasn't until she'd started seeing Dr. Hellman that she'd begun to see the ramifications. At fourteen, Krysta had learned to repress her sexuality and minimize any outward signs of femininity. Then, safe in the bastion of her denial, she'd decided relationships, even casual ones, weren't in the cards.

Yet, for all the talking and analyzing, she wasn't ready to let go of her disguise, or venture out of the safety zone. Her work still was her be-all and end-all, and she couldn't afford distractions.

Case in point, she thought as she got to the wall in the deep end and hung on, instead of doing a racing turn and continuing. Thinking about Francisco Carvalho had made her lose count of her laps, when usually she could keep track of them effortlessly, even while thinking about other things. If he could so easily shut down a function of her brain, one she considered automatic, what could he do to the rest of it, if she let him?

Yet, she knew he wouldn't be as easy to dismiss from her mind as the other men she'd been attracted to. There was definitely something different about Francisco, something compelling. It wasn't his looks, although she thought him handsome. Looks alone would never be enough to pique her interest.

Treading water, she considered exactly what it was about him that gave her goose bumps, and made her heart race, but couldn't pinpoint any one thing.

That, in itself, was additionally frustrating. Krysta was used to being able to work though almost any puzzle and find a logical solution.

Perhaps you're looking for the answer to the wrong question.

Her therapist's voice sounded in her head, making her wrinkle her nose. It was one of Dr. Hellman's more annoying sayings, especially when she never seemed willing to let on what the right question was. The only statement more annoying was, "You need to step out of your comfort zone."

Well, she had, hadn't she? Agreeing to come to Brazil and lecture. Dr. Hellman had seemed pleased when Krysta had told her about the trip. Of course, she'd also told her to take the opportunity to stretch herself even more. There were, according to the psychologist, so many things Krysta had missed out on growing up. Not because her parents had pushed her, but because Krysta had pushed herself.

Realizing she'd done it not just because she wanted to succeed, but because it was a great way to isolate herself socially and feel safe, had been revelatory.

Shoving back from the wall, she floated into the middle of the pool, looking up at the ceiling, drifting lazily in the water, rather than cleaving through the way she usually did.

She'd thought she was fine the way she was, but she'd had to reevaluate that supposition. After all, no one had forced her to make that first appointment with Dr. Hellman. It clearly had been something inside her telling her it was time to get things right in her head. Perhaps telling her a full, successful career wasn't all there was in life. Warning that if she didn't make some changes soon, she may be leaving it too late.

"You're a forward-thinking innovator at work," Dr. Hellman had said, her eyes glinting behind her glasses. "Someone who develops new techniques and isn't afraid to move forward boldly into the future. Why not do that in the rest of your life? Isolating yourself, thinking only about work, isn't healthy."

Hearing those words at first made Krysta feel powerful, in control of whatever might happen. But later, alone at home, they'd come back to mind and scared her almost silly. Why they filled her with such trepidation, she hadn't wanted to contemplate.

Perhaps it was because to go down that road would be to have to acknowledge exactly how much she *had* missed out on.

The friendships, like those she'd seen her brothers develop with others, and her parents had nurtured, even when distance divided them from those closest to them.

The family ties, which she'd neglected so badly in the pursuit of excellence, using work as an excuse to avoid the functions and get-togethers others took for granted.

Meaningful relationships, such as the one her parents shared with each other.

Just now, though, it was the putting aside of her sexuality that felt most important.

Apparently, her body thought giving it free rein was long overdue. Just being around Francisco Carvalho brought all her senses to life, arousing sensations she'd never experienced before.

What she was going to do about any of it, she had no idea. But even if she did get brave enough to try to act on these feelings, it would have to wait until after Enzo Dos Santos's surgery.

She wouldn't allow anything, neither Francisco Carvalho nor her own carnal urges, to interfere with her concentration.

Francisco stood under the shower, trying to get the streams of warm water to unravel his knotted muscles. It wasn't that the day had been terribly stressful. Yes, he'd been called out early in the morning, and had another emergency come into the hospital just as he was getting ready to leave, but he was used to that.

What he wasn't used to was Krysta Simpson.

There was an ineffable aura about her that fascinated him intensely. The more time he spent with her, the more captivated he became—with her confidence, precision, razor-sharp mind and the easy way she spoke to everyone, even while maintaining a certain mysterious distance.

Yet, although all those things would be more than enough, Francisco knew himself to be attracted to her physically as well.

More than once, when she was lecturing and in the presurgery meeting, he'd lost track of what she was saying. Not because he wasn't interested, or enthralled by the subject matter, but because he'd caught himself staring at her lips as she spoke, or at the movement of her hands.

Those hands were both capable and surprisingly graceful, and he'd drifted off into a fantasy of what they would feel like on his skin.

Even now, as he was reiterating to himself just how bad that was, his body reacted to the memory, tightening and hardening against his will.

And it truly wasn't at all a good idea to even entertain any fantasies about Dr. Krysta Simpson, for a number of reasons.

Trying to ignore his burgeoning erection, he silently listed them again.

Krysta Simpson had not, by look or word, expressed the slightest interest in him. She was friendly and professional and, in his estimation, they had a great rapport. But beyond that, he saw nothing to indicate she had any other feelings toward him, and he certainly wasn't the type to push.

Besides, having a months-long affair with someone, who would then quickly disappear, did not appeal to him.

Or certainly *shouldn't*.

Then there was the fact she was a visitor to his country, here to do a job. A colleague whose reputation was stellar, and far above his own. Krysta was a star, world renowned, while Francisco was simply a competent plastic and reconstructive surgeon, good at his job but nothing special. To even spend too much time with her was to court disaster, in the same way being engaged to Mari had caused him untold pain and embarrassment.

All too well could he imagine the whispers, not to mention those, like Delgado, who would say aloud for everyone to hear that he was, once again, trying to sleep his way to success. Using looks and charm to advance into a world where he didn't belong.

He knew the gossip that swirled around him in the hospital, and it made him leery of doing anything to stir the pot. Getting too close to Krysta Simpson definitely would do that.

The thought chilled him, and thankfully his ardor waned. Turning off the water, he stepped out of the shower to grab a towel.

He'd been burned by others' cruelty and lies before, and had no intention of doing anything to precipitate that again.

Instead, he needed to remind himself of how far he'd come, how hard he'd worked to get to where he was. Others could say modeling was easy, or believe the lies told about him—that he'd used his association with Mari to further himself—but he knew the truth. It had been a long, backbreaking and often lonely road he'd taken, and there'd been times he'd wanted to quit, to go home to his family and childhood friends. Only his dream of becoming a doctor had kept him there, working and studying in equal measure.

When he'd met Mari and fallen for her, he'd thought life could get no better. By then he was almost finished medical school, and hadn't cared that she came from a wealthy family. Foolishly, he'd thought it didn't matter. He knew he'd be able to support them, between what he'd had saved and what he would earn as a surgeon. What he hadn't taken into consideration was the different rules by which the privileged lived, where they would steamroll over anyone to get what they wanted, or to get out of trouble.

But he'd learned it the hard way, and discovered it was best not to give yourself too freely, because it opened you up to having what you'd said, done or felt used against you. He'd paid dearly for allowing Mari into his heart, and it wasn't an experience he wanted to go through again.

CHAPTER FOUR

HER DAYS FELL into a routine, which normally would have pleased her, but Krysta grew increasingly restive. It wasn't just that she was used to being far busier, since there was actually quite a bit of research she could, and did, do via computer. Even with the upcoming operation, slated for the following week, there just wasn't enough to fill her time, or quell her almost constant disquiet.

It didn't help that, when at the hospital, she was in almost constant contact with Francisco.

His friendly demeanor had cooled somewhat, though. They still had lunch together, and she did afternoon rounds with him, as well as meeting with the surgical team often, but the connection they'd developed in the first few days seemed to wane. There were no questions now about her family or anything else, other than work.

She should have been happy about that, since it afforded her an opportunity to put her own silly attraction into perspective. Instead, it just made her wonder what had happened to cause his withdrawal. If she had more courage, she'd ask, but while she was willing to do or ask anything in a medical setting to get the answers she needed, in social situations she hadn't a clue.

Sometimes, when he wasn't expecting it, she'd glance

his way, only to find him concentrating intently on her face. In those moments, as their gazes collided, the gleam in his eyes threw her usually focused brain into disarray, and the warmth flooding her system made her want to squirm.

It was disturbing on so many levels, she thought as she was on her way to the director's office. Stabbing the elevator button with unnecessary force brought her no relief.

"Hey. What did that button ever do to you?"

The question, laden with amusement, had Krysta turning, a smile already in place.

"Flávia, don't you see the sheer cheek of it? Its perfection aggravates me."

Flávia laughed with her, but there was a little edge to it. "Yes," she replied, and now there was no mistaking the acerbic tone. "Perfection is definitely annoying. How are things going?"

"Very well," Krysta replied, perhaps not completely honestly. "I know how silly it sounds, but I'm surprised at how fast paced everything is here."

Flávia shrugged. "Hospitals and cities are mostly the same everywhere, aren't they? Way too many people for my liking."

Krysta chuckled, glancing around and seeing Amy Woodell coming in through the front doors. She waved to get the approaching woman's attention, curious to hear how the other woman was getting on. They'd met on arrival in Brazil, in the immigration line at the airport, and spent some time chatting at the welcome reception. But because of being in different departments, they hadn't seen each other since.

As Amy came up, Krysta thought she looked weary. Maybe even frazzled.

"I think I'm having a case of déjà vu," Amy said as she got to where they were standing. "Only, I wasn't this tired at the welcome party."

"We were just talking about how fast paced everything is here in São Paulo," Krysta replied.

Amy nodded, then asked, "Did you already do your seminars? I haven't even looked at the lineup yet."

"No," Flávia replied.

"I've done the first of mine," Krysta said. "One down, two to go."

She glanced at the elevator panel, seeing that the one she wanted was still on the top floor, while another was approaching.

"Which floor are you headed to?"

"Fourth. I'm meeting Roque Cardoza," Amy answered, with a little scowl.

"Is he the one you were sitting by at the party?"

"Yep. He's in charge of me for the next couple of weeks. I have to do anything he says, evidently."

Flávia's head swiveled toward Amy while Krysta raised her eyebrows, fighting the smile she could feel tugging at her lips.

"I mean related to the job," Amy interjected quickly, making Krysta chuckle.

"Com certeza. Só o trabalho."

Flávia's voice had a touch of mirth in it too, letting Krysta know she wasn't the only one who'd found Amy's choice of words amusing.

"It's not like he's hard to look at. If that's your thing."

A rush of rosy color flowed up Amy's face until her cheeks glowed. "You guys… I don't think of him like that at all. Besides, he's really *not* all that good-looking."

As the two elevators Amy and Flávia were waiting for arrived, and the three women took their leave of each other, Krysta saw the man in question step into the car behind Amy.

Had he heard their conversation? She rather hoped not. But as she stepped into the elevator going up to the executive floor she turned her thoughts back to her own dilemma.

What to do about Francisco Carvalho...?

The director welcomed Krysta into his office and fussed about for a few minutes, offering coffee, tea or water, making sure she was comfortably situated in one of the cushioned visitor's chairs. Then he sat forward, placing his crossed arms on his desk, and smiled.

"I hope everything at the hospital is to your specifications, Dr. Simpson?"

Despite the pleasant expression on his face, she thought his eyes seemed watchful, and she knew he was worried she'd come to complain about something, or someone. She smiled back at him.

"Paulista's is wonderful, Dr. Andrade. You know it is. State-of-the-art equipment, and wonderfully trained, professional staff. What could I possibly find lacking?"

He sat back, clearly pleased with her little outpouring of sugar, and his smile widened. "So, what can I do for you, then?"

"I heard one of your residents talking about a planned surgical clinic, and wanted to offer my services. It is slated for my final month here, isn't it?"

Hearing about the clinic hadn't been the only draw. She'd also gotten a peek at the roster, and realized Francisco's name wasn't on it.

Dr. Andrade's brow furrowed slightly, even as he nodded. "Yes, but it will not be held here in the hospital, but in Aparecida, which is about two hours northeast."

She shrugged. "I don't mind traveling to participate.

It will give me a chance to get to see a bit more of your beautiful country."

Still, he looked concerned. "I doubt there will be anything on the surgical roster that falls in with your specialty, Dr. Simpson."

"Oh, I'm not expecting facial transplants, or anything like that, but it was my understanding that there would be a number of cleft lip and palate repairs. I'm quite capable of handling those, or assisting with the operations, if there are already surgeons assigned to the cases."

The director's gaze was searching, and there was a small silence before he slowly said, "If you're quite sure..."

"I am," she replied, making her tone decisive.

"Well, then, I will make the arrangements."

Rising, she gave him one last smile. "Thank you. Let me know went you have it sorted out."

After the usual courtesies, she left him, pleased with herself for having the idea.

This trip would, if nothing else, take her away from Francisco Carvalho. At least for a little while.

Just a couple more days until the Dos Santos operation, and the meeting room was filled with tension.

Or, Francisco thought, was it just the tension in himself he was projecting onto the rest of the team?

All, of course, except Krysta, who was exhibiting her usual cool demeanor, fielding questions and soothing nerves while going through the plan one more time.

"The doctors in London have assured us that the infection Mr. Dos Santos had developed has been dealt with," Jake Cooper was saying. "He's flying in tonight, and I'll be examining him in the morning to confirm their findings. The reconstruction should be able to proceed on the new schedule."

"Nothing has changed, for us," Krysta said. "I will begin with the nerve splice, while Dr. Carvalho prepares the fibula flap for implantation."

There was nothing in the plan Francisco hadn't done before, except in the past he'd had to judge the shape of the bone needed, oftentimes with less than stellar results. Now he would be provided with a template, allowing him to shape the bone properly and achieve the proper fit and height.

He'd also been used to bending the plate that would hold the bone in place on-site, shaping and reshaping until it was correct. According to Krysta, with the 3-D printing, using the patient's undamaged mandible as a guide, and the precision mapping of the injury site, that was no longer a concern.

The plates should fit to exact specifications, and the kit supplied by the company who'd produced them even included the screws needed to fit it. No more hunting for the right screws midoperation.

Yet, the nagging strain twisting his stomach wouldn't abate. Thankfully, he was a master at concealing his emotions. No one liked going into an operating theater with a surgeon who looked as though he were on tenterhooks.

Was it the operation he was worried about, or having to do it with Krysta Simpson, a woman he was fast becoming almost obsessed with?

Suddenly his life, which had appeared so orderly and boring, had become a mass of questions and unwanted sensations. It had been years since his equilibrium had been shaken this badly. And all because of a woman who seemed completely, utterly unaware of him in any way other than as a colleague.

A woman he couldn't stop himself from wanting to know everything about. Intimately. Just watching how she used her hands to emphasize a point, the long, nimble fingers waving through the air, filled him with the kind of blinding desire he had no business feeling.

Just then, as Jake Cooper added something to the conversation, Krysta's gaze met Francisco's, and tingles ran up and down his spine at her dark, intent stare. Her lush lips parted slightly, as though to speak, and then she blinked, and turned away toward one of the surgical nurses who'd asked a question.

A question Francisco missed, completely.

Ridiculous. Get a hold on yourself.

He would be less than useless to the patient if he didn't get his mind back on the job at hand. These feelings, cravings, could be dealt with later.

Dragging his concentration back to the meeting, he made it a point to avoid looking at the alluring doctor for the rest of the time, and took off as soon as everything wrapped up.

Although off shift, going straight home didn't appeal. Whereas up until now he'd been perfectly content with going from work to apartment and back again with few deviations, tonight just thinking about his silent, empty apartment increased his restlessness. Instead, he turned into a restaurant near the hospital, and made his way to the bar.

When his drink arrived, he cupped it in his hand, although he didn't take a sip.

He'd never minded solitude before. Even when caught up in the crazy world of modeling, of being Mari's lover, with its constant whirl of parties and galas and openings, he'd had to sneak away periodically, just to be alone. Never did he feel lonely, at those times when he was by himself in a hotel room, far from home, or even hiding from the press, sequestered in his Rio apartment. Mind you, then he'd also been studying, more determined than ever to make it to, and then through, medical school.

Why, now, did being alone chafe so?

Not even the thought of seeing his family soon lifted his spirits.

A hand on his shoulder startled him from his ruminations.

"Mind some company?" Jake Cooper smiled, and tilted his head toward the bar stool next to Francisco.

Throwing off his dour mood, Francisco replied, "Please have a seat."

Doing as bid, Jake signaled the bartender and, when the smiling woman approached, ordered a Scotch. On receiving it, Jake took a sip, and sighed.

"I needed that," he said with a wry twist of his lips.

"I hope that's not an indication of how much you're enjoying being here," Francisco teased. "I'd hate to think Paulista's is anything but welcoming."

"Not at all," Jake replied. "Just having some personal issues."

Tell me about it.

Francisco didn't pry. Not being the type given to confidences, he rarely asked others to share theirs. He'd heard around the hospital that Jake had brought his nephew, who now lived with him, to Brazil. Perhaps that was where his problem lay.

"So, what do you think of Krysta Simpson?" Jake asked.

Of all the topics, this was the one Francisco least

wanted broached. Yet, there was nothing for it but to reply, "She's brilliant, and nice as well. Not always the case in a surgeon of her caliber."

"Agreed," Jake said, although he sent Francisco a sideways glance as he spoke. "I was a little surprised at Enzo's determination to have her do his reconstruction, but he told me she was recommended to him by a friend at the Mayo Clinic. Once I looked into her record, I could understand why."

"She's a star," Francisco said. "It's the honor of my career to work with her. Under normal circumstances, we probably would never even have met."

"Ah, and here she is," Jake said, without commenting on Francisco's statement. "I invited her to have dinner with me."

He accompanied the words with a wave toward the door, and Francisco turned to see the topic of their conversation hesitating by the doorway.

She was having dinner with Jake Cooper? The confluence of desire and jealousy driving through his chest stole his breath, so much so that when he spoke, his voice was gravelly.

Rough.

"Well, I won't keep you from your meal," he said, unable to tear his gaze away from the woman walking toward them, even knowing he should turn away.

What was it about her that drew him this way?

"Nonsense," Jake said briskly, rising from his seat. "It's a working meal, so you should just join us."

Francisco rose, too, all too aware of her sparkling, somehow serious eyes trained on him as Krysta neared.

"Hi," she said, her gaze holding his effortlessly. "I didn't know you'd be joining us."

Did that mean she was sorry he was? Was she interested in Jake Cooper, not as a fellow physician, but personally?

"I just invited him," Jake said, drawing her attention and finally releasing Francisco from the hold those eyes had on him. "Since we're going to be discussing Enzo's surgery and postoperative care further."

Krysta smiled, and Francisco's heartbeat kicked up a notch. There was something so beautiful in watching those lips curve upward.

"Perfect," she said.

Stupid for that simple comment to make him feel ten feet tall.

As the hostess led them to a table near the windows, Jake and Krysta chatted easily, but Francisco stayed silent, still trying to marshal all his faculties for the discussion ahead.

Just as they sat down, Jake's cell phone rang, and he frowned.

"Excuse me," he said, rising abruptly. "I have to take this."

He left behind a thick silence, which both Francisco and Krysta tried to fill at the same time.

"Are you…"

"What is…"

They both stopped, exchanged a glance, and then Krysta chuckled.

"You go," she said, reaching for her water goblet.

"I was going to ask if you were sure you didn't mind my joining you and Jake for dinner."

She gave him a long look over the edge of her glass, then set it down.

"Not at all," she replied, just as Jake made his way back to the table.

"I'm very sorry," he said, sounding harried. "I'm needed at home, so I'm going to have to leave."

"Oh, nothing serious happening there, I hope?" Krysta didn't sound disappointed, just curious and concerned.

"No," Jake replied with a wry twist of his lips. "My nephew is giving the babysitter hell, and she doesn't know how to deal with him. I'll see you tomorrow, when we go to examine Enzo, and we can talk after if need be."

Then, with a final wave, he was gone, leaving Francisco and Krysta by themselves at the table.

CHAPTER FIVE

KRYSTA STARED ACROSS the table at Francisco, who seemed more interested in looking at the glass in front of him than at her, and wondered where it all had fallen apart.

She'd thought there was a real friendship building between them, but somehow it had devolved into this stiff, stark silence. She knew she was being contrary to let it matter. After all, hadn't she decided it was better to have distance between them, just so she wouldn't have to try to figure out how to manage her attraction?

Yet, she did mind. Finding someone she could relate to, feel truly comfortable with, was rare. Sure, she had colleagues she felt kinship with, but that was strictly on a professional basis. She'd felt there was more to be explored with Francisco, but now...

It was at times like this she felt her inexperience keenly. Someone more worldly, who hadn't spent all their life with their nose in a book, would probably know how to go forward, but unfortunately Krysta had to admit she was stuck.

Then her typical forthrightness reasserted itself.

"I think I must have inadvertently done something to upset you," she said quietly. "I wish you'd tell me what it was, so I can apologize."

His head came up, and she was snared, immediately, by his gaze. It was almost golden in the candlelight, and her breath caught in her throat, a rush of heat cascading down from the top of her head to envelop her.

"Not at all," he replied. "And if I have made you feel that way, it is I who should apologize."

Interesting. And now her curious researcher's brain was fired.

"Then what happened? I thought, when we first met, that we were becoming friends. Was I mistaken?"

He looked away, but not before she saw the shutters come down over his expression.

"No." It sounded as though the word was dragged from his throat.

"Then what happened?"

Almost absently, as though he weren't thinking about what he was doing, he lifted his drink and took a sip. Then he put the glass down with a tad more energy than was necessary.

"It's just me," he said. "I have problems opening up to people, making friends."

If she hadn't seen him around the hospital, had just met him elsewhere and they'd talked like they had at the gala and over lunch, she wouldn't believe him. But she had seen the wall between him and other members of staff, and wondered at it. Just then the waiter came to take their orders, but neither of them had even looked at the menus. Krysta ordered some sort of chicken dish, too distracted to force her brain to interpret the description.

As soon as the waiter left, and she realized he wasn't going to add to his statement, she asked, "Is that because you used to be a model?"

Once more she remembered the insinuations made

by Dr. Delgado on that first evening, and wondered if they had anything to do with his friendless state. Now she wished she hadn't been so noble in not trying to find some articles about his breakup to read. Somehow, she thought they could give her further insight into this most private of men.

Francisco was silent for so long she was beginning to think he wouldn't respond, but eventually he said, "In a way."

She waited for him to expand on his reply, but he just stared down into his glass, seemingly lost in less than happy thoughts. So she took the initiative, and said, "Well, I don't make friends easily, either, so we have that in common."

He gave her a bland look. "Somehow I find that hard to believe. You seem to get along with everyone."

Krysta stared at him, honestly shocked. Then she realized he'd mistaken her work persona, where her confidence was at its highest, for her overall personality.

"That's just work," she said, wondering why she was being so honest with him when she still felt he wasn't being as frank with her. "I don't have friends. I've never fit in anywhere, or felt as though I could trust people not to make fun of me—my lack of fashion sense, the way I always put my work first. Socially, I'm a dud."

"You're not a dud, at anything." He sounded genuinely outraged by her suggesting such a thing, and his reaction made her smile.

"Oh, I know my faults. And if I didn't, my therapist would tell me. I'm afraid of anything that doesn't involve my job. I've never taken the time to make friends, learn new things that aren't work related or even take up a hobby." She shrugged, just as the waiter approached with their meal. "In those regards, I'm the equivalent of a twelve-year-old. Maybe even younger. I know what people say about how I dress, and they're right, but I don't really care. In that respect, you should probably be ashamed to be seen with me!"

Francisco didn't respond until after the waiter had put down their plates and fussed about a little, before leaving them alone again.

Leaning forward, he said, "I don't care about how you dress. You're a brilliant, beautiful woman, and anyone you take as a friend is blessed."

It was her turn to look down, overcome with emotion. What that emotion was, she didn't want to think through, only knew it filled her with warmth and pleasure.

And excitement.

He'd called her beautiful!

Her, who'd had to learn not to react when others made fun of her looks!

"Okay, then," she said when she'd got her voice under control and started shifting her mystery meal around on her plate. "Let's start our friendship over, shall we? If it'll help, think of yourself as my Reintroduction to Interpersonal Relationships 101."

"Sim..." he replied.

But she was sure the hesitation in his voice wasn't her imagination.

Francisco looked down at his plate, not really seeing it, and picked up his fork, although eating was the furthest thing from his mind.

There was a sensation of being pulled into a maelstrom, and it made his stomach roll. He hadn't been able to force himself to tell her about Mari, about being accused of using her to get ahead. Or about being leery of people saying he was doing the same thing with Krysta. Yet, facing that kind of talk didn't seem as imperative right now as it had been.

She thought it important enough to ask what had happened to make him withdraw. It showed she cared and wanted him as a friend, and that's exactly what he would be, despite the simmering attraction making it hard to even look at her for any length of time.

Making him hard, beneath the table.

"What made you go into medicine, anyway?" she was asking, pulling him out of his half-elated, half-agonized thoughts.

"My youngest brother was born with a facial defect, a cleft lip and palate. We were poor. Very, very poor. My parents worried about how they would get him the help he needed, and what would happen to him if they couldn't. Then they heard about a clinic where they could take him for free, and we met a doctor there who agreed to operate on João."

"How old were you?"

"Seven." He smiled slightly, remembering. "João was, not surprisingly, a cranky baby, and I was the only one who could soothe him, so my parents took me with them to see the doctor. I was fascinated by what he was saying, and helped him examine my brother. After the operation, when I saw what Dr. Jimenez was able to achieve, I knew that was what I wanted to do with my life."

Those dark, sparkling eyes were on him, and it felt as though she could see into his soul.

"There's a clinic coming up, in a place called Aparecida. Why aren't you going?"

That surprised him. "I am going. In fact, I am one

of the main organizers this year. How did you hear about it?"

It was her turn to look down at her plate, and it made him wonder what she was trying to hide.

"I overheard a couple of the residents talking, and looked at the roster. I didn't see your name."

"My name wasn't included because it was a given I'd be there."

"Ah," she said, seemingly intent on putting an exact amount and ratio of food on her fork. It was one of those fussy little things she did that amused and enticed him. "I signed up for it, too."

"Oh? You know there probably won't be anything too exciting for you to do, don't you?"

The glance she gave him was scathing. "That's the same thing Director Andrade said to me when I asked if I could go. I didn't get into medicine just to do the flashy stuff, you know. If I can be of help, I'm definitely interested, even if I end up just being a scrub nurse."

Francisco snorted. "I don't think it'll come to that. We're more than happy to have you. Although surgeons come from all around this part of the country, there's always room for more. And it means we can expand the number of patients we see, which is always a good thing."

She nodded, and silence fell between them, but it wasn't fraught, or uncomfortable. Francisco liked that about her—that ability to put him at ease, even when he was supremely aware of her every movement and breath.

Eventually, she looked around and said, "I like this spot. It's cozy, and the food is great."

"Haven't you been here before?" He was a little surprised by that, since the restaurant was near the hospital, and on the route to the apartment building where all the visiting doctors were staying.

"No. I usually eat at home," she said, once more carefully filling her fork.

It made him think about what she'd said earlier, about being afraid, and he had to ask, "What have you seen since you've been here?"

Her reply didn't really surprise him.

"The hospital. My apartment." As though defensive, she quickly added, "The building where I'm staying has a nice pool. I've used that almost every evening."

"Nossa senhora!" He put his hand over his heart, to show how sorry he was. "I have been a poor host, and even poorer friend. We must remedy this, as soon as possible."

The look she gave him, although outwardly bland, sent a streak of fire down his spine.

"After the Dos Santos surgery," she said, and he had the whimsical thought that the operation marked some kind of milestone in her mind. "Then we can discuss it."

But the thought of spending more time with her, breaking her out of her solitary shell, had taken hold of him, and he couldn't stop his excitement and enthusiasm. There were so many things to show her, to watch her experience.

"After the clinic in Aparecida, I'm going to my parents' home to celebrate my birthday with them. You must come, too."

Once more she bent her head to look at her plate, hiding her expression from him.

"We'll see," was all she replied, and he knew, from her tone, not to push.

CHAPTER SIX

ENZO DOS SANTOS was declared fit for surgery, by both Jake Cooper and Krysta, so the schedule was adhered to.

Krysta hadn't allowed herself to think too much about her dinner with Francisco. Doing so would have disordered her usually focused mind. Yet, at night, when usually she soothed herself to sleep with computations and thoughts of work, his image insisted on inserting itself into her head.

For the first time ever, she was eager to get through a surgery. Not because of the help she was affording her patient, but because there was the sensation of life waiting to happen on the other side.

As she scrubbed in prior to the mandibular reconstruction, she kept her thoughts firmly on the surgical plan, doing her best to ignore Francisco, who was doing the same at the next sink. Thankfully, he wasn't a chatterbox, and they completed their preparations in silence, which was only broken by the sounds of running water and the subdued comments of others in the room.

It was a little unusual, in her experience, for the room to be so quiet, but this was, for Paulista's staff, an event of some importance. There was talk. If the surgery was as successful as everyone hoped, and the imaging and mapping models were found effective, the hospital might find it advantageous to use the techniques going forward. It was an opportunity to make Paulista's stand out even more.

Krysta was sure they'd find the new techniques superior to any they now used. The time saved using the preformed plates, guides and the template for modeling the fibula made for a far more efficient operation. And the final results were better than any she'd seen in the past.

Looking through into the theater, she made eye contact with the anesthesiologist, who nodded in return. The gallery above the operating room was full, but she didn't think about that, either.

Strange how if she were going to give a lecture she'd be a frazzled mess right now, but although a man's life and future lay in her hands, she was rock solid. Confident in her abilities.

"Okay, everyone," she said in Portuguese. "Let's get this done."

There was an answering murmur from the assembled team, and then they were in the theater, and beginning.

Surgery wasn't something to be rushed, but as they began, Krysta was highly aware of the time. The longer it took, the less efficient the new techniques would appear to be, and more stress would be put on the patient, who had already gone through one major operation.

"Retractors."

There. Now she could see exactly what she was working with, rather than just looking at scans, and something inside her relaxed, as it always did at this point in a surgery.

It was the feeling of the work truly beginning, although she was totally cognizant of how much it took to get to this point.

"The transplant site looks good," she said, aware that, because of the audience above, she needed to give some kind of running commentary. "Dr. Cooper did a great job of the mandibulectomy, and I don't see any signs of deterioration because of the infection."

They worked apace, each step as laid out in the surgical plan following as it should. Time ticked away, and Krysta kept a sharp eye on the other teams, but didn't try to micromanage them. If there were a problem, they'd tell her.

"Although instant repair of a bisected inferior alveolar nerve is preferred, splicing is still effective if done within three months, and most patients regain some sensation in their chin and lower lip within ten months. Not too long ago, the inclusion of IAN repair in a surgery of this type was considered too time-intensive. Now, with superior facial mapping and virtual surgical planning, it's become viable."

She spoke more for the benefit of the students sitting in the gallery, but it also was a subtle way of letting the fibula team know where they were.

"Performing the osteotomy now, Dr. Simpson."

Right on time. She glanced over in time to see the surgical nurse handing Francisco the Gigli saw, and then looked back at what she was doing. His calm, confident tone fed her own surety in the success of the operation.

"Nurse, make sure you have the template ready."

"*Sim*, Doctor."

There was always a chance that something could go wrong, either with the patient or the process, but Krysta was confident. She was preparing for the insertion of the shaped bone, while the dental implants were being placed.

"Each guide and template we're using today was specifically fabricated for Mr. Dos Santos, sterilized and packaged by a firm in Belgium. Using the template to shape the fibula saves time and eliminates any guesswork from the process. It also allows for preplanning of the placement of the dental implants."

Yet, even with that self-assured pronouncement, Krysta still held her breath for an instant as she fit the bone in place, and heaved a silent sigh of relief when it was, indeed, perfect.

"Less than two millimeters' difference. Good work, Dr. Carvalho."

"Thank you, Dr. Simpson."

Vascular work now, to ensure proper blood flow to the bone and surrounding tissue, and then the fitting of the titanium plate used to secure the bones together. Another silent sigh of relief when it conformed perfectly to the shape of the jaw.

"As you all know, mandibular repair in the past often left patients with malformities of the face, making social interaction difficult. Being able to fabricate a plate that restores the shape of the face as close to normal as possible changed that. But it was up to the surgeon, at the time of the operation, to get the shape and height correct. Now, with all the tools and techniques at our disposal, we can save time in the theater, thereby reducing the stress put on our patients."

She went on to explain, when she could, about the ease of having screws specifically calibrated to the patient's needs.

"No more searching through boxes of screws to find

the appropriate lengths. This particular company even sends correctly sized screwdrivers."

One of the surgical nurses said something under her breath, and Krysta paused to look up.

"Exactly," she said, letting amusement color her tone. "A dream come true."

Soft-tissue work now. She couldn't allow herself to think about the fact that they were on the final lap. If you did, things could be missed, or you could get sloppy.

Check and recheck. Making sure everything was in place, and looked perfect.

"As per usual, the blood flow to the jaw and skin will be monitored every hour for the next two days," she said as she began to close. "Dr. Morales, our maxillofacial specialist, has determined there is no need for temporary arch bars to wire the jaws shut, so I believe we're almost finished here. Mr. Dos Santos has a long recovery ahead of him, but I believe he'll be pleased with the results."

There, the final stitches were in place and, for a moment, she hesitated, running through the entire operation in her mind one more time.

"Good work, Dr. Simpson."

It was Francisco's voice that broke her from her reverie, and she shook her head, looking around at the entire team, even as the bustle of postoperation broke out. Then she looked up, and meeting his gaze—warmly brown now—made her heart stutter.

She turned away, not wanting him to see whatever was in her eyes.

"No. Good work, *team*. I'm proud to have worked with you all."

Muted applause greeted her words and, suddenly exhausted, coming down off the surgical high, she made her way to the door. The surgery may be over, but there was still a long evening and night ahead, to make sure she was available, in case of emergency.

"Five hours and ten minutes." Francisco's voice came from just behind her, made her pause. "I believe that's a record here for us at Paulista's. You were *magnífica*."

"Let's wait and see the results," she rebutted, even though warmth flooded out from her chest at the compliment. "Then we can pat ourselves on the back."

But Francisco just made a rude noise.

"No matter what you say," he replied sternly. *"Magnífica."*

And, in his estimation, she had been.

Krysta ran a tight operation, without fuss or even a hint of confusion, and allowed her fellow practitioners to do their jobs without her constantly looking over their shoulders. She also gave credit where it was due. He'd seen the others relax and do their very best for her—not for the hospital, or even for the praise. Just to please her.

Such character was rare, especially among the people inhabiting the rarefied circles she was known to inhabit.

As he pushed through the doors into the men's changing room, Francisco considered the doctors and surgeons he'd met in the years since he'd started practicing. Just like in any other profession, some were nice, others horrid. Some were snobs, and yet others so full of themselves it was almost painful to behold.

Krysta fell into a class all by herself.

It was almost impossible for him to believe her when she told him of how truncated her life really was. She was the type of woman who should, after a surgery like the one she just performed, be taken out dancing. Be wined and dined and then made long, sweet love to.

Well, not right after surgery, when she would be exhausted and set to spend the night at the hospital, so as to be on hand should anything go wrong. But as soon as things quieted down.

Just imagining holding her, swaying to sweet samba music, pushed the edge of tiredness he felt aside, replacing it with longing.

Pare seu tolo.

Yet, telling himself to stop imagining such things, calling himself a fool, didn't help.

He wanted her, and when his feelings had gone from interest to full-blown desire, he couldn't tell.

"Good work in there." Jake Cooper came over to where Francisco was rummaging in his locker for a clean scrub shirt. The one he'd been wearing was soaked with perspiration. "It went well, from what I saw."

"You were in the gallery?" Francisco pulled off his shirt, using it to wipe at his chest. Did he have time for a shower? Probably not. He still had to check on other patients before he could even think of going home.

"For a time," Jake replied. "I was...otherwise occupied for part of it. Krysta had invited me to be in the theater, but I had to decline. Enzo may be my patient, but reconstruction isn't my specialty, as you know."

Once more Francisco had a moment of white-hot jealousy, and then he shook his head. Being around Krysta was making him a little *louco*, apparently.

"I think you would have enjoyed seeing her work, up close," he said, making sure there was no trace of his self-described craziness in his voice. "She truly is a master at her craft."

"I did get to see you work on the fibula flap. From what I saw, you're not too shabby yourself."

Francisco snorted, the sound caught in the fabric of the fresh shirt as it went over his head. "With the template provided, I would be incompetent if I couldn't get it right."

Jake Cooper just laughed, and turned toward the door. "We both know there was a lot more to it than just cutting out a pattern. Anyway, I'll make a quick check on Enzo in the PACU, then I'm going home." He paused for a moment, then added, "Who knew being a parent could be as exhausting as any day in the hospital?"

And before Francisco could figure out how to reply to that, he pushed through the doors and was gone.

Francisco made his rounds, and everywhere he went it seemed that Krysta's name was on everyone's lips. When he stopped in at the postoperative ward to check on Enzo Dos Santos, it was to hear he had just missed her.

"I sent her to get a little rest," the nurse in charge told him while he was looking at the chart. "She was trying not to hover, but failing, badly."

Francisco nodded, pleased with the readings he was seeing. "Did Dr. Simpson go home?"

That made the nurse chuckle. "Oh, I doubt it. I expect to see her back here in another hour, when we are checking the blood flow again."

He should go home, he knew, but instead, his feet led him to the surgeon's lounge. Opening the door as quietly as he could, he slipped inside. And there, curled up on a couch, he found her.

His heart ached at the peaceful innocence of her relaxed body. Without the force of her personality mobilizing it, the crisp, forthright personality retreated into the background, leaving a softness of lips and face that transformed her into a different woman. One that aroused all his protective instincts.

She needed rest. He could see dark shadows under her eyes, as though she hadn't been sleeping as well as she should.

And had she eaten at all, since the operation? If she planned to stay here all night, as he was sure she was, sustenance was necessary.

As though hearing his thoughts, she sighed, and snuggled deeper into the cushion beneath her head. A part of him wanted to go and set his lips to the curve of her cheek, the indentation between neck and shoulder, and he fisted his fingers to stop from reaching for her. Instead, he forced himself to go in the other direction, slipping back out of the room.

Although he tried to be as quiet as possible coming in less than half an hour later with a tray, as soon as he opened the door, Krysta sat up.

"What time is it?"

"Not time to check on the patient yet," he said as he walked toward the couch. Seeing her look at her watch anyway, he tried to distract her by asking, "Do you always wake up like that?"

That brought her eyebrows up, and then together in a little scowl. "Like what?"

"Fully conscious, as though you could pick up a scalpel and dive right into an operation. It takes me five minutes to figure out which is the floor and which is the ceiling when I first awaken."

Her chuckle was slightly husky, as though sleep still lingered there, if nowhere else, and the sound was delicious.

"No," she replied, watching him put the laden tray down on the table in front of the couch. "I was just dozing. Usually it takes me a minute to get my bearings. What is all that?"

"I thought you might be hungry," he explained, feeling a little silly even as he did. "But I didn't know what you'd want, so I brought some soup, and a salad, and a sandwich. It was all I could get at this late hour without leaving the hospital."

"You're a lifesaver!" She was already reaching for the soup, and her enthusiasm, plus the smile lighting her face, made his heart sing. "I could kiss you."

Ever after, he wondered at how easily the next words slipped from his mouth, propelled by a sudden longing too strong for his control.

"I wish you would."

CHAPTER SEVEN

KRYSTA FROZE, and Francisco did as well. For a long moment neither moved, and then his gaze dropped, to her lips, she thought, and a look she didn't recognize lit his eyes from within. Whatever that expression was caused by, it lit a firestorm inside her belly, and her breath hitched in her throat.

Then, just as swiftly as it had passed over his face, it was gone, and he chuckled, although it sounded forced.

"Desculpa," he said, reverting to his native language and then pausing, before going back to English. "Excuse me. That was out of line, and I apologize."

There was the urge to ignore his comment, or laugh it off. After all, it would be silly to place too much store in an off-the-cuff remark, probably made without thought, in jest.

And yet, she dearly wanted him to mean it, and couldn't help wondering whether she would regret, forever, not finding out whether he did or not.

But the thought of asking him was terrifying. Not only would she be opening herself up to rejection from a man she deeply admired and wanted more than anything in the world, but also risking a friendship she cherished. She could see no benefit to pursuing it.

Unless he *hadn't* been joking...

Then she reminded herself, wasn't she supposed to be conquering her fears, trying new things? It wasn't as though, if he rejected her, she'd have to see him forever and ever. It would just be a matter of toughing it out for a couple of months, and putting the humiliation behind her and moving on.

Even with that staunch pep talk, her heart rate was through the roof and her hands started sweating as she looked at him and said, "Only apologize if you didn't mean it."

He'd adopted his stone face, the one he showed the world most of the time, but as her words sunk in, it fell away to be replaced with an expression she couldn't interpret. Was it pleasure? Hesitation?

A combination of the two?

With a low-voiced mutter that sounded suspiciously like a curse, he stepped forward to sink down onto the couch, as though his legs didn't want to hold him aloft anymore.

Krysta knew the feeling. She didn't think she could stand, she was trembling so hard. How she wished she had even a modicum of poise right now! But she was trying so hard to fake it until she made it, she once more reached for the soup, and then decided on the salad instead. At least if that fell into her lap she didn't risk getting burned.

"I withdraw my apology, then," he said, rather stiffly. "I most certainly do want to kiss you."

Her heart leaped. She'd never known what that meant, only read the expression in books and thought it silly, until now. It leaped and stuttered, and what little sangfroid she'd managed to gather together fled, to be replaced with wild anticipation.

Then she looked over and found him once more staring at her lips, his expression now one of uninhibited hunger. Instinctively, she leaned a little closer, saw him do the same, and everything inside her stilled, waiting.

Wanting.

Then he took a deep breath and, shaking his head just once, reached out to touch her cheek.

"I want to, but not here. Not now, while you are tired and worried about our patient. Away from the hospital, where I can have your undivided attention."

Krysta wanted to argue, disappointment like a cold rock in her stomach. She hadn't given even half a thought to Enzo Dos Santos in the last minutes, much less anything else. But she bit her tongue, and busied herself trying to open the container now perched on her lap. Somehow his words steadied her, made her wonder if he were just trying to brush her off gently.

Or, perhaps, was thinking about his reputation at Paulista's.

Not that she blamed him, really, if that were the case. She'd given in to her curiosity and looked up the articles about his breakup online and realized why he was so cautious. He'd been excoriated in the press, accused of using the young woman in ways Krysta found hard to believe. She'd found herself glaring at a picture of his ex, somehow absolutely certain there was a great deal more to the story than had been reported, but no one seemed interested in asking Francisco for his side. Krysta wished she had the guts to ask for it herself, but didn't.

"Damn it," she muttered, still unable to get the salad open, and when a large, warm hand covered hers, it brought her to immediate motionlessness.

There was a tingle, like static electricity, running up

her arm from where their skin touched, and she suddenly couldn't seem to catch her breath properly.

Turning her head, she looked at him again, was effortlessly caught and held by his tawny, hooded gaze.

"Querida." His voice was low and soft, a caress to her ears that she felt down to her toes. "Spend the day with me, after you feel comfortable with leaving Senhor Dos Santos to others' care. We will find something to do, just the two of us. Then, if you still desire it, we will kiss."

Why not now, or tomorrow?

But she knew why, and was secretly grateful. Tomorrow would be taken up with monitoring Enzo, and finalizing both her next lecture and the planned clinic excursion.

Thinking of the trip to Aparecida made her go hot, and then cold. They would be completely away from Paulista's, and perhaps could spend some time alone, far from prying eyes. Then she stopped her crazy imagination from running away with her good sense. They would be working, surrounded by people, and then, if she agreed to go with him to his parents' home, there would be his family to contend with.

"Fale comigo," he said. *Speak to me.* And she realized she'd been sitting there silently, staring at him like a ninny, while he had no idea what was going through her mind.

"Yes," she said, as though she hadn't had second, third, fourth thoughts. "We'll do that."

He sighed, and gently took the salad container from her hand.

"Good. *Obrigado.*"

"Don't thank me," she said with not a small amount of tartness in her voice. Equilibrium was returning, with a vengeance, and there was so much she needed to think through before that day out with him. "You have no idea what you're getting into."

That made him chuckle as he handed her the now-open salad, and reached to snag her a fork. "I will take my chances," was all he said, and then, much to her relief, changed the subject.

When another surgeon came in, rubbing his eyes and yawning, they were discussing Enzo's operation, and arguing over how much of the new technology could be used in other applications.

After one more check on their patient, Francisco left to go home, as he was operating again early the following morning. Krysta booted up her laptop and tried to do some work, but her brain wouldn't stop going back to their conversation earlier.

That moment when she thought he might kiss her, and how much she wished it had happened.

Had she really opened the door to something more than friendship with him?

Yes, she had. And while it made her sort of proud, it also scared her silly.

It was at times like this she wished she wasn't so solitary and had someone she could confide in.

Unfortunately, she didn't and so had to deal with it herself.

As she made her way back to the PACU to do her hourly check, she wondered how long it would take for the nurses to try to get her to leave. There was, after all, a surgeon on duty in case of emergency, but they'd find it an impossible task to turf her out. She always stayed in the hospital after an important surgery, feeling a sense of responsibility perhaps out of proportion to the situation. While they had used some newer techniques, the operation itself, its risks and long-term effects, were the same, and nothing new to Paulista's staff.

Nearing Enzo Dos Santos's cubicle, she saw Roque Cardoza coming toward her along the corridor. He was leaning rather heavily on his cane, and his face looked a little drawn, as though he had had a long day, and was paying for it.

They met up at the entrance to the cubicle, and she was subjected to an intent look, before he held out his hand.

"We haven't met. I'm Roque Cardoza."

As Krysta shook his hand, she recalled the conversation with Amy and Flávia outside the elevator, and thought:

I think he's rather handsome, too, although not as handsome as Francisco.

But all she said was, "Orthopedics, isn't it? Nice to meet you, Dr. Cardoza."

That brought a lift of one eyebrow, and a twist of the edge of his lips, as though he were remembering when they'd last seen each other.

"I am a friend of Enzo's, so I thought I would check in on him, and see if Lizbet needs anything, but I see she's not here."

Krysta glanced into the cubicle, and replied, "I'm sure she'll be back momentarily. Since she was allowed in, his wife has hardly left his side."

"They are devoted," he said in his deep, accented tones. "One to the other. This has been a trying time for her."

The affection in his voice was clear, and she couldn't help asking, "How do you know the Dos Santoses?"

"Enzo was the owner and manager of the *futebol* team I played on when I was young. It was he who encouraged me to study medicine, after my injury."

"If he hadn't been injured, he would have gone on to play internationally, is what Enzo always said."

At the sound of Lizbet Dos Santos's voice, they both turned. Krysta watched as Roque hugged the older woman, making soothing, nonsense sounds in her ear, which seemed to both please her and bring her close to tears.

"Good of you to come, Roque. I'm sure he would be happy to know you're here."

"I will stay for a while, Lizbet. Has he awakened yet, since the operation?"

"Yes, he goes in and out for a few minutes at a time."

"Which is exactly normal, and how we want it right now," Krysta interjected.

"She is correct, *querida*," Roque said to the other woman. "His pain should be carefully managed."

Then he insisted on taking Lizbet Dos Santos to get a soda in the cafeteria, leaving Krysta and the nurses to do their checks without her looking on.

It was only later, once more ensconced in the surgeon's lounge, while trying to catch a nap, that Krysta remembered how Roque had called the other woman *querida*.

And she couldn't help wondering if, when Francisco used it, it was simply as a form of friendly affection, rather than anything more.

The thought was so depressing she found herself grinding her teeth, had to force herself to stop. And when she fell into a doze, it was to dream about swimming in an unending pool, which offered her nowhere to turn back.

Or to get out.

CHAPTER EIGHT

FRANCISCO KNEW, because of his past career, people viewed him as a playboy, irrespective of the reality of his now rather boring, work-focused life. Yes, there had been some wild times when he was young and travelling with other, far more pleasure-driven people, but at heart he had still remained the same. A man who liked and respected women, almost a traditionalist in the way he felt they should be treated by the men who claimed to love them.

Another thing other people didn't seem to understand about him was the depth of caution life had taught him. At so many junctures he'd leaped without looking, and the results were invariably poor. Even at as young an age as six, the world had tried to teach him to be careful, to think before he acted. Then it was in the form of the spider lurking behind some scraps of wood and metal. His father had told him, repeatedly, to be careful there, but he hadn't bothered to listen. His reward for ignoring Papa's words was a spider bite that brought with it a great deal of pain.

All these things, he knew, had contributed to his not kissing Krysta the night before, when he'd had the chance, but he'd spent all his waking moments since regretting his decision.

Suppose his hesitation caused her to change her mind?

Yet he knew, without a doubt, there was something brewing between them. Something rare and lovely he wanted, oh so desperately, to explore.

This was all new territory to him, but he was determined to make the most of the situation, whatever it turned out to be.

"Are you all right?" Flávia's curt question brought him out of his stupor, and he zoned back in to find her eyeing him curiously. "You look a million miles away."

"Yes," he replied, bringing himself back to their conversation. "When do you think you'll be able to show us around the sanctuary, then?"

She gave a casual shrug, and continued packing her kit. "I'm not entirely sure at the moment. It depends on a few things," she replied, once more sending him a curious glance. "I could arrange for someone else to give you the tour, if you like."

"No," he said. "I think you should do it. Krysta knows and admires you, and she's particularly interested in your research. It can wait."

Flávia smiled, and was still smiling slightly when he left to return to the hospital.

He didn't know when the idea had come to him, but he was glad it had. Krysta had said she didn't make friends easily, yet he'd seen how confident and relaxed she was around others. Perhaps all she needed was to spend more time with people who, like Flávia, seemed particularly to like being around her? Sometimes, when you are used to things being a certain way, it took time and effort to realize they didn't have to remain the same.

He could totally understand where Krysta had learned to rely only on herself, and her own company. She had only been fourteen when she went to college!

When Francisco remembered what he'd been like at that age, he could hardly fathom what she must have experienced. The emotional difference between a fourteen-year-old, no matter how academically brilliant, and the average university student must have been night and day.

Even when he started modeling, he'd been chaperoned by Caro, and so had been somewhat protected. Krysta, although still living with her parents then, would have had to navigate the new world she'd been dropped into on her own.

That was no longer the case, though. She was a well-respected surgeon, a rising star and, most of all, a strong, confident woman. There was no need to hold on to the old phobias and habits. Of course, it was ultimately up to her to realize that, and break out of her shell, but Francisco had no issue with trying to help her along.

It was well-known that Flávia also had the reputation of being rather solitary. She and Krysta may yet turn out to be kindred spirits.

When he'd approached Flávia, he'd seen the wariness in her eyes, and wondered if he was the cause. He was well aware of some of the things said about him at the hospital, and knew his past was the topic of both conversation and speculation. Fighting to put it all behind him, telling himself it didn't matter, and that only his work was important, hadn't taken away the sting.

The shame.

By the end of the conversation with Flávia, he'd realized her reaction probably had nothing to do with him, that he was probably projecting his own neuroses onto her. It had given him pause, made him consider what the situation with Mari had done to his life, despite it being so far in the past.

Yes, there would always be people, like Delgado, who would, without knowing the real story, be prejudiced against him, but he could no longer use that as an excuse to isolate himself. The people who knew him best, his family and oldest friends, knew the stories put out about him were lies, but if he hoped to make new friends, he would have to trust again.

The initial idea to arrange a visit to the sanctuary had started out as a way for Krysta to face one of her fears, but now Francisco wondered if it weren't as important for him to face his, too.

To face them, and get past them.

Making his way into the hospital, he checked his watch. Usually about now Krysta would message him, asking if they were meeting for lunch, but his stomach dropped when the screen was blank.

Had he scared her away last night?

Then his phone vibrated, and he unlocked the screen.

Just checking on Enzo Dos Santos, then I'm free for lunch, if you are.

I was just on my way to look in on him myself. Meet you there.

Not entirely true. He'd planned to make a visit to the patient after lunch, but the opportunity to see her sooner was too good to pass up.

In the ICU, where the patient had been transferred, he saw Roque Cardoza coming out of Senhor Dos Santos's cubicle. It wasn't surprising he would be visiting the patient, since everyone knew Roque had once played on the famous team.

"Oi," Roque said in greeting as they drew abreast of each other. "Enzo seems to be doing very well. Even Dr. Simpson seems happy with his progress so far."

"That is good news indeed," he said. Especially since Enzo Dos Santos's speedy recovery would mean Francisco could get Krysta to himself sooner.

"Funny to see Enzo unable to speak," Roque commented with a wry smile. "But he's already scribbling away on the tablet they gave him, and once he's talking again, the nurses may wish to have the trach reinserted."

Feeling more relaxed than he could remember being in a while, Francisco chuckled, then said, "I should go and take a look for myself, while he's already being examined."

Roque glanced at his watch. "Care to lunch with me? Or have you already eaten?"

"Sorry, I have a previous engagement. Perhaps another time?"

"Of course. *Tchau.*"

Echoing Roque's farewell, Francisco hurried into the cubicle. Krysta was just finishing her examination, handing the nurse the handheld radar machine she'd used to check the vascular flow in the surgical site.

"It looks very good," she said to Enzo Dos Santos, with a look over at his wife, too. "There is less drainage than might be expected, and the swelling is already decreasing nicely. Take a look, Dr. Carvalho."

Francisco performed his own examination, after looking at the chart and readings, and he had to admit the patient was progressing well.

As they made their way to the elevators, Krysta sighed happily. "His recovery so far is going really well.

If he continues at this rate, we might be able to remove the trach and nasogastric tube sooner than I thought."

"It helps that he was in good health otherwise, prior to discovering the cancer."

"Very true," she agreed as the car arrived with its customary soft chime. As they stepped in together, and Francisco pressed the ground-floor button, she continued. "And his attitude toward the surgery and expectations of recovery is important, too. I've told his wife to watch for any changes in mood or personality, explaining sometimes major surgeries can cause depression, or anger, and she's promised she will."

They were alone, facing each other across the elevator car, and suddenly Enzo Dos Santos's operation and recovery were the farthest things from his mind.

Her eyes were shining, and her lush lips were curved in a delicious smile. The urge to take the two steps necessary to press her against the wall and taste her mouth was almost irresistible.

The smile faded, and her cheeks darkened, until they glowed.

"Francisco." It was just a whisper. "Don't look at me like that."

"Or what?" he asked just as they got to their floor, and the conversation was abandoned, although, on his part, anyway, not forgotten.

Her legs were wobbly. It took every ounce of concentration to make them perform to respectable standards and carry her toward the cafeteria when they apparently wanted to fail her completely, leaving her a puddle on the floor at Francisco's feet.

For a moment, he'd looked as though he wanted to devour her on the spot—his eyes heavy lidded and gleaming, his usually stern mouth suddenly, thrill-ingly sensual.

How was she going to get through the next few days until they could be alone?

Did she really have to wait?

It was a question she asked herself repeatedly as lunch progressed, and the conversation between them slowed, then faltered to a stop.

Once more she wished she was more experienced, able to interpret what was happening, and how things were progressing—or not—between them. She'd come to the realization that no amount of intelligence helped when it came to emotions.

Especially for someone like her, without any empiri-cal evidence regarding relationships, casual or serious.

Thank goodness this situation with Francisco would never progress to the latter. She'd never be able to sort out all the feelings, or be brave enough to try taking it even one step further, if she thought it would have long-term ramifications.

When he spoke, she was so deep in thought she started with surprise.

"I thought we could go to Ibirapuera Park this eve-ning, if you are free. There is sometimes live music, and it truly is beautiful at night. And…" He hesitated for a moment, making Krysta's stomach dip and roll, since she didn't know whether what he planned to say was good or bad. "And I have a day off, the day following your next lecture. If it suits you, perhaps we could visit the beach, near Santos?"

She shouldn't feel such an intense rush of joy at the thought of going out with him, but excitement, and re-lief, made her almost light-headed.

"That sounds nice." Even to her, that response

sounded lukewarm, but when she glanced up at him, he was smiling just slightly, that sultry twinkle in his eyes, and she couldn't resist grinning back.

And somehow, once that was settled, they could go back to their usual selves, comfortable together, or as comfortable as she could be with little *zings* of eagerness and desire firing through her veins.

After they'd eaten, and he'd told her he would come and collect her at her apartment at six that evening, he went to do rounds, while she hurried back to the ICU to once more check on Enzo. Knowing he'd suffered an infection after his mandibulectomy, she was paying special attention to his temperature and drains, but so far everything looked perfect. Her anxiety about making sure there were no postsurgical complications was beginning to wane, and she knew the surgeons at Paulista's were competent to handle anything that may arise. Therefore, she felt comfortable telling the nurses she wouldn't be at the hospital during the evening, and hid her amusement when they seemed discreetly relieved. But, of course, she left strict instructions for her to be called, should an emergency arise.

Forcing herself to go up to the small office she'd been assigned and go over her notes for her next lecture felt like punishment, but she did it, anyway. Of course, thoughts of the night ahead kept trying to intrude and, at about three-thirty, she threw in the towel.

She debated whether to go back to the ICU, but decided against it. There was a fine line between being thorough and hovering so much the patient began to wonder if there wasn't something wrong. Everything she'd witnessed at the hospital told her Senhor Dos Santos was in good hands.

Walking through the staff entrance, she found herself holding the door open for Amy Woodell, who was coming in.

"We meet again," she said. "How're you?"

"Good," Amy said. "Hanging in there for all I'm worth."

Krysta chuckled. "Me too. By the skin of my teeth, although with proper brushing I shouldn't have any such thing."

Amy laughed with her, then asked, "You're heading home?"

"Yes, it's been a long couple of days. I need a break."

It wasn't something she could ever remember saying before. Maybe Brazil was changing her even more than she could imagine.

"Ah. The Dos Santos operation." Amy leaned on the wall, as though settling in for a chat. "The whole hospital has been talking about it. Sounds as though it was a success."

"Shh, don't jinx it. But so far, so good."

"We should get together one evening. Have dinner, or go to the Morumbi shopping center. I hear it's fabulous."

"I'd like that," Krysta said, and found that she meant it. There was a part of her ridiculously touched that the other woman actually wanted to spend time with her. "Call me, and we'll set it up."

They spent a few more minutes catching up, with Krysta telling her about the Aparecida trip, and them deciding to wait until Krysta was back from that before embarking on their planned outing.

When they parted company, Krysta made her way outside, and started walking back to the apartment, but there was a thought niggling at the back of her mind, and she found herself stopping on the sidewalk.

What was she going to wear that evening? Despite

assuring Dr. Hellman she would try to get out and about when in São Paulo, she hadn't really taken the promise seriously enough to bring anything even remotely nice.

Not that she really knew, or had even cared before, what would be considered "nice" on her. But tonight she was going out not just with a handsome, intriguing man, but also a man who used to be a model. One who no doubt knew a heck of a lot more about clothing and fashion than she did.

She didn't want to look too frumpy in comparison.

There was a part of her that wanted to scoff at the notion that she could ever be fashionable. Another part was almost petrified by the thought of displaying her body in any way. For so long she'd hidden behind baggy, unattractive clothing, telling herself she didn't really care what she looked like, as long as she was achieving at the highest professional level.

Now she had to admit that she *did* care, that she'd been using her ugly clothes as a shield against being hurt again, and she wanted to get past that painful night.

Perhaps she'd finally gotten to the point where she could, with just a little courage, overcome what had happened to her all those years ago, and begin to truly live again.

However, knowing how to go about it was beyond her talents. Time to find someone who would know better than she did. After all, if a patient needed a coronary angioplasty and a stent, she'd have no problem calling in a cardiologist.

A good doctor knew when to ask for assistance when the issues were outside their purview.

Before she could change her mind, she pulled out her phone and called for a cab.

CHAPTER NINE

THE LOOK ON Francisco's face when she went down to meet him in the apartment lobby made all the effort of shopping worthwhile.

The clerks had fussed over her, exclaiming at her figure, apparently wanting her to try on a mountain of clothing. She'd told them where she was going, and they'd eventually settled on a snug pair of jeans, far tighter than any she'd owned in years, and a beautiful silk top with colorful embroidery at the neck and sleeves. Then, since they said the night air might be a little cool, there was a jacket to go over the blouse.

The two women had argued over which color jacket she should get, one voting for black, the other for a fun orange, which Krysta would never, ever have considered before. Yet, when she put it on, it was instant love.

She'd drawn the line at the high wedged booties they'd wanted her to get and, after some arguing, got a pair of low-heeled boots, reminiscent of hiking boots, but of lovely, soft tooled leather.

Now, as a slow smile dawned over Francisco's face, Krysta felt heat flood her face.

"You wouldn't look out of place at Fashion Week," he said. *"Linda..."*

There he went again, calling her beautiful.

If he weren't careful, she just might start believing him!

Taking her hand, he kissed the back lightly, and then spun her in a slow turn, so he could see the entire outfit.

"I went shopping," she said, her voice sounding strange to her ears. Breathless. Husky. As though she'd just woken up. "I didn't trust my own taste, so I let the ladies in the store help me."

"They did well," he said. "This jacket suits you *à perfeição*."

She didn't tell him the jacket had been her choice in the end, but hugged the compliment to her heart.

The restaurant he took her to seemed a local hangout spot, but the subdued lighting and music low enough to be heard over gave it a subtle romantic tone.

Or perhaps it was the way Francisco kept looking at her that brought romance to mind. For someone who'd never given it a second thought before, she found herself suddenly obsessed.

Yet, they kept the conversation light, speaking about places they'd both visited, and then the conversation turned to their families.

"Are you sure your parents won't mind my turning up with you for your birthday?"

"Not at all," he said. "My mother, in particular, loves having lots of people around. I think that's why she drummed it into us that it's good luck to celebrate your birthday where you were born. There's no such superstition—it's just an excuse to have us come home."

He said it with such fondness Krysta couldn't help chuckling.

"You told me about your brother João. Is he your only sibling?"

"No, there are five of us. My mother always wanted

an even larger family but after my youngest sister was born, Mama hemorrhaged, and had to have a hysterectomy. I remember how sad she was then, for a very long time. So much so I sometimes thought we would never get her back, the way she was before. Eventually she healed, but I know how hard it was for her to watch all her children leave, as they grew up."

In his words she heard the explanation for why he returned home for his birthday, his tenderheartedness toward his mother another wonderful facet of his personality.

"She sounds lovely," she said. And then, to lighten the moment, added, "If she needs a child at home, she could take my youngest brother. He doesn't seem to want to leave at all."

That made him chuckle. "Why not?"

Krysta shook her head, as though in sorrow. "He's an artist, actually a really good one. But apparently he doesn't want to add 'struggling' to the job description. He keeps saying he's waiting to get on his feet before he moves out."

Francisco's eyebrows went up. "How do your parents feel about that?"

She snorted. "Well, I've told you a little about my father, so you can imagine that he's constantly grumbling about it, saying how, when he was that age, he was already out building a life for himself. He doesn't understand why Damon can't work a normal job and do his art on the side, like so many others do. My mom... well...she's a teacher, and always encouraged us to follow our dreams, so she hasn't said much about it. Don't get me wrong. They're both really proud of him, but I think they'd be happier if they felt he was doing better financially."

"Do you see them often?"

"Not as often as I should." There was no sense in lying about it. "I've allowed my life to become centered around work, pushing everything else, everyone else, to the side. It's not something I'm proud of, or planned on. It just happened."

"Well," he said in a deep, somehow serene tone. "It's never too late to embrace a new way of being."

Somehow, when she heard it like that, it made perfect sense, even as she acknowledged it would be harder than it sounded. She'd known, for a while, that her withdrawal from her family had hurt them, yet whenever she thought about going to see them, she allowed herself to be sidetracked by work.

And there was a certain level of guilt keeping her away, too. Not just because she'd distanced herself, but because she felt as though their lives had been turned upside down because of her.

Uncomfortable about admitting that to Francisco, but still wanting to talk about it, she said, "For the last few years, my dad has been saying how much he misses Saint Eustace, and longs to go back there to live. The only reason they left it to begin with was because of me."

Francisco tilted his head to the side, and said, "Why do you think so?"

"It's not what I think," she replied. "It's what I know. Mom went to the island on a teaching assignment, met my father and stayed, instead of going back to Connecticut. From all the stories they tell, they were really happy there, and then they had me. By the time I was two, Mom knew they probably wouldn't be able to give me the education and mental stimulation I needed. That was before easy internet access on the island. They made the decision to go to the States, so I could develop the way she knew I could."

He regarded her silently, his expression serious, eyes intent. Then he asked, "Do you think they regret how you turned out?"

She tried to smile, to keep the conversation light, even as an ache opened up in her chest.

"I don't know." She added a shrug, but knew she hadn't fooled him by the way his eyes narrowed slightly. "I'm not like other people. Not what most parents would expect or even want in a daughter. They never made me feel as though they weren't happy with me, but I never felt…as though I were enough, either."

He was quiet for a moment, then said, "If they cared only for their own pleasure, and had wanted you to conform, they would have stayed on Saint Eustace. But they saw something in you, something special, which needed nurturing, so they took you to a place where you could get what was necessary to thrive, and become what you are."

He paused for a second, as though thinking carefully before he continued. "I think you have come to live inside your head too much, *querida*. So used to trying to find answers to everything when, in truth, there are some things in life meant simply to be enjoyed, not picked over until nothing remains but dry and dusty facts.

"Take what you construe as your parents' sacrifice as a love gift, and be thankful for it. Family is important. There are so many who don't have one, or have ones that cause only anguish and suffering, so those of us who have good ones should be eternally grateful."

He was right. Of course he was. What her parents had done had been out of love, and she was eternally thankful to them. Making it an excuse to avoid them was both pathetic and juvenile and, there and then, she resolved to do better.

"Besides," Francisco said as he reached for his water glass. "If your parents were truly that homesick for Saint Eustace, they could have gone back long ago, despite your brother's determination never to fly the nest. After all, he could have gone with them, too."

That made her laugh, just a little. "That's true. I could see him as a beach bum, to be honest."

He laughed with her, then his face got serious again. "Most importantly, you are a wonderful, beautiful, talented and amazing woman. Any parent would be proud to call you their daughter."

Although she scrunched her nose at him, intimating disbelief at his words, she also looked down at her plate so he couldn't see the sheen of tears in her eyes.

He said all the right things. If only she could trust he meant them, but her insecurities ran too deep, and something stirred inside her, firing a determination to glean the truth. Just as she would if he were a difficult case, demanding facts to get to the basis of the problem.

She met his gaze across the table, and without hesitation said, "I don't have much experience in things like this, Francisco, so I have to ask, are you trying to seduce me?"

The shutters came down over his face, leaving only the stern, haughty look he so often wore around the hospital, and her heart sank.

But there was no anger in his voice when he replied, "Why do you ask? Is it because I call you beautiful, and say how remarkable I think you are?"

"Yes." This was too important to back down, even if backing down were her way, which it wasn't.

"When I speak of beauty, it is not in the way the fashion magazines mean it. I lived in the world they try to make others aspire to, and there is little beauty to be found there. For me, beauty is inside, shining out through the smile, the eyes.

"This evening, when I came to pick you up, it wasn't your new clothes, or even the fit of them, that made me say *linda*." He shook his head slowly, still holding her gaze. "It was you, who stood there obviously feeling good in those clothes. You shone, your natural confidence lighting you from within, only highlighted by the clothes, not caused by it."

He gave her a long look, then asked, "Do you find me handsome?"

"Yes," she said. "You're very good-looking."

That made his lips quirk into a wry smile. "And are you attracted to me?"

"You know I am." Heat gathered under her skin at saying it out loud.

"Because I am good-looking?"

"No," she said.

"Then why?"

"I'm not sure," she said honestly. "I've thought about that quite a lot, but haven't come to a definitive conclusion."

His smile widened, his eyes starting to twinkle. "*Exatamente.* It is the same with me. A fascination I can only feel grow stronger each time I see you. An appreciation of the person you are, and how I feel when I'm with you. It is many things, but not based solely on physical beauty, or physical attraction, although the latter is definitely powerful, too."

A shiver of awareness, of desire, ran down her spine,

and her mind stuttered, shutting down for the moments she spent drowning in his dark, slumberous eyes.

Then she gathered herself together, wondering why he was able to so easily short-circuit her brain that way.

Did it matter, though? Couldn't she simply go wherever this led, without the constant overthinking? After all, this was her Brazilian adventure, to be experienced fully, without fear.

"Maybe one of those things best just enjoyed, rather than dissected?" she suggested, and her body flushed from head to toe at his smile, which seemed laden with promise.

"De fato."

After they finished eating, they drove to Ibirapuera Park, and walked the short distance to the entrance. The grounds were a sight to behold, the trails and fountains lit with thousands of lights, which gleamed on the water, casting a dreamy glow over everything. When Francisco took her hand, Krysta moved a little closer to him, so their arms brushed as they walked. His fingers tightened on hers, his thumb caressing the back of her hand, sending tingles firing up from that point of contact.

"I will bring you back here, in the daylight," he said as they wove through the crowds. "It is the most gorgeous place in São Paulo."

"I believe you."

He pointed out the auditorium, which he explained had been designed by Oscar Niemeyer, and chuckled when she said the red marquee made it look as if the building was sticking out its tongue at passersby.

"He is my country's most famous architect, and this is how you categorize his work?"

She shrugged. "I have no eye for design or even

beauty, Francisco, so my opinion means less than nothing, really."

He tugged on her hand, halting her, and his expression made her heart race.

"Perhaps that is another reason why I like being with
you," he said, his thumb stroking the back of her hand
again. "For many years I was seen only as a pretty face,
no one interested in what lay behind it. With you I know,
however my face may be classified and objectified by
others, you don't do that. You see me, the man."

Then, before she could formulate a reply, he turned
and started walking again, leading her on toward an
outdoor pavilion, where a crowd was gathered.

The trio played a type of instrumental music she'd
never heard before, but instinctively liked. It was called
choro, Francisco explained, and was an older musical
form that few performed much anymore. To Krysta,
the guitar sounded as though it were singing, but in a
language she couldn't speak, so she could only hear the
words, not understand them.

It moved her, and she swayed in time to the enticing
beat. When Francisco put his arms around her waist
from behind, and they moved to the music together, the
night took on a sweet, sultry aura.

Krysta let herself go with it, not thinking about it,
just living in the moment, something she never did
enough of.

As the final note played, and he let her go to join in
the applause, there was a sensation of being lesser than
she had been just moments before.

They followed the dispersing crowd along the road.
Ibirapuera closed at midnight, Francisco had said, and
it was getting on to twelve when they came to a metal
bridge spanning part of the lake. They climbed to the

top, and then paused on the landing to lean on the railing and look down into the water. As though the crowd was suddenly in cahoots with fate, the people who'd been there before them climbed down, and no one came to take their places.

It was as though they were suddenly the only ones in the park, and it was there just for them.

In the distance the lights of São Paulo gleamed, adding to the ambience. His arm went around her shoulders, pulled her close to his side, and she couldn't stop the little sigh of contentment that broke from between her lips.

She sensed him looking at her profile, and turned to speak, but the words died unspoken in her throat. The gleam in his eyes, that softening of his lips, sent her pulse skyrocketing.

Contentment fled, heat firing out from her core to swirl and whip through her body. Need flooded her as she stared at his mouth, so gorgeous in the low light. Stark shadows cast on his face would have made him look ferocious if it weren't for his eyes, the desirous set of his lips.

"This is one of my favorite spots," he said, his voice low and intent. "But tonight its beauty cannot hold my attention. May I kiss you now?"

Krysta didn't reply, simply lifted her face, angled her head and set her lips to his.

What she knew firsthand about kissing could dance on the head of a pin, but there was no fear or trepidation, just need. There was no one she trusted more to guide her, no one she'd ever desired the way she wanted Francisco.

It was a moment frozen in time, that first touch of

his warm, firm lips on hers, and she shivered, the sensation so exquisite as to be almost surreal.

Then a deep, arousal-struck sound growled from his throat, and his arms banded around her waist to pull her in close. When his lips moved on hers, seeking, searching, her mouth instinctively softened, opened to the sweet sweep of his tongue.

For the first time in her life, her brain stopped whirring, thought ceased, and there was just Francisco and her and the glory of their kisses.

A sudden burst of laughter from a group of young people passing by had Francisco lifting his head, and slowly Krysta came back to herself.

Not entirely, though. There was, it seemed, a part of her that wanted to hang on to his neck and drag his lips back to hers, which was an urge contrary to the person she'd thought herself to be. Her cool control had been shattered by his taste and touch, the sensation of his warm, hard body against her.

"We should go, *querida*." His voice sounded rough, his smooth tones seemingly having deserted him. "The park will be closing soon, and we are expected at the hospital in the morning."

She didn't want to leave. If they could stay there, forever, his lips on hers, she thought she could be content.

But common sense won the day, and she let her arms slip from around his neck, wondering when they'd actually made their way there in the first place.

"Of course," she replied, surprised that her voice sounded so normal when her insides felt like melted wax. And it was only when he turned her back the way they'd come that she realized her legs were shaky.

The walk back to the car and drive to her apartment was a quiet one, both of them seemingly lost in their own thoughts. This was new territory for Krysta, and she couldn't help wondering if he'd found their kisses as thrilling as she had. If not, he would be too polite to say, and she wasn't sure if it would be appropriate to ask.

"I enjoyed the night," he said quietly as they stood in her lobby.

"I did, too." How tame that sounded, totally unbefitting the way little shock waves still fired through her system. Should she invite him up? Would he expect kisses to turn into something more? Was she ready to cross the next hurdle, whatever that may be?

Before she could find answers to any of those questions, Francisco pressed the button for the elevator. Then, putting his hands on her shoulders, he smiled gently. "Sleep well," he said before brushing her cheeks, one after the other, with his lips. "I'll see you tomorrow."

Then, as she stepped into the elevator, he left, and the bottom seemed to drop out of her world.

CHAPTER TEN

FRANCISCO BELIEVED IN patience, and in making good, well-considered choices, but on the morning after his dinner with Krysta, he awoke with a nagging sense of opportunity lost.

The taste of her mouth, the sensation of her pressed against his body, still lingered in his senses, and had him craving more, and more. The memory left him moody and frustrated.

Yet, in his heart he knew he needed to go slowly with Krysta Simpson. That, if he were not careful, she could turn out to be the heartache of a lifetime.

He'd also seen the hesitation in her eyes as they stood in the lobby of her apartment building, and felt she was worried about what might happen next. It had made it right to walk away, although no easier.

He knew if he'd stayed, gone to her apartment, he would want to kiss her again, perhaps go even further.

Not make love. He wasn't ready to take that step, might never be ready. Already his emotions were being engaged, his heart wanting to get in on a situation that was completely temporary. There could be no good ending for him if he allowed that to happen.

Krysta was too special, as a friend, as a colleague,

to risk it all on physical satisfaction, no matter how much he wanted it.

He also sensed a deep vulnerability in her, no matter how well masked it was by her outward confidence. Perhaps the confidence stemmed from surety of her competence to do her job, but hadn't truly spilled over into her personal life. That would also explain why she'd immersed herself so fully in her job.

If nothing else, he could introduce her to a different kind of life. One where leisure played as important a role as work.

At the same time, it would allow him to ease out of the rut he'd fallen into as well. She truly had illustrated to him just how insular he'd become. It probably wouldn't have been long before he, like Krysta, had left a full life behind. But unlike her, he had no doubt he'd have turned into a lonely, bitter man, eaten up by regret.

He had her to thank for saving him from such a fate.

As he arrived at the hospital, he was called into surgery, and didn't have a chance to see Krysta, or even check on Senhor Dos Santos. He finished just prior to lunchtime, and made his way to the room their patient had been transferred to.

Enzo Dos Santos was sitting in a chair by the window, his leg elevated, a smile on his face at seeing Francisco.

"How are you feeling, *senhor*?" Francisco asked as he picked up the chart to scan it.

Dos Santos had a computer tablet in his hand, and scrawled with the stylus.

Ready to play football.

Francisco chuckled, and replied, "You may want to wait a couple more days before you get back on the field, sir."

The patient pouted, his eyes twinkling.

Still chuckling, Francisco checked Enzo's leg, and the outer area of the transplant, finding both to be healing well. The chart showed that the surgeon on duty had checked the reconstruction site not long before, and had made meticulous notes at what he found, so Francisco didn't check inside the patient's mouth again.

Enzo scribbled on his tablet, then held it out to Francisco.

Where's my pretty doctor? You're the second man I've had poking at me today. I prefer when she does it.

"I'm sure she'll be along soon to see you," Francisco said, but inside he felt a sinking sensation. It wasn't like Krysta not to check on her patient at least twice a day. In fact, he'd been hoping to run into her here, in Enzo's room, since this was one of the times she usually came by.

Had what happened last night made her stay away?

But that was ridiculous. He didn't see her allowing anything not of the utmost importance to interfere with her work.

After leaving Senhor Dos Santos's room, he found the charge nurse and asked, "Has Dr. Simpson not been in, at all, today?"

"She called earlier for an update on the patient's status, and said she wouldn't be by until later this afternoon."

Thanking her for the information, Francisco made his slow way to the elevator, wondering if he should call her, or not. Then he asked himself a simple question: If they had not kissed the night before, would he hesitate to contact her today because she wasn't in?

The answer to that, of course, was no, so he took out his phone and dialed her number. When it went to voice mail, he left a message, asking if she were going to be at the hospital for their customary lunch date.

Ten minutes later, she called back.

"Sorry I couldn't answer before," she said. "I was on a conference call. There's a problem in New York I have to deal with as quickly as possible. I won't be able to make lunch."

She sounded brisk, a little impatient, and he knew mentally she was still wrestling with whatever was going on, so he said, "I am sorry to hear that. Let me know when you are free, and we will meet then. Perhaps for dinner?"

"Sure," she replied, and then added, "I'm sorry to miss lunch with you. I look forward to it every day."

Before he could answer, there was a chime in the background, and Krysta said, "I have to go. There's a video call coming through."

And she hung up without waiting for him to say anything more.

How silly to feel gratified at her saying the time spent with him was one of the highlights of her day, but it was small consolation when he went to the cafeteria and ate his solitary meal.

Apparently, being with her was taking on a great importance in his life, and he wasn't at all sure what to do about it.

* * *

"And can you at least tell me why the funding was withdrawn?"

Krysta tried to keep her voice level, but it was difficult. She'd gotten very little sleep the night before, reliving Francisco's kisses, wrestling with the emotions and sensations they brought to life inside. The last thing she needed was to wake up to the news her next research project was being canceled.

"I'm not at liberty to say," the hospital administrator replied. "But you know research funds are limited, and sometimes one project leapfrogs in significance over another."

A nice way of saying someone else had commandeered her funding!

"Is there a possibility of sourcing funding elsewhere? As you know, in the past my research has sometimes been subsidized by private sector individuals."

"Well, if you wish to try to find alternate funding, that's your prerogative, although you'll also have to get it passed by the board of directors."

That would set her back months.

By the time she hung up, she was seething with frustration. They knew full well her past research had garnered the hospital both acclaim and financial benefit. Knowing they'd pulled her funding and given it to someone else was infuriating.

But it wasn't the first time something like this had happened. In her earlier days it had occurred with anxiety-inducing regularity. She'd thought she was past that point in her career, but apparently not.

Throwing herself back on the couch, she stared up at the ceiling, trying to decide what to do next. She loved being on rotation at the hospital, diagnosing otolaryngologic diseases and operating whenever something fell within her specialty, but research had always been even more important. It filled her life, keeping her engaged and at the forefront of new technology and methods.

Maybe she should fly back and petition the board in person? It felt as though they were taking advantage of her absence to mess around with the funding. With her contract coming up for renewal, was this someone's way of making her seem unimportant to the hospital? Expendable?

The thought infuriated her, and she'd actually sat up and pulled her computer closer, to look up flights, when she realized she was shaking, and her stomach was rolling. Despite the cool air of the room, a sheen of perspiration covered her face.

That brought her up short, and forced her to take a long, hard look at herself.

She'd made a commitment to Paulista's, to Enzo Dos Santos, and yet she was contemplating jumping on a plane, risking her reputation for reliability, just because her funding fell through? When had she allowed her love of work to become such a driving obsession?

And *why* had she allowed it?

Work was the altar on which she'd sacrificed everything—family, friendships, relationships—and now, looking out the window at the blue Brazilian sky, she felt hollow. Not at the thought of losing the grant, but at what her life, such as it was, had become.

Her work defined her, was the yardstick by which she measured herself. So much so that any disruption in it threw her into a tailspin.

Dr. Hellman had tried to get her to see it, in the weird, roundabout way psychologists had of getting their point across. When she'd expressed guilt at missing her parents' anniversary party, instead of focusing on the guilt, Dr. Hellman had made her explain why she'd missed it. When she'd admitted to not having hobbies, or good friends outside of work, the other woman had asked why. Almost every question regarding her lack of a normal, healthy social and interpersonal life had the same answer.

Work.

Research.

Staying relevant in her field.

Now she considered herself the poster child for dysfunction when it came to life.

Real life.

And she had to ask herself: Was this any way to live?

Even the resolve reached last night, when speaking to Francisco, about doing better by her parents had flown out of her head the moment work entered the picture.

What was the worst that could happen should her project get shelved?

The thought of it made her stomach roil. The physical reaction made her gasp, and blink against the tears suddenly prickling the backs of her eyes.

Her first instinct was to push the thought away as untenable. Then she forced her mind to hold it, sit with it, let it percolate.

As she did, her stomach settled, and calm descended.

What would happen?

She'd have free time, to see her parents, go wherever she wanted, although where that was, she had no idea just yet.

There would be time to do other things, learn something new, not because it was important for work, but just because.

Allow herself to be spontaneous occasionally, rather

than letting her compulsion to plan every little thing order her days.

And all the prep work she'd been doing while in Brazil would no longer be necessary, and she could spend more time with Francisco.

Once more her stomach dipped, but it wasn't just fear causing her reaction this time. There was an element of excitement mixed in, and the memory of being in his arms, his lips on hers, pushed trepidation aside.

Settling back against the couch, she closed her eyes to heighten the recall of those moments.

His muscular body fitted against hers, firm mouth softened and sensual with passion, the satiny sensation of his hair between her fingers. It all rushed back, and a little moan of pleasure whispered from her throat.

It had been delicious. Sublime. And left her with an interminable ache she'd never truly experienced before but recognized for what it was.

Sexual need.

Another facet of life she'd never explored, out of fear, and now wanted to.

The thought of only being in Brazil for a short time shouldn't be an impediment to sleeping with Francisco, if he were willing. In fact, it would be the perfect opportunity. She wasn't interested in a long-term relationship, but she liked him, a lot, and found him more attractive than any man she'd met before. He, no doubt, would be glad to know she wouldn't be around for much longer, and therefore wouldn't be expecting a commitment of any kind.

Would he be willing, though? And how on earth would she find that out?

She wasn't so naive as to think a few kisses in a romantic setting meant he wanted to sleep with her, or that there mightn't be some other reason why he wouldn't want to.

Despite her just-made choice to be more spontaneous, this wasn't something she wanted left to chance. No, there needed to be a plan.

Could she somehow seduce him, like she thought he had been doing when he complimented her last night?

That seemed a nonstarter, since she hadn't the first clue how to go about something like that, and deemed the possible humiliation quotient too high if she got it wrong.

But how else did people signal their sexual interest in someone else? Should she research it, and try to glean more information?

She stopped herself. While she was a champion researcher in the medical field, thinking about hunting for the answers to this conundrum online felt wrong. Forced. Instead, wouldn't it be better to simply be herself, the new self she was discovering, and take it from there?

A glance at her watch told her Francisco would have had lunch already, and be on his rounds. While there was an urge to rush over to the hospital right away, she also had a lecture to give in the morning, and needed to make sure all her notes and slides were in order. One thing that helped her overcome her horrendous stage fright was meticulous planning, so she at least knew she was fully prepared. If she went to check on her patient now, she could spend the rest of the afternoon going over her presentation, one more time.

It would mean not seeing Francisco until dinnertime, but although she'd decided to turn over a new, less-strict leaf, today wasn't the day to wing it.

After all, even if Brazil changed her fundamentally,

she still needed her reputation to keep her job, and that was, in the end, what was most important.

No matter what any other part of her anatomy tried to say!

CHAPTER ELEVEN

THE NEXT DAY seemed to pass at a rate best described as glacial, but she'd surprised herself with her reaction to having to once more speak in front of the crowd of doctors. While, when she awoke in the morning, she'd felt her usual queasiness, by the time she got to the hospital and entered the building, it had started to wane.

Seeing Francisco waiting for her didn't hurt, either.

"Ah, here you are," he said, that tiny smile playing around his lips, making her salivate for another taste of them. "How're you feeling?"

"Good," she replied as they walked together toward the lecture hall, and she sternly admonished herself to keep her mind on business. "How did your operation go last night?"

There had been a horrendous accident in the late afternoon, and the survivors had been brought to Paulista's. Francisco had been in theater when she arrived to check on Enzo, and had texted at five thirty to say he was unfortunately unable to make their dinner date.

She'd been disappointed, but took it in stride. After all, how many times had she been in theater only to find out that what she thought would be a two-hour operation stretched on to five?

"The facial trauma was severe. So much so that she

lost her eye. The orbital structure was shattered, and I spent most of the operation trying to retrieve as many bone splinters as were safely possible."

They got to the door of the waiting area beside the auditorium, and he opened it for her, allowing her to precede him into the room as he continued. "Should she survive, which is still in question, she will need extensive reconstruction, including of the orbital floor. Since her other eye socket is undamaged, it would be a perfect case for your techniques, but unfortunately I doubt she would be able to afford it."

"Well, some of the companies are willing to do some pro bono work, or at a lesser cost, in the hopes of developing a relationship with a new hospital. Let me know, I'll approach the Belgian firm."

They'd discussed the injuries and future prospective operations and, before she'd known it, an assistant came to tell her it was time.

"Before you go," Francisco said quietly as she got up to head for the stage. "Are we still on for tomorrow?"

"Sure," she replied, trying not to let how much she was looking forward to it show.

And from that moment on, it felt as though the day ground almost to a halt. Never before had she been so impatient to finish giving a lecture, and less than completely focused. Getting through it felt sort of like a slog through mud, despite her love of the subject matter.

Then, before she could leave, the director cornered her, and invited her to lunch with him and the head of surgery. It wouldn't be politic to decline, so off they went to a restaurant a few miles from the hospital, and had the longest lunch she could ever remember. Both men were charming and articulate, so it wasn't boring, but she chafed at having to be there, rather than with Francisco.

Figuring it was as good a time as any, she floated the idea of approaching the 3-D printing firm about fabricating orbital floor mesh for the accident victim.

"Is it the same firm that worked on Senhor Dos Santos's case?"

"Yes," she replied to the director. "I've worked with them a number of times, and have found them reliable, cost-efficient and quick. It might suit Paulista's to have them as a contact, in case of need."

The two men exchanged glances, and then the chief of surgery said, "Let us see if the young woman survives, but even if she doesn't, I think it would be advantageous for us if you would put us in contact with the right person there. The director and I have been discussing the possibility of developing a program using the techniques and information you're imparting. It is just talk, so far, but if we decide to approach the board, it would be good to have additional information to give them."

She felt a little thrill of achievement. If they were talking about offering 3-D mapping and a more extensive virtual-surgery plan, her visit was already a success.

Getting back to the hospital, she went to check on Enzo Dos Santos, and found him not only in good spirits but also healing nicely. Once more, Roque Cardoza was keeping him company, since Lizbet Dos Santos had gone home for a couple of hours. With Enzo's permission, she did her checks with Roque in the room, and thought, perhaps, her patient wanted a second opinion on how things were going. Luckily, she didn't think there was anything the other doctor could find fault with. Things were going exceedingly well.

"I won't be by to see you tomorrow, Senhor Dos Santos." Then she had to chuckle when he held up the tablet and he'd written *Enzo* in big bold letters. It had been an ongoing battle since the first day they'd met, but maybe it was time to let him win.

"Very well, Enzo. I'll see you in two days."

He scribbled for a moment, then she read it.

Going on a date?

She wrinkled her nose at him, but at the same time a wave of heat washed through her, and it took everything in her to keep her face neutral and her tone unchanged as she replied, "Going to see some more of your beautiful country. A place that shares your name—Santos."

His eyes lit up, and he nodded, then wrote.

Beautiful beaches and gardens. Coffee museum.

Krysta chuckled. "I'll make sure to visit that museum. I'm a huge fan of coffee."

"If you have the time, and the inclination, there is also a lovely orchid garden there, too," Roque added. "And although the water may be too cool for swimming, if you surf you can rent a wet suit and board on the beach, close to São Vincente."

"I swim in the lakes up north, so I might risk the ocean," she said, without telling him the thought of trying to surf made her anxiety rise. Doubtful her athletic prowess would be sufficient for that!

There was no sign of Francisco, but a message came up on her phone, telling her he was going into theater again. The fates weren't being kind to them, but Krysta thought it was just as well. She still hadn't come to any kind of conclusion about what she wanted to do when it came to Francisco.

That evening, after taking a swim in the pool, which, for a change, did nothing to ease her stress levels, she impulsively picked up her phone and called her mother.

"Hello, darling," her mother said, answering after one ring. "Is everything all right?"

"Does something have to be wrong for me to check up on my parents?" she said, trying to sound amused, but in truth riding out a little wave of guilt. Her calls were few and far between, with little silences her mother always filled with chitchat, which always made Krysta feel worse.

"Of course not. How are you? How are you enjoying Brazil?"

"I'm great. Brazil is amazing. I think you and Daddy would love it."

"I've always wanted to go." Then her mother chuckled. "But getting your father to commit to a plane ride longer than it takes to get to Saint Eustace? Not an easy task!"

Krysta laughed with her. Her father's dislike of planes was a source of constant amusement to the rest of the family. A few times, while abroad working, Krysta had suggested her parents join her for a week, but it never happened, because her father always found an excuse as to why he couldn't go.

Now that she thought about it, maybe she'd inherited more from her father than her ears and the shape of her lower face.

"Well, if you were on Saint Eustace, it wouldn't be as long a trip. It's something to think about." How much smoother this conversation seemed, as if once Krysta allowed herself to relax into the give-and-take, it all became ridiculously easy.

There was a little silence, and then her mother said, "If you were going to stay there in Brazil, we'd definitely make the trip, but otherwise I doubt it will ever happen. Your father is just too set in his ways. I mean, he keeps bawling about wanting to move back to Saint Eustace, but if I try to talk to him about making actual plans? He's suddenly too busy to think about it."

Oh, she'd definitely inherited some of her father's fear-induced deflection and avoidance!

Then her mother's words struck straight through her heart.

"Is…is that really why you've never moved back?"

"Of course," her mother said in her serene way. "Once you were old enough and we were convinced you could manage on your own, there was no excuse, other than your father." She laughed. "He's such a fuddy-duddy. But one day I'll pin him down and get him moving."

Krysta laughed with her, but there was a manic edge to her amusement, and relief made her light-headed.

It wasn't her fault that they hadn't gone back. She wasn't to blame. It was just her head, and maybe her ego, messing with her judgment.

Which other long-held beliefs was she holding on to that were, in fact, false?

Something more to think about.

And that night, when she finally fell asleep, it was to dream once more of that never-ending pool. But this time there was a current pulling her inexorably on, and a muted, distant roar that made her wonder if there were a waterfall at the end.

* * *

Francisco dragged himself out of the hospital after midnight, and drove home almost on autopilot. The last two days had been almost as bad as some he remembered from his years of residency, and at times the only thing keeping him going was the knowledge of the approaching day off.

And the time he'd get to spend with Krysta.

Yet he still hadn't been able to decide how to proceed with their relationship. There were too many variables to make it an easy choice.

As work colleagues, it could be deleterious to one or the other of them, or both, if they got intimately involved and then it fell apart badly. He'd learned that lesson a long time ago. When he'd started dating, he'd chosen young women in the fashion industry—models, makeup artists, stylists—because those were the people he was constantly around. But on more than one occasion, with both casual and serious relationships, the ending had caused untold misery on jobs.

He'd wised up, and stopped doing it, hating the drama and the feeling of being judged a bad person because others said he was. Stupidly, he'd not stuck to his decision, and gotten involved with Mari, which had led to the ultimate in betrayal and character assassination.

He knew he was constantly under scrutiny at Paulista's, and didn't want anything to jeopardize the life he was building in São Paulo. There was often the feeling that there were some, like Delgado, who would be ecstatic to be given an excuse to get rid of him. It didn't matter the other man wasn't his direct supervisor. He and his family still had enough clout at the hospital to force the board to let him go.

Then there was the fact he wasn't into casual sex

anymore, but on the other hand, neither was he looking for a serious relationship, having been so badly hurt before and being unwilling to risk it all again. It was a dichotomy that had kept him single and uninvolved, and sexually starved, far longer than perhaps was healthy.

When he was young, and ran with a wild crowd, he thought nothing of sharing a night, or day, with a woman, and then moving on. There had been a couple more involved affairs, but only until he'd met Mari. He'd been crazy for her from the first moment they met, not realizing sexual attraction and insane emotional highs and lows didn't necessarily signify love.

After their breakup he'd become leery of entanglements, preferring to concentrate on his career, rather than open himself up to additional hurt. The women who'd expressed interest in dating him seemed more enamored with the thought of dating "Cisco" the ex-model than Francisco the man. None of that held any kind of appeal. Truly, no one had attracted him enough to make him change his solitary ways, until Krysta came along to make him wonder what, exactly, he wanted.

He had no answers, only knew he enjoyed spending time with her, and wanted to kiss her again, as the memory of those moments on the bridge replayed on a loop over and over in his brain.

Soft lips and body pressed to his. The sensation of sinking into their kisses, going down and down, until he drowned in her little sighs and sounds of pleasure. He hadn't wanted to stop. Indeed, he'd wanted more than was possible or feasible or even legal in such a public place. She'd aroused him almost beyond bearing, so that he had, for an instant, felt once more a callow youth, straining with desire, hungering for the fulfillment of sexual release.

Letting her go had been a task almost too difficult to achieve, leaving her in the lobby of the apartment building an exercise in willpower he still wasn't sure how he managed.

And tomorrow they would spend the entire day together, and he knew, without a doubt, he would be tempted to kiss her again.

He *would* kiss her again.

Which led him right back to the question of how far their relationship could go, should go.

It was a question that circled in his head until the moment his head hit the pillow, and exhaustion claimed him.

CHAPTER TWELVE

KRYSTA WAS UP and ready long before the agreed-on nine o'clock start of their day out, but at a quarter to, Francisco texted to say he was running a little late, but would be there in thirty minutes. It gave Krysta far too much time to stress over her appearance some more.

When she'd gone to the mall the day of their trip to Ibirapuera, she'd also bought a few more things, assisted, of course, by the salesladies. One of them was a new bathing suit, which was very different from her usual choice of traditional, all-encompassing, one-piece designs made to conceal rather than enhance her body.

They'd called it a trikini and, at first, she'd refused to even consider trying it on. Everything about it, from the brightly colored pattern to the cutouts on either side of the torso, had screamed "no." But the two ladies wouldn't stop until she agreed to at least put it on. If, when wearing it, she truly hated it, they would find her something else.

She didn't hate it, and had stared at her reflection for the longest time, wondering if it were really her staring back. The shape had emphasized her breasts in a way that should have made her uncomfortable, but instead merely reminded her she was a woman. The curved cutouts made her waist seem even more slender, and then made her hips flare.

Buying it, and the three sundresses the women swore were made just for her, had seemed a no-brainer at the time. Now, however, she was wondering if she were really ready to step out of her shapeless fashion box in this way. The sundress was fine, even if it did seem to cling to every curve when she moved, but the swimsuit she had on underneath filled her with disquiet.

Even reminding herself she was going with Francisco, a man she trusted explicitly, didn't help, and if he hadn't arrived a little earlier than he had said he would, she would have talked herself into running back and changing into her old stretched-out and unattractive one-piece.

Then he was there, smiling at her as the elevator opened on the ground floor, and her consternation fled.

It was the first time she'd seen him so casually dressed, in board shorts and a tight-fitting T-shirt that left nothing to the imagination. He was gorgeous, and she tried not to melt away to nothing just looking at him.

"Querida," he said, holding her shoulders and bending to kiss first one cheek and then the next. "I am sorry I am late. I overslept, which is not like me."

"Well, that's what happens when your operating schedule explodes the way yours has over the last few days," she replied, glad he'd kept his greeting so casual. Mentally berating herself for wanting to have grabbed him and given him a far more thorough set of kisses. "You must be exhausted. Do you really want to drive so far on your day off?"

"Hush," was his reply as they walked toward his car. "It is only a little more than an hour, and I want to show it to you. It will be far more relaxing than staying here."

Probably because he knew the chances of seeing any-one they knew while at Santos was remote. She didn't know whether to be annoyed or grateful he was being so careful about keeping their growing relationship pri-vate, although she couldn't help wondering why he did.

But she put the question aside, and they set out, Fran-cisco handling the traffic with casual ease, until they had left the city behind. With it being a weekday, he ex-plained, the traffic wouldn't be as bad as on the week-end.

"I thought we would take the older road, Rodovia Anchieta, on our way there, and the newer Rodovia dos Imigrantes on the way back. To me, Anchieta is more picturesque."

He went on to explain that the newer road was built to ease the congestion between São Paulo and the coast, since the traffic comprised both the movement of cargo and pleasure seekers. When the congestion was excep-tionally heavy, the two highways would become uni-directional, with all vehicles going in one direction routed along one, and vehicles going the other way using the other.

A truck, going in the opposite direction, whizzed by at what Krysta thought an unsafe speed, making her gasp. Francisco's lips twitched in one of his little smiles, and he said, "I'm afraid you will have to trust me today. Sometimes the traffic can be a little fright-ening, but I am used to it."

"It's okay," she said. "In this I trust you."

That earned her a flicked sideways glance, but he didn't comment further.

The scenery fascinated her. Sometimes it was as though they were on an American highway, with care-fully manicured grass on the wide verges; at others, the jungle seemed to press in on either side. Then there were the mountain cuts, which had her craning her head to see up along the slopes, where tenacious trees loomed above them. If occasionally she found herself wondering at the engineering it took to have built the road in the first place, she quieted the analytical part of her mind, and just enjoyed the scenery instead.

Arriving in Santos, Krysta was surprised to find herself in a place that reminded her of the fancier part of the Fort Lauderdale beachfront. When she said as much, Francisco nodded.

"It is a very popular resort for tourists and Paulista's as well," he said. "On the weekend, it's a bit of a madhouse, especially when there are cruise ships in port."

She could see why people flocked to the town. When she saw the beach, bordered where they were by a strip of garden, it looked amazing, with clear, light blue water and one of the widest expanses of sand she'd ever seen.

"We will go to the beach when it gets a little warmer," he said. "There are many places to see and explore here. I thought we'd start in the town and work our way down to the water later."

"Sure," she said as he parked and turned off the ignition. "Enzo said there was a coffee museum," she added hopefully.

Francisco chuckled. "Do you really want to visit the museum, or are you craving some coffee?"

"Both," she replied, making him chuckle again.

"Then both is what you shall get."

They stopped at a café, and had coffee and a pastry, and then continued on to the Museu do Café. As they approached, even Krysta had to be impressed with the remarkable building.

"Once this was the coffee-exchange building, and

they built it to illustrate the importance of the crop. Would you like to take a guided tour, or just wander around?"

She opted to wander around, looking at the displays, recognizing the majesty of the building, with its intricate marble floors, stained-glass panel in the ceiling, and general opulence.

They ended up in the coffee shop, where Krysta sampled some of the different blends available, and had another cup.

"You will not sleep for days, at this rate," Francisco teased, but he had one as well.

They visited the orchid gardens, which had a small zoo attached. The flowers and birds were beautiful, and she enjoyed watching the animals, too. The elevated walk through a tropical jungle got their appetites going, and after they finished nosing around, looking at the statues and arguing over which of the animals were cuter, they decided to go to lunch.

They found a restaurant with an outdoor seating area, and Francisco got her settled, then excused himself to go to the restroom. Krysta turned her face up to the sun, and realized she couldn't tell when last she'd been more relaxed. And happy. There was something about Francisco's company that allowed her habitual tension to dissipate. Most of the time she wasn't even aware she was stressed, muscles knotted, mind racing. It was only in the absence of those things she could appreciate how bad they usually were.

Lunch was a leisurely affair. The food was delicious, and she even had dessert because, as she told him, who could resist more coffee, this time in the form of ice cream?

"Do not call me at two in the morning when you are

still wide awake," was his stern admonishment, but the twinkle in his eyes belied his words.

Then they got in the car and drove toward São Vincente, where he took her to see the sculpture by Tomie Ohtake, commemorating the arrival of Japanese immigrants to Brazil. She thought it looked a bit like a dragon, but then became fascinated when a gust of wind made the statue produce a low, whistling sound.

"It makes different sounds, depending on the speed and direction of the wind," Francisco explained, making Krysta wish there was more of a breeze, so she could hear more of the tones.

They left the rocky shoreline where the statue was, and drove back to Santos, as Francisco insisted the beach was better there. There were few people on the sand, probably since the wind had picked up a little, but that didn't deter them. Francisco led her down through the gardens to the shore. Taking off her sandals, she sank her toes into the warm, soft grains, and sighed.

"Oh, I've missed the beach. I never realize how much until I get back to one," she said. "When I go to Saint Eustace, I practically live by the water the entire time."

"Do you miss it, the island?"

She thought about that for a moment as they walked toward the frothing waves, the sound of their ebb and flow like a lullaby to her.

"I didn't grow up there, so I don't have the deep connection my father has to it, but yes, I do. There is a part of me intrinsically linked to it." She hesitated, wondering if she should share something so deeply personal with him. Then decided she would. There was something about Francisco that called her to share confidences with him she wouldn't with anyone else. "There are times when I almost feel it calling to me, like a whisper on the wind, and I long for it so badly it's like an ache around my heart."

"We have a name for that feeling of homesickness, or longing. *Saudades.* I feel like that about Brazil whenever I am away from her for any length of time. Do you go back when that happens?"

Guilt tried to push its way to the forefront, but she wouldn't let it. The woman who ignored that kind of calling was slowly dying, leaving a new person to rise from the ashes. But she would always be honest about her past, too.

"Rarely," she replied. "I went more often when I was young, and before my grandparents died, but as I got older, the time between visits grew longer and longer. I'm going to change that, though. It's a part of my life I shouldn't neglect any longer."

"That is good," he said. "You need to feed your soul, as well as body and mind. I'd forgotten that up until recently but, like you, I plan to do better."

Curious, she asked, "Was there nowhere else, in all the places you've traveled, that called to you?"

"Strangely enough, only Paris. I know there are many people who are not fond of it, but I loved it, very much. Perhaps because the French know how to balance those things that are important in life."

They had reached the water, and Krysta waded in up to her ankles, holding up the end of her dress. It was chilly, but nowhere as bad as the lakes she was used to back home.

"Surely, you don't plan to swim in there?" Francisco said, staying back from the waterline, amusement echoing in his voice. "It can't be more than twenty-two degrees."

Even though she was completely familiar with the

Celsius system, she decided to tease him. Giving him a saucy look over her shoulder, she said, "Twenty-two? If it were that cold, it would be frozen. I'd say it's about seventy or so."

"You Americans and your Fahrenheit," he teased in return. "But however you want to express it, that water is cold."

"Not cold," she rebutted, reaching for the zipper at the side of her dress. "Here, hold my dress while I take a dip."

The flare of awareness in his eyes almost caused her fingers to fumble, almost made her change her mind and retreat to her old bastion of fear. But even more overwhelming was her need for him to see the new her, which, mostly because of him, was emerging.

So, before he could reply, she pulled the garment off over her head and then tossed it to him, the gesture far more symbolic than he could ever imagine.

He caught it, but as if by sheer instinct alone, for his gaze was fixed on her, and she saw his eyes slowly skim down her body, and then back up. When their eyes met, there was no mistaking the desire flaring in his, and her body responded, as if touched by a jolt of electricity.

For an instant, neither moved, caught and held in place by the knowledge of deep want, of arousal unleashed.

Then Francisco stepped forward, as though to walk into the sea to her, and the motion broke her free. Turning, she took a couple running steps into deeper water, then executed a shallow dive beneath an incoming wave.

The chill of the water did nothing to alleviate the heat sizzling through her blood. How could he do that to her with just one look? Swimming out a little ways, only the horizon ahead brought her dream back to mind, and she paused to float in the water, turning her face up into the sun in an attempt to quell her disquiet.

What was she going to do with these feelings?

Instead of giving her any insight, the ocean replied by sending a wave crashing over her head.

Treading water, she wiped her face, and started back to shore. Although she wouldn't admit it to Francisco, it really was too chilly for a prolonged swim.

Thankfully, he had brought a towel with him from the car for them to sit on, because the breeze, which had seemed merely cooling before, now nipped at her skin, raising goose bumps.

But he was there, waiting to enfold her in the soft terry, rubbing at her arms and back.

"You must be freezing," he said, deep concern in his voice. "Come up to the boardwalk and have a hot drink to warm you up."

"Coffee?" she asked, infusing as much hope into the words as she could through her chattering teeth.

That made him chuckle, even as he was leading her back along the sand, his arm around her shoulders.

After he had her ensconced at a table at an open-air restaurant with a lovely view of the ocean and heard she had a change of clothing in her bag, Francisco went back to the car to retrieve it. When he returned with not only her bag but also a dry towel, she thanked him, and went to the ladies' room. Luckily, because it was a seaside restaurant, there was a tiny shower stall, and she rinsed off the salt water before changing.

Coming back, she paused just outside the door to watch Francisco, who was unaware of her presence.

He was looking off into the distance, the set of his lips and angle of his head speaking of thoughts perhaps not entirely happy. His pensive expression tugged at her, made her wonder what he was thinking to look that way.

Then he turned his head toward the door and saw her, and the smile lighting his face made her knees tremble.

CHAPTER THIRTEEN

AS HE WATCHED Krysta walk toward him, Francisco tried to push the thoughts nagging at him from his mind, but wasn't completely successful.

He'd had to acknowledge to himself, as he watched her run into the ocean, the intensity of desire she aroused in him, and it was a little frightening. When she'd pulled off her dress, revealing her body clad only in that trikini, it was as though he was a troll turned to stone by the sun. He'd been unable to move, to breathe, and then, like a tsunami, need swamped him, almost bringing him to his knees.

Instantly hard, desperate want shutting his brain down, he was about to go after her, take her in his arms—take her, there in the water—when she turned away, breaking the spell.

Thank goodness she had. He had been about to make a spectacle of himself, and that feeling of being on the verge of losing control, completely, didn't sit well with him.

He'd tried that in the past, and it had been the worst experience of his life.

"That's better," she said, sliding into her seat and putting her beach bag down on the adjacent chair. "The water wasn't too bad, but once I got out and the wind got me…"

She shivered.

"Are you warm enough now?" he asked, scanning inside the busy restaurant to see if there was any space. "We could go inside."

"No, this is perfect," she said. "Or it will be, when they bring my cappuccino."

As though on cue, the waiter appeared with their drinks, and she put both hands around the cup, as though for warmth, before lifting it to her lips. Her little sound of appreciation made him, once more, have sexual thoughts, and she looked up and caught him staring.

"What?" she asked, but he could see how her cheeks darkened, and knew there was no need to reply.

As if in an attempt to dissipate the thick, sensual aura between them, she said, "How is your car crash victim doing? Did she survive?"

He didn't want to speak of work, but simply answered, "She is still in ICU, but the neurologist thinks there is hope she will make an almost complete recovery."

"I spoke to the director and chief of surgery about her, and they seemed willing to let me speak to the Belgians about supplying the orbital floor mesh. I'll follow up on it tomorrow."

"And I will apprise you of her condition, and when I think she will be strong enough for the reconstructive surgery."

Silence fell between them again, and it was the first time since they'd met that it was fraught, uncomfortable. She was looking down into her cappuccino as though the answers to all the mysteries of the world lay within it, but she was also worrying the corner of her lip with her teeth.

Francisco couldn't help thinking of how she'd said she had confidence in his driving, with the intimation that there were other areas where she might not be so willing to trust. There was so much he wanted to know about her, but wondered if she would answer his questions. One, in particular, he'd been mulling on since the night they'd gone to Ibirapuera, and felt compelled to ask. In the answer might lie another piece to the puzzle she presented.

"Krysta, may I ask you a very personal question?"

Her lashes lifted, and he was caught in the shadows of her gaze. The whimsical thought came to him that perhaps it was there, in her deep brown eyes, rather than the coffee cup, that the answers truly lay.

"Sure," she said. "I don't mind."

"Why is it, day to day, that you hide your body the way you do?" The shutters came down over her gaze, and the look of mild curiosity she'd worn melted away, leaving her expressionless.

Now there was the sensation of being on unsteady ground, but there was no way to turn back. So, he plowed ahead instead, wondering if everything would give out beneath his feet.

"You have said you're not interested in fashion, and I see nothing wrong with that. It is not something that is important to everyone. But even those who don't care about latest fashions usually try to at least buy clothing that fits. You seem to go out of your way to buy everything too big and, in my experience, that means there is a reason."

"In your experience?" she said, her voice cool and

level, and just a touch sarcastic. "I wasn't aware you were a trained psychologist, too. Or are you a psychiatrist?"

He didn't take offense. "Neither, of course, but I used to work in the fashion business, and it is littered with enough neurosis and dysfunction to swamp the entire world. I know the signs."

Looking away, her shoulders stiff and high, she gave him her profile, as though ignoring his words. Her lips were tight, thinned by the pain he now knew she had squashed deep down inside.

Then she looked back at him, and he saw it all there in her gaze—an agony of spirit she probably rarely unleashed or examined.

"When I started college, my body was already quite mature, to the point where my mother used to joke that it was as if it was trying to keep up with the development of my mind. I never gave much thought to it. After all, at fourteen all I was interested in was my studies, nothing else, really."

She paused, looked down into her cup. Her long, nimble fingers moved over the porcelain, as though unable to remain still. Perhaps seeking purchase in a slippery, sliding world.

"I was still a normal teenager, though. I wore what everyone else wore. Tight jeans and tank tops. Short shorts or miniskirts when it was hot. I never gave my clothes more than a passing thought, although I didn't mind shopping with my mom and getting new stuff. And then, one night, when I was leaving the library, I was attacked. A man came out of the shadows, put his arm around my neck and tried to choke me, while dragging me toward some bushes."

Francisco froze, the ice flowing out from his gut inundating his entire being. And then it melted under the hellfire of fury. Keeping a neutral expression was the hardest thing he'd done in a long time. He wanted to rage, to demand to know what had happened, but reined all emotion in, to be what she needed.

Someone to listen.

Lifting her cup, she took a swallow, but now Francisco could see her hands were trembling.

Then, with a sharp clack, she set the cup down, straightened her back and lifted her chin to look right into his eyes. Now the fear was gone, replaced by something stronger, more resilient.

"I was lucky. My father was waiting to drive me home, and heard me scream. He'd also made sure to teach me some basic self-defense, so when I was grabbed from behind, I went limp, became dead weight, rather than starting to struggle. The attacker wasn't expecting that, and partially lost his grip. I got him right in the face with my bag, and then Daddy was there, and my assailant took off running."

A little smile tried to form, but died before it fully flowered.

"Daddy chased him, took him down and punched him hard enough to break his jaw. I was bruised, but alive, and I hadn't been raped, so I was very, very lucky. But I couldn't stop it from changing how I viewed my body. I didn't trust it not to get me into trouble, I guess, and started to hide it with baggy, ugly clothes. And even when I was old enough to know better, it had become a habit."

"I am sorry," he said, his voice a rasping mess because his throat was tight with anger and pain. "Sorry that you had to go through that, and sorry to have brought it all back. I should never have pried."

But she shook her head, and now a smile was not only achieved, but also reached her eyes.

"It actually felt good to talk about it, to air it out again and release it. He pled guilty, so thankfully there was no trial, but my parents didn't want to talk about it, and I had no one to confide in, so it festered. Coming to terms with it took a long time, but letting go of the effects has taken even longer."

Her smile widened, and Francisco's heart clenched at the beauty. It was a benediction, a bright, proud flame to chase the darkness of horror away.

"Here in Brazil, I've found parts of myself I didn't even think were missing," she said. "And I believe I have you to thank for that. So, thank you."

"No," he croaked, still unable to get his voice to come back to normal. "Thank you for sharing yourself with me. It is more than I deserve."

She shook her head, but said nothing more, and lightened the mood by asking what she should wear to his birthday party. Yet, even that innocuous question was laden with meaning for him, and he felt overfilled with emotion, proud of her bravery, touched by her confidence in him and moved by how desperately he wished he could have known her then, and kept her safe.

Daylight was waning as they made their way, hand in hand, to the car for the drive back to São Paulo. They'd fallen back into their easy ways, chatting and laughing, Krysta teasing him about his unwillingness to go swimming with her, Francisco snorting with disgust.

"I prefer my water warm, thank you very much."

"So, I suppose if, as Roque Cardoza suggested, I wanted to go surfing, you wouldn't be willing to teach me?"

"Not today," he stoutly averred. "Not even in a wet suit would I brave that water."

She just laughed, and called him a coward, and he readily agreed with her assessment, which spoiled some of her fun but didn't stop her needling.

By the time they were back in the city, it was dark, and he pulled into a well-known casual dining restaurant so they could have dinner.

"Ooh," she said, sending him a teasing glance. "More coffee."

"Are you sure you're not Brazilian? Your obsession with coffee rivals that of any of my countrymen."

After eating, he drove her home, and walked her in, as always. The lobby was empty, and as he reached out to push the button for the elevator, Krysta put her hand on his arm, stopping him.

"It's my turn to ask a question," she said, and something in her gaze caused his very soul to still. "Something very personal. More like a favor."

He tried to relax, to speak, but could only nod, and hold his breath, although why he did so wasn't clear to him.

"Would you take my virginity?"

Krysta saw a flash of desire in Francisco's eyes so intense she shivered, but then it was gone, and his habitual mask fell into place, leaving his expression carefully blank.

For her part, she felt no trepidation. He was the one man she'd ever met who she both trusted and wanted. The worst that could happen is he declined, and they continued on the way they were.

Or not.

It mattered greatly to her, but she was used to making decisions and sticking to them, and sometime during the day she'd realized she couldn't bear the desire without knowing whether or not it would be fulfilled. If he said no, then she'd at least have an answer, and could figure out how else to manage the changes she was going through.

He was still just looking at her, the arm beneath her hand tightening to rock hardness.

"Fale comigo," she said to him as he once had said to her, and she saw him swallow.

"You would ask me this, here? In the lobby?" His voice was as hard as his arm, but it wasn't frightening. In fact, it gave her another *zing* of awareness, edged her arousal a little higher. "Tell me, in one sentence, that you want me but are still a virgin?"

"Is that a bad thing?" she asked, not allowing her voice to display anything but mild curiosity, and a touch of amusement, even though, inside, her stomach twisted and her heartbeat was a ragged, unsteady thing.

"Meu Deus. Is this a joke to you? For it isn't to me. I cannot discuss this here with you now."

Releasing his arm, she reached back and pressed the button for the elevator, and then stepped in when the doors opened immediately.

Placing her hand to stop them from closing, she said, "We could discuss it upstairs, if you prefer more privacy."

He covered her hand with his. "You make me *louco.* I should walk away, but I do not want to."

"Then don't," she said, her insides melting in the way they so often did when she was around him.

"If I come upstairs, it will not be to take your virginity, but I cannot promise I will behave the perfect gentleman, either. Choose carefully, *amor*, before you tell me to stay, or go."

Should she be having second thoughts at his fierce

pronouncement? If so, she'd missed some vital piece of information, because it did nothing but make her want him more.

She wrapped her fingers around his wrist, and gave it a tug. It wasn't enough to budge a man as strong as Francisco, but apparently all the impetus he needed to step into the car.

They didn't touch as the doors slid closed and she pressed the button for her floor, but their gazes locked, and the air in the elevator grew thick with anticipation.

Still silent, he stood back to let her pass when they got to her floor, and the doors opened once more. The ride had been only seconds long, but to Krysta it seemed to have taken forever. Beneath her skin her entire being vibrated with want. She still remembered how he'd felt in her arms, that hard, delicious body against her softer, more yielding one, and craved that again.

When she'd unlocked the door and stepped a few paces inside, she turned to watch him follow. He prowled in slowly, his gait reminding her of her initial reaction on meeting him, when she'd likened him to a wolf.

And when he circled her, making her have to turn to watch him, his gaze never straying from her face, the effect was heightened to a thrilling degree.

"You are still a virgin?"

He fired the question like a shot at her, and she started, her heart rate kicking up another notch.

"Yes."

"How? Why?"

At any other time, she would have laughed at the thought of explaining the "how," but nothing about this was amusing. Arousing, frustrating and a little frightening, yes. But not amusing.

"Lack of interest, would be the first guess. Not finding anyone I wanted, the way I want you, would be the second."

His eyes darkened, and his prowling, stalking revolution around her stopped.

"Fear? Because of what happened when you were young?"

She'd always been honest with him. No need to stop now.

"Yes."

"Are you afraid now?"

"A little, because this is all new to me. But somehow I trust you not to hurt me."

The fierce expression faded, and he scrubbed a hand over his face. When it fell away, she saw a man conflicted—need and worry at war with each other.

"Eu te quero," he said.

I want you.

Then he continued, "But you must realize, sex changes everything. I am afraid that if we make love, nothing will be the same, and perhaps not for the better."

She lifted her chin, and said, "I'm willing to take that chance. Are you? And if you're not, I think you should leave now, before I come over there and climb all over you."

CHAPTER FOURTEEN

Now SHE HELD her breath, waiting for his decision. When he finally moved, she thought it was to leave, and her heart stopped for an instant, but he only went as far as the door, locking it. Then he turned, and now her heart raced again.

"I know I should leave," he said, his voice so low it was just above a whisper. "And yet, the thought of not holding you again, not kissing you, never being able to know what it is like when we are intimately together, is untenable."

Once more he stalked her, closing in slowly, and her legs trembled from seeing the heat in his eyes. Then she was in his arms, and her brain stuttered and shut down as their lips met.

He kissed her with muted ferocity, and she returned it in kind. She'd spent too many nights longing for this moment, dreaming of it, and she couldn't get enough. The remembered taste of him fired into her blood, more potent than any liquor, and when he exhaled, she took the air into her body, held it for a moment.

His lips left hers to slide along her jaw, and then up to her ear.

"Amor. Eu te quero," he whispered. "I want to touch you, feel your skin on mine. I crave it, like water, or air."

"Yes," she gasped. "I want that, too. So very much."

Yet, he took his time, guiding her to the couch and pulling her onto his lap to kiss her some more. It was the sweetest of agonies as his hands skimmed her back and belly, the lower swells of her breasts through her clothes. Impatient, she tugged at his T-shirt, and he leaned forward to help her get it off.

The sensation of his flesh under her fingertips, the muscles rippling beneath, was fascinating and oh so arousing. Touching him became her focus, and he let her explore his torso and arms to her heart's content.

But when she circled his nipples, watching them contract to tiny peaks, he growled her name and pulled her hands away.

"Hey, I was enjoying that," she groused.

"I'll show you why I stopped you," came his rough reply.

He unzipped her dress, and she shivered as his fingers brushed her flesh. When he pushed the straps down, the garment fell to her waist, leaving her upper body clad only in her strapless bra, which he didn't hesitate to unclasp with a quick flick of his fingers.

Then his hands were on her, fingers drifting over her skin, raising trails of flames wherever they touched. She arched, wanting more, desire whipped to a wildfire in her body, immolating her from the inside out.

Just like she had, he circled her nipples, and she trembled, lost in the glorious torture. Then his lips closed over one, and she jerked, grabbing the back of his head to hang on, afraid she'd pass out, it felt so good.

He rolled her off his lap, lying her down on her back on the sofa, leaning over her to lick and suck from her throat to her belly. Krysta twisted beneath him, shocked at her body's response, the immensity of her need. Sud-

denly frightened, she pushed at his head, and he sat up.
Whatever he saw on her face had him pulling her up
into his arms.

"Shh…" he whispered, holding her, stroking her hair.
"I forgot I need to be gentle, to take my time. Do you
want me to stop?"

"No. I don't know." The breath was sawing in and
out of her lungs, making it difficult to speak. "I'm overwhelmed right now, but I don't really want to stop. I
don't know what I want."

"Krysta, have you ever had an orgasm?"

She snorted. "Are you asking if I masturbate? The
answer is no. I told you, I locked everything to do with
sex away, and refused to give it a thought."

He was silent for a moment, then he asked, "Will
you let me give you one? I think, perhaps, that's what
your body wants right now."

"Okay." She said it into his throat, suddenly shy, although she knew how ridiculous that was. After all,
wasn't she the one who initiated this?

"Tell me to stop if you want to," he said, and then
eased her back onto his lap. She leaned on his chest,
her face tucked into the space between his shoulder
and neck.

He didn't take off her dress, just slowly slid his hand
up under the skirt, caressing her calves, then her knees,
and thighs, moving up to the apex of her legs. It relaxed
and aroused her, all at the same time.

How was that even possible?

Her legs fell open of their own accord, giving him
access, and she found herself tilting her hips, longing
for the touch that would take her over the edge.

When his finger slid under her panties and between

her folds, gently exploring, she had to remind herself to breathe.

"Easy, *amor*," he whispered. "Let me take care of you."

His finger circled, awakening nerve endings, sending another wave of shudders through her body. Then the circle tightened, found its mark, and she stiffened, shaking and mewling and wanting to beg for culmination.

"There," she cried, her thighs tightening on his arm.

"Yes," he crooned. "Let it happen, *amor*. Come for me."

Somehow the words made it perfect, took her from frustration and need and threw her, body and soul, into swirling, beautiful, orgasmic satisfaction.

"Better?" he asked when she finally calmed.

"Yes," she said, feeling wonderfully lethargic. "But can we do that again?"

He chuckled, but it was strained, and she could feel the hardness of his erection beneath her bottom.

"Francisco?"

"Hmm?"

"If you won't make love to me tonight, maybe we should stop. I don't want to cause you more discomfort."

"Ah, *amor*, even if we stopped now, I would be hard for you all night. You are like fire in my blood."

She lifted her head to look at him, and immediately she felt another surge of desire chase away her lethargy. There was something about his heavy-lidded eyes and softened mouth that did things to her insides.

Krysta tried to move, but Francisco held her in place with his arm.

"Where are you going?"

"Nowhere," she said. "I just wanted to change position." When he let her up, she slid off his lap to shimmy

out of her dress. Feeling bold, she pulled off her panties, too, and stepped out of them. His face tightened,
and her nipples beaded just from the way his gaze caressed her body.

Then she straddled him, her thighs on either side
of his, and he groaned as his arms banded around her
waist to pull her in tight. His lips found the pulse at the
side of her throat, and she arched, loving the sensation
of his mouth on her skin.

"*Nossa senhora.* I want you so much."

"Why not have me, then?"

"I don't know if it is the right thing to do, Krysta. I
need to think it through, and I can't when I have you
naked in my arms."

Leaning back, she lifted his chin, so as to see his expression when she asked, "If I weren't a virgin, would
you still hesitate?"

"Yes," he replied without pause. "There is something
between us, something I'm a little afraid of. You'll be
gone in less than two months. I don't want to do something I, or we, will regret."

She nodded. "I know what you mean, but I looked at
it from the other side. When I left, would it be with re-
grets for not taking this chance? Would I forever wonder what it would be like to kiss you, touch you, make
love with you? And I knew the answer would be yes."

Taking a deep breath, she said what she thought
they'd been skirting around the entire time.

"What we've found in each other is special, at least
it is to me, but I don't want to fall in love with you. I
don't want you to fall for me. Soon, our lives will once
more diverge, me heading back to the States, you staying here. We have careers we're proud of, and want to

keep building. Your family is here, mine is back home. It's a recipe for disaster, if we let it come to that.

"But this…" She gestured between them, touching his chest and then her own. "This I will never, ever regret, no matter what else happens."

His gaze bored into hers, as though he were trying to see into her soul. It amazed her how dark his eyes got, his pupils dilating until there was just a hint of lighter brown around them. And the knowledge it was passion for her that made them so gave her huge satisfaction.

"So, you feel we should make memories to carry with us, without worry or fear of the future? Slake this desire, and gorge ourselves with passion, because we already know it is all to end when you leave?"

"Yes." She nodded. "That's exactly what I think."

He was silent for a moment more, and then inhaled deeply.

"So be it," came his reply as he lifted to his feet, his hands on her bottom to hold her aloft. "Where is your bedroom?"

He knew Krysta spoke the truth, as she knew it, but Francisco suspected it was already too late for him.

That he was already more than halfway in love with her.

There was no future in it, as she had already so succinctly stated, but he couldn't resist her, didn't want to resist the passion that arose in him every time she was near. There might never be another chance like this, and he would grab hold of it with both hands, even if the end result was heartbreak.

So, he made love to her, taking pride in being the man who opened to her the world of passion, reveling in her responses, and the knowledge he gave her satisfaction.

Her body was beautiful, her lack of self-consciousness a turn-on unlike any he'd experienced before. She was a woman who, now that she had broken out from beyond the barrier of her inhibitions, embraced physical pleasure with the same enthusiasm as she did her work.

In a strange way, he felt as though it was his responsibility to introduce her fully to her body, and it made him more sensitive to her every reaction.

"Oh, Francisco." Her voice was hoarse, the words strained, as her hips tilted up toward his lips. "That's so good."

"You like that, *amor*?" He was teasing her, wanting her ready for his body. "Will you come for me again?"

Her body tightened around his fingers, and her thighs trembled.

"I want you. I need you. *Please*."

He didn't want to wait anymore; he wanted to be inside her with a kind of ferocious desperation he wasn't used to feeling.

Thank goodness he still had a condom in his wallet, although *Deus* alone knew how long it had been there. The last thing either of them would want or need was for her to get pregnant.

Yet, the thought of it brought him no fear, only a rush of longing so strong it stole his breath, and it took a moment for him to regain his composure.

Well, as much composure as one could muster when faced with the woman of your dreams, naked, begging for you to make her yours.

He'd done his best to prepare her but, as he positioned himself between her thighs, he watched for any sign of pain, or indication she'd suddenly changed her mind. Instead, what happened was, as soon as he started to slide into the gloriously wet heat of her body, she wrapped her legs around his waist and tried to pull him in, all at once.

"Gently." It rumbled from his throat like a groan. "Gently."

She only tilted her hips and tugged harder.

He lay over her, kissing her over and over, letting her get used to him, watching the play of emotion over her face. When he started to move in long, slow strokes, her eyes flew open and her lips parted on a gasp so redolent of pleasure it almost made him lose control.

Her hips flexed beneath his, adding a thrilling new sensation, and Francisco knew he wouldn't last long.

The feelings were too sublime, the emotions in him too strong.

Going up on his knees, he resumed his thrusts, but reached between them to find her clitoris and stroke it with his thumb.

Her eyelids fluttered, tried to close, but she kept them open, her gaze on his, as she whimpered a plea.

And when they found bliss together, Francisco knew, without a doubt, he was already in too deep.

CHAPTER FIFTEEN

KRYSTA WASN'T AT ALL sure what she'd gotten herself into, but whatever the outcome, she didn't want her affair with Francisco to end one moment sooner than it had to.

The memory of his kisses, touch and lovemaking intruded on her brain at the most inopportune moments, sending waves of heat through her body. Sometimes it felt as though she were constantly blushing. Keeping it all together, not betraying the change in their relationship at work, was exceedingly difficult, and she finally thought she knew what he'd meant when he'd said sex changes everything.

Keeping their interactions businesslike and professional at the hospital took reserves of strength she didn't even know she had.

It appeared, however, that she was doing a good job, as she discovered one day while in the ladies' room near the cafeteria.

"What a strange pair they make—Cisco and the American. Him so handsome and put together, her so strange and unfashionable. Do you think there's something going on between them?"

There was a giggle, and another voice answered, "She's not so bad. If she dressed better, I think she'd be more attractive. But as for if there's anything happening, I haven't seen any signs. Besides, he could have his pick of women. Why would he choose her?"

Krysta didn't recognize the voices and, trapped in the stall as she rearranged her clothing, couldn't see the two women talking. Her Portuguese had improved a lot since her arrival, so she had no problem following the conversation.

The two women went into separate stalls, but continued the conversation.

"Well, you know what they say about what he did to Mariella Guzman—used her for her money and connections, then dumped her. Maybe he thinks the American can help his career."

Letting herself out of the stall, Krysta made her way to the basins. Talk about eavesdroppers hearing no good of themselves!

"I, for one, don't know if I believe that story," the other woman said. "I've worked with Dr. Cisco, and I can't see him doing that to anyone."

After washing her hands, thankfully unable to hear any more of the conversation, Krysta grabbed some hand towels before quickly leaving the room.

She didn't believe that story, either. The man she'd come to know had too much integrity to harm another person in the way it had been rumored, and too much pride to defend himself, probably.

What it did bring to the forefront of her mind, though, was the fact she didn't know the real story. While she'd bared her soul to him, Francisco had held so much of his own life experience back, as though reluctant to share it with her.

Did he not trust her?

That was a sobering thought, and one that made her

even more determined to keep their relationship on a casual level.

They'd decided, since all the other visiting specialists were housed at the same apartment building she was in, they would meet instead at Francisco's place. It all took on a sort of cloak-and-dagger aura contrary to her forthright persona, yet made perfect sense in light of the transient nature of their relationship.

No matter how difficult it was to maintain the discretion, she knew she wouldn't change any of it. Coming to Brazil had not only given her a new perspective on the world, but given her a lover for the ages, too. Passionate and masterful, yet gentle and caring.

What more could a woman ask for, especially in her first affair?

Sometimes when she asked herself that, she knew there was an answer she wouldn't want to consider, so she pushed it aside.

She'd put off finding funding for her next project, realizing she needed some time to work on spending time with her family, and getting a life.

As she explained to Francisco, "It doesn't make sense to go back to exactly what I left, when I've realized it wasn't healthy. I'll still be practicing at the hospital, and probably be called in on some outside cases, like the one I assisted with in France, but I'll also have the opportunity to build a more normal life."

He'd nodded and agreed, but something about his closed expression made her wonder what he truly thought, but she didn't want to ask.

There were areas of life they didn't speak about. In particular, what would happen when they parted.

Francisco's accident patient began the long road to recovery, and Krysta had contacted the Belgian company about 3-D printing the orbital floor mesh for the reconstruction. When she explained that Paulista's was considering creating a program where the doctors would be using the virtual surgical mapping and 3-D printing technology, the Belgians were happy to work with her on a price.

"She won't be strong enough for another month or so," she told the company rep. "And I probably won't be in Brazil anymore. But the surgeon handling the case worked with me on the Dos Santos case, and is more than competent to get you all the information you need, as well as perform the surgery."

Enzo Dos Santos was getting ready to leave the hospital soon, too, and although she still had a month before she left, Krysta was starting to feel things coming to an end. At least she still had the clinic trip to Aparecida, and the visit to Francisco's home, to look forward to. Yet, she could feel the time slipping away far more quickly than she'd like, especially when she looked at her calendar and realized she only had one more lecture to give.

It made her stomach feel hollow, empty, although she knew it would be a new and improved woman going back to New York.

Or would it be?

Somehow, here in Brazil, it seemed easy to change— to get in touch with her femininity, to contemplate a more balanced life. Yet, not even here could she bring herself to make any alterations to her work persona, still fearful doing so would undermine the respect she'd built up.

It all felt as though she were playing a role not really suited for her, and she couldn't help wondering if she were just fooling herself.

She'd always been an outsider, the one who didn't fit in, allowing her to stay safe and unhurt. The outer trappings could change, but had the inner woman truly changed as well?

And what was she risking, spending this time with Francisco?

Impossible to view him as anything but a holiday fling. Despite everything that had happened, she knew there was no future between them. How could there be? They were from different worlds. His experience, in comparison to her lack thereof, must make her seem like nothing more than an amusing diversion.

No, there was nothing serious between them, no matter what emotions she felt when they were together. As he was her first lover, she might be forgiven for thinking there was more to their affair, but as an adult, a woman who thought things through, she knew better. She had to keep that in mind because, although she had no fear of him physically, it would be all too easy to be hurt by him otherwise.

She had to protect herself.

Yet, that night, as she lay in Francisco's arms, she dreaded the moment she'd once more be on her own. Rolling over, she let the last of her inhibitions slip away, so she could make love to him the way she wanted, make him crazy—*louco*—the way he made her every night.

And as she took them both to orgasm, she had to hide her eyes from him, so he wouldn't see her tears.

They drove together to Aparecida, leaving São Paulo at five in the morning to make the drive. Although the clinic organizers had arranged accommodation, Francisco had opted to rent them a room at another venue.

"Aren't you afraid people will talk? After all, they'll know we're staying together."

He shrugged. "It doesn't matter. Any gossip about us will fade quickly."

After you're gone.

He didn't say it, but she heard it in her mind, anyway.

When they arrived at the hospital where the clinic was taking place, Krysta was surprised to see the number of children and adults waiting to be seen or operated on.

Francisco explained, "Often when we have these clinics, parents whose children didn't make the list, or who heard of the clinic too late, will turn up, hoping their child will be seen. The administrators will do the best they can, but it's almost a triage situation at that point. The children with the highest need will get seen if there is time."

It gave her the impetus to work as quickly as she could on the cases she was given, which included two adult cleft-palate repairs. It wasn't something she'd ever seen in the States, where the repairs were generally done on infants, but she'd been forewarned of the cases, and was prepared. Taking a quick break after the second operation, she was walking through the waiting area, on her way outside, when a child and mother caught her attention.

The child was supposed to be feeding, but after every couple of pulls on the mother's breast, the child went limp. When Krysta took a closer look, she could see a blue tinge around the baby's face, and at the ends of the tiny fingers.

Concerned, she approached the mother, and said, in Portuguese, "I am a doctor. May I examine your baby?"

"Sim," she replied, holding out the tiny mite to Krysta, who could hear the relief in the mother's voice.

"What is his name?" she asked, trying to keep the mother calm and engaged as she sat next to her and put the little boy on her lap.

"Paavo," she replied, watching as Krysta opened a package and took out a tongue depressor.

A quick examination confirmed what she suspected, and had her looking around for one of the administrators. When she stood up and caught one's eye, she waved her over. The woman bustled over, looking a little put out.

"This baby should be looked at, preferably by a pediatric surgeon," Krysta said.

"There are only two here today, Doctor," the woman said firmly, in English. "And they are fully booked up. If this lady had applied like the other parents…"

"Whether she did, or she didn't, doesn't matter. This infant needs help. I suspect he has Pierre Robin sequence, and his airway is obstructed each time he tries to feed."

"But…"

Krysta was still holding the baby, keeping him across her arm, his head angled down to allow his airway to remain open. Despite her fragile burden and the mother sitting right there, she was ready to let the other woman have it, when Francisco's calm voice came from behind her.

"Is there a problem here?"

The administrator's attitude and demeanor changed immediately, becoming suddenly sweet. And she reverted to her native language as she replied, "Oh, no. I was just explaining to the American doctor that we have to follow procedure and can't take on patients who weren't preregistered before the rest of the listed patients are seen."

Francisco turned to Krysta, eyebrows raised, and the annoyance she'd felt dealing with the other woman flared a little higher. But she kept her voice cool, almost cold, as she said, in Portuguese, "And I was explaining to the Brazilian administrator that this child has severe glossoptosis, leading to airway obstruction each time he tries to feed. He needs to see a surgeon."

Francisco looked down at the tiny scrap of a baby lying across her arm and, for an instant, she saw pain flash across his face. Perhaps he was remembering his own brother's problems at that age?

"Pierre Robin sequence, you think?" he asked, looking up at her.

She nodded. "Looks like it. The mandible looks foreshortened, too, although I couldn't be completely sure without a more comprehensive examination."

He turned to the administrator and said, "I will take this case if the pediatric surgeons are too busy."

Then, before the woman could even find her tongue to say anything more, he held out his arms to take the child from Krysta, saying to the child's mother, "Please come with me, so I can examine your baby properly, and then we will see what can be done."

The tears immediately overflowing the mother's eyes, and her obvious gratitude, filled Krysta with satisfaction, and when she put the baby in Francisco's arms and met his gaze, she had a revelation. One she'd been avoiding for, oh, all these many weeks.

This man was one like no other, and she'd fallen for him ass over teakettle, as her granny used to say.

But there was nothing she could do but try to keep a cool head, and hand the child over. Holding the new knowledge close to her heart, but keeping it off her face and out of her voice, was difficult. She thought she did a credible job when she said, "Thank you."

Then she turned and walked away, back to the one thing she was counting on to keep her sane and give her solace in the future.

Work.

Francisco performed the cleft-palate revision surgery and a tongue-lip adhesion on the infant boy, hopefully giving him the help he needed to begin to grow properly and ultimately thrive. The mother, who lived in a remote area, hours away from Aparecida, had only heard of the clinic two days before. She'd left her home immediately, in hopes of getting her child seen and at least diagnosed.

What the baby really needed was a mandibular distraction osteogenesis, but that operation demanded the child be in the NICU for the entire period needed to lengthen the jaw. There was no hospital near where they lived that could perform the surgery, even if the family could afford it, or have it subsidized. At least with the other two issues dealt with, baby Paavo would have a better chance of survival.

As Francisco washed up after the surgery, he remembered the look on Krysta's face as the administrator had tried to brush her off. He wouldn't be surprised if he hadn't saved the administrator from getting a thorough tongue-lashing. He'd never seen Krysta even slightly ruffled, but at that moment she'd looked ready to go to war.

She was, in every sense of the word, *magnifica*.

He wasn't sure what he was going to do without her. When she'd told him her next research project had been canceled, he'd felt a brief spurt of hope that perhaps it meant she could stay a little longer in Brazil. But that was just a pipe dream, and he knew it. She was on sabbatical from the hospital, and they would expect her back as soon as her tenure at Paulista's was over.

Really, as much as he wanted to simply enjoy the time they had left together, there was a part of himself already in retreat, trying to salvage whatever he could of pride and heart and soul. Then she goes and does something like going to battle for a tiny baby, one who reminded him so much of João, and he fell in love with her all over again.

Shaking his head at his own folly, he went to speak to Paavo's mother, making sure to tell her she needed to have the tongue-lip release surgery done the following year. Then it was on to prepare for the next surgery.

They ended up not leaving until after dark, and when they got to their hotel, all they could do was shower and fall into bed, exhausted, hardly saying more than two words to each other the entire time.

Then they woke up the next morning and did it all over again.

"Good job, everyone," Francisco said to the team after the last patient of day two had been taken to recovery. "Thanks to your fine work, we were able to see many more patients than we had originally planned, and the clinic was a great success."

Walking out to the car, Krysta looked as though she were asleep on her feet, but she turned to him and said, "So, where are we going dancing?"

He laughed, shaking his head at her silliness as he opened her door and helped her slip inside. "There'll be time for dancing two nights from now, at my parents' home. All the dancing you want."

She yawned, putting her head back against the head-rest. "I'm warning you—I have no idea how to samba, or cha-cha, or merengue, so you may be disappointed."

Leaning on the door, he met her gaze and said, "The cha-cha is Cuban, and the merengue is from the Dominican Republic, so you're okay not knowing those. But the samba? You will learn the samba, even if one of us dies in the effort."

And she was giggling as he shut the door.

It was, he mused, one of the things he loved about her, and being with her. She took her work seriously, but not herself. She had no problem laughing at herself, or just at silly things, and it brought a lightness to his life he'd not known for far too many years.

She made him, his life, better, just by being herself.

Settling into the driver's seat, he said, "Good catch on that baby yesterday. The diagnosis of Pierre Robin sequence was spot-on."

"What were you able to do for him?"

"Tongue-lip adhesion, as well as the cleft-palate repair. Seeing him lying there, prone, in your arms took me back in time."

"Your brother?"

"Mmm, although this little boy today was actually worse off, since João didn't have the glossoptosis. Little Paavo's airway obstruction was severe, and he's in the lowest growth percentile for his age. Hopefully now he can feed without choking on his own tongue, and put on some weight."

"And thank you," she said quietly with a note in her voice he didn't recognize. He glanced at her, but couldn't see anything in the dark interior of the car.

"For what?"

"For taking on the case. For being you."

He wanted to say something in return, but his heart was full, and ached, and it was better to stay silent, rather than say too much.

Not that he should have worried. When he glanced at her at the next stoplight, she was asleep, so that when he whispered, *"Eu te amo,"* it was because he knew she wouldn't hear.

CHAPTER SIXTEEN

KRYSTA AWOKE THE next morning still exhausted, but when she opened her eyes and saw Francisco lying on his side, watching her, she smiled and held out her arms. He'd already warned that they'd be sleeping in separate rooms at his parents, so it would be another couple of nights before they were back in the same bed.

The made love slowly, sweetly, taking their time, finding maximum satisfaction. Having finally admitted to herself that she was in love with Francisco added a new dimension to the experience, and she found herself trying to capture each moment in her memory. It made her stretch out every touch, every kiss, seeking the most she could get out of each one.

"*Amor*, you are torturing me," Francisco groaned.

Torturing herself, too, but in the best possible way.

"Happy birthday," she said, sipping at his skin until he was trembling, goose bumps rising where she touched.

When they achieved orgasm, first her, and then him, her ecstasy was heightened, knowing she'd wrung that deep, pleasure-drunk sound from his throat.

"You know my birthday isn't until tomorrow, don't you?"

"Mmm-hmm. Think of this as an early present."

"Puxa vida," he groaned. "The real gift is going to kill me, isn't it?"

She just laughed softly, and kissed the nipple nearest to her, making it pucker.

After a leisurely breakfast, they left Aparecida and drove south for a short time, before turning west, farther inland. He'd told her it shouldn't take more than a couple of hours to get to his parents' house.

"I was glad to get the offer to work in São Paulo, since it is closer to my parents. Mind you, when I was in Rio they didn't complain half as much about my not visiting, because they knew it was farther to come."

Krysta chuckled. "I have the opposite problem. Since my parents moved to Georgia three years ago, they're constantly complaining that they don't see me, although when they were still in Rochester, they hardly said a word."

They laughed together, and Francisco suggested she take a nap, but she refused. She didn't want to miss any of their time together. She could catch up on sleep in her lonely bed when she got back to New York.

Partway there, he stopped at the side of the road for them to stretch their legs and buy fresh, cold coconuts for them to drink the water.

"This reminds me of the Caribbean," she said, watching the vendor wielding his machete to cut off the top of the husk, then creating a hole in the nut inside.

When he handed her the coconut, he also tried to give her a straw, which she declined, telling him, "I'm sure I remember how to drink these the way my grandfather taught me." And thankfully she did, getting the cool fresh liquid from the coconut into her mouth, rather than down her chin and the front of her blouse.

"Brava! Brava!" the vendor cried, the two of them laughing together.

She took that spirit of fun with her for the rest of the journey, determined to enjoy the trip. When they pulled up at Francisco's parents' home, she got out of the car and stretched, just as the door flew open and what seemed like a battalion of people spilled out, all seemingly talking at the same time. They engulfed the car, Francisco and, to her surprise, Krysta, too.

It was a whirl of names and faces as she was grabbed and kissed on both cheeks by everyone. Not knowing what to expect, it was a little overwhelming, but she smiled and tried to remember who was who in the crowd.

Finally, Francisco's mother shooed everyone back inside. "Let them breathe. Let them breathe. João, take Krysta's bag into the house. Your brother's, too."

"I believe he's quite capable of carrying his own bag," was João's saucy reply. "Irrespective of him being so very old now."

That led to a mock wrestling match, with fake blows thrown, and some trash talking. This was a Francisco she'd never seen before, although the ghost of it came out sometimes when they spoke and laughed. Relaxed, teasing and being teased. Just a part of a family that obviously shared great love and respect.

"Ah, boys," Senhora Carvalho said with a smile as she tucked her arm through Krysta's and pulled her toward the door. "They can be doctors and architects, but a part of them never truly grows up."

The house was large and rambling, but smelled wonderfully of good food, and sounded like a family home should—ringing with laughter and teasing remarks shouted down corridors.

"You're in here with me," Francisco's youngest sister, Teresa, said, leading the way down the hallway. Raising her voice, she added, "Because although Mathile has the biggest room, she takes up more space than I do!"

"You would as well, if you were eight months pregnant," came the shouted reply, and Krysta exchanged a laughing look with Teresa.

Even as she tried to be as unobtrusive as possible, neither Francisco nor the rest of his family would allow it, pulling her into conversations, slowing their speech when they realized her Portuguese may not be up to the rapid-fire quips and barbs flying around.

Although the *festa* in honor of Francisco's birthday wasn't until the following day, everyone seemed in a party mood already, and his mother had cooked a feast of a dinner.

"Take Krysta and show her the animals," Francisco's father suggested, and she was glad of a small reprieve from the noise and crowd.

Senhor Carvalho had a small farm, which augmented his salary as a water-quality inspector for the area, Francisco explained, but he thought the real reason for the farm was that his father loved animals. There were at least three dogs underfoot in the house, and a cat that stayed up on a high shelf in the living room, surveying the surroundings with feline superiority.

Now Krysta found herself meeting chickens and ducks, a large sow and a donkey that was far friendlier than any she'd met before.

"The last donkey I came in contact with tried to take a chunk out of me," she said, smiling up at Francisco while scratching the donkey's muzzle. "This one is sweet."

Another cat slunk out of the barn, giving them a disdainful glance before disappearing into the nearby bushes.

"Mama said she has kittens in the barn. Want to look?" he asked.

Of course she did, and they found the four little wriggling fluff balls in a disused stall, their eyes not even open yet.

"How darling," she crooned, stroking them lightly with her forefinger. "So soft."

When she stood up, she found Francisco barring her way to the door, and it seemed the most natural thing in the world to go into his arms, and exchange a long, drugging kiss.

After she'd seen the vegetable garden and coffee trees, it was back inside to clean up for dinner, which was served on the courtyard at the back of the house.

Since she hadn't contributed to fixing the meal, Krysta offered to help with the cleanup, and found herself absorbed into a laughing, chattering swirl of women. At first she didn't notice, and then she realized they were determined to winkle any information about her relationship with Francisco out of her, by hook or by crook. But she was used to keeping her own counsel and deflected the interrogation as best she could.

Yes, she thought him very nice.

No, they were work colleagues and friends, and he'd wanted her to see as much of Brazil as she could before she left.

It was like being in a sword fight, she thought as the last dish was washed and put away, but with multiple opponents all coming at you at the same time, and it was a relief to escape back outside, where the conversation was more general.

She went to bed with a wave to everyone, being careful not to single out Francisco in any discernible way, and, not surprisingly, she fell asleep as soon as her head hit the pillow.

The day of the party was another whirl of activity, and the preparations made the time fly. Before she knew it, it was time to change, and the music was already beginning outside.

If it had seemed like there was a mass of people with just the family there, now it was a crush. The party spread out from the house to the courtyard, and beyond. She was taken around and introduced to so many people her head was spinning, and her usually good memory all but deserted her.

Just before dinner was served, she found herself standing with Francisco and his other brother, Antonio, the latter taking her hand and kissing it lightly.

"I don't think you will want to be with this old man anymore," he teased. "Not now that you've met his younger, more handsome brother."

Francisco rolled his eyes, and smacked his brother on the back of the head. "Why don't you go try out your smooth lines on some of the little girls making eyes at you? They will probably appreciate them more."

"*Oi!* Watch the hair," was the testy answer.

"Come and dance with me," Francisco said, insisting when she demurred, saying she should go and help his mother in the kitchen. "She has five hundred women in there already," was his reply. "She won't even miss you."

But it wasn't that she wanted to be in the kitchen, or even that she didn't know the steps. It was knowing being in his arms, even for a dance lesson, would be the ultimate in pleasure-filled pain. Especially since they were trying not to let his family know what lay between them.

Yet still, she gave in, unable to resist.

"Since it's your birthday," she said, infusing her voice with disgruntlement.

He just laughed, and led her to where some of the partygoers were already making use of the dance floor.

To her surprise, she caught on to the steps fairly quickly, although cognizant of the fact he kept it simple for her, not expecting her to do any of the fancier footwork going on around them. And she enjoyed it, finding herself laughing with delight, loving the way the swaying lanterns above their heads cast intriguing shadows on his face, and how easily he laughed with her.

It was a night to remember, and as the party wound down, Krysta found herself beside Senhora Carvalho, who had finally decided she'd done everything necessary and could sit for a moment. Francisco was dancing with a lovely blonde woman he'd introduced as his cousin, and they were putting on a show. It was beautiful to watch.

"My Francisco is a good dancer, isn't he? I think it's important that a man know how to move to music."

"Yes, he is," Krysta agreed, trying to tear her gaze away from him and having a hard time of it.

"But even more important," her companion went on, "is that he is a good man."

Krysta turned to find the older woman watching her, not the dancing, and schooled her own face to stillness. "Yes, he is," she agreed again.

"He was hurt, very badly, by people he thought friends, by a woman he held dear. I would hate to see that happen again. He deserves better. Just as I believe you do, too."

"Yes," Krysta said again, sadness washing through her, her gaze drawn back to where Francisco undulated, his feet flying faster than she could follow.

It was a warning his mother offered, obviously not fooled by their attempt to seem to be only friends. But it was a warning that, for Krysta, had come far too late.

As always, Francisco enjoyed his time with his family, but he was eager to get back to São Paulo, not for work, but to have Krysta to himself again. The time was ticking away, even swifter now than ever.

He listed what was yet to come in his head, trying to take comfort in the fact none of them had yet occurred.

One more of her lectures.

A postoperative checkup of Enzo Dos Santos.

A conference call with the manufacturers in Belgium, so she could guide him and the rest of the team through the steps they'd need to take to work with the company.

The farewell dinner, back at the place where it started. A circle closing that he wished could turn into a Möbius strip, so it never had to end.

These were the landmarks he would use to mark the final days with her, and as hard as he tried to not think about them, the more they weighed on his mind.

It didn't help that she was unusually quiet on the drive back, seemingly sunk deep in thought. When he questioned her, she just shook her head, sending him a little smile.

"I'm just tired. It's been a hectic few days."

With that he could definitely agree, but then he knew he was in trouble when she asked to be dropped at her apartment, rather than coming home with him.

He wanted to beg, and the impulse angered him, so

he just agreed, without asking why, or trying to discover what was wrong.

Yet, there was one thing he absolutely had to know. So, as he pulled into the parking lot outside the apartment building, he turned to her and asked, "Did someone in my family, or at the party, say something to upset you? Did I do something?"

"No," she said. "They were all lovely. You know they were. And so were you."

But she wasn't looking at him when she said it, searching her handbag instead, coming out with her keys.

Self-preservation insisted he not push, so he got out to open her door, and walked her into the lobby, wheeling her bag behind him.

Should he kiss her good-night? He didn't know, couldn't read this new mood she was in.

"Até logo," she said, reaching up to kiss him on his cheeks, as though they were nothing more than the friends they'd pretended to be at his parents' house. "See you tomorrow."

Then she took her bag from his suddenly nerveless grip, and stepped into the elevator. But although she tried not to show any emotion, she kept her gaze on his until the doors closed, and he could have sworn there was deep pain glimmering in her eyes.

CHAPTER SEVENTEEN

KRYSTA LET HERSELF into her apartment and deflated like a popped balloon. She felt like an idiot, a coward. She should have spoken to Francisco, at least made an attempt to tell him what she was feeling, and why she was so distant, but she didn't feel equipped to do it right now. There was a tender, hurting space around her heart that didn't feel as though it could take any more blows.

She'd tried to call on the old Krysta—prosaic, practical Krysta—to come up with a solution to her conundrum, but unfortunately that woman seemed to have taken a holiday, at the worst possible time.

So she had no answers to the question she kept asking herself, over and over again.

Which would be better, less painful, for both herself and Francisco: Break it off now, or see it through to the end?

Leaving her bags by the door, she wandered into the apartment, and sat down on the couch. The memories of their first night together tried to intrude, but she pushed them back. If she thought about him in a sexual way, she'd never work it all out. Besides, it was no longer about just physical satisfaction, at least not for her.

When they were together, she felt lighter, better, freer, than she ever had before. He'd helped her become stronger. She'd always been confident in her abilities as a doctor and surgeon. That had never been in question. But as a woman? She'd known she was lacking. It was why her work became her be-all and end-all. If you don't put yourself out there, you don't have to try to figure things out. You can just drift along, secure in your little space.

And now, hurt and confused, as much as it was tempting to retreat back into that little space, she knew she'd no longer fit in it. She'd grown in ways she'd never imagined she could, and there was a part of her eager to keep growing, but right now it felt as if without Francisco she might not be able to.

A foolish notion, she was sure. There were few things she'd set her mind to that she hadn't been able to achieve, and she was determined to rebuild her familial relationships, expand her horizons and keep moving forward in life.

She could do that, without anyone's help.

But she would love to have Francisco beside her, encouraging her, stretching her when she'd be tempted to lapse back into her old ways.

That, too, was just a dream. Nothing had changed from the first night they'd been together when she'd so boldly, so foolishly, thumbed her nose at love. They would still be going their separate ways, his life here in Brazil, hers in America.

No, nothing had changed, except her feelings for him, which had grown and expanded until they seemed to inhabit every corner of her being. How was she to know he'd fill her so completely, so thoroughly, the thought of being without him created a physical ache?

Yet, there was also more than just the divide caused by their work lives to consider. For all the time they'd spent together, Francisco still held a part of himself in abeyance. Not physically, but in other ways. He'd never talked about what happened between him and his ex-fiancée, or even much about his modeling career. Not that it was terribly important, just that it seemed to show he didn't totally trust her, nor did he want to allow her access to the deepest parts of his heart.

She wished she had the courage to simply ask him, to demand that of him, but she didn't. To do so and be rejected would hurt even more than his reticence. He'd have to volunteer the information himself, and without that openness, she knew there couldn't be a long-term relationship between them.

But for all that, she'd hurt him this evening. It had been plain on his face, and considering all they'd shared, the way she'd handled it was unforgivable. She'd definitely lapsed into old, selfish ways, where the only person she'd had to think of was herself, and that was *all* she'd thought of.

Like his mother said, he deserved better, and although she couldn't be his forever, the least she could do was be better now. After rummaging through her bag, she found her phone, and called him. Even texting would be cowardly tonight, and she was determined to do the right thing.

He answered immediately, traffic noise in the distance telling her he hadn't got home yet.

"Oi," he said, and hearing the caution in his voice made her ache even more.

"I'm sorry. I behaved like a child, running away."

There was a little silence, and her heart raced with fear and self-recrimination. When he spoke, his voice was softer, and her eyes prickled with tears.

"What were you running away from, *amor*?"

"Myself. My feelings. My fears."

He sighed, a long, hard exhale. "I understand. Sometimes it's easier than facing them, yes?"

"Definitely," she agreed. "Especially when you don't know the right thing to do."

"I don't know, either."

"I'm so confused, Francisco."

There was another pause while he thought. It was one of the many things she loved about him: the careful consideration he gave decisions. When he spoke again, there was a tone in his voice she didn't recognize.

"Forget right or wrong at this moment. What do you *want* to do?"

That was easy. "Be with you."

"Then come back downstairs, or I will come upstairs, and we will spend tonight together. Tomorrow is soon enough to try to find the answers."

"How soon will you get here?" she asked, her heart thumping now with joy, fear fleeing at the thought of even one more moment with him.

"I never left. Like a lovelorn young boy, I have been sitting in the parking lot, wondering what next to do. How I can make right whatever I did to wrong you."

She should laugh, but the air was stuck in her lungs, and the tears had made a lump form in her throat. Swallowing it hurt, as though the lump was mixed with shards of glass, destined to lacerate her heart. But she forced it down and, wanting to be where they'd spent so many beautiful nights together, said, "I'll be right there."

They drove silently to his place, going inside still without speaking. There was a sense that what there was between them had grown fragile and words might cause it to break into a million, irredeemable pieces.

Any questions to be asked and answered tonight were posed through looks, and touches.

Do you want to make love with me?

He asked with fingers spanning her wrist, his thumb moving gently against the pulse point. Although the only point of contact, she felt it down to her toes.

Yes.

She answered with a kiss, set against the side of his mouth, gentle and tempting, but not demanding. Then she walked into his bedroom, leading him, despite the fact it was he who held her.

They made love slowly, almost carefully, until the passion overtook them, and thought fled, leaving just sensation. His mouth on her. His hands. His skin beneath her fingertips and palms. The hard length of him filling her, taking her to ecstasy.

Grateful for the surcease from conflicted emotion, she rode the waves with him, feeling the moment he, too, let go, and they could fly together.

Drifting into sleep, she held on to that, letting the memory lull her, wishing she could hold on to it—to him—forever.

Francisco woke first, and turned his head to watch Krysta sleep.

Despite the beauty of the night just spent with her, he ached. Not physically. That would be bearable. No, this was deeper, harder to heal.

He'd thought he'd known what heartbreak was. Had known what love was. But looking at the woman beside him, he realized what he'd felt before had been an illusion. The emotions of a young man, still inexperienced and susceptible to the lure of a pretty face and the right words.

And he knew the heartbreak coming would be devastating.

He'd known the relationship with her wouldn't last, but still he had dreamed.

Had acknowledged to himself that, as her first lover, it was assured she would move on, find others. Hopefully she would think of him fondly and, should they meet at a conference or seminar, share with him a smile redolent of good memories.

But there, too, he'd dreamed—of being her first, her last. Of being enough that she would never want another.

Foolish to dream. He wasn't in the dreaming business. Medicine demanded logic, foresight, patience, determination. Those were qualities he'd cultivated, but none of them had stopped him from giving his heart where it wasn't safe. From loving more than was wise.

Yet, there was a little sense of having failed her— them—in the way he held parts of himself back. He hadn't found the courage to open himself up completely to her, to put himself on the line, and ask her to stay.

Theirs would be the kind of love story without a happy ending, and he couldn't lay bare his heart to her, knowing she would walk away.

Krysta stirred, as though hearing his thoughts in her dreams, and when her eyes opened, he thought he might drown in the emotion swirling in them.

"I know I said I wouldn't, and I didn't want to, but I've fallen in love with you."

She spoke softly, in her habitual matter-of-fact way, and for a moment his heart leaped with joy. If they loved, truly, deeply, they could find a way, couldn't they? But before he could voice that thought, she continued.

"Besides that, nothing in our circumstances has changed. I'll be going back to New York in two weeks. You've built a life for yourself here, in a place that you love, where you belong. I wish I could say I would give everything I've worked for up for you, but I can't. I know I'll resent it and, eventually, you. I've changed a lot since I came here, but not enough to throw my life's work away."

And he knew then what the right words were. Not what he'd been thinking, for they were born of dreams, not reality.

"And I would never ask you to. You've done great things, and there is so much more you have to contribute. To even consider asking you to give that up would be sacrilege."

They both knew Brazil could offer her nothing like what she already had, and despite the connectivity of the world, eventually she would start to fall behind.

As for him, he didn't know how to get around the thought that perhaps she only believed herself in love with him, because he was her first love affair. Only too well did he remember how all-encompassing those emotions could be, and how they could, in reality, be false.

"What do you want to do?" Her voice trembled, and he knew she was fighting tears. Her eyes glistened with them. "Do you want us to stop seeing each other now?"

"Will that make our parting any less painful?" he asked, knowing for him it wouldn't.

"No." She shook her head, lifted her hand to dash away the tears spilling down her cheeks. "No, it won't."

"Then let us enjoy each other until the very last moment. There will be time enough to mourn this beautiful thing we created, later."

And he still believed that, even as the days rushed, one into the other, and their lovemaking became increasingly frantic, as the nights fled by, too.

He heard from Flávia, and told Krysta he'd arranged for a tour of the sanctuary.

"Will you be coming, too?" she asked.

"If you promise to keep me safe from spiders," he said, making her chuckle, as he intended.

So they went, and although it wasn't anywhere he'd rush back to, it had been informative, and Krysta had seemed to know just the right questions to ask.

At the end, Flávia had hugged her, and asked, "Can we keep in touch? I do like you."

"Of course," Krysta replied. "I don't know when next I'll be coming this way, but if you're ever in the States, no matter where, let me know."

The new Krysta, he believed, would keep that promise, and perhaps the two often-isolated women would remain friends.

Her last lecture came and went, and his pride knew no bounds at her poise beforehand, so different from that first day when she'd had to throw up. And he'd clapped harder than anyone during the standing ovation at the end.

The time for Enzo Dos Santos's last checkup with her arrived, and they both forced a laugh when Enzo said to Francisco, "I still prefer her, over you, but I suppose you will have to do."

"Your recovery is remarkable," she told him, obviously pleased at his progress, especially in regard to his speech therapy. "And I'll be checking on you from afar, so make sure you behave."

He'd sketched her a salute, making her laugh again, and then that milestone, too, was past.

And then, suddenly, far too soon, there were just two days left before she was to leave.

He took her back to Santos, and this time he braved the water with her. Taking her to the beach where the surfers hung out, he rented wet suits and boards, and taught her to surf in the relatively gentle waves. Why he'd thought of it, he wasn't sure. Perhaps because he wanted to give her one more reminder of how much she'd changed. One more proof of her courage.

She was surprised at how well she did, but he wasn't. There was an indomitable spirit within her that, along with her intellect, would assure her success in whatever she turned her mind to.

It was something he believed with all his heart, and he told her so.

When her face lit up with pleasure at his words, his heart broke just a little more at how beautiful she was when that inner light shone out from her soul through her eyes.

One more walk on the beach, another coffee. Dinner at the outdoor restaurant they had been to before. A kiss beneath the moonlight on their way to the car.

All these things he stored in his memory, wishing they could go on forever.

Then the second to last day was done.

And he still hadn't confessed his own feelings to her, just held them close to his breaking heart.

CHAPTER EIGHTEEN

THE CLOSING RECEPTION passed in a blur. Throughout the dinner, speeches and schmoozing, all Krysta could do was wonder where the time had gone.

Hadn't she blinked, and the months flew by?

The last weeks with Francisco, in particular, had gone by in a flash, and even though they'd made their decision, agreed on how their affair should play out, there was a part of her that refused to believe it was about to be over.

Yet, what did she know about love, really? How could she know whether in a week, or a month, or a year, she'd wouldn't stop yearning for him? That the memory of his smile, his kiss, his touch, wouldn't fade into insignificance?

And despite the beauty of his lovemaking, the way he looked at her, especially when he didn't think she'd see, Francisco hadn't actually told her how he felt about her or their relationship, still holding an integral part of himself locked away. It made her think she was doing the right thing, even as she desperately wanted to hold on to him, however possible.

It was a fight with no winners. A riddle with no answer.

It was their last night together. She'd packed all her things and moved them to his apartment, so they could go straight there from the closing reception. They'd been quiet with each other, perhaps each making a defensive retreat in the face of the parting ahead. In Santos they'd talked and talked, as though to fit in a lifetime of stories into one sun-drenched day. And they'd laughed, even though there was already a painful edge to their amusement.

At the reception, she saw Dr. Delgado glaring across the room at them, and couldn't help asking, "Why does that man dislike you so much?"

Francisco's lips tightened, and then he relaxed, and sighed.

"He is a distant cousin to the young woman I was engaged to, and is determined to think the worst of me."

"Just shows how little he knows you," she said as casually as she could, knowing this was probably her last chance to hear his side of the story. "I've heard the rumors. What really happened?"

The look he gave her scorched her to her toes, and for an instant he looked as though he wanted to kiss her, right there, in front of everyone.

"You are the first person to ask me that," he said, his voice low and rough. "Most just assume what they read or heard was true."

She kept her gaze level, wanting him to know she meant it when she replied, "Then obviously they're not particularly good judges of character. I think you'd find there are a number of people in the hospital who don't believe the stories, either."

His gaze was so intent, as he searched her face, she felt it like a physical touch. Then he took her hand and led her to the side of the room, where they wouldn't be overheard.

"I fell for Mari when we were both models. The difference between us was that she came from a wealthy family, and, well, my family was much poorer than it is now. Our upbringings were worlds apart, but I thought we had something special, and between the money I'd saved from modeling and what I'd make as a doctor, we'd have a good life. I asked her to marry me, and she agreed, but then I found out she was hooked on cocaine, and told her I couldn't marry her unless she got clean."

He shook his head, a rueful smile tugging at one corner of his lips.

"She left me, after taking most of my money, apparently wanting the drugs more than she wanted me. But she couldn't let anyone know why things had ended between us. So, she and her friends began telling everyone that I had deserted her, and when her father found out she was using, she told him she had only started because of the breakup. By then, I had just finished medical school, and the general consensus was that I had used her, and her wealth, to get what I wanted and then discarded her."

"I'm sorry." She touched his wrist in sympathy, but inside she was shaken and angry on his behalf. No one deserved to be treated that way, least of all Francisco, who was so proud, and had so much integrity. "Addiction is a disease that makes people do things the rest of us can't understand."

"Sim," he replied, the warmth in his eyes melting her heart. "Thank you."

"For what?" she asked.

"For believing in me, even when you didn't know the whole story."

Walking into the apartment after the reception, she paused, took a deep breath. In these rooms she'd spent the happiest days of her life, and had discovered herself in a way she couldn't have done on her own. Turning to him, she wanted to tell him that, make him understand she'd never forget him, never be ungrateful for the time they'd spent together, but there was something in his eyes that stilled the words on her tongue.

"Come to bed, *amor*." He held out his hand and, without reservation, she laid hers in it. "I don't want to talk anymore. I want only to feel."

They made love far into the night, and he didn't say anything when, as she lay above him, her tears fell on his face. Instead, he just held her tighter, and kissed them away, making her wish with all her heart that he could love her, too, the way she loved him.

The next morning, he drove her to the airport, although Paulista's had offered a limo to take her. A part of her thought they should have said their goodbyes at his home, but the bigger part still was greedy, demanding every last moment she could have with him.

She checked in, and afterward they looked at each other, neither wanting to suggest she go through security, both knowing she should.

They walked slowly to the security barrier, and stood, hand in hand, watching the crowds. Needing one last point of contact, one last memory, she turned, and found his gaze trained on her face, a look of such longing in his eyes it made her heart clench, the pain making her gasp.

Then she was in his arms, his face in her neck, her tears dampening the front of his shirt.

"Eu te amo," he said. *"Eu te amarei para sempre."*

She froze, her brain scrambling to understand, to accept what he was saying. Desperate thoughts ran through her mind, about staying, asking him to come

with her, as, at that moment, she knew she would love
him forever, too.

Then common sense took over. He was playing their
affair out to the end, with the perfect goodbye to put a
period on their time together. If that were not the case,
wouldn't he have said something earlier, rather than
wait until now, when there was no more time to talk,
to negotiate?

So, although there was so much she wanted to say,
to ask, to tell him, all she whispered was, "I love you,
too, Francisco."

And then she forced herself to walk away, uncaring
of the stares her tearstained cheeks garnered her.

Rochester seemed flat and bland after the colors of Brazil, but she threw herself back into work, trying to regain the momentum she'd had before she left. Yet, she
really wasn't the same, and the cutthroat world of ap-
plying and securing grants didn't hold the same appeal as before.

Without the new research project, she had some time
on her hands, and used it to visit first her parents, and
then her older brother, his wife and two kids. Sitting in
Kelvin's backyard, in Houston, he finally broached the
subject of the change in her.

"Mom told me not to ask, but I have to," he said.
"What happened in Brazil? You're a different person.
You even look different."

Even after a month, the thought of Francisco brought
tears to her eyes, and she looked away, so he wouldn't
see.

"You can tell me," he said quietly, putting his hand
on her arm. "Whatever it was couldn't have been a totally bad thing."

"I was a wonderful thing," she said, sniffling. "His name is Francisco."

"Wait, what?" Kelvin leaned forward, searching her eyes. "What the hell… You fell in love! So where is he, and when do we get to meet him?" Then his eyes narrowed. "Or do I have to fly to Brazil and beat the crap out of him?"

That made her laugh, as he knew it would.

"No, you don't have to beat him up. The reality is, I'm here and he's there, and our jobs don't leave us much option to be together. We decided it would be better to just end it, rather than torture ourselves until it fizzled out."

Kelvin was an engineer, with the kind of mind that cut through the nonsense to the meat of any problem. So, she wasn't too surprised when he said, "Does it feel like it's fizzling out?"

"No, it doesn't. In fact, it hurts a little more every day."

He leaned back, and took a long swig of his beer.

"I think you should find a way to be together. Love doesn't come along every day, especially not for people like us."

She knew what he meant. They were both driven and hyperfocused, sometimes unable to see past whatever they were concentrating on. Somehow Ginny, his wife, had gotten through to him, and they'd been happily married for over six years.

Could she hope for a similar happy outcome? She highly doubted it.

Yet, even through her misery, her brain kept cycling back to that moment at the airport, when Francisco said he'd love her forever. She'd attributed it to a whim on his part to make their affair end as romantically as it had played out, but was that really the type of man Francisco was?

No.

His integrity would never allow him to say something as monumental as that if he didn't mean it.

And yet, she'd walked away, rather than gather her courage and try to work it out.

Was it too late for them?

"Put your mind to it," Kelvin said. "If anyone can find a solution, it's you."

Francisco let himself into his apartment, and hung his keys on the hook by the door. Then he inhaled, deeply. Although it had been over a month since Krysta left, every time he came home, he swore he could still smell her distinctive fresh scent in the air.

He didn't know whether that made him insane, but if he wasn't there yet, he soon would be.

Missing her was a constant ache, so much so he'd realized he couldn't go on this way. Soon his work would suffer, and Delgado was still making snide remarks, going so far as to question his abilities. One slip, and he knew he'd be out. Delgado would see to it.

Before he'd met Krysta that would have made him incensed, but losing her had made him realize there were far more important things than work, or his pride, or even opening himself up to pain. Looking back, he could no longer understand the reasons he'd used for letting her go. Now they seemed flimsy, rather than anything important.

He'd refused to allow them the chance they deserved, because he was afraid it would all turn to dust. Yet, deep inside, he knew what they'd shared was extraordinary—

a once in a lifetime connection. One that he'd foolishly thrown away out of fear.

Moving to the sofa, he threw himself down on it.

Today he'd given in to his craving for her, and tried to call, but couldn't get through. Her cell phone had gone to voice mail, and the hospital in Rochester had said she was away. They wouldn't give out any further information. He'd left a message, asking her to call.

Maybe she was visiting her parents. He hoped, wherever she was, she was having a good time. Trying something new. Living her best life.

Even if it were without him.

She'd said she loved him, but when he'd finally admitted he loved her, too, she'd walked away. He knew it was because he'd left it too late, had agreed with her when she'd said nothing had changed about their lives.

Everything had changed for him. Meeting her, loving her, had caused the kind of seismic emotional shift only love can. There was the knowledge he'd give anything, do anything, to be with her again.

Life was too short to waste any more of it on wondering whether they could make it together or not. If he couldn't contact her by phone, he would go and find her, ask her to take him for her own, for as long as she might want him, in whatever capacity she wanted.

He was so lost in thought when his phone rang it startled him. Not even looking at the screen, he clicked it on while lifting it to his ear.

"Oi." There was a pause, and he almost hung up.

"Francisco?"

Joy, unfettered and complete, fired through him, and he found himself on his feet.

"Krysta? *Amor?*"

"Yes."

The joy he felt echoed back at him from her voice, and his heart began to race.

"Where are you?"

She didn't reply, just asked, "Am I still your *amor*? Do you still love me?"

"Yes. And yes. I ache for you. I don't want to live without you anymore."

He heard her gasp, and then he heard a sniffle. Was she crying?

"Don't cry, *amor*. I can't bear it if you cry and I am not there to wipe your tears."

"Then let me in, darling. I'm outside."

For an instant he thought she was joking, but he knew she would never be so cruel. And when, in a matter of minutes, she was in his arms, he swore he would never let her go again.

He couldn't stop kissing her, touching her, his hands and lips seeking to make sure she was actually there, and not a figment of his love-crazed imagination.

When they finally came up for breath, he asked, "When did you arrive? Why didn't you let me know you were coming?"

"I flew in today, and it was only when I was in the air I realized you might not even be here." She shook her head, a smile tilting her lips. "I wasn't thinking straight. You know how I am. I get an idea and run with it, full speed ahead. I wanted to tell you something, but face-to-face, not on the phone."

"Tell me," he said. "And then I will tell you mine."

"I don't want to be apart from you anymore, so I'm thinking of leaving the hospital in Rochester after my contract is up, and the French transplant team has offered me a job. I know it's asking a lot, but you said you love Paris, and the Belgians are looking for a representative in France—someone to demonstrate the products, hands-on—if you think you might be interested—"

"Yes," he said before she could finish. Then kissed her again to seal the deal. "Yes. And yes. And yes."

"Oh, Francisco. *Eu te amarei para sempre.*"

Heart soaring, he picked her up and, carrying her to his bedroom, he echoed her words. "And I will love you, forever."

"What was your news?" she asked as he laid her down on his bed, and came to rest above her.

"I was going to tell you that I will go anywhere with you, and be happy, as long as I am by your side. I planned to go to Rochester to tell you in person, but you beat me to it."

"You snooze, you lose, my love."

She grinned up at him, and he bent to kiss the smile off her lips, but paused with their mouths millimeters apart, to say, "No, *amor*. In this case, we both win."

* * * * *

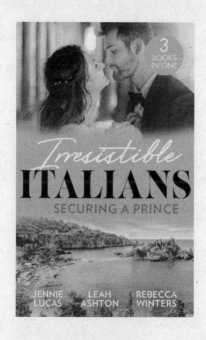

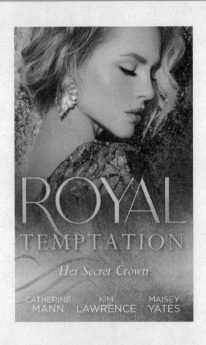